FLESH AND BLOOD

MAYA BARTON #BOOK 3

KATE BENDELOW

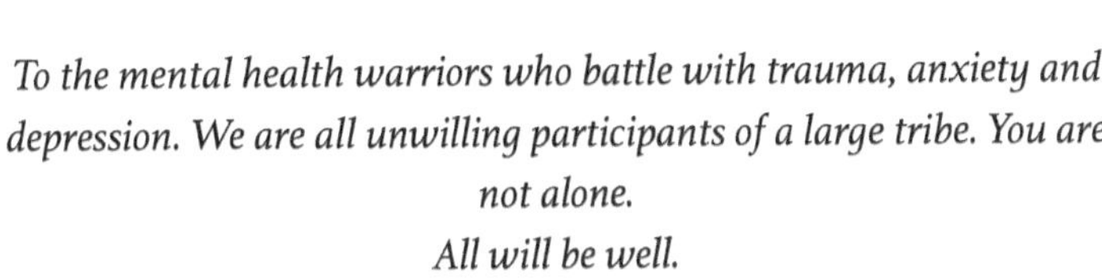

To the mental health warriors who battle with trauma, anxiety and depression. We are all unwilling participants of a large tribe. You are not alone.
All will be well.

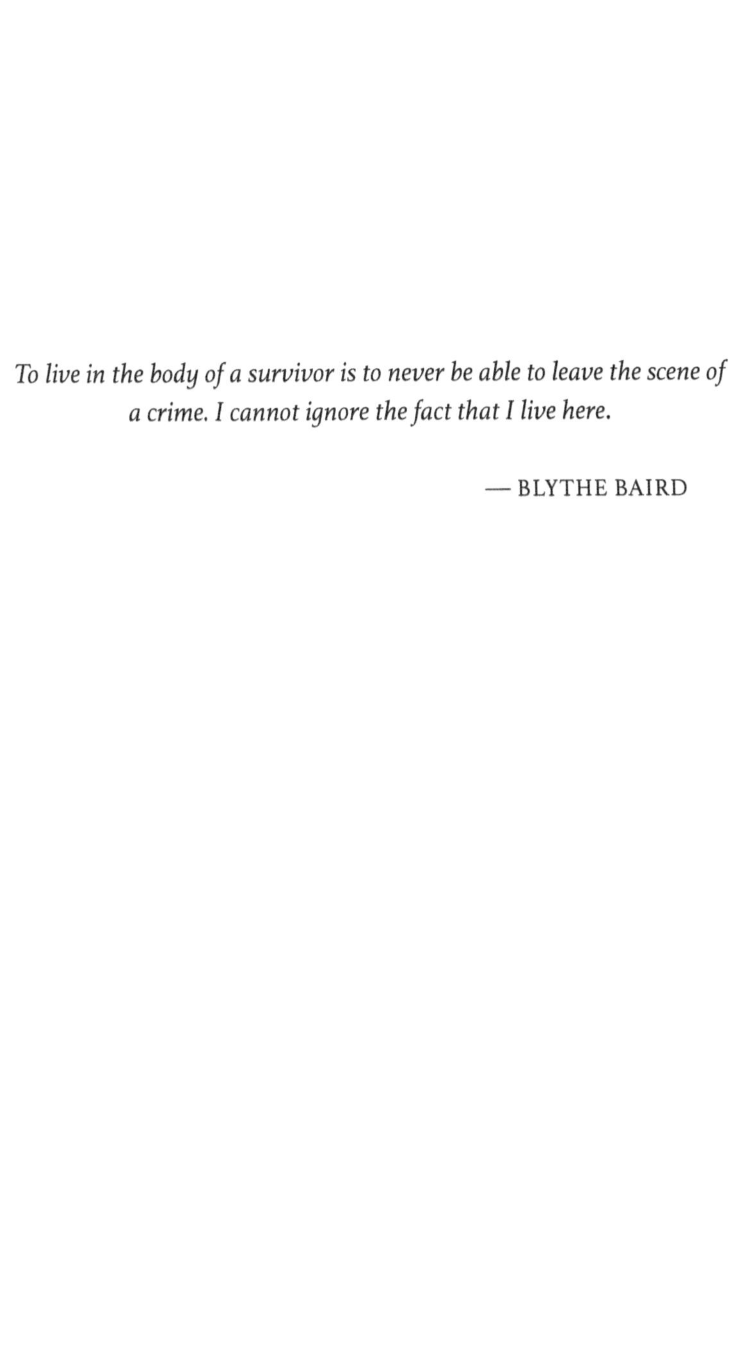

To live in the body of a survivor is to never be able to leave the scene of a crime. I cannot ignore the fact that I live here.

— BLYTHE BAIRD

PROLOGUE

They say hindsight is a wonderful thing. How true. With hindsight, Maya Barton should have known exactly when her estranged father, Marcus Naylor was going to strike. On 26th November the previous year, he had finally been released from prison. In his warped, twisted mind, he blamed her for his incarceration, so it was fitting he would choose this date, his first anniversary of freedom to wreak his revenge.

Oh, for the gift of hindsight.

She should have known.

She should have realised.

She wished she had the hindsight as, in a perverse way, she would have welcomed the date because the anticipation of knowing he was coming, but not knowing *when* he was going to strike was excruciating.

Hindsight would have allowed her to prepare for the day he would come back to kill.

She would have drawn a red circle around 26th November and made a note that death was coming on that day.

She would have been ready to meet her maker, but God knows she would have put up one hell of a fight first.

$$1$$

The fugitive moved like a shadow, unremarkable and unnoticed. He was surprisingly light on his feet. Remarkably agile for a man of his size. He was fully aware of Edmond Locard's Exchange Principle, the theory that 'every contact leaves a trace'. He was careful to leave barely a hint of scent in the air as he moved from place to place. He had learned a lot over the years. He had used his time in hiding to educate himself. He was much more astute than he used to be and that made him even more of a dangerous man.

Being invisible wasn't always easy but it was necessary. He was a wanted man. If the police caught up with him, he could be sent away for a long time. That couldn't happen. He wouldn't let it happen. Staying hidden was no longer an option though. As much as he valued his freedom and anonymity, there was something he valued even more. Something that had forced him from his refuge.

The fugitive wanted to right a wrong and get revenge for someone he had loved. Retribution had given him a hunger. It had turned him into a hunter.

He surveyed his new quarters with satisfied eyes and nodded to himself, gratified that he'd chosen the perfect location. Smug at the fact he was hiding in plain sight. He drew noisily on his e-cigarette, savouring the menthol flavour and nicotine hit before he exhaled slowly. He much preferred cigarettes, but that meant discarding tab ends rich in his DNA. He was too astute to make such a foolish mistake.

Locard be damned.

The murky window mirrored his reflection as he sat in the Stygian room. Even the sun was reluctant to cast its rays near this place. The light from his mobile phone lit up his face as he began his ritual of scouring search engines, eager for any new information. He regularly checked social media too but continued to be frustrated by the fact that all her accounts were private. They would be, she was like him – careful. But was she careful enough? Surely even she would make a mistake one day, and then...

His interest was suddenly piqued by an online news article reporting a life-threatening stabbing. His heart began to race, his mouth grew dry as he scanned the article. He enlarged the photographs from the scene to take a closer look at a figure clad in a white scene suit. She was near the edge of the police tape, talking to a young-looking plain-clothed officer. She had lowered her face mask to speak to the detective. In that instant, her image had been caught with perfect timing as she'd turned obliviously towards the angle of the journalist's camera. The photo had clearly been taken from some distance, but her identity was unmistakable. He would recognise SOCO Maya Barton anywhere.

The fugitive read the article again, slowly this time, taking in all the repetitive detail typical of an online newspaper. He did a quick search of the location and smiled. He was less than a mile away from the crime scene. He subconsciously reached out and ran his finger along the blade of the knife that rested across his lap.

He was getting so close; he could practically smell her.

2

___

Mallon Lodge was a derelict care home that had long since gone to seed. Metal sheets plugged the windows and doors. Ivy permeated its crumbling walls and appeared to be the only thing holding the building up. In the six years since its abandonment, it had been stripped of its copper, used as a squat and set alight numerous times. Its sprawling car park was lined with shrubs and trees allowing its insalubrious visitors the privacy they craved. Its secluded location made it the go-to place for local drug dealers and sex workers to ply their trades discreetly without attracting the attention of any neighbours, passers-by, or more importantly, the police.

The car park of Mallon Lodge was also the crime scene where seventeen-year-old Kyle Brogan had been stabbed. It was Kyle's regular stomping ground. Always the first stop of his day when selling drugs. If he had any nous about him, he would have spotted something was amiss as he cycled in the car park and realised his regulars were notable by their absence. But Kyle was seventeen, still incredibly gauche, with his mind on nothing but money and what lay between his legs.

He'd been intercepted by rival drug dealers and his lack of

acumen resulted in a good kicking and a nasty stab wound to his abdomen. To add insult to injury, while his intestines spilled out onto the asphalt, his drugs had also been stolen. This was colloquially known as being taxed, when a rival drug dealer steals from another. Overall, it hadn't been a good day for poor Kyle.

The last light of the day was fading fast, typical for late October. Maya hated this time of year. The memory of summer was being snatched away hour by hour, replaced by shorter days and longer black nights. She didn't find the onset of autumn comforting like some people did. She'd rather be baked by the sun than warmed in front of a log fire and the thought of a pumpkin spiced latte made her want to heave. She resented the shorter days and relentless black nights. It was like a melancholy ending.

Maya perused the area one final time so she could satisfy herself she'd not overlooked any vital evidence.

'How are you getting on, mate?' DC Sean Stevenson was an experienced and efficient detective, much to the surprise of anyone who first met him due to his boyish, unkempt ginger hair and freckles.

'I'm all done. Before we close the scene though, you'll need to get street cleansing out to remove the claret.' Maya nodded her head towards the thick pool of blood which had already started to congeal like the coating on a toffee apple. 'Also, give them the heads-up there's a load of needles in that top right corner.'

Sean nodded. 'Will do. I've just been on the phone to Malone, he's had an update from Kyle's consultant.'

'How's he doing? Do they still think it's life threatening?'

'He's not making any promises, but claims the operation went well. Only thing is, he'll be shitting in a bag for the rest of his life.'

Maya shook her head and let out a sigh. 'Poor sod.' She was about to comment further but was interrupted by the ringing of Sean's mobile.

'Sorry, Maya, it's DI Redford. He's probably after an update.'

Maya nodded and walked over to her van so she could start to take off her scene suit. She perched on the edge of the driver's seat while she wrestled the suit over her boots, her eyes met Sean's and she frowned with concern at the obvious change in his pallor. He finished his call and was at her side in an instant.

'What is it? Something wrong?'

'Okay, try not to panic but DI Redford has taken a call. There's been a sighting of Marcus Naylor.'

Maya felt her breath catch as she stared numbly at Sean. Bile threatened to flood her mouth and it took several seconds for her to gain composure. Marcus Naylor was her estranged father. A violent man who had spent years in prison and had made various threats to Maya and her mother, Dominique.

He had been on the run for several months since his involvement in plotting to set fire to Dominique's house. This had resulted in a fatality, which he needed to account for. Since he had left without trace, he was subsequently breaking the conditions of his licence, which meant he was wanted for recall to prison. Despite many public appeals by the police for information on his whereabouts, he had evaded capture or even any definite sightings. Until now.

'When. Where was he seen?'

Sean shifted uncomfortably. 'About an hour ago. On Glendale Avenue. I'm sorry, Maya, but it coincides with a photo of you working here that has been shared online by the *Evening News*.'

Maya winced and wiped a hand across her mouth as she let out a frustrated groan then her eyes drifted to the edge of the overgrown car park. It had been flooded with October sunshine when she arrived. Now, with the ensuing twilight, the shadows seemed to stretch menacingly, creating pockets of refuge for anyone wanting to creep closer to the crime scene without being noticed by the uniformed scene guards.

An evening breeze carried across the car park, causing Maya to shiver. Sean's eyes had been flitting across the same area as hers and he moved instinctively closer to her.

'C'mon, mate, let's go. I'll jump in the van and head back with you. Uniform can stay here and wait for street cleansing before they shut it down. They can drive my car back to the nick.'

Maya didn't need telling twice, she was eager to get back to Beech Field and find out exactly what DI Redford knew. Then she needed to ring Dominique and check her mother was safe. Moments ago, her priority had been scouring the scene for clues as to who had stabbed Kyle Brogan. Now she was desperate to get away, terrified she might meet the same fate.

3

Owen Walsh was feeling anxious, which was ironic as it was usually him who caused other people's sphincters to twitch. Aged nineteen, he was scrawny looking, with gangly limbs and a sallow complexion smattered with crimson acne which he'd attempted to disguise under a beard. The result was pitiful as straggly, mousy wisps of bumfluff clung in patches along his bony jaw and hollow cheeks.

Although woeful to look at, for the last six years he had gained a reputation for being a violent thief, bully, and drugs courier. He was known as Wheeler due to his predilection for steeling anything with wheels – pedal cycles, cars, motorbikes and infamously once, a mobility scooter. All modes of transport attracted Wheeler like flies to shit. He had been expelled from school and arrested more times than he could care to remember.

And that was the problem; he just didn't care about anything, authority, his family, education; nothing until now. Now he cared desperately about having to deliver bad news to his boss, Liam Reilly. The prospect terrified him.

Reilly had found Wheeler on a freezing winter's night when he had left the children's home determined to move to a new city and start a fresh life away from school, social services and his alcoholic mother. His plan was to leave the northwest completely and travel to London, but he'd been kicked off the train at Crewe once the conductor discovered he didn't have a ticket.

Wheeler had been following an elderly lady out of the train station, waiting for the opportune moment to grab her handbag. Reilly had been watching him and had intervened before Wheeler could make his move. With an avuncular arm around Wheeler's shoulder, he had steered the lad away from the train station, pointing out the undercover police officers deployed to target thieves.

He had taken Wheeler back to his house and the lad had been impressed with the size of the television, games consoles and surround sound system. Reilly had ordered a Chinese takeout and provided Wheeler with cans of cider and cannabis. Wheeler thought he was in paradise. He was flattered by Reilly's attention and impressed by his lifestyle.

Reilly talked Wheeler out of running away, encouraging him to return home, but also to gain some independence by selling cannabis to his classmates, so he could earn money of his own. Wheeler had jumped at the chance. The following morning, having spent the night on Reilly's sofa, he was sent home with a rail card and a burner phone.

Wheeler had been recruited in what the police referred to as *county lines*. He was a pawn in a criminal network controlled by Reilly and used to flood his local area with drugs. The younger Wheeler had started off selling cannabis, but had quickly been tasked with selling heroin and cocaine. The supply had become thicker and faster, resulting in him having to employ a trusted ally to become part of the network and courier the drugs. Now that courier, Brogan, had been seriously injured and a break in the network meant that the drugs would not be delivered as quickly, and profits would dwindle.

Wheeler had driven to Crewe in a stolen black Golf, which he'd fitted with false registration plates. He parked it a street away from Reilly's new-build townhouse, knowing his boss would skin him alive for bringing a stolen motor to his doorstep. Rounding the corner, his heart sunk at the sight of the Audi gleaming on the drive. Its presence meant Reilly was home and he couldn't put off the inevitable any longer.

Reilly's posh house was all fur coat and no knickers. Although swollen at the seams with designer clothing, jewellery, aftershave, and top of the range electrics, the house itself was a dump. Reilly's car, however, was his pride and joy and always pristine. Rumour had it that a passenger of Reilly's had once dropped an empty packet of crisps in the footwell resulting in Reilly smashing the passenger's hand in the door so many times, the surgeons were unable to repair his shattered bones.

He knocked on the door, shifting from foot to foot until it was eventually opened by Sully, a stocky mass of toned muscle and Reilly's right-hand man. A man of few words, Sully didn't so much as acknowledge Wheeler, but headed towards the lounge where Reilly was sprawled across an expansive sofa, surrounded by McDonald's food wrappers, and playing a shooting game on his PlayStation 5. His eyes flickered fleetingly from the flat-screen television to Wheeler.

'S'up,' he said with a grunt. Just the utterance of that one syllable conveyed to Wheeler that he was already irritated by the intrusion. That didn't bode well.

'Sorry, boss, we've got a problem.'

Ostentatious, diamond-studded rings covered Reilly's hands as he gripped the games controller. The glinting jewels paused for a split second until the shooting recommenced. Wheeler could barely hear Reilly's words they were uttered so quietly, his soft Gaelic tone dripping with menace.

'I'm having a grand day; *you* have problems so that I don't have to. That's what I pay you for.'

Wheeler shifted awkwardly, unsure how best to respond. This was the thing with Reilly. Although not as physically intimidating as Sully, he had a scheming way with words and could twist and manipulate a conversation in such a way you'd be left doubting your own name by the end of it.

Reilly sighed with annoyance as he propped a foot up on the sofa and turned his attention to Wheeler. Late-thirties, he was shaven headed, with steely grey eyes. He had a puckered scar across his right cheek, and as much as the gleaming flesh looked menacing, Reilly's demeanour suggested his attacker had undoubtedly come off worse.

'Sorry, Mr Reilly.'

Reilly smiled pleasantly. His lips peeled back in a shark-like grin, revealing a set of pristine white veneers.

'What are you sorry for, Wheeler?' Reilly cooed. 'Being an annoying little prick or for daring to come here and breathe the same air while you tell me *"We"* have a problem.'

Wheeler began to pick nervously at a spot on his forehead, his gaze glued to the floor, unable to meet his boss's eyes.

'Erm, all of it. Sorry for being a prick... and the breathing... and that.'

'Jesus, to think you're the fucking sperm that won,' Reilly said, causing Sully to snort with laughter. He was leaning against the doorframe, his thick forearms crossed over his bull-like chest. Wheeler suddenly felt like a mouse being baited by two vicious cats.

'Tell us all about your little problem, Wheeler. Then perhaps me and Sully can help. Do you think we can help him, Sully?'

Sully grunted his assent.

Reilly wafted his hand encouragingly. 'Come on, don't be shy. You're amongst friends.'

Wheeler's trepidation grew, not fooled by Reilly's honeyed tones. He was physically sandwiched between the two men in a room which seemed to be closing in around him. The music from the game was fraying his already shot nerves.

'Kyle Brogan's been taxed on his first drop, at Mallon Lodge. He's been shanked up good and proper.' He could detect the tremor in his own voice.

Reilly and Sully exchanged a glance. Reilly cleared his throat before he spoke.

'You really do have a problem. Doesn't he, Sully?'

Sully nodded.

'I do.' He spoke the words like a question. He was so scared now; his mind had gone blank. He picked at the spot again, even though he suspected it had started to bleed.

'Wheeler told us Brogan would make a good courier. He recruited him, didn't he?' Reilly asked Sully.

'Yeah, his old mate from the scary children's home.' Sully made a show of rubbing his hands against his cheeks in a crying motion.

Reilly nodded. 'He said they were like brothers. *Said* we could trust him. That neither of them would let us down. But you have, haven't you?' Reilly asked as he arched an eyebrow. 'The pair of you have let us down.'

'Yes. Sorry.' Wheeler's eyes grew wide, his panicked face visibly paled. His mouth opened and closed wordlessly as he wrestled for the right words to say.

'How badly injured is poor Kyle?' Reilly asked, as if chatting to a toddler.

'Bad. He's in intensive care.'

'Oh dear. I'll ring Interflora and arrange some flowers.'

Sully let out a snort while Reilly just sat and stared at

Wheeler, who didn't know whether he should speak or even so much as move. After an age, Reilly placed the games controller on the arm of the sofa and spoke again.

'So, if it was his first drop, how much gear did he have on him?'

'About five hundred quid's worth.'

'Okay. Because he's your friend and I know you're worried about him, I'm going to tell you how to deal with *your* little problem. First of all, find out exactly how poorly he is. Don't go bumbling up to the hospital, it'll be crawling with filth, so use that one paltry brain cell of yours and think before you act. If he's going to die, let me know. If he doesn't, as soon as he's discharged, tell him he owes me a grand.'

Wheeler's head shot up; his eyes widened. 'A grand? But he only had a monkey's worth of gear on him.'

Reilly smiled pleasantly. He sighed as he heaved himself up off the sofa. In two paces he was in front of Wheeler, gently patting his spotty, bumfluff-covered cheek.

'Only? That's my money and you say *only* a monkey? It's interest, isn't it? If he does live, tell him to get my money or I'll kill him. And if I ever set eyes on his gormless fucking face again, I'll kill him. In short, so you both understand, he better get my money and fuck right off. And you?'

'Me, boss?'

'Yes you. You need to find another courier. By the end of the week. And if this one fucks up, I'll be very, very cross.' Reilly's sing-song tone and close proximity were breaking the last of Wheeler's resolve. For the first time in his life, he was terrified.

'We're expecting a big delivery soon, so I also need you to find somewhere safe to stash the gear. Where are you staying at the moment?'

'Between my mum's and Susie's, but I can't use either place for that. Mum's a liability and Susie's parents are too straight.'

'You better start looking for somewhere else to stay then.' Reilly patted his cheek again. Then he took a step back and winced. He opened his palm, looked at it and shook his head. He took a step back towards Wheeler and purposely wiped his hand down his top. Then, he turned back to the sofa and picked up the games controller. Wheeler's shoulders slumped with relief as it looked like he was being dismissed.

Wheeler turned towards the door, but Reilly was at his side in an instant. He didn't have time or the reflexes to protect his face as Reilly began to smash the controller into his head. Wheeler dropped like a stone, instinctively curling into the foetal position.

Reilly continued to rein blows on him with the controller, punctuating each blow with a word as he screamed, 'That's... for...making...me...touch...your...skanky...fuckin'...skin.'

The blows eventually stopped, and Wheeler heard Reilly panting with the exertion of the attack as he returned to the sofa. Cautiously, he lifted his head, his ears ringing from the blows. He glanced at Sully who was still leaning against the doorframe. He made an imperceptible gesture with his head, giving Wheeler his queue to leave. Just as he reached the hallway, Reilly's voice called from the lounge.

'You owe me a new games controller. Get one here within the hour.'

Wheeler closed the front door quietly behind him before running to his car. He felt a trickle of blood snake down his face and swiped it away with his sleeve. He couldn't help envying Brogan his temporary sanctuary in intensive care.

4

Maya and Sean strode through Beech Field police station in silence, both lost in their own thoughts. Maya found herself having to take measured breaths in an attempt to stay calm. The sheer thought of Naylor was enough to make her scream out loud, and she bit back the urge as she marched down the corporate-blue-carpeted corridors towards DI Redford's office.

Sean gave Redford's door a perfunctory knock before they entered the room. On seeing Maya, Redford rose from his desk and gestured towards the conference table.

'Please, take a seat. Sean, would you mind fetching Kym for me?'

'I'll not insult you by asking how you are, but rest assured we're doing everything we can, and well, we're optimistic that, er...' Redford tailed off. His usual efficient demeanour escaped him as he smoothed down his tie before busying himself with pouring Maya a glass of water from the jug in the centre of the table. Redford was tall and lean, his buzz-cut hair revealing enough stubble to hint at his auburn colouring. He was always immaculately dressed, and little fazed him, which was why it unnerved her to see him so ill at ease.

'Maya, love. Are you okay?' SOCO Chris Makin bustled into the office. She stood to greet him as he enveloped her into a huge bear hug. A stocky man with thickset eyebrows, black-rimmed glasses and salt and pepper hair that made him appear older than his current age of late forties. Despite the difference in their age, Chris had become one of Maya's closest friends and confidants and she was relieved to see him.

Kym Lawson, the senior SOCO, bustled into the office accompanied by Sean. She appraised Maya with a steady eye before letting out a sigh. 'Thank God you're okay.'

Maya gave her a wan smile. 'But for how much longer?' She turned to Redford. 'What do we know?'

He indicated for them all to take a seat and cleared his throat before he continued. 'We received a call earlier today from a member of the public. They stated that a man matching Naylor's description had been seen on foot near Glendale Avenue. Patrols were scrambled to the area, but there was no trace.'

'Who called it in? How can they be sure it was him? It's been months since the fire and him going on the run and this is the first sighting of him. Surely the informant is mistaken, it could have been anyone.' Maya could detect the desperation in her voice and took a deep breath, determined to appear pragmatic and unemotional.

'Sean said my face has been plastered across the *Evening News'* website. It would be reasonable to expect that the informant had seen it and imagined they'd also seen Naylor close to the crime scene.'

Redford coughed again as he shuffled some paperwork around. 'The informant is a Mrs Gillespie. Adila has been and spoken to her and is confident that the woman is a good witness. For the last few years, she's run a neighbourhood watch group in the area. As you know, Glendale is a cut-through to access the woodland trail and fields. As much as it's popular for walkers, it used to attract a lot of antisocial behaviour, which led to her becoming the eyes and ears of the local community. Her words – not mine.'

'Any CCTV?' Chris asked.

'Unfortunately, no.'

Maya let out a derisive snort. 'Jesus, a neighbourhood watch without CCTV. Does she keep her spare front door key under a plant pot too?'

'I know it's frustrating. Adila has shown Mrs Gillespie the photofit we have of Naylor and she's adamant it's him.'

Maya craned forward eagerly. 'I think this woman, well intended as she may be, has made a mistake. He's been missing for months, surely if he was going to make a move, he would have done it by now. He knows if he gets caught, he's going away for a very long time. I can't see why he would risk it now. And if he were to come back, trust me, he wouldn't slip up so easily and chance getting caught.'

'Even so,' said Kym, 'it would be remiss of us not to take a sighting, however improbable, seriously. I think we should err on the side of caution and in the meantime, Maya, we'll make sure you're doubled up on your shifts.'

Maya straightened up. 'I don't need babysitting.'

'I'm fully aware of that, but it's the most common-sense approach. It's either that or you'll be office based for the foreseeable, and just that look on your face tells me that's not an option.'

Chris nodded. 'I agree with Kym.' He smiled reassuringly at Maya. 'It's not forever, love. Just until we're satisfied it's not him. I agree with you, I think it's a false sighting, but just to be on the safe side, eh? I can shift my hours around and double up with you.'

Redford nodded. 'It is the sensible option. I've obviously made MIT aware of the sighting and they're doing everything they can and will keep us informed of any developments. I will also be speaking to the *Evening News* and reiterating the importance that your image is not to be shared online and I want to know who the hell took that photograph in the first place.'

'It was Dave "The Bastard" Wainwright,' Sean said with disgust. 'I swear his previous dealings with Maya have made him obsessed. I specifically told him, no photos of her from the scene.'

'Parasite,' muttered Chris as the others nodded in agreement.

'Right, well leave that with me and rest assured Wainwright will be strongly advised, I'll get hold of his boss straight away.' He rose from the table, stacking his papers together to indicate that the meeting was over.

Maya, Chris and Kym headed back to the SOCO office. They were greeted by office administrator Amanda Mayhew and SOCO Tara Coleman. Chris made a beeline for the duties board and began looking at his and Maya's shifts.

'Amanda,' Kym said, 'we're going to make some interim changes to the duties so that Maya and Chris work the same shifts for now. If you could make the necessary updates, I'd be obliged.'

Amanda nodded and reached efficiently for pen and paper. Meanwhile, Tara popped her head above her computer monitor and pouted like a sulking child.

'If this is because her dad has been seen, don't you think we should all be double-crewed. I mean, he's a complete madman, isn't he? What if he decides to target all us SOCOs. It's not fair that Maya is looked after, but I'm just left to my own devices. No offence, but I don't want to get dragged into your dysfunctional family business.' She threw Maya a caustic look.

Kym's expression gathered like thunder. Despite being short and trim, she had a reputation for being formidable. She was attractive, with large brown eyes and dark hair styled elegantly in a pixie-cut. When she smiled, she had the ability to put people at ease, but right now, she looked like she was going to explode.

'For once, Tara, this isn't about you and I'm satisfied, under the circumstances that there is no risk to–'

Maya held up her hand to interject. 'Tara has every right to be concerned, Kym. It's natural for her to want to know. I'm sure the others will be considering their own risk assessments too. It would be wrong if we didn't address that and at the very least allay their fears.'

Kym nodded in acquiescence, but still narrowed her eyes in Tara's direction as Maya continued.

'I can assure you that *if* Naylor was spotted today and to be honest, I personally think it's a big if, then the only person he's interested in is me. He hates me with an absolute passion. For some warped reason, he seems to hold me responsible for the fact he was sent to prison.' Maya shook her head inconceivably.

'I appreciate your concerns, Tara. He is a dangerous man and possibly mentally deranged, but I'm confident you'll all be way under his radar. It's me he wants, and honestly, I worry that if he *is* back, he won't stop until I'm in the mortuary.'

5

Best friends Jordan Gaffney and Lewis Mellor left school together in a companionable silence. The place was deserted other than the rest of the stragglers who'd just finished an after-school detention like Lewis or had stayed behind for football practice like Jordan. The final few teachers looked as morose and bedraggled as the kids as they scuffed across the car park to waiting vehicles. Jordan nodded towards the bike shed.

'Are you getting the bus, or do you want a backie?'

'Backie please, I'm saving me bus fare for smokes,' Lewis said as he climbed onto the back of Jordan's mountain bike.

Jordan hesitated as a black car he recognised pulled out of the staff car park and idled towards them, the window down. 'You played really good again tonight, Jordan,' said Mr Ramos, the PE teacher who also ran the school football team. 'Just remember not to lean back when you shoot. Come to practice a bit earlier next week and we'll have some one-on-one time and I'll show you what I mean.'

'Thanks, sir, I will. Enjoy your squash game tonight.'

'Thanks, son, I will. You have a good evening.' He smiled at

Jordan, but it died on his lips as he glanced at Lewis, who he gave a brusque nod. 'Bye.'

As the teacher drove off, Lewis leaned into Jordan's back and mimicked, 'Enjoy your squash game, wish you were slamming my balls about, can't wait for our naked one-on-one.'

'Sod off, he's a nice guy and you're just being a dick,' replied Jordan as they began to pedal towards the estate. They carried on in silence until they got to the brow of the hill near the wasteland at the back of the precinct, which was only ever frequented by homeless drunks. The gravel was loose which, combined with the weight of a passenger and a steep incline, made cycling difficult.

Jordan hunched his weight forward over the pedals as he powered them onwards. He adjusted gears as he neared the top, then swore as he felt the chain come off. They both climbed off the bike and Jordan swiped away beads of sweat from his forehead as he flipped the bike upside down so he could fix the chain.

Lewis dropped his school bag to the ground and pulled out a hand-rolled cigarette from his blazer pocket. He made several attempts to light it, but his lighter was out of fluid. He swore and threw it across the gravel, slumping against a wall as he watched Jordan wrestling with the chain.

'All right, lads. Got a problem?' Wheeler had coasted into the area unnoticed and was now hanging out of the driver's window. A perma-tanned blonde was peering at them from the passenger's seat as she chewed open-mouthed and noisily on a piece of gum.

Jordan straightened up and eyed the pair cautiously. Wheeler's reputation preceded him; the two schoolboys knew all about his notoriety. Jordan couldn't help but wince at the myriad of fresh cuts and bruises on Wheeler's face. Being bruised and battered made him look more intimidating.

'We're good, thanks. Just fixing my chain,' Jordan said breaking eye contact, so he didn't have to look at the bruises.

Wheeler nodded as he climbed out of the car. He approached Lewis and handed him a cigarette lighter. 'Cheers, mate,' Lewis said as he took a drag of the roll-up and began posturing as he handed Wheeler the lighter back.

Wheeler watched Jordan fumbling with the bike, before eventually breaking the silence. 'Want any gear to liven up your day?' he asked nonchalantly as he patted the man-bag that he wore crossed over his torso.

Jordan eyed Wheeler steadily, ignoring the sense of trepidation that was beginning to build in his gut. 'We're good, thanks,' he said a second time. He indicated with his head to Lewis that it was time to go.

Lewis took a long steady drag as he eyed Susie before casually asking, 'What have you got?'

'Nah, man, don't be a dick,' Jordan hissed at Lewis. 'C'mon, let's go. Thanks though,' he added reverently to Wheeler, wary of antagonising him. 'We haven't got any money,' he added by way of explanation.

Wheeler nodded. 'No worries, little-man; we're cool. Where do I know you from, you look familiar?'

Jordan shrugged. 'Probably just from around here.'

'Where do you live?'

'Langtree estate.'

'Yeah, I know Langtree. Near the Glendale fields. Which road?'

Jordan swallowed drily. He was struggling to maintain composure and just wanted to get away, but he was sensible enough to know not to risk alienating Wheeler.

'Bideford Avenue.'

Wheeler grinned as he peeled himself away from the car,

giving Jordan his full attention. 'I know who you are.' He clicked his fingers and furrowed his brow as he concentrated.

Lewis was leaning sulkily against the wall, irritated at being ignored while Jordan earned all of Wheeler's attention. He was blissfully unaware that Jordan would happily have traded places with him.

'Craig Gaffney's little brother!' Wheeler announced triumphantly. 'I knew I recognised you. I haven't seen your kid for a while, how's he doing?'

Jordan nodded. 'He's good, thanks. I'll tell him you were asking after him.'

'We was in remedial classes together for a bit,' Wheeler added. 'I skipped that much school I was always behind. And obviously with your kid being a bit, well, you know. No offence, little-man...' Wheeler tailed off.

'Fuckin' special,' added Lewis as he laughed nastily. 'Don't fink he can even tie his own shoelaces, can he?' Lewis cackled to himself, oblivious to the cold stare from Jordan.

'Nasty prick,' said Susie, with a scowl. She'd emerged from the car and had perched herself on the bonnet, crossing and uncrossing her legs, hoping to get Wheeler's attention.

Wheeler was staring at Lewis as if he'd just defecated on the ground. His eyes narrowed thunderously as he glared at him. 'Shite-mouth,' he hissed before turning to Jordan. 'Not gonna stand for that, are you?' he asked challengingly.

'He's not worth it.' Jordan shrugged as he turned to climb back on his bike. Fuck Lewis, he could walk the rest of his way home after that, he was still riling after the snide comment about the PE teacher, but insulting Craig was a step too far.

'Little-man, he's just dissed your bro. You can't let that slide. Word gets round and everyone'll be disrespecting you and your family. Stand up for yourself, mate.'

Lewis was looking nervous now and he began to stutter an apology, but Wheeler silenced him with a raised hand.

'He needs teaching a lesson,' Wheeler said. His voice was low and his tone full of menace. Susie had stilled, sensing the change in atmosphere, and eagerly anticipating how things were going to play out.

Jordan and Lewis locked eyes, both as unsure how to react or what to say.

'I *said*, he needs teaching a lesson.' Wheeler was emulating Reilly now, speaking in a sing-song fashion; enjoying seeing how much it made other people squirm. His earlier slight was behind him, and he was feeling like the big man again, buoyed on by the fact that Susie was turned on by his hard-man act.

Wheeler moved towards the car and leaned through the driver's window so he could fish something out of the door pocket. He turned towards Jordan and opened his palm, revealing a lock knife. Open-mouthed, Jordan looked at the knife and then wordlessly at Wheeler. The air was charged with violence as Wheeler thrust his open palm towards Jordan.

'Shank him up,' he said simply.

Jordan turned to look at Lewis who was open-mouthed, silently pleading with Jordan not to. Jordan swallowed and looked back at Wheeler. 'Nah, I can't, he's me best mate.'

Wheeler smiled sweetly as he dipped his head towards Jordan and spoke again in the sinister sing-song fashion. 'If you don't, I will and once I start I might not stop.'

Jordan's eyes widened as they shot towards Lewis's. His friend had grown pale, and he was shaking his head furiously. 'Just do it, Jord,' he said pleadingly.

'No. Sorry, I can't.'

'You sure?' Wheeler leaned in and lowered his voice. He was so close to Jordan he could feel his breath on his face. 'If you don't do it, not only will I stab him, you'll be next. Then I'll be going for your brother and that mum of yours. From what I remember she was a bit of a MILF. Bet she'd be begging for a bit of this to make me stop,' he said as he grabbed at his crotch with one hand and held out the knife with another.

Bile flooded Jordan's mouth as he thought of his mum and Craig. The last thing he wanted was to stab Lewis, but he had no choice, if he didn't Wheeler would, and then he would be next. Even worse than that, he would then hurt his mum and Craig and there was no way he could let that happen. He would protect his own flesh and blood over Lewis.

With a shaking hand, Jordan took the lock knife from Wheeler. He would just give him a superficial slash wound. Just a scratch. Whatever he did to Lewis would be nowhere near as bad as what Wheeler would do; he'd have no qualms about killing his best friend. This was the only way he could get them both out of this nightmarish situation relatively unscathed.

He fumbled with the handle, unsure how the mechanism worked so the blade could be released. His heart was ricocheting around his ribcage and his legs were trembling. He was vaguely aware of Wheeler laughing as he produced his mobile phone and started to record proceedings.

With a click that seemed to resonate like a gunshot, the blade flicked out. Although he'd never used a knife in violence before, Jordan could see how sharp it was as he turned it in his hand. He innately knew it was long enough to cause serious damage. He pressed his fingertips to the flat part of the blade, amazed at how much threat an inanimate object could pose. He was now in absolutely no doubt that Wheeler would cause his friend much more damage with it than he ever could.

'Do it,' Wheeler goaded as he walked around the two teenagers, honing his phone in on them, ready to capture every moment. Swallowing again, Jordan looked at Lewis and his friend gave him a consensual nod. Jordan stepped toward him, his hand shaking so much, he could barely keep hold of the knife. As he grew closer to Lewis, he whispered an apology, but the first syllable had barely left his lips and Lewis lunged forward, shoving him away.

'What the fuck!' Jordan staggered backwards, one leg dropping towards the ground as Lewis loomed over him. His mind went into overdrive, the two-faced bastard was going to turn this on him. Instinctively, Jordan knew that if he hit the ground, things would turn bad for him. Likewise, if he lost his now, vice-like grip on the knife. It was stab or be stabbed. Then what would Wheeler do to Craig and his mum?

A guttural roar escaped his lips as he propelled himself forwards, driven by rage and fear, lunging the knife towards Lewis as the blade swept through the air. Lewis arched back, dodged the blade, turned on his heel and sprinted away. Jordan was taller and fitter though, much more agile than Lewis. Within several paces, he had closed the distance between the two of them, although driven by fear, Lewis was running faster than Jordan had ever seen him run before.

Lewis's mistake was to glance over his shoulder to see where Jordan was. The lapse in concentration caused him to slip on the loose gravel. An uneven piece of ground catapulted him forward. Then there was no distance between the two boys. As his friend slammed into the ground face first, Jordan lunged forward again.

Only this time the blade didn't cut through the air.

It carved into Lewis Mellor.

6

Dominique Barton's CCTV system alerted her to the fact that someone had arrived outside her house. She viewed the camera on her mobile phone and smiled as she saw Maya pull up on her motorbike. She'd placed the Bonneville on its kickstand and was already shaking her hair out of the helmet by the time Dominique opened the door. The two women grinned at each other and anyone watching would be left in no doubt that they were related.

They were both tall and slim and shared the same magnetic smile. Late twenties, Maya had honeycomb skin, her hair was a halo of dark-brown, corkscrew curls. Dominique was darker skinned, with close-cropped hair, a style which accentuated her cheekbones.

'Is everything okay? You sounded harassed on the phone?' Dominique asked as she embraced Maya.

'Let's go inside.' Maya locked the door behind her and followed Dominique through to the kitchen. Her mama still had a noticeable limp having previously broken her pelvis after jumping from her first-floor bedroom window when her house was set on fire, and it pained Maya to see her suffering.

Dominique gestured for her to sit down while she clicked the kettle on. She currently lived in a rented house which was new and equipped with all mod cons but seemed too sterile and characterless for Dominique's tastes. She knew Dominique missed having a decent-sized garden, as the one here only had a small square patch of lawn to the rear.

Despite Maya's encouragement to go and look at new houses since the insurance had paid out, Dominique seemed reluctant. The threat of Marcus had hugely affected Dominique's confidence and Maya knew that while he was still on the run she couldn't move on with her life. After all, Maya felt the same. They were in limbo whilst trying to carry on as normal, they were both constantly aware that Naylor was still at large and could strike anytime. This new sighting, whether genuine or not, was a stark reminder of that.

Maya made small talk as she prepared the tea before eventually joining Dominique at the table and telling her that Marcus had possibly been spotted nearby. Dominique remained silent as she listened to Maya. Her brow puckered as she traced her fingers across the grain of the kitchen table.

'What do you think?' Dominique asked eventually.

Maya sighed and shook her head. 'Honestly? I think the informant has made a mistake and spotted someone she *thinks* looks like Marcus. There's hasn't been sight nor sound of him since the fire. If the supposition is that he's come after me because he's seen me on the *Evening News*' website, it doesn't sit right with me. He's on the run, so why would he chance being spotted in daylight in an area surrounded by cops? You and I both know, when he decides to surface, neither of us will see it coming.'

Dominique nodded and reached across the table for Maya's hand to stop her from gnawing at her cuticles, a habit she'd had since childhood. Maya could detect a trembling in Dominique's fingers and squeezed them reassuringly. She nodded to Dominique's cup as she stood up. 'Forget the tea, have something stronger.'

'I should keep a clear head,' Dominique insisted.

'I'm making you a G&T, not passing you the meths. One drink won't do you any harm, it'll take the edge off the shock.'

Dominique watched Maya busy herself around the kitchen as she mixed the drink, which she set before her as she stifled a yawn.

'You're tired. Has work been busy?'

'So-so. I've not been sleeping too well, that's all.'

'The nightmares again?'

'Not really,' Maya said, keen to minimise things so Dominique wouldn't worry. 'Just the shift pattern. It's tiring coming off a late shift straight onto a day.'

Dominique nodded but didn't seem too convinced. 'The journalist who's written the piece about you and shared your photograph online. Isn't he the same one you've had problems with before?'

'Yeah, Dave "The Bastard" Wainwright. DI Redford is going to pull rank and speak to his boss to make sure it doesn't happen again. And I'm going to be double crewed at work with Chris until this all blows over, so there's no need to worry about me.'

'That makes me feel better. Do you think this will all blow over though?' Dominique sounded sceptical.

'God only knows. I feel like a child again, walking on eggshells and not knowing what each hour of the day is going to bring. Then another part of me refuses to be intimidated and live in fear, and just carry on regardless. I can't figure out why he hates me so much. He blames me for being sent away, but he committed all those offences of his own volition. All I did was phone the police to stop him hurting us. If he wasn't such a violent bastard in the first place, then they would never have locked him up like the animal he is.'

Dominique began once again to trace her finger across the grain of the kitchen tabletop. 'How's Spence?'

'He's good, thanks. Obviously worried about me and you. The thing is, Mama, there's just so much about the past I can't remember. It's like I have this fog – a Swiss-cheese memory that has deliberately blocked things out to stop me getting hurt. I think it would help if we talked about it. Jayne, my counsellor, suggested it and has said if it helps, we can both go and see her together. That way she can support you too.'

Dominique looked up, her eyes wide. 'No, Maya. I can't, it's too much. Talking to a complete stranger. I think all this counselling is having a negative effect on you. I don't think it's helping. You're starting to dwell on things. You have such a strong faith, won't you feel better talking about this at church? It's helped in the past.'

'Not with this it won't. I need professional help so I can remember things. I'm not dwelling. That's the thing. The more I can remember and understand what motivated Marcus back then, might help me figure out where he's coming from now. Don't you think?'

Dominique remained silent; eyes fixed on the table. Maya could sense she was uncomfortable with the conversation, but pressed on regardless, convinced that as difficult as it was to revisit the past that it would definitely help in the long run.

'The night the police came and arrested Marcus, I can't remember–'

'Maya, stop. Please.' Dominique gripped her hand, her eyes brimming with anxiety. 'I appreciate what you're saying, love, but I can't do this, I can't revisit the past. It's too painful and it won't help. You should be glad you can't remember. If I'm honest I can't either. Our minds block things out for a reason, to protect us from the damage of the past. What's done is done. I can't help because a lot of it is patchy in my mind too, but unlike you, I don't think it will help to look back.' She took several large gulps from her glass and rose from the table to make another, leaving Maya wounded by the rebuff.

'Sorry, I didn't mean to upset you.' Maya rose from the table as she picked up the keys for the Bonneville, signalling it was time for her to leave.

Dominique smiled weakly. 'I know and you haven't. It's just the shock of the sighting, you know? And I'm sorry, love, but talking about it might help you but it really doesn't help me. I don't want to remember, I just want to forget. It's the only way I can deal with things. Please don't push me on this.'

'Okay. I'm sorry I said anything.' Maya kissed Dominique on the cheek before she escorted her back up the hall and the two women hugged briefly. Dominique was uncharacteristically quiet, and Maya felt guilty for digging up the past. Normally Dominique would stand at the door and wave her off, but this time, Maya heard the door close and double lock before she'd even reached her bike. She rode away with a heavy heart and an all-too-familiar sense of foreboding.

7

If Dave Wainwright, lead journalist of the *Evening News*, knew that Maya referred to him as 'Dave the Bastard', he would have been inclined to agree it was quite a fitting title. As would his long-suffering wife, Leonora. As would his equally long-suffering boss, Peter, who had just sent him a passive-aggressive email demanding he attend his office urgently.

Wainwright, comfortable in the knowledge that Peter's bark was worse than his bite, had read the email, nipped outside for a brew and a couple of cigarettes, taken a leisurely shit, and flirted with Chantelle from accounts before giving a perfunctory knock on Peter's door and strolling in before he was invited.

'You wanted to see me?' Wainwright announced rhetorically as he took a seat.

Peter was a reedy-looking man with thin, wispy, strawberry-blond hair that covered his head like down. His Adam's apple protruded, blade-like from his neck and tended to bob up and down erratically when he was animated.

'Maya Barton,' Peter said without preamble.

Wainwright shrugged. 'Nice-looking piece. Bit fiery too. I'd love to know the history behind her and her old man. There's a front-page story if ever I saw one.'

Spots of colour pinched at Peter's cheeks as he slammed his palm down on the desk. 'DI Redford has made it perfectly clear that any further breach of Maya's privacy will be treated as harassment. You've really crossed the line this time, and I'm not prepared to sit back and–'

'Speaking of nice-looking pieces,' Wainwright grinned wolfishly as he cut Peter off mid-sentence, 'me and a couple of the lads are heading to Legs & Lashes on Friday if you fancy joining us. I'm sure I can shout you a couple of pints.'

Peter's Adam's apple quivered as he began to stutter unintelligibly. Wainwright sat back and basked in Peter's discomfort. He knew he had his boss by the short and curlies. Last Christmas he had coaxed the inebriated man into the lap-dancing bar and taken a few souvenir snaps. Peter had phoned him, frantic the next day, asking Wainwright to delete the photographs for fear his wife would see them. Wainwright had reassured his boss that his discretion was guaranteed as long as they maintained a mutual back-scratching agreement at work. The mention of Legs & Lashes meant that any imminent bollocking had been well and truly nipped in the bud.

'Look,' said Peter as he battled to maintain an element of calm. 'If you show up on Redford's radar again, you're on your own. There's nothing I can do to keep you out of the shit. It'll be between you, him and the Press Complaints Commission.'

Wainwright hunched forward in his seat. 'Redford's all talk. I'm telling you, there's a story there. A bloody good one. I just need to be a bit more discreet in future.'

Peter wiped his palm across his face as he sighed. 'I'm asking, no, *telling* you to leave her alone.'

Wainwright flashed his wolfish grin again. 'And I'm *telling* you, I'll be more careful in future.' He stood up and smoothed his crumpled shirt down, the fabric straining against his rotund stomach.

'You could be looking at criminal charges. It's harassment!' Peter called after him as he left the office.

Wainwright walked off, whistling contentedly to himself. Peter had always been a naysayer. It'd be a slap on the wrist if that. It'd be worth it once he'd published the scoop of his career.

8

Jordan Gaffney hadn't slept the night of the stabbing. He had relived the sensation of the knife slicing into Lewis's leg again and again. He could hear his best friend's screams, a cacophony of noise against Wheeler's cackling and Susie's shocked exclamations. The blood had come so quick. A scarlet river, pumping from Lewis's leg, so much more blood than he could ever have anticipated. He could still smell it, the metallic tang so thick, he could almost taste it.

Jordan had looked on stunned, frozen with shock. Screaming, Lewis had attempted to cover the wound with his hands, futile as the blood continued to trickle through his fingers. Lewis's face grew deathly pale as he'd pleaded for help. The knife lay discarded on the ground, until Wheeler ceased his cruel laughter and snapped into action. He had demanded a tissue from Susie's bag and used it to pick up the knife before concealing it in his pocket. Then Wheeler had screamed at Jordan to go. To get back on his bike and get out of there, quick.

Jordan hadn't needed telling twice. He was desperate to put as much space between him and the nightmare as possible. He had left his best friend, bleeding and terrified and now he was tormented by not knowing if he was dead or alive. Sleep eluded him as he lay in bed, shivering with shock and tossing and turning as the nightmarish events played on a loop in his mind. He had eventually crept downstairs to make himself a hot drink, hoping it would soothe him to sleep.

'Jordan?' As the kettle clicked off, his mother had appeared in the doorway, wrapped in her dressing gown. 'Are you okay?'

'Sorry, I didn't mean to wake you. I'm feeling a bit rough and thought a brew might help.'

She had approached him, concern pinching her brows as she placed a hand on his forehead. 'Hmm, you don't feel like you've got a temperature, but you do look pale and you're shivering. Go and get back to bed and I'll bring you a hot chocolate up. I'll phone school first thing and tell them you won't be in today.'

He had felt like a young, innocent boy again as she brought him the drink and tucked his duvet around him to warm him up. Impulsively, he had reached for his mum, embracing her tightly as he buried his head against her neck. 'I love you, Mum,' he had muttered into her dressing gown. It smelt freshly laundered with a hint of her perfume and the smell soothed him as much as the feel of her arms around him.

Claire Gaffney had laughed softly as she ruffled his hair. 'Blimey, you must be feeling rough. I love you too. Now, go and sleep it off.'

Eventually, he had managed to capture several hours of fitful sleep and was now lounging in bed. His brother Craig had come to see how he was and had stayed to keep him company and watch a film with him. Jordan watched Craig. His mouth hung open, as his eyes flickered across the screen, absorbed in the film. For the first time ever, he envied his older brother. Craig lived happily and peacefully in his own quiet world. He was a contented soul, although not much of a conversationalist. Craig viewed life from a different perspective than other people and sometimes conversations could confuse him.

Various SEN co-ordinators had suggested Claire have Craig tested for conditions such as autism, dyslexia and dyspraxia, but she had refused – she hadn't wanted him to be labelled. He was so much more than whatever condition he may or may not have. She appreciated the fact he was different and had his ways, but she loved him unconditionally and wouldn't change a thing about him. It was enough for her that steps had been put in place to support Craig educationally and keep him in a mainstream school, albeit through the remedial hub.

The brothers' contented reverie was broken by Claire suddenly bursting into the room, mobile phone clutched in her hand. She was dressed in her purple carers uniform, a bottle of hand sanitiser clipped to her lanyard, brown hair secured into her usual flawless chignon.

'When did you last see Lewis?' she demanded.

'Lewis?' Jordan straightened up, attempting to feign nonchalance despite the churning of his stomach.

'Lewis is your best friend, Jord,' Craig said, ever helpful.

'Shut up, Craig.'

'I've had Sarah on the phone. Lewis is in The General. He was stabbed last night. He's lost a lot of blood and is described as poorly. When did you last see him?'

'I dunno. After school, I guess. Not at finishing time, later. I'd been at footie practice, and he had a detention.'

'And did you come home together?'

'I think so.'

'You "think" so? You either did or you didn't, Jordan. It was less than twenty-four hours ago. You must remember.'

'All right, all right, we did come home together. I gave him a backie to the precinct, and I came home.'

'He's not saying anything to Sarah or the police about what happened. Do you know anything?'

'The police?' Jordan's stomach lurched again as a squeeze of fear gripped his bowels.

'Yes, Jordan, the police. Did you not hear me, he's been stabbed so of course the police are involved? And it strikes me as a little more than coincidental that Jordan has been assaulted the same time as you're suddenly taken too ill to go to school. What's going on?'

'I don't know what you mean.'

'She means do you know who stabbed Jordan and is that why you're pretending to be ill?'

'Shut *up*, Craig. Look, Mum, I genuinely do feel rough, and I don't know anything about Lewis being stabbed. I left him at the precinct, he was going on about wanting to try and get some drugs and I didn't want anything to do with it, so came straight home. You know what he can be like sometimes, he likes pretending to be the big man. He's probably rubbed someone up the wrong way. Can I go and see him?'

Claire eyed him dubiously as she weighed up what he had said. God knows Jordan had his faults, show her a teenager that didn't, but drugs and knives weren't his thing. Never. He was a good kid – studious and polite. She'd raised both her boys the right way. Fine, she might not have much, but what she did have was kept pristine and more importantly than that, she had raised her boys to have manners and respect for other people. If Jordan said he didn't know anything, then she believed him. She'd have to give him the benefit of the doubt for risk of alienating him. If she did that then there would be little chance of him coming and speaking to her.

Sighing, she shook her head. 'I doubt Sarah will want you hanging round the hospital, love. Wait until he's home, you can go and see him them, but if he tells you who did it you must promise to tell me straight away.'

Jordan nodded mutely and Sarah let out another sigh as she gave her boys a smile. 'I'm off to work, I'll see you tonight.'

Both boys mumbled their goodbyes. Craig was distracted by his mobile phone, and this piqued Jordan's interest as his brother rarely texted.

'Who are you chatting to?' Jordan said as he reached for the phone.

Craig nudged his arm away as Jordan's own phone bleeped. 'My mate Owen Walsh who I used to go to school with. He wanted your number, so I've just sent it to him.'

'Why? I've never even heard of him.'

'You might know him as Wheeler,' said Craig as Jordan's phone chirruped. His eyes widened as he saw an image of the lock knife he had used yesterday accompanied by the message:

> Got the blade with your prints all over it and the
> video too. Meet me after school at the crime
> scene. I've got some work for you.

'Has he texted you? What does Wheeler want with you?'

Jordan blinked back tears as he grabbed his phone and slammed out of the room. '*Shut up*, Craig!'

9

<hr>

'Good morning, people. It's looking like another busy day, so let's get to it.' Kym did her customary double clap and the pockets of chatter in the office died down. 'Connor, the stabbing you attended last night, is that all done and dusted?'

'The scene is done, for what it's worth. There's no sign of the weapon and we have nothing to help us identify the offender. CCTV has captured a black car near the scene, but no registration. CID were struggling to get information from the victim. His clothing has been seized and placed in the drying cabinet and Adila has asked if we can arrange injury photos later today. The nurse has said if we let her know what time we're going, she'll arrange to change the bandages at the same time so we can record the stab wound. He's also got injuries to his face and hands.'

'Which ward is he on?' Amanda asked as she scribbled notes on the job sheet.

'Children's ward.'

'Bloody hell, how old is he?'

'Fourteen,' said Connor.

'A year older than you,' quipped Chris. At twenty-two

Connor was the youngest member of staff. He had previously only attended volume crime scene such as burglaries, but several months ago had been promoted. Initially, he thought he would have to leave Beech Field and work elsewhere, but his colleague Nicola Warne had successfully applied for a temporary crime-scene manager's post, so Connor had taken her position and was delighted to be able to stay with his team.

'I know I'm getting on, but seriously I swear our victims and our offenders are getting younger,' said Elaine. She was the eldest of the SOCOs with fading blonde hair and a plump, rosy face.

'You're right, there certainly wasn't the level of knife crime there is today when I first joined,' Amanda said.

'If I had the choice, I'd rather someone shoot me than try to stab me,' said Tara as she twirled a piece of hair around her finger.

'Is that something you fantasise about often?' Maya said with a laugh.

Tara grinned. 'No, it's just that in the majority of shootings we attend, people miss. You've got to be up close and personal for someone to stab them, so there's more chance they'll do more harm.'

'I'd take either of those options rather than drown,' said Chris. 'That must be horrendous.'

'Or die in a fire,' added Connor.

'Falling from a height would be my–' Elaine was cut off by a clapping of hands.

'Sorry to interrupt such a light-hearted, jovial conversation, but can we get back to discussing our workload?' asked Kym, her face contorted into a scowl.

'We have the victim at hospital, several burglaries and a raft of cars at the garage which we really need to break the back of today. Sean has also made me aware of a rape suspect that is currently being booked into custody. If you'd like to chat amongst yourselves and decide who is doing what rather than your worst-case scenario of violent death, I'd be ever so obliged.'

With another double clap, she spun on her heel and headed for the sanctuary of her office.

⌇

The car park of The General was busy as always. Maya and Chris had been circling it for over fifteen minutes trying to get a space as close to the door as possible so they wouldn't have to hike too far with the camera kit. There were usually designated bays for police and CSI vehicles, but these had already been used up as several police cars and vans had parked up hurriedly, two with their blue lights still flashing.

Beech Field's response officers had been depleted as several had been required to accompany a violent prisoner who had taken ill in custody. They had admitted to taking an overdose and started to attack the custody nurse, knowing they would administer Naloxone which would reverse the effects of opiates.

Whereas most people would be grateful to a healthcare professional for administering a drug which could potentially save their life, seasoned drug users knew it would instantly reverse the effect of their high and the money they had desperately procured to pay for the hit would be wasted. Such is the grip of addiction.

In addition to that, a female had been pulled down from a motorway bridge and was having a psychotic episode, which also meant that police were required to assist in restraining her and keeping her safe, whilst ensuring she didn't flee the hospital. Maya didn't need to walk into A&E to know how many members of the public would be sat cross-legged and judgemental as they overlooked their own ailments in favour of criticising the large police presence, which in their inexperienced eyes would appear heavy-handed and a waste of resources.

'Do you want to stay with the van and I'll head over to the ward?' Maya asked Chris as she glanced at the time. 'The nurse is due to change the victim's bandages, so we need to get in there to photograph his stab wound.'

Chris frowned as he perused the busy car park. There were so many people coming and going it almost felt disorientating.

'I dunno, love. Let's just circle round again and go in together. The victim's mother knows we're coming so I'm sure the nurse will wait. A space is bound to come free eventually.'

'If you're worried about me being targeted by Naylor now, you needn't be. There are more cops here than at Beech Field, plus the fact a hospital is a bit too public, don't you think? All the CCTV cameras for a start. I'm sure the nurse is far too busy to wait around for me, it wouldn't be fair on the rest of the patients. You know how busy it is in there.'

'I suppose so,' he said without much conviction as he continued to scowl around him.

'Honest, I'll be fine. If I need you, I'll ring you.' Maya grabbed her camera bag and began to weave her way along the hospital corridors until she reached the children's ward. She waited at the intercom until she could introduce herself to a nurse, give the password and be led to Lewis Mellor's room. The teenager had been given a side room to himself and was reclining moodily in bed.

'Hi, Lewis. Miss Mellor? I'm Maya, we spoke before.' Maya hovered at the doorway and gave a little wave. Sarah Mellor stood to greet her and inclined her head towards the corridor. Maya followed the pale woman out of the room. Her eyes were rimmed with mascara stains, and she looked utterly drained.

She was incredibly thin, dressed only in leggings and a tight T-shirt. She wrapped her arms around herself for warmth.

'Have you heard anyfink from the detective investigating Lewis's stabbing?' she asked, desperation pinching her face.

'They're doing everything they can to track down any potential witnesses or CCTV footage, but unless Lewis can provide us with more information about who did this to him, we're struggling.'

Sarah sighed and ran a hand through greasy blonde hair, her blue eyes pooling with unshed tears. 'It's not good enough.' She pleaded, 'You need to do more.'

'We are trying, Sarah, I can promise you that. DC Adila Laghari is one of our most dedicated detectives and she's all over it,' Maya said reassuringly.

'Five millimetres. Five bloody millimetres.'

'I'm sorry, I don't understand.'

'That main doctor, the one with his tie tucked funny in his shirt said the blade had missed Lewis's somefink artery by five millimetres. If it had caught it, he would have bled out in no time. Do you realise that? My boy would be dead.' A sob escaped her lips as tears began to stream down her face.

'I know he acts like he's some bloody hardman. You lot probably think he's just some two-bit scrote not worth bothering with because he's in bother at school and he's been done for shoplifting a few times, but he's a child, Maya. He's fourteen. He's on a bloody children's ward for Christ's sake. There are teddy bears on the curtain around his bed.'

Sarah suddenly lost the fight in her as she slumped forwards and Maya gathered her in her arms. She held the woman and stroked her cigarette-scented hair until the noisy sobs subsided. Maya guided Sarah towards a chair in the corridor and handed her a tissue as she knelt in front of her.

'None of us think anything bad about Lewis. You said

yourself, he's a fourteen-year-old boy. A child. I promise you we will do everything we can to find out who did this to him. I believe Lewis was reluctant to hand his phone over to our digital investigation team, perhaps you could try and persuade him otherwise as they might find information on there that Lewis is too scared to tell us.'

'I've asked him several times and he won't. You know what teenagers are like with their phones. You've more chance of getting blood out of a stone.'

A nurse Maya recognised from a previous ward visit arrived and Maya gestured that she'd be with her shortly. 'The nurse is here to change his bandages, so I'll pop in and take the photographs. Do you want me to try and talk to him?'

Sarah shrugged hopelessly. 'You can try, but I honestly don't fink he'll speak to you. He's coming out with some bullshit about "not talking to the feds" like he's some thirty-year-old American gangster. The reality is, he still gives me cuddles and cries his eyes out when I know he's missing his dad. He still sleeps with the stuffed rabbit he's had since he was a baby for Christ's sake.' She gave Maya a wan smile and squeezed her hand. 'Ta for being kind.'

Maya nodded and returned to Lewis's room where the nurse was busy checking his temperature and blood pressure, allowing Maya time to set up her camera. Before Maya had a chance to ask Lewis anything he turned to her, concerned.

'Was that my Mum crying out there, is she okay?'

'She's upset and worried, Lewis. She's terrified by the fact you could have been killed. However grown-up you are, you'll always be her little boy, you know that, right? It's just how parents are. My mama is still the same way with me at my age. To her, you're her world and she can't cope with the fact that something this awful has happened to you at your age.'

Lewis was staring at the wall, deliberately avoiding eye

contact, but a slight tremor of his lower lip suggested that her words were resonating. She decided to chip away a little more in the hope she could persuade him to start talking.

'To be honest, mate, what she seems most upset about is the fact you won't tell us who did this to you. I know a lot of people your age are told it's wrong to "grass" and talk to the police. If it helps, I'm not a police officer. I'm a civilian member of police staff, a member of forensic services, so if you talk to me, it's not really the same thing, is it? We'd just be chatting, right?'

He turned to look at her but remained resolutely silent.

Maya ran a hand through her hair. 'What worries me and your mum, is that you've obviously popped up on someone's radar for this to have happened. So, you could at least tell me if it was a disagreement over something or if you're being bullied? If you don't talk to us, we can't help you and who's to say that whoever did this won't do it again.

'And I know you must be scared. I've taken injury photographs of people much older than you who have been terrified by what has happened to them. It's only natural. I've also seen a lot of bodies in the mortuary too, of people who haven't been as lucky as you.'

She paused to let that sink in. Lewis's eyes had widened at the mention of the mortuary.

'And you have been lucky, mate,' Maya continued as she made a gap using her thumb and forefinger. 'That is five millimetres.' She turned to the nurse. 'Didn't the specialist say that was how far away the knife had been from cutting into Lewis's artery?'

The nurse nodded and Maya turned back to Lewis. 'If that had happened you would have been dead within minutes. You would have bled out, all alone on the floor like nothing more than a piece of meat a butcher had just slaughtered. If you think your mum is upset now, can you imagine how devastated she would have been if that happened? And from now on, every time you walk out of the house, she's going to be worried sick that it's going to happen again. You need to start talking.'

And talk he did.

~

Back at Beech Field, Maya left Chris to park the van and practically sprinted to CID. Jack Dwyer, the acting DI, was strolling towards her from the kitchen. His arrogant swagger would normally cause her to walk in the opposite direction, but she eagerly followed him into his office.

'Lewis Mellor,' she stated breathlessly.

'Ah, yes. Did you manage to get his injuries recorded?'

'Yes and he told me what happened.'

'Oh, Maya, you're fantastic.' He indicated for her to take a seat and reached for his policy book so he could take notes.

'Lewis said he was with his friend, Jordan Gaffney. They'd both left school late and Jordan had offered him a backie on the way home. They were near the wasteland at the back of the precinct and Jordan cross-chained. Lewis said Jordan started trying to fix it and he made some piss-taking comment about the state of the bike, which led to the two lads having a row. Lewis said Jordan rode off without him and he stayed to have a smoke and calm down before he went home.'

Jack was scribbling away furiously and held his hand to pause Maya while he caught up with his notes. She surveyed him as he wrote, he was tall and lean with a shaven head and dark eyes. He was a good-looking man, but arrogant with it, which had caused them to have clashed several times in the past. Whilst he was a good detective, he tended to make assumptions and wasn't always keen to take on other people's views unless he could pass them off as his own.

'Then what did he say happened?'

'He was trying to light his roll-up. But his lighter was out of gas. He said an older guy approached him, late thirties, scruffy-looking. Lewis was under the impression he might be a rough sleeper. He handed Lewis a light and started chatting to him. He asked Lewis for a spare smoke but got irritable when Lewis told him it was his last one.

'Then Lewis said the guy made him feel uncomfortable. Asked him if he wanted to come and sit next to him on the ground so they could share the roll-up. Lewis said he was looking him up and down, licking his lips. That he had his hands in his trouser pockets and appeared to be rubbing himself.'

Jack nodded and Maya continued. 'Lewis said he got freaked out, called the guy a nonce and started to run off. He was chased and Lewis tripped on the loose stones and that's when the offender stabbed him. His account of being on the ground is certainly consistent with his injuries and he has gravel rash on his knees, chin and the heel of his hands.'

'Could he describe the man?'

'He was vague about it but said he'd try. He was starting to get upset at that point, so I didn't want to push him. I've already spoken to Sian in the Imaging Unit; she's going to arrange to see him tomorrow so they can work on an E-FIT.'

'That's great work. Can you keep me posted on that, please? If he does come up with a decent image, I'll get the team to circulate it right away. I don't like the sound of this. The stabbing is bad enough, but the predatory element is disturbing me. Especially because, as always, it's an area where there's limited CCTV.' Sean sat and thought for a moment before he continued.

'Does the offender know that do you think, and he's been hanging round on the off-chance of preying on someone? I'll speak to DI Redford about getting a warning out to local schools today ahead of a press release tomorrow. I'd be happier if the kids were warned to avoid the area, at least for now.'

Maya nodded her agreement. 'From talking to Connor earlier, I believe the crime scene gave us nothing other than a few blood swabs which are bound to be his, no. There was no sign of a weapon. He was eventually found by a delivery guy who called the ambulance. Fortunately, he came along when he did, it sounds like our victim was in too much of a state of shock to have the sense to call someone.'

Maya was about to leave, when Jack swiped his face with a hand and let out a sigh. 'Bloody teenagers.'

Maya felt her hackles rise as she assumed Jack was going to spew out a tirade of rants about how Lewis was nothing but trouble and not worth his time. How a kid his age already had a criminal record and lived with a mum who Jack deemed common. She was surprised when he turned to her with a look of compassion.

'Do you remember being that age?' he asked rhetorically. 'I bloody do, and God, it was hard enough back then. Bound to be even worse now with them all having mobile phones and social media. It means they never have the chance to get a break from the pressure of their peers. Something like this is bound to have a huge impact on the poor kid and it won't help when everyone knows about it. I believe he can be a bit of a loose cannon and I hope this doesn't push him further down the wrong track.'

'His mum is clearly supportive and engaging. Apparently, his dad walked out years ago and is inconsistent with contact, so she's raised him on her own, with no other family support,' Maya said.

'Cases like theirs are why school is so important. How many of us listened to our parents or family at that age anyway? I didn't, more's the pity. It was a teacher who got me on the straight and narrow. Mr Roberts, PE teacher and ex-army. He was a real stickler for the rules. He caught me playing truant and smoking a joint one day. He tore a strip off me and said he'd give me the choice to either visit a prison cell or mortuary because if I carried on the way I was going, I'd end up in either one by the time I was twenty. I was such a little gobshite back in the day.'

'Past tense, are you sure?' Maya grinned. 'Which did you choose?'

'Neither. I couldn't decide which scared me more. He dragged me to the local police station, and I was convinced he was going to get me locked up. Instead, he introduced me to a friend of his who was a sergeant at the time. He was in charge of the police cadets and gave me the option to join up with them instead, so of course I didn't hesitate, and the rest is history,' he said with a shrug. 'Adila is taking the lead on this case, but I might go and see Jordan and have a word with the lad, see if I can get through to him,' he muttered as an afterthought to himself.

'I'll keep you posted about the E-FIT,' Maya said as she left him to it. She was surprised at someone as egotistical as Jack firstly sharing something so personal, and secondly appearing uncharacteristically empathetic. She shook her head as she mused that no matter how well you thought you knew someone, they could always surprise you.

10

The fugitive knew he was taking a huge risk. Hiding in plain sight was all well and good, but even he questioned if he was pushing his luck. He pulled his hat down to cover his face as he ambled along the perimeter of Beech Field police station. He reached the bus stop, grateful that there was nobody else waiting. From here, he had optimum view of the staff entrance.

He kept his head lowered, allowing his eyes to flit from behind dark glasses and scour the windows of the building. He wondered which office she worked in and whether, if she looked out now, she would be able to see him. Would she recognise him? His eyes drifted to the stairwell; perhaps he would see her there?

He didn't know how long he stayed there. He lost all track of time, watching police cars come and go, some on blues and twos. He was consumed only with thoughts of her. Occasionally, he had been joined by fellow commuters. First, there had been the gaggle of schoolgirls, then the old man who he worried might want to strike up a conversation. Clearly, his size and the fact that even uncommunicative, he could radiate aggression, kept them all at bay.

Eventually, his patience was rewarded. He watched as her Triumph Bonneville approached the white barrier. He heard the engine idling as the barrier rose slowly, steadily. He saw her approach the junction, indicating right, she eventually joined the queue of traffic as a delivery driver waved her out. His eyes burned into her helmet as she rode towards him. She even glanced in his direction and for a millisecond, her eyes settled on the reflection of his glasses. Then she spotted a gap in traffic, increased speed and weaved away.

She had been so close. She had even looked at him. He had taken a huge risk, but his patience had paid off. He stretched out the stiffness in his limbs and walked away from the bus stop. Walked away from Beech Field police station. Being at her place of work was one thing, but he needed to get closer.

He needed to be at her apartment.

11

____

Being back at the scene of the crime made Jordan feel physically sick. His eyes scoured the gravel, convinced he could still see traces of Lewis's blood. He was half-expecting undercover police to come bursting from out of nowhere. It was a common adage wasn't it, that offenders always return to the scene of the crime, so who was to say they weren't lying in wait. After all, he *was* back here, wasn't he? Jordan's agitation continued to build as he waited for Wheeler's arrival.

Eventually, Wheeler's car crawled towards him. Despite the windows being up, Jordan could hear the deafening bass from the stereo within. Wheeler gave him a Machiavellian grin as he parked up. Susie offered him a curt nod. She remained in the car chewing on gum while she checked her overly contoured make-up in the vanity mirror. Wheeler climbed out of the car and swaggered over to Jordan, accompanied by the smell of weed.

'Ait, little-man. How's that mate of yours doing?'

'Not so good. Lewis, he'd lost a lot of blood by the time they got him to hospital. They're saying he's described as poorly, whatever that means. Look, about that video and the knife–'

Wheeler laughed as he sparked up a joint. 'Not so fast, little-man. You're even keener than Susie and that's saying something. This little meetup is all about us building trust. Have the police been to see you?'

'Not yet. Mum said they're coming to take a statement in an hour. That means Lewis must have grassed on me.'

'And what are you going to tell them?'

'Nothing. Maybe something. I don't know.'

Wheeler laughed again and gathered Jordan into a man hug. 'You're going to tell them the truth. You gave Lewis a ride after school. When you got to here, your chain came off. You were fixing the bike and he started to take the piss. You had words and told him to fuck off. You left him here and cycled home. You've not heard from him since. A lot of fact mixed in with the twist of a lie and trust me, you'll get away with attempted murder. Get me?'

Jordan nodded and reached for his bike as he thanked him. 'Whoa,' Wheeler exclaimed. 'Where do you think you're going?'

'Home. I told you; the police are on their way to take a statement. I need to be back in time or my mum will kill me.'

'And I told you, this meeting is all about us building trust. Now I like you, little-man, and the last thing I want to do is to have to share what I know about Lewis's little accident. I know you didn't mean to do it, but the fact is you did. You stabbed him and left him for dead.' Wheeler took a drag of the joint and blew the smoke in Jordan's face.

'I mean, let's face it, look at you with your tight little ass and slim figure. They'd love you inside. You'd be so popular you'd be dead within the week.'

Jordan's sphincter tightened at the veiled threat and his legs began to tremble violently.

'No, please. I couldn't cope with that. And there's my mum to think of. Please, I'll do anything, don't grass me up.'

Wheeler's eyes narrowed as he flicked the remains of the

joint at Jordan's chest. 'Did you just call me a fucking grass?!' he screamed in his face, causing the boy to shrink back so much he nearly fell to the ground.

'No, no, I'm sorry, I... I...'

Wheeler let out a manic laugh which was nearly as terrifying as the deranged look in his eyes. 'I'm messing with you, little-man, I know we're good. We're building trust, remember?'

Jordan nodded eagerly. He glanced towards the car, hoping Susie would intervene in the nightmarish situation, but from what he could see, she was too absorbed in taking selfies and hadn't been paying any attention to the exchange.

'So, I have a situation which has dropped me in a bit of shit with my boss and he's the type of man you really don't want to upset, know what I mean?'

Jordan nodded again.

'It would really help *me* help him, if you could run a few errands for me. Nothing too taxing, I just need you to take a parcel to an address for me. Drop stuff off now and then, you know?'

'Not drugs?' Jordan could feel his sphincter twitch again.

'As me old nan used to say, "Ask me no questions and I'll tell you no lies". Look, you don't need to know what's in the package, you just need to do as I ask, otherwise it'll make me think I can't trust you and this is...'

'All about building trust,' Jordan mumbled.

'Good lad,' said Wheeler as he gave him a playful punch on the arm, which nearly knocked the lad over.

'Here,' Wheeler reached in his pocket and handed Jordan a small mobile phone, 'this is a burner phone. You keep it on you at all times and don't ever contact me on anything other than that. I've put my number in it.'

Jordan watched with horror as Wheeler then fished around

in the crotch of his boxer shorts before pulling out a cellophane-wrapped square package about the size of his palm. 'All I need you to do is take this to the flats on Jowett Row. Knock on flat number three and ask for Taz. He won't give you anything in return, just leave it with him.'

Jordan turned the package around in his hands; it felt uncomfortably warm and knowing where it had come from, Jordan had a yearning to sanitise his hands. He glanced around him and swallowed nervously as he followed Wheeler's lead and secured the package down the front of his boxer shorts. He knew it was drugs he was carrying and he also knew there was no way he could refuse Wheeler's demands.

'When does it need to be there for?'

'Now.'

'But I told you, the police–'

Wheeler let out his manic laugh again. 'Trust me, little-man, if the police are at your house the last thing you want to do is roll in with that tucked next to your cock. If you don't want to be late for them, I suggest you start pedalling.'

Jordan didn't need telling twice as his feet flew over the pedals, powering him towards Jowett Row.

12

Wheeler and Susie drove towards the shops where he parked up and lit a joint. He took a deep drag and exhaled slowly. It wasn't just the cannabis that was relaxing him, but the fact he'd also managed to pacify Reilly with the news he'd found a new drugs courier. Jordan was the ideal candidate, he'd never been in trouble with the police before and was so terrified of Wheeler that he'd do whatever he demanded of him, whenever.

With his boss off his back and Jordan at his beck and call, things were looking good. Wheeler took a last drag of his joint before flicking it out of the car window. He turned to Susie and gave her his best smile as he reached across to squeeze her thigh suggestively.

'Fancy picking up a chippy and going back to yours?'

'Yeah, I'm starving, but I'm not sure about going back to mine.'

Wheeler's relaxed reverie was broken in an instant. 'Why not?'

'Thing is, it's me dad. You know he's not keen on us going together as it is and now he's said he doesn't want you at the house anymore. He said you don't respect the place and you speak to me Mum like shit.'

Wheeler glared at her as he began to pick away at the persistent patch of acne on his forehead. 'Cheeky bastard,' he muttered.

'What about going back to yours?'

Wheeler thought briefly of his alcoholic mother sipping vodka in her dirty dressing gown. He thought of her greasy hair and the smell of her unwashed body. How she got teary when she saw him and tried to cling to him; her bony fingers digging into his skin. He shook his head. 'No, not mine.'

He sat gloomily and stared at the row of shops in front of him whilst he considered his options. The thing was, he couldn't fault Susie's family for not wanting him, he *had* taken the piss and spoke to her parents like shit. It was just his way.

If Susie's dad had been any kind of man, he'd have kicked him out of the house before now, not just told her he wasn't welcome anymore. He considered racking up there anyway and fronting it out. Perhaps he could turn on the charm, or failing that, threaten Mr Smith with a slap. But then the pathetic bastard would probably just phone the police and that was grief he didn't need.

What he needed was a new place to stay. Somewhere he could have privacy especially with the new shipment of gear coming anytime soon. He needed a safe place and quick. Somewhere the police wouldn't come looking. Somewhere he could hide in plain sight and go about his business without people interfering.

Just as he was considering his options, he watched an elderly man navigate his wheeled shopping bag out of the corner shop. He looked rather unkempt and dishevelled and judging by the way he was attempting to manoeuvre the bag down the small set of stairs, he didn't have too much strength.

'C'mon,' he said to Susie as he indicated his head towards the old boy. They raced over and Wheeler grinned at the man. 'Can I help you, sir?'

The wizened man scowled suspiciously at Wheeler, his face softening slightly when he saw Susie clutching his arm and smiling brightly. 'I'm okay, it's just these steps, you know.'

'May I?' Wheeler grinned again as he reached for the shopping bag and lowered it down the steps. 'There's your problem,' he said as he dropped to his haunches. 'One of your wheels is loose. I could fix that for you if you've got some tools?'

The man hesitated, grateful for the help but wary of the skinny-looking youth. 'I... well... I have a few bits at my flat.'

'I can't fix it until it's empty, see?' Wheeler said as he lifted the bag, which was weighty with the shopping.

'We can walk you back if you like?' Susie offered. 'He can carry your bag.'

The old man weighed up the precarious lift and the imposing stairway. 'I would appreciate your help,' he said tentatively.

'It'd be our pleasure, wouldn't it, Suse?'

'Yeah course.' Susie smiled reassuringly whilst Wheeler effortlessly scooped up the shopping bag.

'What's your name?' Wheeler asked congenially.

'Mr Bennett.'

'Pleased to meet you, I'm Owen, but my friends call me Wheeler, and this is Susie. I tell you what, Mr Bennett, Susie and I were going to treat ourselves to a chippy tea if you'd like to join us. My treat, of course.'

Bennett beamed at the thought. It had been a long time since he'd had a chippy. His pension hadn't stretched to a treat like that for such a long time. The mere thought of fish and chips swimming in salt and vinegar left him salivating. He looked at the young man and smiled, feeling bad about his earlier misgivings.

'That would be lovely if you're sure you don't mind? I can make us all a nice cup of tea to go with it.' He nodded towards the shopping bag. 'And there's a nice bit of Battenberg in there too, for afters. That's if you don't mind putting up with an old man?'

'It'd be our pleasure, Mr Bennett,' purred Wheeler as Susie leaned in to link the old man's arm.

He beamed at the pair of them. 'Please,' he insisted, 'call me Albert.'

13

———

Maya had arrived home later than anticipated. She had called to the gym and then to Dominique's, so it was turned 8pm by the time she parked the Bonneville up. It was a miserable evening, biting wind hurled rain at her, the shrouded night sky felt oppressive and sinister. Maya ran to the rear door of the apartment block and was annoyed to discover it had been left unlocked again. Some of the residents were far too complacent about security and she was sick of reporting it to the property developer who owned Miller Court.

Just as she stepped through the doors, her mobile rang with a number she didn't recognise. She considered ignoring it, but her curiosity was piqued and if it was a scam caller, she could always block it. She answered but didn't speak straight away. There was a pause before she heard a familiar voice she couldn't quite place.

'Hello? Maya, is that you? Are you there?'

'Yes, it's Maya speaking. Who's this?'

'Hiya, Maya. It's only me, Dave Wainwright, *Evening News*.'

'How the hell did you get my number?'

'Oh, come on, Maya. Don't be frosty. We're on the same side.

Journalists can be just as canny as detectives. I just want to give you the opportunity to give your side of the story, about your dad? It may garner some public sympathy and help flush him out from wherever he's hiding. I can help you, Maya. Wouldn't you like that?'

'Go to hell, you parasite!' she screamed before hanging up and immediately blocking his number.

Shaken, she called for the lift and shivered as she waited. The inclement weather felt like it had pinched through to her marrow despite the rage she felt towards 'Dave the Bastard'. The lift creaked ominously as it climbed to the eleventh floor. The doors groaned open, and Maya stepped out to an eerie glow from the corridor. The ceiling light had become faulty and was flickering on and off. Maya swore under her breath as she walked down the corridor, the light giving a horror movie feel that unnerved her.

An instinct made her turn, and she was relieved to find herself alone in the corridor. Her mind had conjured up a Dracula-esque figure lurking in the flickering shadows. She swore again, cursing herself for letting the phone call unnerve her so much. The urge to get into her apartment was overwhelming. With shaking hands, she fumbled with her keys but in her haste dropped them.

'Shit!' She picked her keys off the carpet and swung them frantically towards the lock. Except the lock wasn't where it should be. The door had opened suddenly, and Maya let out a scream.

'What's the matter?' Spence asked as he instinctively pulled her towards him before glancing down the corridor.

'What the hell are you doing here?' she chided.

'Lisa wanted to swap shifts last minute, so I thought I'd come to you and make a start on dinner. I heard the lift and guessed it was you so came to open the door. Are you okay, has something happened?'

Maya buried her head into Spence's chest as his arms encircled her.

'Jesus. I'm a paranoid mess,' she mumbled into his shirt. 'It's the shitty weather, that bloody light and "Dave the Bastard". I'm overtired, and it all just spooked me.'

'What about him?' Spence asked, a pulse throbbing in his jaw at the mere mention of the journalist as Maya told him about the call.

'Mention it to Redford at work again tomorrow. Make sure he follows it up as another complaint to Wainwright's boss. This is deliberate harassment.' Spence dropped a kiss on the top of her head and led her through the flat and onto the sofa. 'It's not just him though, you've been really jumpy lately,' he said cautiously as he handed her a glass of wine.

Maya threw him a caustic look as she gulped her drink. 'You think? My psychotic estranged father is on the loose and has recently been sighted and you wonder why I'm a bit tense.'

Spence raised his hands placatingly. 'Hey, I'm not criticising you. And I know the reasons why. I'm on your side, remember.' He drew her to him for a hug and she smiled apologetically.

'You were so restless in your sleep again, no wonder you're overtired. You're clearly shattered and that's not going to help your nerves.'

She rubbed her eyes as she sank back into the sofa. 'I am tired,' she acquiesced. She looked at Spence and as always, her heart lurched at the sight of him. He was dressed in jeans and a polo shirt, his dark wavy hair looked unruly and his electric-blue eyes were as dazzling as ever. She reached for his hand and smiled at him, and he smiled back, flashing the dimples she loved so much. 'I'm glad you're here,' she said as she squeezed his hand.

Spence worked as the bar manager at the local pub The Eagle. He shared the role with his friend Lisa and they each took it in turn to stay at the pub when they were on a late shift. The rest of the time he preferred to stay with Maya and had all but moved in. He was due to begin studying to become a personal trainer in the hope that the job would bring more stability and better pay.

'Did you see Dominique tonight – has she said anything else?' he asked.

Maya shook her head. 'I tried to hint at the subject of Marcus and what happened when I was younger, but she was deliberately evasive again and then started getting snappy. I'm not probing it any further. It's not fair, it's clearly upsetting her and pissing her off and the last thing I want is to fall out over it.'

'Okay,' said Spence as he took a sudden interest in some fluff on the arm of the sofa.

Maya straightened up. 'What does "okay" mean?'

'Nothing.'

'You used a tone.'

Spence sighed. 'I don't want to rile you.'

'Jesus, Spence, this is me. You don't have to walk on eggshells, just tell me what's on your mind, because something clearly is.'

'It's Dominique and her refusal to talk to you about the past. I don't think it's fair that she's refusing to engage with you. I appreciate how upsetting it is for her, but I really think it would help you to get some answers. Without clarity, I don't see how you can move on. She's leaving you with more questions than answers.'

Maya nodded her agreement. 'But what can I do about it?'

'Like I said, I know it's distressing for her, but she's your mother, she's the parent. I think she should tell you what you want to know. Maybe give it a couple of weeks for things to settle down after the sighting, then broach the subject again. But this time, don't take no for an answer.'

Maya nodded again. Spence was right, she wanted more than anything to be able to fill in the blanks from her childhood and Dominique was the only person who could do that for her. Spence wasn't the only person who had suggested it. Her counsellor Jayne had pretty much had the same conversation with her during their last session.

Maya sighed as she sank back into the sofa again, finishing the glass of wine in one greedy gulp. It was time to face up to the fact that as difficult as it might be, Maya needed to speak to Dominique and make her confront the past.

14

———

Claire Gaffney stood at the kitchen door; arms folded with a face like thunder as she watched Jordan wheel his bike into the yard.

'Where have you been?' she hissed. 'The police have been here for forty-five minutes. They were just getting ready to leave. Do you have any idea how bad this looks?'

Jordan was panting with the exertion of having cycled back at speed after the drugs drops at Jowett Row. It had been a horrendous experience. He had knocked on the battered door of flat number three and been greeted by Taz, a terrifying-looking man with a tattooed face wielding a baseball bat. Taz had insisted Jordan follow him inside, revealing that the Stygian property was a squat which reeked of dirt and drugs.

Taz had examined the package before secreting it down the front of his dirty jogging bottoms, then he had turned his attention to Jordan. He had slowly looked Jordan up and down, the baseball bat dangling loosely, but no less menacingly in his hand. Jordan had become rooted to the spot with fear as Taz had approached him. Without saying a word, he had leant towards Jordan so closely, for a moment he thought he was going to kiss him. But even worse, Taz had licked him, running his nicotine-furred tongue up the side of his face from his jawbone to his temple.

Jordan had recoiled in horror, desperate to swipe the stinking saliva from his face. He had wanted to run out of the flat, but his feet wouldn't move. Taz had stood grinning at him, before eventually leaning forward again. Jordan had tensed and closed his eyes, anticipating being licked again. He had felt Taz's hot breath in his face as the maniac suddenly screamed 'Boo!' Jordan's legs had become unstuck, his heart pounding in his throat as he ran out of the flat and jumped on his bike.

Now home and safe, his stomach lurched again at the thought of the police. He had hoped they would have been and gone by now. Surely, they were too busy to hang around and wait for the likes of him. Solemnly, he followed Claire through to the freshly polished lounge where an Asian lady with a thick dark fringe sat smiling pleasantly at him over the cup of one of Claire's special filter coffees.

'Hi, Jordan. I'm DC Adila Laghari from Beech Field police station.'

'Hiya, nice to meet you. I'm so sorry to have kept you waiting, I lost track of time.'

'That's okay, I'm glad you're finally here. I know your mum has told you already that it's really important that I ask you a few questions about Lewis.'

Jordan shrugged. 'I wasn't there when it happened. I didn't see anything, and I don't know who did it.'

Adila smiled reassuringly. 'It would just be useful if you could talk me through what happened from leaving school and the last time you saw Lewis. You might recall something important to us that you didn't think was relevant at the time, okay?'

Jordan nodded reluctantly as he talked Adila through the

sequence of events, fact mixed with fiction, just as Wheeler had advised him. After what felt like an age, Adila finished making notes and closed her policy book before reaching into her messenger bag for a piece of paper.

'One last thing, Jordan. Lewis has very bravely managed to produce what we call an E-FIT. It's an electronic picture of the person who attacked him. I'd like you to look at the image please and tell me if you recognise the person in it.'

Jordan hesitated. Was this a trick, was the police officer going to show him a picture of himself? Was he about to be arrested? With trembling hands, he reached for the paper and turned it over. He glanced at the picture for a moment and felt a bubble of hysteria rise in his stomach. It took all his effort to quell it as he shook his head and handed the picture back.

The police officer had returned the E-FIT back to her bag and Jordan had excused himself as he fled up the stairs to the sanctuary of his room. He had covered his face with his pillow as his body was wracked with laughter, tears rolling down his face as he thought of the image he had just been shown.

Lewis wasn't such an idiot after all and he was clearly trying to protect Jordan, which was a huge relief. The E-FIT he had allowed to be produced was a scruffier, long-haired version of Mr Ramos, their PE teacher.

15

———

DI Redford, acting DI Jack Dwyer and DS Mark Turner were gathered round the conference table in Redford's room, ready for their daily briefing. Redford steepled his fingers under his chin as he surveyed his colleagues. 'Let's start with Kyle Brogan,' he said as he pushed paperwork across the desk. 'What's the latest, Mark?'

'Sean tried to engage with him in the hospital after he was moved from ICU, but with no joy. Brogan's sister rang Sean last night to say he'd discharged himself from hospital and hasn't been seen since.' Turner shrugged. 'Same old story, he's never going to tell us who did it and he's too scared of repercussions to hang around.'

Redford glanced in his policy book. 'Have we had any intelligence to link him to our local dealers?'

Turner shook his head. 'We don't know who he's working for, but Ivo Zlatan's name keeps coming up and we believe his lot are responsible for Brogan being taxed.'

Redford ran a hand across his chin. 'I'm going to make some enquiries with neighbouring forces. I can only guess that if we don't know who Brogan was working for, he could have been recruited by county lines.'

'It's like looking for a needle in a haystack though. We can barely keep up with our own criminals, how the hell are we supposed to police offenders outside our jurisdiction?' Jack asked.

Redford gave him a hard stare. 'Because as we know they'll get too arrogant and slip up eventually. If it is a gang out in force, then dealers like Zlatan won't like their customers being poached. We keep eyes on our criminals and our ears to the ground, they'll lead us to who we're looking for. You know the saying *if you lie down with dogs, you'll get up with fleas*, that's what I'm relying on here. We let it play out and the evidence will come to us.'

Jack and Turner both nodded, but neither felt convinced. It was more like wishful thinking than a positive plan of action, but in reality, they had little else to go on.

'What's the latest on the Lewis Mellor stabbing? Please tell me we've at least had a result back from that.'

'The laceration to his leg is healing well and he's been sent home. He's been able to provide an E-FIT of the offender, which we've released to local press and on social media and Adila is chasing up a couple of lines of enquiry,' Jack said. 'I spoke to Lewis myself and although he's given a reasonable account of the attack, again, there's nothing for us to work with in regard to names and the motive is woolly. I'm doing some work around the predatory element of the attack as I'm confident we're looking for a repeat offender and likely one with a sexual motivation.'

'Good. Keep me posted on that and make sure any press releases advise caution in that area, particularly for youths. Try and word it in a way that won't have the vigilantes out in force or people too scared to leave their own homes; certainly at this point avoid the predatory angle.'

As Jack and Turner both stood to leave, Redford indicated that Jack should remain. He waited until the door was shut before taking Jack into his confidence.

'It's about Maya,' he said, the concern etched on his face. 'You know that MIT are leading the search for Naylor, but I get the impression that they're running out of leads and they're even beginning to doubt the latest potential sighting. Personally, something in my gut is telling me that it was him. I want to make sure we're doing everything we can to keep an eye on her and the other SOCOs. If Naylor does reappear, they could all be cannon fodder.'

'Understood,' said Jack. 'Is Kym aware of your concerns?'

'Yes, but it stays with us for now. The only other person who knows is Amanda, as an ex-cop I trust her instincts and she's an asset to us. Both Kym and Amanda are as concerned as I am and it's clear Maya is struggling.

'What isn't helping is the continued harassment from Dave Wainwright. Despite being warned off by his boss, I believe he's somehow managed to get her mobile number and has been ringing her offering to write an exclusive which will supposedly help unearth Naylor.'

'Jesus, hasn't she had enough to deal with the last year or so without having that parasite on her back too.'

'Exactly. I know you and Maya have locked horns in the past, but I want you to keep things amicable at least. She doesn't need any more stress.'

'We've had our issues but the last thing I'd ever do is cause problems for her. For what it's worth I care about her and I'm as keen as anyone to see Naylor back behind bars.'

'Good to hear.'

'This instinct of yours. What are you thinking?'

Redford rubbed his chin and let out a sigh. 'Strictly between you and me, mate. I think he's a disaster waiting to happen. He's been hellbent on revenge for years and is clearly deranged. I don't think for one moment he's had it away on his toes with no intention of returning. I think it's only a matter of time before he's back.'

'But is he really going to risk going back to jail just for revenge?'

'Maya will really need to watch her back. We know better than anyone how retribution can cause people to act. My concern is that it's such a powerful emotion, Naylor will be prepared to kill. He won't let the fact that Maya is his own flesh and blood stop him from murdering her if that's what he's got planned. We just need to pray to God that we can find him and stop him before that happens.'

16

Maya arrived at occupational health with a heavy heart. Although she was fortunate to have gelled with her counsellor, the sessions exhausted her. Each hour left her feeling fatigued and drained, as if she'd endured an hour of physical exercise. She knew the sessions were beneficial to her mental health, but the fact she couldn't remember her past, and Dominique was reluctant to help, always left her feeling frustrated and unable to move on.

Maya paced the waiting room, staring without really seeing the familiar corporate posters until she heard heels clattering down the stairway.

'Come on up.' Jayne Harding was a tall lady with long blonde hair. She had a mischievous smile and radiated warmth. Maya believed that if they had met in different circumstances, Jayne would have been the type of woman she'd happily go for drinks with. Maya followed her up the first flight of stairs to her office, where she was invited to sit down in the familiar comfy chair.

Chairs were positioned either side of a low desk, which contained a box of tissues and a basket of stress balls and fidget spinners. The room was softly lit and adorned with ferns and posters depicting Buddhist quotes. The usual smell of lavender was also evident and instantly soothing.

'How has your week been?' Jayne asked without preamble.

'Frustrating. I tried to speak to Mama as you suggested, but to say she shut me down would be an understatement. I can't ask her again, it's obviously too painful for her to talk about, and things have been a bit tense between us since I raised it. It's become a huge elephant in the room and the last thing I need, particularly at the moment is to risk alienating her. We need to stick together now more than ever.'

Jayne nodded. 'We always knew that a reaction like that would be possible, but the situation still needed raising regardless. It's just a shame she can't be more forthcoming or tell you what you so clearly need to know.'

Maya began to pick at her cuticles. 'So that's that. I'm not going to get the answers I need to move on. So where do we go from here? More talking therapy to help with the anxiety?'

Jayne removed her glasses and leaned across the desk. 'We get the answers you're looking for from you.'

'How? I've told you, other than flashbacks, I can't remember anything.'

'There is a treatment, but it's not for everyone. Have you ever heard of EMDR?'

'No. God, it's not some sort of electric shock therapy, is it? My hair is curly enough!'

Jayne grinned. 'It's an acronym for Eye Movement Desensitisation and Reprocessing. In layman's terms it's an approach to treating trauma by reconnecting you to the images, emotions and sensations your body associates with trauma. It's possible that it could help you recall and process whatever Naylor put you through when you were a child.'

'So, it's like hypnosis? You're not going to make me cluck like a chicken every time I hear the word *egg*?'

'I wouldn't be so cruel. EMDR is quite a complex process to understand, so if it helps you to compare it to that you can, but the fundamental difference is that you will never lose consciousness or enter a trance state. You will remain aware and coherent. I'll use a technique called bilateral stimulation where I'll either guide your eye movements with my fingers or use a tapping method, depending which you find more comfortable.'

'Okay, this all sounds very technical. What does the stimulation do?'

'When we experience a trauma, that memory becomes incorrectly stored in the brain. As a result, you can experience PTSD and symptoms will arise similar to yours such as the stress, anxiety, nightmares and trouble sleeping.'

'Can it affect my concentration too, because that's been a problem lately. I've just put it down to stress. And I keep having brief flashbacks connected to my dreams, but there's nothing vivid enough that I can make sense of.'

'All of those things are associated with PTSD. Remember how we discussed the amygdala? It's the primal part of the brain which triggers an alarm system when it thinks there is danger. It would have been useful during prehistoric times when a sabre-toothed tiger was about to attack a caveman, but now, in your case, it's problematic as the amygdala has been too overactive and is causing the symptoms you have described.

'The bilateral stimulation, the side-to-side movement I will make with my fingers, will help deactivate the amygdala so you will not feel as scared. It will simulate REM sleep and allow the brain to process the memory and elevate the trauma associated to it. EMDR slows the amygdala down and synchronises brainwaves which will help identify and process the traumatic memory making it more manageable and allowing it to be stored in the correct part of the brain.'

'What if the memory is too painful to cope with? What if recalling it makes me feel even worse than I do now and causes more damage?'

'This is where you have to trust me. I know it's a hugely daunting process facing your fears head-on, especially when, for you, you don't even know what your demons look like. We'll go at your pace. I'll be monitoring you at all times to make sure you're comfortable and if I feel like the recall is becoming too much, we'll pull back.'

Maya sat in silent contemplation for a while and Jayne took the opportunity to turn her attention to her computer to allow her some time.

'How soon can we start?' Maya asked eventually.

The printer sprung to life as Jayne reached over and plucked a sheet of paper from it. 'Not today. I want you to go away and think about what I've said. There's a fact sheet here with more information. Talk it over with your loved ones and let me know if you want to go ahead. Absolutely no pressure.'

Maya took the paper from her and uttered her thanks.

'If you do want to proceed, we can start next week. Just leave me a message.'

Maya bid Jayne goodbye and left, folding the paper away carefully so she could read it when she got home. She had to admit she was intrigued. This way she could finally get the answers to the past she so desperately wanted. But now it was a real and valid option, she questioned whether she was doing the right thing. Should she leave the past behind her or take the risk and hope that on this occasion, curiosity wouldn't kill the cat.

17

Albert Bennett was beginning to rue the day he met Wheeler. Despite his initial misgivings when he first saw the youth, Wheeler had charmed him with a fish and chip supper. He had fixed his shopping trolley and carried out a couple of other odd jobs around the flat that Albert had been meaning to get round to, but never quite had the motivation. Susie was a lovely young lady. She enjoyed listening to his stories about life in the 'old days' and had an infectious laugh that ricocheted around his dreary flat.

It was late in the evening when they announced it was time to leave, and he had surprised himself when he realised he was sorry to see them go. He had already asked how Wheeler had come about the myriad of cuts and bruises that made Albert wince to look at. Wheeler had become coy and hinted at problems at home. As he was due to wave them off, he had assumed that Wheeler would be staying the night at Susie's.

'My dad won't let him stay,' Susie had said, addressing her feet, unable to look Wheeler in the eye.

'We don't get on. I don't think he likes me.' Wheeler had shrugged nonchalantly.

Albert had felt the bite of the fresh autumnal evening air and shivered involuntarily. 'Where are you going to go then, lad?' he had asked, as he weighed up the scrawny youth in his jeans and a lightweight hoodie.

'Either one of me mates or I'll kip in the car again,' he had said.

With hindsight, Albert should have left it at that. Wheeler was old enough to look after himself. But at that moment, his pitiful frame, battered face and the increasing chill in the air caused his soul to flood with pity. Albert himself had survived on the kindness of strangers over the years. God knows some of his darkest hours had been aided by people giving him a much needed helping hand. And hadn't the young couple done a good turn for him that evening? They'd carried his shopping, helped around the flat and been the most company he'd had in years.

He had offered to let Wheeler stay the night on his couch. It was meant to be a one-off, but over a week had passed and there were no signs of the lad leaving. He had made himself very much at home. Too much so, in fact. And not only that, but Wheeler's demeanour had also begun to change. The polite young man he had first met had turned into a surly, acerbic tyrant. His language was appalling. He had begun to smoke in the flat, rather than using the balcony as Albert had asked. It wasn't just tobacco either, Albert had been around long enough to know the earthy smell was cannabis.

Wheeler had also begun to taunt the old man whenever Susie wasn't around. It was just a few jokes at first that quickly turned into nasty jibes and bullying. He knew he should stand up to him, but at eighty-three, he had neither the strength or the stamina and if truth be told, the lad scared him. He had no one he could turn to for help. He had no family and most of his friends had passed away. Those still living were as frail as him, if not worse.

His best hope was that Wheeler would get sick of hanging round the tiny flat and leave. He complained often enough that it was too small and old-fashioned. The only saving grace was that Susie called often which pleased him as she was good company. He couldn't understand why a sweet girl like her was with someone as vile as Wheeler, but he seemed to have manipulated her in such a way that she was wrapped around his little finger.

Credit where it was due, Wheeler also brought food home and had kept the electric meter topped up, but that was becoming little salvation compared to the increasing hostility and underlying threat that Albert was now living under. He had a cuckoo in his nest and no idea how to get rid of him.

Whilst Albert Bennett was lamenting over his new living situation, for Wheeler, it was currently the only good thing going for him. He had been summoned to Crewe the previous evening where Reilly had metaphorically ripped him a new arsehole. He was raging that Brogan had disappeared without a trace and more importantly without paying his debt.

'I'll find him,' Wheeler had gushed placatingly, 'and I'll get your money. Honest, by the end of the month.'

The blow to his stomach had sent him sprawling across the room and left him so winded, he thought he'd never draw breath again. Reilly had towered over him, screaming expletives and kicking him like a football.

'End of the fucking month? It's been too long already. This is on you. I took him on because I trusted *your* word and now you've just let him disappear knowing he still owes me money? What sort of message does that send out? It makes me look weak and a pushover and I'm one step away from kicking you to death to send out the message that I'm neither of those things.'

Wheeler was cursing himself for not keeping a tighter rein on Brogan. He had been a fool to blindly trust that his mate would do the right thing and do whatever it took to pay the debt off. In fairness he couldn't blame him for doing a runner. Raising a thousand pounds without having gear to sell was impossible. Even if Wheeler did find Brogan, it was still unlikely he'd have, or be able to raise, the cash. He knew what was happening even before Reilly picked him from the floor by his scruff and screamed in his face.

'It's only by the grace of God and because the shipment is pending that I'm not going to end you now. You have got two weeks to clear his debt off or you're a dead man walking, understood?'

He had nodded mutely, unable to speak because of the grip Reilly had on him. 'And in case you're thinking of being stupid and running off to join your mate, remember what I've told you before, I'll rip your piss-can mother limb from limb if you cross me. By the time I've finished with her, an archaeologist will need to piece her back together like a fucking two-hundred-and-six-piece jigsaw.'

Reilly had then headbutted him for not realising that that was the number of bones in an adult human body. Just as he had solved one problem, another arose. He had secured Albert's flat ready to receive the shipment of drugs when it arrived, but now he had to find a grand to keep Reilly from putting him in intensive care. Wheeler lit a joint and took a large drag as he draped his leg over the arm of the old man's sofa. He leant back and something tickled his neck. Irritated, he threw the beige antimacassar across the room and took another long pull.

The cannabis soothed him as he knew it would. It would take the angst away and allow him to think more clearly, as if things had shifted focus and he was viewing his problems from a more comfortable distance. That made him think of Reilly telling him that he had problems so Reilly wouldn't have to, and his thoughts drifted to Jordan.

Problem solved. Little-man could get his finger out of his arse and raise the money. That was what he was there for. Smiling, he settled back and shouted to Albert to make him a brew. It was good to be in charge.

18

'Ooh, what a sight for sore eyes. You smell amazing,' said Chris.

Maya leaned in to kiss him on the cheek. 'So kind of you to say, but you did only see me a few hours ago.'

Chris grinned. 'I wasn't talking to you, I was talking to the takeaway.'

He took the bag of food from her and carried it through to the dining room. Two beers were already open on the table. Maya, familiar with Chris's house, slung her jacket over the newel post and followed him. She glanced through the window into the garden. It wasn't a huge space but Chris had made it look lovely with a nice patio furniture set and a few pot plants. The wall, which had originally been part of the outdoor toilet, had been painted white and he'd strung up a row of fairy lights which gave the yard a warm and inviting look.

'I love this house,' she said as she clinked bottles with Chris. 'It always feels so cosy and homely.'

'It suits me,' he agreed as he began to serve their food. Chicken tikka madras for Maya and lamb jhalfrezi for him as well as rice and naan breads.

'It's not like you not to have a starter, are you feeling okay?' Maya said.

'Grand, me and Amanda had a chippy at lunchtime while you were at your appointment.'

'Greedy git,' she quipped. 'That diet you've been planning is going well then?'

Chris stretched and rubbed his tummy. 'Life's too short, love, I could be dead tomorrow.'

'Don't say that,' she said seriously. 'What would I do without you?'

He reached for her hand and squeezed it. 'Don't worry about that, you'll never have to find out. I'll always be here for you. I'm like haemorrhoids, difficult to get rid of.'

'You can be a pain in the arse.' She laughed.

'How's things with Spence?'

Maya smiled and Chris was delighted to see his friend's face light up at the mere mention of his name. 'Really good. He's at mine most of the time when he's not working the late shift.'

'And long term? It's not ideal that you can't stay together all the time and I know you don't like staying over at the pub. Have you not talked about moving in together permanently?'

'We've talked about it. It's one of the reasons he decided to sign up for the personal trainer's course, so once he gives up the bar manager's position it would make it easier to move in together.'

'I take it he'd move into your apartment?'

'Initially,' Maya said coyly.

Chris grinned. 'Go on, what have you got planned?'

'Well, my apartment is okay, but ideally it would be nice to have somewhere a bit bigger and a garden. A bit like this place.'

'And room for all the babies,' said Chris excitedly.

Maya closed her eyes and shook her head. 'I bloody knew you'd be like this. One step at a time, okay? Babies are a long way off in the future. I want to concentrate on my career for now and there's loads of places we want to travel to.'

'But babies are on the cards,' pressed Chris. 'I can at least dream about being a surrogate grandad.'

Maya laughed at his enthusiasm. 'If... when we do have kids, I'd be honoured if you'd be in their lives. But like I said, it's years off, so don't go getting too excited. I know what you're like, you get too carried away. You'll be knitting by this time next week.'

'It pays to be prepared. Might give the spare room a lick of paint so it's ready for sleepovers.'

'Chris!'

'I'm sorry, it's just that I take my grandad duties seriously. Last I'll mention of it, I promise.'

'Good, thank you.'

'Other than to say, you should think about taking folic acid.'

'Have you ever been slapped across the face with a naan bread before?' Maya said as she wielded it towards his face.

Chris laughed and went to fetch them a couple more beers.

'Hey, what's up? I'm sorry, I didn't mean to go too far with the baby thing,' he said when he returned, noticing Maya looking sullen.

'It's not you. It's the bloody elephant in the room. How can I even think about the future? I can't even nip to the shops without it feeling like a military manoeuvre because I'm double-checking I'm not being followed. Mama and I are both living in a home that feels like Fort Knox and I even have to double up at work. None of this is going to stop until Naylor is locked up, but what are the chances of that happening and when? I'm stuck in limbo and there's absolutely nothing I can do about it.'

'Right, so explain to me what this EMDR is all about.'

Maya explained in more detail than she had when she'd returned to the office after counselling. She'd confided in Chris and Amanda that Jayne had offered her the treatment. Jayne had told her to discuss it with a loved one, but Spence was working and she knew Dominique wouldn't be receptive to the conversation, so Chris had been the natural choice, which is why he had invited her for dinner, to talk about it in greater detail.

'So, what do you think. Should I go for it?'

'It depends on how much you want to know the truth. Uncovering it may lead you to face something you wish you didn't know, and you can't shut the box once it's open. That said, I know how much *not* knowing is unsettling you.'

'It's such a difficult decision, honestly, I'm completely torn. Make it easy for me, Chris. Tell me whether I should go through with it or let sleeping dogs lie.'

He shook his head. 'I can't do that, love. This has to be your decision. I'm sorry because I know that's not what you want to hear. Whatever you decide, I'll be behind you every step of the way.'

Maya sighed. 'I know that, thank you. I guess I'll sleep on it, only I *don't* sleep. I keep having really disturbing dreams, I guess they're flashbacks, but nothing I can make sense of. Perhaps if I could unravel the dreams then they'd stop.'

Chris reached for her hand. 'There you go then. I guess you have your answer. If the EMDR is going to help you remember what you need to know, then I guess you should give it a try.'

19

———

Jordan was trapped like the proverbial fly in the spider's web and there was nothing he could do to get out. Wheeler was becoming more incessantly demanding, meaning that Jordan had started to miss a lot of school. His deliveries were keeping him out later and later, meaning his mum was constantly on his back, checking where he was and demanding he come home.

Wheeler had also demanded that Jordan always kept his phone on so he could be at his beck and call, and it was a nightmare trying to get out of classes to answer it without his teachers noticing. Lewis was back at school but refused to even look, let alone speak to him. Craig remained in his own world, oblivious to the nightmare his brother had become embroiled in, and Jordan had never felt so out of his depth or so lonely. He was constantly on edge, trying to keep school and his mum off his back as well as doing Wheeler's bidding.

Even now, just as he was hoping to go home for tea and do some homework, he had been summoned to see Wheeler at an address he didn't recognise. The lift was broken, so he had to leave his bike chained downstairs and panted his way up the six flights of stairs. He'd arrived at the maroon-coloured front door and peered at the kitchen window. It was covered with a heavy net curtain, the kind he usually associated with old people. He checked his phone to make sure he had the correct address before knocking.

His heart was heavy with trepidation as he wondered who would answer the door. He was anticipating someone as unhinged as Taz, so it was a huge relief when the door was opened by an old man. He was tall with stooped shoulders, and a mop of wiry, white hair. He was dressed in grey slacks and a green cardigan and his plastic, black-framed glasses looked oversized on his gaunt face. Jordan's relief was replaced with confusion as he wondered who the man was. Could it be Wheeler's grandad?

'Sorry to bother you, sir, I'm not sure if I've got the right address. I'm looking for Wheeler.'

The old man leant forward, prodding a finger in Jordan's chest as he hissed urgently, 'Now then, you're not coming in here at your age. You're far too young to be taking drugs, away with you.'

His sour breath made Jordan wince. 'I'm not, I mean I've never taken drugs. I've just been asked to come and speak to him.'

'Do yourself a favour and go now. Don't get involved.' The old man was about to shut the door when Wheeler appeared behind him and barged him out of the way.

'I hope you're not getting involved in my business, old man,' he shouted as he pulled Albert back into the hallway. Albert cowered as Wheeler pushed his face into his. 'I've told you before, keep your nose out and we'll carry on getting along just fine. Go and have a nap.'

Jordan glanced at the old man pityingly as he scurried to his room. 'Wanker,' muttered Wheeler as he indicated for Jordan to follow him through to the lounge.

'Got a little job for you,' he said as he sparked up a joint.

'I've done all the drops you asked me to already. My mum is starting to ask where I am all the time, I can't do any more.'

'Can't or won't?' Wheeler snapped. 'Think I'm fucking bothered about your mum? Tell the bitch to quiet down or I'll happily pay her a visit. I need to raise some cash and you're going to get it for me.'

'How, I haven't got any money?'

'No, but you've got a bike and you're quick.'

'I don't understand.'

'Course you don't because you've not got the brains, little-man. You're too used to being told what to do, rather than using your own initiative, which is why it's a good thing you've got me looking after you, as well as keeping your dirty little secret.'

'What do you want me to do?'

Wheeler took another pull on the joint as he studied Jordan. 'Have you heard of snatch and grab?'

'I... erm, I don't think so.' Jordan could feel dread creeping up his spine. This didn't sound good.

'Get yourself around places like College Road or outside the bus station. Mind for CCTV cameras though and cover your face. Keep an eye out for all the zombies walking down the road with their faces in their phones. Half the time they're oblivious of anyone else around them, especially when they've got headphones on. Then all you have to do is ride past and grab the phones. It's like taking candy from a baby.'

Jordan was mortified. It had been bad enough dropping drugs off, but this was something else. Now Wheeler was expecting him to steal from innocent people, it was too much.

'I'm sorry, Wheeler, I can't. It's wrong and I don't have the bottle for anything like that. Surely there must be something else I can do?'

Wheeler flicked the joint into an ashtray and stood up. In a flash he had Jordan gripped in a headlock with one arm as he began to rain blows along his torso with his free hand. 'It's wrong, is it? It was wrong to stab your best mate, but you had the bottle to do that, didn't you? Do you want to watch the video to remind yourself what you can do if you put your mind to it, or shall I just send it straight to the police?'

Wheeler's grip was so tight Jordan felt like his skull was being crushed and the punches were excruciating. He desperately tried to wiggle free. He was no stranger to being in fights with someone bigger and stronger than him, he'd had plenty of play fights with Craig over the years, but this was different. It was clear that Wheeler was intent on hurting him, whereas gentle-giant Craig never had.

'What are you doing? Let him go, you're gonna hurt him.'

The grip was released so suddenly that Jordan dropped to the floor as Wheeler turned towards Susie. She read the room quick as a flash and was wise enough to know that Wheeler needed calming down.

'Babe,' she said placatingly as she entwined her arms around his hips, 'what's going on?'

'Little-man here has decided to stop following orders. I've told him we need more cash coming in and he's refusing. I was just convincing him otherwise.'

Susie glanced down at Jordan. He was slumped on the floor, panting and rubbing his head. 'Well, it looks like you've persuaded him.'

'I hope so,' Wheeler said as he gripped Jordan by the arm and pulled him from the floor. 'I'll be in touch, keep your phone on. Now get out.'

As Jordan headed down the woodchip-covered hallway, he

noticed the old man peeping through a crack in his bedroom door. As their eyes met, they exchanged mutually desperate glances. Jordan was a good lad at heart and knowing that the old man appeared to be in trouble would usually cause him to raise the alarm. Now though, with the weight of the world on his shoulders, he turned away and left the flat. However the old boy had become embroiled with Wheeler, it was his problem to sort out, Jordan had enough of his own.

Ivo Zlatan was parked in his silver Tesla watching the flats where Albert Bennett lived. The car was a new purchase and so far, Ivo was pleased with it. For him, the benefit of an electric car was the quietness, no noisy rattling exhaust. He felt like he could creep the streets even more surreptitiously than he usually did without being seen or heard. And Ivo liked to creep these streets. They were his playground and his workplace, the source of his income where he could sell drugs and tax rival drug dealers.

He was a cautious man and rather than getting his hands dirty and risk getting caught, he employed a handful of trusted soldiers to do the job for him. Unlike Wheeler, he didn't rely on fear to keep people where he wanted them, he baited them with honey. His boys were paid amply and treated well. They were like family to him, and his generosity and graciousness was rewarded by their loyalty. As far as Ivo was concerned, loyalty was more sacrosanct than love.

Ivo had so much respect for his soldiers that he didn't issue them work until he had checked out the risks himself. He would only give them the instructions to tax rival dealers when he knew who they were dealing with. He would never risk any of his boys getting injured or arrested. That was why he had been personally following the young schoolboy Wheeler appeared to have recently recruited. He assumed the kid was a replacement for Brogan who his lads had left bleeding out on the car park of Mallon Lodge. He was surprised at Wheeler taking a chance on recruiting someone so young though. But in his opinion, Wheeler was a loose cannon and certainly didn't have his business acumen.

Ivo had long since suspected that there was someone above Wheeler pulling his strings, but as yet, he hadn't discovered who. It certainly wasn't someone local or he'd know about it. He knew all his rival dealers and gang members, including the has-beens such as Aiden Donnelly, Piotr Nowak and the McCluskey brothers. They'd all been top of the tree at one time, but now it was Ivo's turn and he'd be damned if he'd be challenged by a rat like Wheeler or whoever he was working for.

His patience was rewarded when he saw the kid emerge from the flats. He looked harassed, and Ivo would have loved to know why as he watched him pedal off. He laughed to himself as the kid veered across the footpath. A kid, an old man and a girl with a face full of fake tan and chewing gum. If that was the extent of Wheeler's army, then the scrawny little scrote had no chance.

His business was ripe for the taking.

20

Maya and Chris pulled up outside a nondescript-looking semi-detached house not far from Beech Field.

'Another day, another crime scene.' Chris yawned and scratched his belly.

'And the cavalry is just in time.' Maya nodded to a white Toyota that had pulled up in front of them. Sean strode from the car waving to them enthusiastically followed by Malone who offered them both a perfunctory nod. He exuded his usual sense of boredom and disinterest.

'Do you know anything about the job?' Sean asked.

Maya shook her head. 'Other than it's an assault, no. We were on the other side of the division finishing up at a scene and comms asked us to come and meet you here.'

'What's the score? I hope there's not much in it, I'm starving,' Chris said, causing Maya and Sean to exchange a grin. Whatever he was doing, Chris's thoughts were never too far away from his next meal or snack.

'It's a ball of shit,' Malone grumbled as he headed over to the scene guard for a chat.

'What's up with him. Is he hungry too?' Chris asked.

Sean laughed. 'No, he's been tasked by Jack to try and keep tracks on one of our dealers, Ivo Zlatan, but he's getting nowhere with it, mainly because every time he does, another job like this comes in. We're just firefighting all the time and not having a chance to get anywhere with past cases.'

'What can we do to help you with this then?' Maya asked.

'We've got two brothers in their late fifties in custody for assaulting the elderly father. Apparently, all three were drinking heavily last night, which is normal for them. Neighbours rang us at about five to complain about the noise, but we had no patrols free to attend. Then they rang back at seven reporting sounds of a disturbance. When we got there, all three were heavily intoxicated. Dad was covered in blood, so he was taken into the kitchen to separate him from the other two so he could be questioned, and he collapsed.'

'What's his prognosis?' Maya asked.

'He's sustained a head injury which is giving the doctors cause for concern, but they are hoping he'll stabilise more when the alcohol has passed through his system. Both brothers have got superficial cuts and bruises too.'

'Right, we'll go and have a look and see what the scene can tell us.'

Maya and Chris chatted briefly to the uniformed officer guarding the address as they signed the crime scene log. Then they entered the address; the hallway was cluttered with coats and an array of different footwear, mainly trainers and work boots. Maya eyed the dark wood of the interior door and was struck by their familiarity; Dominique used to have the same style of doors when Maya was younger.

'I'm guessing this is the lounge,' she said to Chris as she reached for the door handle. As she opened the door, she could see bloodstains on the carpet, and she was struck with an overwhelming sense of déjà vu. It stopped her in her tracks. She closed her eyes and remembered another time when she had opened a door similar to this. She remembered seeing blood on the floor...

'Maya, you okay, love?' She opened her eyes and saw Chris looking at her curiously and the moment passed.

'Yes, fine. I just remembered something.'

'You look like you've seen a ghost.'

'I feel like I have.'

'What have you remembered?'

She shivered. 'Mama used to have the same doors as these. I remember opening it and seeing blood on the floor, like that.' She nodded towards the bloodstains on the carpet.

'Whose blood was it?'

Maya shook her head. 'I don't know. It's a complete blank. It must have been Mama's.' Naylor's name hung in the air unspoken.

'Go back to the van and have a minute. I'll make a start in here.'

She nodded gratefully and returned to the van where she let her head fall back against the driver's headrest as she closed her eyes and tried to reach again for the distant memory, but it was gone. The recollection had slipped back into the confines of her subconscious, and it was too deep to access. She was certain though, that however fleeting that recollection had been, it was important and was clearly one of the things her mind had blanked out over the years.

She reached for her mobile phone and rang Jayne's number. She listened to the familiar voice of her counsellor's voicemail asking that she leave a message.

'Jayne, hi, it's Maya Barton. I'm just ringing to let you know that I've been thinking about the EMDR and I've decided to try it. I'll see you at my next session.'

She said goodbye and hung up, confident that she'd made

the right decision. It was time to face up to whatever secrets lay hidden in the past. Next, she rang Spence, eager to hear his voice and reassurances that she was doing the right thing. She knew she should also go and see Dominique to at least let her know what she had decided. But she also knew she wouldn't approve and would probably try and change her mind. It was a conversation she didn't want to have.

21

———

Jordan was fraught with nerves. He'd been hanging around College Road for nearly an hour watching people come and go. Wheeler had been right. So many people scurried past him absorbed in their phones and oblivious to the world around them. It would be so easy to cycle past and just pluck the phone from their hands. He just needed to work up the nerve to do it.

It wasn't just the morality of the situation but the fact that the majority of students were a damn sight bigger than him. He was still hurting from the beating off Wheeler and couldn't face the thought of getting another hiding for stealing someone's phone. He couldn't countenance stealing from someone older and frailer. The more he sat and watched the throngs of people surging around him, the more adamant he became that he couldn't do it.

His phone bleeped and he eyed it warily. He had already been dodging calls from his mum and her text messages were getting more irate with each one he received and ignored. He was mortified to see it was a text from Wheeler:

Have you made me any money yet? I want at
least ten phones by the end of the week or else.

His heart sank to his toes. Ten phones? The thought of just
stealing one made him sick to his stomach, but the threat of 'or
else' made him feel even worse. Wheeler had him well and truly
over the proverbial barrel. Sighing, he climbed on his bike and
slipped on a face mask and gloves. He also pulled his hood
down so his eyes were shielded. He waited, poised on his bike as
he watched people move around him. A bus pulled over and he
watched as a group of passengers alighted.

A middle-aged man was ranting into his phone. He was
clearly incensed as his face was flushed and he seemed oblivious
to the woman he barged past to get onto the pavement. He
ignored her shouts of admonishment as he continued his angry
phone call, his rudeness making him Jordan's obvious first
target. He watched the man as he strode down the street and
began to pedal after him. He looked over his shoulder to make
sure the road was clear before picking up speed.

Within seconds he was at his side. He swerved towards him
and reached for the phone, snatching it from his hand. He felt a
rush of exhilaration as he deftly pocketed it and cycled away at
speed, cutting across the road and making for the sanctity of
Victoria Park. He could hear the man screaming obscenities at
him and he laughed manically as he pedalled harder. Wheeler
had been right; it was like taking candy from a baby.

22

———

The fugitive was grateful for the light rain. It meant he could loiter with his hood up and not arouse suspicions. He glanced surreptitiously at his watch. It was 9.30pm and chilly, a hint of frost in the air. Still, the cold didn't bother him, he was hardened to extremes of weather. In fact, he was hardened to most things. Little affected him; a psychologist would probably conclude he was a psychopath and he smiled at the thought – he was so much more than that.

He heard a car approaching and pulled his head lower as he tugged on his vape. Nothing to see here, he thought, just a man stretching his legs and vaping outside. Hiding in plain sight was the best way for someone with his huge stature. From the corner of his eye, he watched the taillights of the vehicle as it swung into the car park of Miller Court. The electric gates groaned open. He waited until the car had driven through and was out of sight, then quick as a flash, before the gates closed, he slipped through the gap with ease.

He made his way to the covered communal bin area and listened to the sounds of the driver locking the car and walking away. Although the bin area was dimly lit, it was still too bright for his liking. Satisfied he was alone, he reached into the waistband of his jeans and pulled out his knife. Using the handle as a butt, he reached up and smashed the bulb. That was better, he preferred the sanctity of the dark. He eyed the layout of the car park and was pleased to note the lack of security cameras. Most of the apartments had their blinds or curtains drawn at this time of the evening and it pleased him.

He took another drag of his vape before making his way across the car park to the communal door. He smiled to himself as he opened it. People who lived in places like this were naturally complacent. They thought the electric gates afforded them the security they needed and never bothered about the lock that always tended to stick because of overuse. He studied the post boxes in the hallway and reached for his phone to photograph the names of the occupants on the eleventh floor.

He called for the lift and rode it to the tenth floor. From there he took the flight of stairs up to the eleventh. He doubted many people, if any, used the stairway at this height. Still, he decided not to take any chances and reached for the knife again, this time smashing the ceiling bulb.

He eased the stair door open and peered down the corridor of the eleventh floor. It was muffled in silence; a faulty bulb threw flickering shadows against the apartment doors. He retreated to the sanctity of the stairwell. Engulfed once again in the darkness, he smiled, satisfied at how easy it was to get into Maya's apartment building.

Surprisingly light on his feet, he skirted down the stairs, making himself dizzy as he circled around each flight. He reached the ground floor in no time and flitted out through the front door onto the street. A fleeting, unnoticeable shadow.

23

___

Most repeat offenders, whether they are car thieves, burglars or shoplifters, tend to have one thing in common. The first offence they commit is an arse-clenching, heart-racing moment. A pivotal life-first. They know the risks; they take their chance. Whatever their motive, be it greed or desperation, once that first offence is committed the die is cast.

When the offender commits again, their confidence grows. The more they accrue without being caught, the more they gain a sense of overconfidence and complacency. The offender begins to believe they are untouchable; infallible. This bullishness causes them to make mistakes and this is when they will shed a plethora of evidence.

Jordan Gaffney fitted that mould perfectly. Despite his initial reservations, Jordan found the snatch and grab an addictive thrill. He had easily met his quota of phones that Wheeler had demanded. He made peace with the fact what he was doing was wrong by only stealing from people who seemed arrogant like his first victim. People who he perceived deserved it.

He eased his conscience by telling himself he was nothing like Wheeler. He would never target the elderly or vulnerable.

Just men of a certain age who he sensed could afford the loss. Plus, didn't everyone who had a phone have insurance, so where was the harm really, other than the initial inconvenience?

It had now been three days since his first snatch and grab, and the relief that he had met Wheeler's demands so quickly was a huge weight lifted from his shoulders. Today had been a good day. He'd emptied the dishwasher before school, which had pleased his mum. He had been on time for school and had been praised for his participation in several of his lessons. For the first time since stabbing Lewis and becoming embroiled with Wheeler, he was feeling good. Life felt back to normal.

He was cycling back from school when his phone rang. Thankfully not the burner phone Wheeler had given him, but his own phone. He grinned when he saw it was his mum.

'Hiya. If you're ringing to see where I am, I'm nearly home.'

'Okay, love. Craig is in, but I'm ringing to let you know I'll be late. Janice has phoned in sick this afternoon, so I just need to cover a couple of her rounds.'

'Can we get takeaway for tea then?' he said, his mouth salivating at the thought of pizza or maybe even Chinese.

'Sorry, love, not tonight, I can't afford it.'

'But you're doing overtime,' he said, painfully aware he sounded like a petulant kid but unable to mask it. It had been ages since they'd had a takeaway. Surely he wasn't asking for the world.

'Yes, Jordan, but I've also just paid a huge electricity bill and I did a big shop yesterday. I've pulled a tuna bake out of the freezer. Heat that up when you get in. Love you.'

Claire hung up and Jordan's mood soured. He was sick of them always being skint. She worked stupidly long hours, and they had nothing to show for it other than 'the roof over their heads'. Granted, the house was lovely and always spotless, the cupboards full of snacks, but most of the other kids at school had a fortnight abroad each year, takeaways every week and wore whatever clothes they wanted. He and Craig had sodding tuna pasta bake, which incidentally, he hated.

Swearing under his breath he continued home. He decided to take the Delaware Road as it was the quickest route. He cycled past the restaurants and bars, and just as the boutique on the corner was in sight, he saw the back of a woman emerge. She was laden down with shopping bags and a large handbag in one hand, whilst chattering excitedly and animatedly into her phone.

He slowed his pace and held back. He knew if she turned left at the corner, she'd be heading to the pay and display car park. His irritation at being skint fuelled him forwards as he watched her bending under the weight of the bags. It wasn't fair that one person had so much, and he couldn't even have a bloody pizza. He thought of his mum working all hours and the indignity and frustration seared through him.

As he neared her, he could hear part of the conversation as she shrilled into her phone, '...and honestly, Tabitha, the dresses are divine. I can't wait to show you the shoes. I know Stephen will say I've bought far too many.'

She let out a gay laugh as the person on the other end responded. Jordan looked around as he balanced his weight on the pedals. There were just the two of them now on the back road and she was too engrossed in her conversation to even have noticed him. If he was going to do it, it had to be now, before she got to the car park which was monitored by CCTV.

'You're right!' shrieked the woman. 'A princess can never have too many shoes!'

This fuelled the fire in the pit of his stomach further as he cycled towards her, hand outstretched, ready to pluck the phone from her. Like candy from a baby.

Except it wasn't.

He was taken aback by a steely grip. So much so, he wobbled precariously on his bike. He attempted to pull at it again, but she resisted. The shopping and handbag dropped to the ground as she clung to the phone with both hands.

'No!' she screeched as she wrestled it away from him, in the process, snagging his glove, which she managed to pull off.

It all happened so fast. Mere seconds. The shock that she'd fought back. The horror of seeing his glove pulled from his hand. He instinctively reached for it, desperate to claw it from her, but she stumbled over the bags. It was only then he noticed her distended stomach as she fell forwards, her bump slamming into the ground.

Pure fear powered his feet as he pedalled away. The sickening shriek and cries of, 'My baby!' clawing at his soul like nails down a chalkboard.

24

Maya and Chris were driving back to the office after finishing all their burglary scenes. Chris was driving, which is why, when Maya's mobile rang, she could check who was calling. She disconnected the call straight away.

Chris arched an eyebrow at her. 'Problem?'

'Another number I don't recognise and I'm not answering it in case it's Wainwright again.'

'Surely he wouldn't be that stupid. Redford made it perfectly clear after last time that he's not to contact you again.'

'Yeah, I know, but he's a stupid man. That's if it is him. Whoever it is isn't leaving any messages, so unless I know who it is, I don't want to know.'

'Fair enough.' Chris was about to say something else when a call came over the police radio and he stopped to listen.

'Any patrols free to assist the ambulance please, Delaware Road.'

'We're passing that way,' said Maya as she reached to turn the radio up.

A patrol shouted up to confirm they were nearby and asked for the circumstances.

'Passer-by has rang ambo after discovering a heavily pregnant woman on the ground. She's the victim of an attempted street robbery and has managed to remove a glove from the offender.'

Patrol confirmed they were en route and Maya reached enthusiastically for the radio. 'SOCO Barton, comms, can you show myself and SOCO Makin attending that job too, please. Can you ask patrols to ensure the glove isn't disturbed and make CID aware. We're about ten minutes away.'

'Result.' Maya grinned as Chris high-fived her.

They were at the scene in no time and headed straight to where an officer was speaking to the victim in the back of the ambulance.

'How are you?' Maya asked with a reassuring smile.

'Very shook up and apparently my blood pressure is through the roof. They're going to take me in to get the baby checked out, but she's thrashing around a lot, thank God.' The woman stroked her stomach protectively.

'That's good to hear. I hope you're both okay. I believe you managed to get the offender's glove, is that right?'

'Yes, it should be under one of the shopping bags. Oh, it's my own fault.' She swiped at a sudden stream of tears that spilled down her face.

'Hey, it's not your fault at all. You didn't ask for this to happen. Did he manage to steal anything?'

She shook her head as she blew her nose. 'No. He was after my phone. I was talking to Tabitha, my boss. With hindsight I probably shouldn't have been, should have watched where I was going, but I was so excited. I finished work last Friday for maternity leave and Tabitha and the others had arranged a collection and bought me some vouchers for the boutique on Delaware Road. God knows I couldn't afford to shop there otherwise.

'Anyway, I rang her to let her know what I'd bought for the baby. The next thing I know this guy appeared from nowhere on his bike and tried to steal my phone. I know I should have probably just let him have it, but it was just instinct, you know? I grabbed it back and managed to pull his glove off in the process. He tried to get that back and I ended up falling over the bags.'

'Okay, I'm going to recover the glove, and have it sent off for DNA analysis so hopefully we can find out who did this to you. I'll bring your bags over so you can get to the hospital.'

Chris was on his mobile when Maya joined him. He grinned at her as he ended the call. 'That was Sean, apparently there has been a series of similar snatch and grab robberies the last few days. Lad on a mountain bike stealing phones from commuters, just like our victim. No clear description because he's been wearing a hood and face mask, but a couple of the victims think he's only high-school age.'

'Young and daft, the dream combination for shedding DNA at a crime scene,' said Maya as she nodded towards the glove. 'That, my friend, is a DNA hit waiting to happen.'

Chris nodded in agreement. 'Let's get it recovered so we can nail the little bastard.'

25

Jordan was close to tears by the time he got home. He'd ignored Craig's greetings and locked himself in his bedroom. Fully clothed, he lay in the foetal position under the duvet. The screams from the pregnant woman were echoing in his ears. He groaned as he recalled the dread of seeing her swollen stomach. What if he'd harmed the baby? What if she lost it? He flew from his room and barely made it to the bathroom in time before vomiting noisily. His stomach was soon empty, but he continued to dry heave as he thought about what he'd done.

'You okay, mate?' Craig appeared wide-eyed and worried-looking at the bathroom door.

'Yeah, I'm great, bro. Never felt better,' Jordan replied sarcastically as he flushed the chain and began to rinse his mouth at the sink.

'Really? I always feel really wobbly when I've been sick. It hurts my throat and tummy.'

'Obviously I'm not okay. Just leave me alone,' he snapped. Then he saw the hurt in Craig's eyes and hated himself even more.

'Sorry, Craig. I'm okay. I just need to lie down. I didn't mean to have a go.'

'Shall I ring Mum?'

'No, she's working. I'll be okay in a bit. Give me half an hour and I'll sort our tea out, okay? Go and watch some TV, I'll be down in a bit.'

Jordan returned to his room and lay on the bed, willing the panic in his chest to subside. He desperately hoped the woman and the baby were okay. God knows, he hadn't meant to hurt them. If he had known she was pregnant he would never, ever have targeted her.

He thought about his glove and his stomach churned again. What if the police got hold of it, his DNA would be all over it. But then how would they know it was his DNA? He'd not been arrested before. Not yet anyway. He could deny it, of course. In fact, he'd get rid of his other glove. He'd bin it on the way to school tomorrow and if anyone asked, he'd say his gloves were stolen or he'd lost them. She'd not seen his face; it had been too well covered, so he couldn't be identified that way.

He ground the heel of his hands into his eyes as a moan escaped his lips. He cursed his stupidity. He had let anger, frustration and jealousy fuel his actions. He hadn't even needed to steal the phone; he'd met the quota demanded from Wheeler. He sat up suddenly as he thought about why he had stolen it. Yes, he'd been angry and jealous when he saw the woman laden down with shopping bags. He recalled the half-overheard phone call as she had talked about having bought too many shoes and how this had convinced him she deserved it.

Then he visualised her stomach slamming into the ground again and thought of the innocent, unborn baby and knew he was wrong. He had been fuelled by jealousy and worse, greed. He didn't need to steal that phone; he had wanted to and that made him as bad as Wheeler. What had happened to him that in a few short weeks he had stabbed his best friend, was pedalling drugs and was now stealing from pregnant women? Things were spiralling out of control and there was nothing he could do to stop it. He buried his face in the pillow and cried like the young boy he was.

It was nearly midnight by the time Claire Gaffney arrived home after covering the extra shifts. One of Janice's old dears had taken a funny turn and Claire had waited with her until a doctor arrived. She had no family so Claire had felt obliged, plus, despite putting a brave face on, the old woman was clearly scared. The least Claire could do was stay and keep her calm and comfortable. The doctor had suspected a kidney infection and had the woman admitted to hospital, so that was one less visit to cover tomorrow.

She kicked off her shoes and clicked on the kettle. She was pleased to see the boys had eaten and washed up after themselves. She smiled to herself; they had their moments, but they were good kids. She felt a pang of guilt at denying Jordan a takeaway earlier. It's not as if the lad asked for much. She made a pact with herself that she'd cover Janice's shifts for the rest of the week and then treat the boys to a pizza at the weekend.

She set about making a quick sandwich before bed and ate it while watching a soap. Then as always, she looked in on both boys. As she peered in Jordan's room, she spotted his bulging school bag and tutted to herself at the thought of the stinking sports kit sat inevitably in there. She smiled to herself as she heard him snoring and reached for his school bag. Just as quietly, she carried it downstairs to the kitchen table so she could fish out the dirty clothes and put them in the washing machine overnight.

The open mouth of the bag gaped at her as she reached in and pulled his sports shirt, hoodie and football socks from the top. She dug deeper, searching for any more rogue items of clothing. Her jaw dropped open, almost comically like a cartoon character's when her hand wrapped around a Samsung mobile which she knew wasn't Jordan's.

It dropped further still when she discovered another ten phones.

26

―――――――

Colin Parkes had his mobile phone gripped between his ear and shoulder. Although he was in the middle of a call, all his attention was focused on the newspaper in front of him as he doodled around the crossword he was studying.

'Light on the eleventh floor is flickering and the one in the bin area is broken, yes, got it, writing that down now,' he mumbled as he studied seven across. The clue was *slothful*.

'The rear access door from the car park being left open. I'll put a sign up,' he agreed. Eight letters beginning with I.

The conversation lasted a further three minutes as he made appropriate responses and even managed to add a little sincerity to his tone. Hanging up, he tossed the phone on the cluttered desk of the caretakers' office and told it to sod off.

Giles McGowan, the property developer of Miller Court was a mithering bastard. He'd already been onto Colin about the faulty light on the eleventh floor. Like he always said to his nagging wife, he'd get round to it eventually, he didn't need reminding of things every six months.

Colin was a man who liked to pace himself and right now, his priority was his crossword. The light could wait and as for the door that the residents kept leaving open, he'd print out a passive-aggressive sign at some point. No need to worry about it for now.

'Aha,' he said as he scribbled in the word *indolent*.

The irony was lost on him.

~

Spence was the antithesis of workshy Colin Parks. It was mid-afternoon in The Eagle and unusually quiet, so he was taking the opportunity to clean glasses, whilst also making adjustments to the rota. He was trying to fit in dates he could attend his personal trainer course alongside his shifts.

It would be tight for a few months as it would leave him with very little spare time, but he knew the outcome would make it worthwhile. Being bar manager was okay for now, but he was ready to commit to a vocation with better prospects and long-term, more stability for him and Maya.

He was so engrossed in the rota, tapping the pen against his teeth, brow furrowed in concentration, that he didn't realise anyone had approached the bar until he heard, 'Hello, love.'

Looking up, he was pleased to see Dominique.

'Hello, you, this is a lovely surprise. Maya didn't say you were coming. You know she's at work, right?'

'Yes. It's why I'm here actually, I wanted a word with you on your own.'

'That sounds ominous. Drink?'

'Orange juice and lemonade would be lovely, thank you.'

He prepared her drink, noticing how Dominique positioned herself at the door so she could see who was coming and going. This was a habit Maya had fallen into since she'd started working for the police, but he recognised that Dominique was doing it as she was scared who might have followed her here and could come walking through the door any moment. Since the house fire, he barely recognised the strong-willed woman he used to know. She was becoming a nervous wreck and it broke his heart to see it.

Spence carried her drink round the other side of the bar so he could sit with her.

'How have you been?' Dominique asked.

'Good, thanks. I start my personal trainer's course next week, so just been juggling a few shifts around. I reckon if I can reduce my sleep down to just three hours a night, I can squeeze everything in.'

'Ha, who needs sleep?' Dominique said as she took a sip of her drink. 'I'm worried about Maya.'

'I know.' Spence gave Dominique's hand a light squeeze. 'I'm worried about both of you.'

Dominique shook her head. 'I don't just mean about Marcus. It's this therapy that Maya wants to start, she mentioned it to me the other day.'

'The EMDR?'

'Yes. I don't think it's a good idea and I've told her as much. I want you to talk to her too and persuade her to change her mind.'

Spence frowned. 'But why? I don't understand why you're so against it. I think it's a good idea.'

'There's things you don't understand.' Dominique slapped her hand on the bar. 'Marcus is a very dangerous man. Her childhood wasn't always... it's a blessing that she can't remember those earlier days. There are certain things that children shouldn't be exposed to. And I don't want her exposed to them now. No good will come of it. It'll just cause more heartache.'

'I love how much you want to protect her, but I honestly don't think it's helping. The not knowing – all these blank spaces in her childhood are what's causing the nightmares to become more frequent. She even had a flashback at a job the other day, but thankfully she was with Chris.'

'Spence, if she goes through with this therapy, she might uncover things that she can never come back from.'

'Like what? What's so bad that it's worse than what she's going through now?'

Dominique stared at him impassively. 'I can't recall a lot of it in detail myself. It was a long time ago and I've blanked stuff out too. For good reason. I need you to help me, Spence. Promise me you'll talk to her and persuade her not to do this. If she remembers the past, I'll have to as well and I can't go through all that again.'

The silence hung ominously as Spence thought about what Dominique was asking from him. Eventually he shook his head. 'I'm sorry, Dominique, I respect your opinion and I need you to know I'm here for you as much as Maya. I'll do everything I can to support both of you through all of this. Until Marcus is back behind bars and beyond.'

He reached out for Dominique's hand and held it this time. 'But, I honestly think this therapy will help. She can't go on like she is at the moment. The nightmares are torturing her; they're making her ill. She's made her decision and I support her fully. I'm not going to ask her to change her mind.'

Dominique pulled her hand away.

27

The silence of the house was ominous. Jordan knew something was wrong the moment he woke up. Normally, this time of day would be filled with the sounds of the shower running, the radio playing, and breakfast being made. This morning there was nothing other than a heavy stillness. He assumed Claire was up already as her bedroom door was ajar. He washed quickly and pulled on his uniform, reaching under his pillow for the burner phone. It wasn't there. He was so upset last night; he must have left it in his school bag.

It was whilst he was straightening his tie, he was horrified to realise that his bag wasn't lying next to his desk where he'd left it. 'Shit!' He stepped onto the landing and saw Craig emerging from his room, rubbing his eyes and yawning.

'Have you seen my school bag?'

'No, have you tried looking for it? Need a pee.' Craig pushed past him into the bathroom as Jordan braced himself for what he knew was coming.

As he entered the kitchen, he realised that things were worse than he could have anticipated. Claire was sat at the kitchen table nursing an empty mug. She wasn't dressed for work and despite still being in her pyjamas it was evident from the dark shadows under her eyes, she'd not been to bed.

Eleven mobile phones were lined up on the table in front of her, the ten he had stolen and even more terrifying than that, the burner phone that may well ring any minute as he always kept it on as ordered. Perhaps it had even rang already and she'd answered it; spoken to Wheeler.

'Who the hell do these belong to?' Claire asked, her tone flat but heavy with menace.

'What were you doing going through my bag?' Jordan asked, affronted by the invasion of his privacy. His sense of being wronged flitted away the moment Claire stood and slammed her hand down on the kitchen table.

'I SAID who the hell do these belong to? And don't even fucking think about trying to bullshit me!' she roared, her face puce, spittle flying from her lips. He had never, ever seen her so angry. His usually quiet, diminutive mother certainly had a bark worse than her bite, but she looked like a stranger in that moment. And he had never heard her swear like that.

Jordan wracked his brain for answers as Craig appeared wordlessly next to him.

'Jordan, answer the bastard question,' Claire hissed.

'Just some kids at school. They're broken and I said I'd have a go at mending them for them.'

Claire closed her eyes as she wiped a hand across her face, her shoulders slumped towards the table. 'I told you not to lie to me. I'm not stupid.'

Her voice was quieter now, barely a whisper. She eventually looked up and Jordan was mortified to see tears brimming in her eyes. He hated that. He would rather the shouting and swearing – even for her to hit him – but he couldn't bear the tears. When his dad first left, she had cried continuously for weeks until one day she suddenly seemed to compose herself overnight. Either that, or she literally had no tears left. This was the first time he had seen her cry since and he had been gone ten years.

'Mum.' He sank to the floor and reached for her hands, but she pulled away. 'Okay, if you want to know the truth they're Lewis's.'

Her curiosity piqued, she looked him in the eye, a frown furrowing her brow. 'Why has Lewis got *eleven* phones? What does he need that many for?'

'Does he want mine too, Jord?' Craig offered helpfully from where he was slumped against the doorframe, anxiously watching events unfold.

Claire smiled at Craig kindly. 'It's okay, hon. Jordan?' Claire tuned back to him, her expression demanding an answer as he desperately thought on his feet.

'I don't know where he got them or why he needs them, and I don't want to know. I know he's in trouble since the stabbing–' Jordan left the words unspoken long enough for Claire to nod her understanding. 'He just asked me to mind them for a couple of days and then he said, the stuff he's involved with will be over.'

Claire frowned as she chewed on a fingernail. 'I need to speak to Sarah. She's his mum, she has a right to know what he's got himself into.'

'Mum, no. Please. That will only make things worse. I assume he needs the phones to pay off some kind of debt and once he's done that, he'll be safe. If his Mum gets involved and she goes to the police, it'll cause all sorts of trouble for him. He won't be able to pay off his debt and they'll make him pay for getting the police involved.'

'I don't know, Jordan. If it was you, I'd want to know. I'd *need* to know what was going on.'

'But it's not me, Mum. This has got nothing to do with you. Just pretend you never saw them; that this never happened. I'll give Lewis the phones back like he asked and then he'll get whoever is giving him grief off his back. Then everything can go back to normal. This is his mess to sort out, not ours.'

He saw her hesitate and decided it was time to resort to something he wouldn't have thought possible of himself.

'Mum, he's already been stabbed once. They could have killed him. I'm genuinely worried that next time they will if he doesn't do what he's been told to with these.' He gestured his hand towards the phones on the table. Claire eyed him warily, caught between her head and heart. 'Pretend we've never seen any of this, and it can all go away. Trust me.'

Eventually, she gave an imperceptible nod. 'I do trust you. And I love you. But now is your last chance to tell me the honest truth. If you've got involved in something over your head, stealing or drugs or whatever, tell me now and I can help you.'

'I haven't, Mum. Honest.'

She leant forwards and grasped his face between her hands, her forehead pressed to his. 'Good. Because I'm telling you now, Jordan, if I suspect for one minute that you're involved in any of those things, drugs, stealing, gangs – whatever. As much as it would kill me, I would rather take a knife to you myself then sit and wait for some bloody stranger to do it. Because that's how it will end. It's how it always ends.'

With that, she stood up, pushed the phones across the table towards him and shuffled back to bed, worn and broken like one of the octogenarians she cared for.

28

As Maya arrived at Beech Field for her mid shift, her curiosity was piqued by the array of television cameras clustered round the front door. Experience taught her the press were waiting for an official briefing, but she hadn't heard of any incidents overnight. She saw Chris's car pull in and walked over to join him. As she waited, she could see some of the reporters gathering near the car park fence. She was horrified to find herself locking eyes with the meaty-faced 'Dave the Bastard'.

She turned away quickly but it was too late. He had clocked her and began to approach the fence hurriedly, waving for her attention.

'Maya, love, just a quick word.'

She was about to reply, but quick as a flash, Chris had appeared at her side. 'Two seconds to back off, Wainwright, or I'll have my boss ring yours and you can kiss your scumbag career away.'

Without waiting for a reply, he put a protective arm around her shoulder and wheeled her towards the staff entrance.

'Thanks, mate. God, he doesn't give up, does he?'

'You okay?'

'Yes thanks. I was actually having a nice morning until I saw him. Managed to get to the gym for a swim and fifteen minutes in the sauna so I *was* feeling quite relaxed. What's going on?'

'You've not seen the news?'

'No, don't tend to watch TV when I'm swimming and the radio on my bike is as broken as the ashtray.'

Chris grinned at her as they pushed their way through the doors. 'Remember the pregnant lady from the street mugging? She was taken in for an emergency section last night. She works for a PA company apparently and her colleagues have been all over it, highlighting it to the press in a bid to get the lad caught.'

'Are they okay, mum and baby?'

'Not heard yet, hopefully Kym will be able to give us an update.'

They hurried up to the office, both of them willing for good news. 'She said in the ambulance that her blood pressure was sky high, which was understandable, but the baby was moving around okay,' Maya said anxiously as they walked into the office. Kym's office door was shut, and through the slatted blinds, they could see her in a meeting with Redford, Jack and Adila.

Maya said hello to Amanda and nodded towards the office door. 'Have you heard any update?'

Amanda shook her head. 'Not yet. They've been in there about forty-five minutes so I'm hoping they're nearly done.'

'The glove I seized, has that been submitted for DNA work?'

'Yes, it went yesterday, but I'm anticipating it may well be fast-tracked as an urgent case today.'

'Hopefully,' said Chris and Maya together.

They waited a further agonising ten minutes, making brews and logging on to computers before eventually Kym's office door opened and CID filed out, each with a nod to Maya and Chris.

Kym emerged too and didn't need to bother with a double clap, the sea of expectant faces enough to know she had their attention. 'First of all, baby Eden is still giving us cause for concern. There were complications last night, which could possibly be contributed to the fall, but Eden was safely delivered and is being constantly monitored. She's described as poorly but stable.'

Kym repeated what Chris had told Maya about the PA team contacting the press in order to identify the assailant. 'A press statement has been prepared and will be read out by the chief super in a few hours. Adila is going back to the hospital to let the parents know and to be there for any update on Eden. Jack is arranging a fresh round of house to house in the area.'

'Are they going to fast-track the glove?' Maya asked.

Kym nodded. 'The lab have already been contacted.'

Conversation turned to the rest of the day's jobs until they were interrupted by the office phone ringing, which Maya turned to answer. 'Hello, Crime Scene Investigation Unit, Maya speaking.'

'Maya, it was rude of you to ignore me just then. How many times do I need to tell you that you'll benefit from telling your side of the story.'

Maya felt the blood draining from her face at the sound of 'Dave the Bastard's' all too familiar voice. 'I have told you before, I'm not interested. Now stop phoning me and leave me alone.'

She slammed the receiver down so hard, she was worried it would crack.

'Who the hell was that?' Kym asked sternly, her mouth twitching with disapproval at the treatment of the phone.

Maya ran a hand through her hair. 'Sorry, Kym. It was Dave Wainwright again. He's just tried to speak to me outside which is why he knew to ring the office. He can't ring my mobile anymore because I blocked his number and I'm deliberately screening any other unknown numbers.'

'And have you had many?' Pinpricks of colour flushed Kym's

cheeks, an indication that she was about to embark on a full-blown rage.

Maya scrolled through the call list on her mobile. 'About a dozen since I blocked him. Obviously, I don't know if these other numbers are him other than the first landline number which I looked up. It's the switchboard number for the *Evening News*.'

'Can you send me a screenshot of those calls, please. I'm going to speak to DI Redford. He's more than pushed his luck this time. We'll have him suspended by the end of the day.'

29

Wheeler was pacing the flat, smoking a joint as usual and trying to get his thoughts in order. He knew he needed to lay off the weed, it was making him sluggish and right now he needed to be on top of his game. Reilly had rung him the previous evening to let him know the drugs would be arriving tomorrow. He had to take Reilly the thousand pounds from Brogan's debt, and then return back here with the drugs, which would then need to be bagged and dispatched to old and new clients.

If he was honest, the thought of ferrying the drugs back terrified him. All it would take was one tug by the police and with so much gear on him, he could be looking at a life sentence. Also, securing new clients could be risky if he stepped on a rival dealer's toes. On the other hand, once the drugs started getting shipped out, if everything went according to plan, he was confident that Reilly would give him a nice big payout. Maybe enough to start looking for legitimate lodgings.

The sound of the television broke his chain of thought. He snatched the remote control off the coffee table, turned the TV off, and hurled the remote at the sofa where Susie and Albert were snuggled together. They were getting more and more pally, and he didn't like it. Not only that, but the old man was looking shabbier by the day and it was starting to grate on him.

'What's up with you?' Susie snapped, as she placed the remote next to a cold mug of tea. 'That's Albert's favourite programme.'

'I couldn't give a shit. I'm trying to work out the logistics of how to keep money coming into this shithole and can't even hear myself think because of that sodding TV. Who pays for the electricity to keep it running, eh? Me, that's who and I deserve some fuckin' respect.'

'Okay,' said Susie. 'I can see you're stressed but there's no need to shout.'

Albert wisely decided it was time to get out of Wheeler's way.

'Where are you going?' Wheeler shouted at him as he began to shuffle off.

'My room.'

'Yeah, think again. There are going to be some changes around here. Shift your shit out of there, that's my room from now on.'

'Where am I supposed to sleep?' Albert asked.

'You can have the couch. It's been good enough for me for the last few weeks. At least then you'll be nearer your precious bloody TV.'

Albert was too scared to argue. He'd long since learnt that the best way to soothe Wheeler's moods was just to do as he asked. He scuttled off, leaving Wheeler to turn his attention to Susie who was frowning unhappily at seeing Albert unsettled.

'You can move in then, babe,' Wheeler cooed as he wrapped his arms around her. 'We've talked about having our own place for ages and this isn't a bad start, just for a while. Once the gear arrives tomorrow, it's safer if you stay here rather than keep coming and going. That's just asking for us to get taxed. Plus, I need someone I can trust to help bag up.'

Susie frowned. 'I don't know. I don't really want to get involved in all that.'

'But who else can I trust other than my best girl?' he said as he nuzzled her neck. 'Plus, just think, once the gear is sold, Reilly will have to give me a decent payday and we can look for somewhere else. A nice place near town maybe? And it means I'll have the cash to take you shopping. Get you whatever you want.'

The cajoling worked and Susie brightened at the thought of the clothes that amount of drug money could buy. Not to mention the fact she could get her hair and nails done and regular spray tans. 'What about Albert? We could treat him too, thank him for letting us stay?'

'Yeah, dead right.' Wheeler nodded, despite thinking there was no chance. 'We'll cover his bills and maybe get him a better, bigger television, he'd like that, eh?'

Susie pondered on it briefly before nodding agreement. 'Right, get to your mum and dad's and pack your stuff. Little-man is coming to chat some business, so I could do with you out of the way.'

He watched as she applied a gelatinous slick of lip gloss before blowing him a kiss and sweeping out of the flat at the same time as Jordan arrived. He looked as pale and nervous as always, and Wheeler questioned exactly how much use a kid like this really was to him.

'Phones,' he said, hand already outstretched. He watched with mounting irritation as Jordan fished around in his school bag and he lit another joint to calm himself before he snapped and gave the kid another good hiding. He watched Jordan spread the phones across the table and was quietly impressed that he'd managed to grab a stash of decent models. There was definitely a few quid in that lot, more than a grand by the looks of it. And he'd managed all ten, when in reality, Wheeler had only expected half a dozen.

'Not bad, little-man,' he said reluctantly. 'Any bother getting them?'

Jordan suddenly seemed fascinated by the threadbare beige carpet, as he nudged the material with the toe of his trainer. The silence pulsed menacingly.

'Well?' Wheeler kicked at the coffee table, causing tea to slop on it which riled him even more.

'Honest, they were all like you said, a piece of cake other than the last one.'

Wheeler raised an eyebrow at Jordan as he took a long drag on the joint, before slowly expelling the joint in his face. Jordan tried not to wince or splutter as the smoke stung his eyes and seared the back of his throat.

'What have you done, little-man?' Wheeler asked warily as he flicked the joint into an ashtray.

'So, there was this lady. She had all these bags and things. Looked dead rich. And she was miles away, chatting on her phone. I just thought it was too good an opportunity to miss, so I went for it. Only she didn't let it go and she kind of fell over.' Jordan babbled on, as if the faster he could get the words out, the less impact they would have.

'Wait, is this you?' Wheeler reached for his phone and brought up a breaking news story on Instagram. Jordan's mouth dropped open when he saw the headlines about the pregnant woman. He could feel the colour drain from his face and his legs start to turn to jelly.

'The baby. Is the baby okay?'

'I don't know, they haven't said. What the fuck were you

thinking?' Wheeler hissed as he jabbed a forefinger into the boy's temple. 'Are you stupid?'

Jordan was about to reply, but Wheeler silenced him with a raised hand as he stared at the phones on the table. 'I asked you for ten phones, you got me ten phones.'

Jordan nodded mutely.

'Then why the fuck did you go for another one?'

'I told you; it was too good an opportunity to ignore–'

Jordan was cut off mid-sentence as Wheeler raised his hand and brought his palm across the boy's face. The stinging blow caused him to stumble backwards. He raised his hands instinctively, but was too slow as the second strike, this time with a curled fist, sent him crashing to the floor. It felt like his nose had exploded and the pain from his face made him disorientated.

Wheeler reached down and grabbed the boy by the collar and hauled him to his feet, shoving him roughly against the wall. 'You're a greedy little bastard!' Wheeler screamed as he smashed the back of Jordan's head against the wall. 'What are you?'

Jordan was unable to speak, his ears were now ringing, and it felt like the latest assault had caused every tooth in his head to rattle.

'I'm waiting to take delivery of the biggest drug deal I've ever had, and you bring attention to my door because you can't keep your thieving fingers to yourself? Do you realise how stupid you've been?'

Jordan's continued silence caused him to snap as he slapped the boy across the face again and then, before he knew it, his hands were wrapped around his neck. Wheeler was squeezing Jordan's throat like it was nothing more than a stress ball. Jordan felt his eyes begin to bulge. The grip was so tight he couldn't move his head and the crushing of his windpipe was excruciating. Jordan was convinced Wheeler was going to squeeze every last breath out of his body.

Wheeler was too far gone to be aware of his actions. Jordan's vision began to swim, and as his lungs screamed for air, stars appeared on the periphery of his vision as darkness descended.

30

Maya arrived home from her shift mentally and physically exhausted. She'd spent most of it in custody with a particularly irate prisoner, which was never ideal when she needed to get up close and personal to not only photograph him, but swab blood from his hands and photo any cuts and bruises as his clothing was removed.

His unpredictable mood had unnerved her and meant that the process had become more protracted than usual. On top of that, it was evident that personal hygiene wasn't on the suspect's list of priorities, and she would hazard a guess he'd not bathed in weeks. As she said to Chris later, she'd worked with dead bodies that hadn't smelt that bad.

The vile odour in the cramped room had increased like a fug with every item of clothing that was peeled away. It was like being in the presence of a real life Pig-Pen from the *Peanuts* comic strip. And once his shoes and socks had come off, well, she didn't think even several hours' intensive counselling with Jayne would ever eradicate that unsavoury memory.

The highlight of the shift had been the welcome news that

baby Eden was much improved and there were no longer any serious concerns for her health. Both mum and baby would remain in hospital where they could be monitored until they were deemed fit to return home. In the meantime, Maya was hoping for a DNA hit on the offender's glove.

She called for the lift and once inside allowed her head to rest on the wall as it began its creaking ascent to the eleventh floor. She wanted nothing more than to be warm in bed with a hot chocolate and a good book. For once, Maya didn't mind that Spence would be spending the evening at The Eagle. At least she could stretch out and hog all the duvet and spray the sleep-inducing pillow mist that he always complained gave him a headache and made him sneeze.

The lift shuddered to a halt, and she stepped out into the hallway, frowning at the dark corridor. The faulty light fitting must have finally blown. Colin the caretaker was as much use as a cock in a convent, and rather than wasting another phone call to the property developer, she vowed to track him down herself tomorrow and give him a piece of her mind.

Maya fished her phone out of her pocket to use the torch to help locate her door key but was mortified to see her battery had died. The darkness consumed her as she fumbled with the keys. Hair rose on the back of her neck as she became consumed by panic, causing her to drop them. This was the stuff of nightmares.

Willing herself to stay calm, she crouched down to pick the keys up. Her fingers grazed the carpet as she searched for them. The fabric was coarse and static beneath her trembling hands. The darkness seemed to be swallowing her. Rather than the familiar smell of home, her nostrils were tainted with the smell of the suspect she had been dealing with. It added to her panic.

She let out a gasp of relief when she discovered the edge of her key ring. She straightened up and was horrified to feel a hand on her shoulder. The scream stalled in her throat as a sour-smelling mouth hissed into her ear the word, 'Bitch.'

31

Jordan felt the last of his breath leave his body as Wheeler squeezed his neck even tighter. He willed the darkness to take him; anything to make the agony stop.

'Let him go.' The usually frail voice was surprisingly strong and so was the sharp crack across the shoulders from Albert's walking stick. It was enough to break Wheeler's red mist. He let go of Jordan who fell forward across the coffee table coughing, spluttering and gasping for precious breath.

Wheeler turned on Albert who was standing resolute, although there was a noticeable quiver in the hand that gripped the walking stick. 'Now then, if you hurt that young man, you'll have the police on you,' Albert cautioned. 'He's just a boy,' he added as he leant towards Jordan to check he was okay.

Albert's reasoned tone sobered Wheeler up enough to take stock of his actions. Truth be known, had he not intervened, he would easily have choked the life out of him, and then where would he be? On a murder charge and up to his neck in it with Reilly who would have no qualms about having him targeted inside. Wheeler let out a sigh and swiped away spittle from his acne-riddled chin.

'We're all right, aren't we, little-man?' he said as he ruffled the boy's hair. 'Go and fetch him a glass of water,' he ordered Albert, as he reached for the joint.

Jordan managed to stagger to his feet and collapse onto the sofa where he rubbed at his neck, simultaneously sucking in the air. Although thick with the fug of cannabis smoke, Jordan thought it was the sweetest thing he'd ever inhaled as his oxygen-starved lungs re-inflated.

Albert appeared and cupped the lad's face gently as he held a glass of water to his lips. 'Now, lad, gentle sips, don't gulp.'

Jordan nodded as he sipped the water, each gulp feeling like his Adam's apple was being lacerated. Sated, he sank back, allowing the sofa to embrace his weight. Albert nestled next to him and began to carefully place some frozen peas that he'd wrapped in a threadbare tea towel against the boy's throat.

Wheeler watched on dispassionately as he continued to smoke. 'You don't have to mother him. He's okay, aren't you, little-man?'

'You could have killed him,' Albert said. 'You could at least get him to hospital and have him checked.'

Wheeler stubbed the joint out angrily. 'Nobody's going to hospital. He's fine. The last thing we need is to attract any attention, he's done enough of that. Finish your water and get yourself home and sleep it off. You, go and carry on moving your stuff out of my room.'

Jordan watched reluctantly as Albert scuttled off. He carried on sipping his water and clutching the cold compress to his tender throat. Wheeler disappeared into the kitchen and appeared a short time later, clutching something that made Jordan gasp. He was wielding a menacing-looking kitchen knife and for a split second, Jordan thought he was going to have his throat slit.

'Don't worry, little-man, this is for you to keep safe. You're gonna be carrying more gear from tomorrow, which means more money for us, but it also means you risk other people trying to tax you. D'ya get me?'

Jordan nodded although he didn't have a clue what Wheeler was talking about, and it was evident by his blank expression.

'For Christ's sake. Taxed – it means a man's gonna try and steal our drugs, right? So, keep your eyes and ears open while you're doing deliveries. And keep moving, yeah? You think you're in any bother, then use this right away. No hesitation. Better you shank them up first,' Wheeler said as he passed Jordan the knife and nodded for him to put it in his school bag.

'And this,' Wheeler continued as he passed him several wraps of weed. 'Help take the edge off so you can relax. Might help the pain later.' As an afterthought, he even offered a pre-rolled joint to Jordan along with a spare cigarette lighter.

Jordan realised that this was the closest Wheeler would ever come to apologise for strangling him. He stuffed the knife and drugs into his bag and darted out of the room as quick as he could, considering the pain he was in. He hovered in the hallway, from where he could see Albert standing sadly by his bed. As much as he was desperate to get out of the flat and away from Wheeler's violent mood swings, the sight of the old man and the tenderness he had shown him, glued him to the spot.

'Are you okay?' Jordan croaked.

Albert raised his head and Jordan could see the defeated look in his eyes, accentuated by the stoop of his shoulders and sluggish movements. 'Not really, son. Are you?'

Jordan gave a thin smile. 'Not really.'

'You need to stay away from him, he could have killed you,' Albert hissed.

'I can't. If I don't do what he says, he'll kill me, then come after my mum and brother. I can't let that happen.' Jordan straightened up resolutely. 'It'll all stop soon. I'm not sure how yet, but it will. I'll find a way. We'll be okay.'

Jordan gave Albert a wan smile and left. He took the stairs two at a time, ignoring the feel of the blade in his bag as it bounced against his shoulders. Outside, the cold bit him, icier than the compress Albert had given him for his throat. He started to climb on his bike, when he noticed a man approaching him. He was older, about his dad's age and smartly dressed.

'All right, son, mind if we have a little chat? Let's walk and talk, yeah?' The man's eyes darted upwards toward the flat, suggesting he knew where Jordan had come from. Jordan felt a fist of fear squeeze his stomach; was he police? He looked around frantically for any police cars or uniforms but saw nothing.

The man gave an easy laugh as he clapped him avuncularly on his shoulder. 'Don't look so nervous, there's nothing for you to worry about. What's your name?'

'Jordan.'

'I've noticed you about, Jordan. You've been running a few errands for Wheeler, haven't you?'

Jordan's eyes widened with panic as he looked around again. The man had led him round the back of the flats, and he was now stood with his back to an isolated car park with nowhere to go. If he wasn't police, why had he been watching him? Fear had silenced him; all he could manage was a surly shrug.

'I'll take your silence as a yes. I also assume that red mark around your throat is down to him too. You don't need to put up with that.'

'Who are you?'

'My name's Ivo. I'm in the same line of work as Wheeler, but let's just say I'm more successful and better to work for. I look after my couriers – there's no need for that,' he said as he nodded towards the bruising.

'What do you want?'

'I'm offering you a job. I'll double whatever Wheeler's paying you and I can guarantee you'll be well looked after.'

Jordan shook his head and gave an incredulous laugh. What was it with him, he was being courted by drug dealers like a debutante at a prom. 'Thanks, but I'm not interested. I've got too much going on at the minute. I don't need this.'

Ivo raised his hands. 'No pressure. Here, give me your phone. Let me put my number in. That way if you change your mind, or if that happens again,' he said, pointing to Jordan's neck, 'you can phone me.'

Jordan hesitated, wondering if Ivo would be able to get him out of the mess he was in. But what if this was some sort of trick set up by Wheeler to test his honesty. He felt trapped in the car park with Ivo and didn't want to cross him and risk another beating. He handed his phone over and watched as he typed his number in.

'Here,' he said as he reached in his pocket and passed Jordan a handful of twenty-pound notes as he gave his phone back. 'Go and treat yourself, you look like you could do with a decent feed.'

Jordan's eyes lit up at the sight of so much cash. 'No, honestly, I couldn't–'

Ivo waved his objections away. 'It's peanuts to me, kid, don't worry about it. Ring me if you change your mind. And, probably best if you don't mention our little conversation with Wheeler, eh? I don't think he'd be too happy about it. See you around.'

Ivo flashed an easy smile and walked away leaving a cloud of expensive aftershave in his wake, and Jordan wondering how earning this amount of cash on a regular basis could help his mum and Craig.

32

Maya finally let out a scream that reverberated down the corridor. The moment the hand was placed on her shoulder, she instinctively donkey-kicked her heel backwards. The reinforced soles of her biker's boot scraped sickeningly down her assailant's shin, and she heard him grunt in pain.

She heard her neighbour's door open, the light from within illuminating the corridor. Turning, with keys gripped in her hand, she made a pre-emptive strike towards a face that was already cowering backwards, covered by hands. The fear and sheer panic she had experienced moments ago was replaced with an anger equally strong.

'You bastard! What the hell!?'

'Maya, are you okay?' Her neighbour, Keith, was at her side in an instant and it was only his presence and a distant reflex that prevented Maya launching her boot in her would-be-attacker's face.

'Yes, but could you call the police, please. This man has been harassing me.'

'Dave the Bastard' cowered on the hallway floor as he raised his hands in defence. 'Maya, love,' he said, his voice thickened with alcohol. 'I only ever wanted to talk to you. There was no need to get me sacked.'

'How dare you. You've made my life a nightmare. Printing pictures of me you were told not to post on your shitty online rag. Phoning me on my mobile and work and now *this*. How dare you – this is my *home*. I've had enough to contend with over the last twelve months without being harassed by you, just so you can write a story that no one wants to read.'

'But they *will* read it. Everyone is dying to hear about the truth between you and the notorious Marcus Naylor.'

'I can't tell you what I don't know!' Maya shrieked.

Keith moved closer and put a comforting arm around her shoulder. 'Don't upset yourself. The police are on the way. He can wait at mine until they come. Go and get yourself inside.'

Keith hauled the inebriated Wainwright to his feet. For a moment it looked like he was going to put up a fight, but the alcohol dulled him, and he raised his hands in a peaceful gesture.

'I'll come with you and wait to speak to the police,' he slurred. 'This is all just a misunderstanding. It'll all blow over.'

Wainwright followed the man into his flat, pausing briefly to glance back at Maya. He had the audacity to give her a wounded look, as if he was the victim. She slammed her front door so hard, it rocked on its hinges.

33

Maya arrived for her first EMDR session with Jayne. She had attended the previous week and Jayne had talked her through the process, including what to expect and how the sessions would be controlled if recalling the trauma became too much. Then the rest of that session had been spent teaching Maya some tricks to calm her anxiety.

Sitting in reception, she was using one of those techniques now, recalling the alphabet backwards as a type of grounding and distraction. Her phone chirruped with the sound of two messages arriving simultaneously She smiled as she read the good luck messages from Spence and Chris. She turned off her phone and continued to wait. She thought of Dominique and how much she wished she could be sat here with her right now. She was the only other person who would be able to understand and interpret whatever memories were uncovered during these sessions.

Dominique had arrived at Maya's the moment she heard about Wainwright turning up at her apartment. In true Dominique style, she had also located Colin the hapless caretaker and demanded there and then that the lighting on the eleven floor be fixed. Afterwards, they had shared a takeaway and a bottle of wine and Dominique had stayed over so Maya didn't have to be alone. Despite the distress caused by Wainwright, it was the most fun they had shared together in a while, especially as all mention of Naylor remained unspoken. As did any mention of the EMDR as Dominique had made it clear that she still didn't approve.

Jayne's familiar voice invited her up and Maya took the stairs with heavy legs. The room was warm and welcoming; an oil burner was releasing puffs of lavender and chamomile and the lights were soft and unobtrusive as always. Despite her nervousness, Maya shucked off her heavy jacket and began to feel herself relax.

'How was your week?' Jayne asked as always, and Maya filled her in with a succinct, profanity-free precis of the previous evening's events with Wainwright.

When Maya had finished, Jayne had puffed out her cheeks and exhaled. 'That man sounds like he has some serious issues. So, I assume he's been arrested?'

'Yes, for harassment. He's on bail with conditions not to come anywhere near me at home or work, or to contact me directly or indirectly.'

'Well let's hope he finally listens this time. Hopefully that's one last stress behind you. Want to talk about anything else?'

'No, I don't think so. I'm feeling nervous actually. I think I just want to make a start before I change my mind.'

'Which is completely understandable. I know how daunting this process is, but you also know that I honestly believe you're doing the right thing. It can really help you.'

'Let's give it a try. I'm ready.'

'Okay, before we start, remember we discussed your safe place, think of that for a while, get comfortable and start to feel stabilised.'

Maya nodded, closed her eyes and concentrated on her breathing and relaxation, whilst picturing her safe space. Once relaxed and ready, she opened her eyes and nodded at Jayne.

'Just to remind you, we're going to use eye movement for the bilateral stimulation. I'm going to move my fingers from left to right, like this, and I want you to let your eyes follow the movement.' Jayne held her right hand up, her index and middle finger pointed towards Maya as she swung her hand from left to right.

Maya nodded again.

'Okay, in our previous session, we discussed the flashback you had in the hallway. You recall opening a door, which you believed led to the lounge and you could see bloodstains on the floor. Is that right?'

Maya swallowed. 'Yes.'

'When you think of that memory, how anxious would you say it made you feel on a scale of one to ten. One being least anxious, ten being distressed?'

'Very, I'd say nine.'

'As we work through this process, that anxiety should decrease, allowing you to process that memory and explore a bit deeper. We'll go at your pace. When you're ready, I want you to take a breath and picture yourself in that hallway. Start to allow your eyes to follow the movement of my fingers.'

Maya did as Jayne asked. She pictured the scenario and allowed herself to be present in the hallway, her eyes following Jayne's fingers. After a while, Jayne stopped.

'Okay, tell me what you're feeling.'

'It's dark. The hallway light isn't on but the one on the landing is. It's too dark.'

'Go with that.'

Jayne repeated the process again. 'What are you feeling now?' she asked when she stopped.

Maya shivered involuntarily. 'It's cold. It must be night-time. The smell...'

'What about the smell?'

'I know I'm definitely in the hall at Mama's, but it doesn't smell like her house. That smells like cooking and soap powder. There's cigarette smoke.'

Jayne let Maya's mind permeate the image more before continuing. 'Now what do you feel?'

'I'm scared–'

'You're safe.'

'No, I mean in the hall. I'm scared. It's dark and cold. I want Mama. I need to go in the lounge.'

'Go with it.'

'Something's stopping me.'

'Okay, take a breath.' Jayne gave Maya a moment before continuing moving her fingers in the insistent, pendulum-like sway.

After what might have been seconds, minutes or hours, Maya didn't know, she was too consumed with absorbing the image. It was astounding that despite the warmth of the room she was sat in, she could feel the chill of the hallway. The lavender-scented air had dispersed into a dirty smell – the antithesis of Dominique's.

'What can you feel?'

'I want to go in the room, but something's stopping me. I think it's a noise. Something in there is scaring me, but at the same time I want to go in. I *need* to go in. The door is open slightly. I can see in the room.'

'Go with that, Maya.'

'I can nudge the door open. There're bloodstains on the carpet. A lot of blood.'

'Stay with it, you're safe, remember. What else can you see?'

'There's a hand. On the carpet. Someone's lying on the carpet, and they're covered in blood. I can't–'

'Okay, Maya, if you need to use your safe space you can. Take a moment. Remember your breathing and there's a glass of water just in front of you if you need some.'

Jayne gave Maya the time she needed to compose herself. 'You've done really well. You've made great progress for the first session. How are you feeling now?'

Maya let out a dry laugh. 'Exhausted.'

'That's natural, we talked about that, remember. How do you feel it went?'

'Surreal. Good though, I think. Good probably isn't the right word, but we've made a start, haven't we? There was some development, however small, and I at least responded to the treatment when part of me was doubting whether or not I would.'

'When you think of yourself stood in the hallway now, where is your anxiety on a scale of one to ten?'

Maya pondered for a while. 'It's surprisingly not as heightened as when you first asked, I guess. I'd say eight.'

'Which is amazing for our first session. You've taken the very first, brave step in exploring this memory and allowing yourself to dig deeper. The fact you were able to put yourself back into child Maya and stand there in that hallway is amazing. Are you ready to try again on our next session?'

Maya nodded. It wasn't going to be easy, but now she'd made a start, she needed to see it through. She needed to see who was lying in that room. She needed to know what had happened to them, even though she already knew who had caused it.

34

By the time Maya arrived home from counselling, she was exhausted. Jayne had finished the session with some grounding and relaxation so she was happy that Maya was fully recovered before riding home. Maya had stepped out of the session into a full-blown autumnal storm and was relieved to be off the bike and riding the lift, knowing Spence would be waiting for her. Today had been the first of his personal trainer courses so they had lots to talk about.

As the lift stopped, she found herself looking out into the hallway before leaving the sanctity of the elevator. 'Dave the Bastard's' visit last night had unnerved her more than she cared to admit. That said, any anxiety alleviated the moment she put the key in the lock and opened her front door to a myriad of delicious smells coming from the kitchen.

'You've cooked.' Maya beamed at Spence as she wrapped her arms around him.

'Yes, lasagne just for you. I guessed you'd need some soft-soaping after your session. There's profiteroles for afters, *not* home-made, and some Prosecco chilling in the fridge. As you're off tomorrow, I thought it would be nice to share a meal, relax, catch up and just spend some alone time.'

'Sounds perfect. And these flowers? They're gorgeous, thank you.' Maya buried her nose in the huge bouquet stood proudly on the hall table.

'Ah, can't take credit for them I'm afraid. Dominique dropped them off for you earlier. She said to ring her later and let her know how it went.'

Maya snorted. 'That's so kind of her, but I know she doesn't want to know about the session. She's made her feelings perfectly clear on that score.'

'I know, but she still just wants to know that you're okay. You don't have to go into details.'

'You're right. It's a lovely gesture, it would be more helpful though if she'd just get on board with it–'

Maya was interrupted by the buzzer. 'Are you expecting anyone?'

Spence shook his head, and on seeing Maya's hesitation, pushed past her to see who was there. She hovered nervously in the kitchen until she heard a familiar voice booming down the corridor. 'Not interrupting, am I, mate?'

Maya stepped into the hallway and grinned at the sight of Chris. 'Don't tell me you could smell Spence's lasagne from your house.' She laughed, then hesitated. 'Hey, how did you get to the lift without buzzing us?'

'One of the other tenants or their visitor held the door open for me as she was leaving.'

'Jesus, the security at this place is a joke.' Maya was about to build up into a rant about the uselessness of Colin the caretaker but was intercepted by Spence who asked Chris if he'd like to join them for dinner. 'There's loads to go around,' he reassured.

'I've already eaten, but I'll stay for a taste if you don't mind, just while I hear how this one got on with her session.' Chris was already rubbing his stomach as he took off his jacket and Maya laughed. Anyone else dropping in as they were about to enjoy their couple's quality time would probably be an issue, but she knew Spence loved Chris as much as she did, and it was always a genuine delight to see him.

Spence had already cracked open a beer and was pouring it into a glass for Chris as they settled around the table. Maya quickly filled them in on how the session had gone.

'Honestly, the strangest thing was even though I knew I was in the room with Jayne, I could imagine being in that hallway as a child with such detail. Even the temperature and smell. I'd forgotten I'd been scared of the dark as a kid. In fact, I was wondering if that was why the hallway out there has been freaking me out so much. You know the flickering bulb before it blew?' she asked Spence, who nodded. 'I think it may have been a subconscious thing, a kind of memory peg to that childhood recollection?'

Spence nodded. 'Maybe. But to be fair, love, all the stress of Naylor, it's no wonder you're jumping at shadows. And after that trick Wainwright pulled last night, well, I just hope they throw the bloody book at him for that. He's made you scared to be in your own home.'

Maya took a sip of Prosecco. 'To be honest, I've not felt safe here for a while. Not since Lurch broke in.'

Lurch, whose real name was Sydney, had previously been ordered to break into her apartment while she was sleeping and give her a message from Naylor, who was still in prison at the time. Lurch had been an intimidating looking man, his bulging forehead accentuated by his receding mousy brown hairline. His protruding eyes were rimmed with dark shadows, his nose looked like it had been broken several times and he had several missing teeth all of which added to his sinister appearance. Despite being involved with a criminal gang, Maya believed

Lurch was a good man who had been taken advantage of and she had encouraged him to flee the country to avoid being arrested.

'And security is so lax,' Maya continued. 'The fact this reprobate snuck in unannounced is proof of that,' she said with a grin as she tapped Chris's foot under the table.

'Actually,' said Chris as he scratched his belly, 'this is the reason why "this reprobate" is here. I have a suggestion and need you both to consider it?'

'Intriguing,' said Spence as he leant forward in his chair. 'I'm all ears, mate.'

'You've so much going on as you've said. It's been heartbreaking for me watching how much the last sighting of Naylor has unnerved you. Whether it was him or not, it's always going to be there until he's locked up and you've got all this therapy in front of you. I know you've not felt safe here for a while and I'm so proud of how well you've been trying to cope and put a brave face on.'

Maya gave a watery smile as she reached across the table to squeeze his hand. 'So,' he continued, 'I would like to suggest a house swap.'

'Eh?' Maya and Spence said simultaneously, causing Chris to laugh.

'How about I stay here for a while and you two move into my house? You're closer to work and Dominique's and, Spence, my place is easier to get to your PT course. It's not as close to the pub, granted, but it would mean on the nights you're working there, hopefully Maya will feel more comfortable on her own at my place. There are more pros than cons.

'Plus, Maya, you said yourself, you love my house. You feel comfy there. You don't need to decide now, have a think and let me know and if you think it would help, we can give it a try, eh? Just until things settle down and you're feeling more stable.

We've nothing to lose, if it doesn't work out, which I can't see why it wouldn't then we just go back to normal – no harm done.'

'You'd honestly do that, for us?' Maya reached for his hand again, her eyes brimming with tears.

Chris gripped her hand and gave her a soft smile. 'Maya, love, I'd do anything for you.' He coughed as he swiped a hand across his brow and continued nonchalantly. 'Wouldn't have suggested it otherwise. I've been thinking about if for a while to be honest. It suits me because I fancy a change of scene, and if it helps take some of the pressure off you two, it's worth giving it a go, eh?'

Maya and Spence exchanged a look.

'We don't need time to think about it, it's a definite yes. We honestly can't thank you enough.'

Then with a squeal of sheer happiness that Spence and Chris hadn't seen for months, Maya leapt from the chair and wrapped her arms around Chris's neck.

'We really appreciate it. We really appreciate *you*. Thanks, Chris,' she said, her voice thick with emotion.

'No need for thanks, you daft sod,' he said as he hugged her back. 'But if one of you could start dishing up that lasagne, I won't say no. Pudding would be nice, too.'

35

———

W heeler's day had started well. It had been nice to wake up in a proper bed with the ever-willing Susie by his side. After they'd given Albert's mattress a good pummelling, he'd made a good deal with a fence he knew and accrued over fifteen hundred pounds for the stolen phones. Despite the trouble he'd caused with the pregnant woman, little-man had clearly stolen well and might not be completely useless after all.

With money to pay off Brogan's debt and change besides, Wheeler was feeling optimistic as he drove a rented hire car to Crewe to collect the drugs from Reilly. There was no way he was risking driving a stolen car on false plates, which was his usual go-to. Today, he was doing things legitimately.

He arrived at Reilly's with the usual trepidation. The beating he had sustained last time was still fresh in his memory, and the irony that he had inflicted twice as much pain on Jordan would have been lost on him if he'd realised. Sully had the door open before he even had a chance to knock.

'Kitchen,' said the man-mountain. Wheeler nodded to him as he as he walked down the hall pleased he wasn't following behind him. Reilly was leaning nonchalantly against an

American-style fridge-freezer. The sight of the bundles of drugs on the kitchen table made Wheeler baulk.

'Problem?' Reilly asked in his honeyed Gaelic tones.

'No, boss. Just... all that gear. How much of it am I taking?'

'All of it, dickhead. Why, are you going shy bride on me?'

'No, it's just a lot more than I expected. There's a lot to shift.'

Reilly shrugged. 'Not scared of a bit of hard work, are you? You told me you'd recruited another runner. Please don't tell me you're going to disappoint me again.' Reilly shook his head slowly and tutted, before calling out in his sing-song voice, 'Sully, could you come in here, please? Wheeler is being difficult again.'

Wheeler was rooted to the spot with fear as Sully appeared almost from nowhere. His arms were folded over his broad chest, which was so wide, they could barely cross.

'Want me to snap him?' Sully asked.

He approached Wheeler and pressed his face so close, their noses were nearly touching. 'I'll fold you like a fucking pretzel,' he said softly, the words barely audible.

Wheeler leapt back, hands raised. 'Honest, boss, it's not a problem. It's just more than I anticipated. And here. Here's your money.' In his panic he pulled out the full fifteen hundred, no longer bothering about keeping five hundred back for himself. 'It's to clear Brogan's debt. With more besides to say sorry for all the bother, like.'

Reilly arched an eyebrow. 'Good lad. Maybe you're not so completely fucking useless after all. Sorry, Sully, no snapping today. So, back to business, there's a pick-and-mix of delight. Coke, weed, ket. And some ecstasy tablets. Is the car ready?'

Wheeler nodded. He'd already removed the spare tyre so he could pack some drugs in the boot as well as other areas in the car. He also had some McDonald's bags that he could stash some of the gear in, so if he was pulled by the police, God forbid, it would all look innocuous. On the surface anyway. If he was caught with all this lot, he would never see the light of day again. And it was so much more than he was expecting to shift. How was he supposed to manage this lot by himself? Jordan was next to bloody useless.

'All good, boss. I'll start loading up.' His smile masked his apprehension. Showing any signs of trepidation in front of these two would be akin to signing his own death warrant. He'd get the drugs back to the flat and take it from there. He'd come up with something.

'Sully will help you load up,' Reilly said pleasantly. 'Keep your phone on, sweetheart, I'll be in touch.'

With that, Reilly headed for the lounge. Sully grinned at him as he raised both of his meaty paws and made a snapping gesture. Wheeler looked at him, then he looked at the drugs on the table and it was all he could do not to spill his bowels on the kitchen floor.

36

───────────

Jordan would normally relish the thought of a Saturday at home. No getting up for school and so far, Wheeler hadn't phoned him with any of his usual demands. Things almost appeared relatively peaceful. That was until Claire had returned from her shift early and spotted the bruising on his neck. He had managed to hide it from her the last few days either because her shifts meant he was in bed when she returned home or by covering it with his hoodie. He had tried to deflect the agony he was feeling from his injuries and claimed he had just been play-fighting after school earlier that week.

'Doesn't look like you've been playing, Jord. It looks really sore,' Craig had offered unhelpfully.

'And you stink,' Claire said, suddenly suspicious as she had grabbed his jacket from the back of the kitchen chair and buried her nose in it. 'Have you been smoking cannabis? Your coat reeks of it.'

'No, not me. One of the lads was.'

'Which lads? Who have you been hanging about with?'

'Just lads from school. No one you know.'

'Well, that's convenient. Has this got anything to do with Lewis? I've warned you about drugs and gangs and stuff.'

'God, Mum, as if. It's nothing to do with that. Just get off my case. Just because a few of my friends smoke weed, doesn't mean I'm going to. I know better than that, I'm not an idiot.'

'I know you're not but look at it from my point of view. You're coming and going at all hours; you've been missing school and you're jumpy and snappy all the time.'

'Because you're always on my back. You don't give me a chance to breathe. I'm a teenager; we're all moody. Just because I'm not a cute little ten-year-old anymore. You hate that, don't you? You wish I was little again so you'd be the centre of my world and you can control me all the time. God, I bet it wouldn't be like this if I lived with Dad.'

The moment the words were out of his mouth, he regretted them. He didn't think he could have hurt her more if he'd put a knife through her heart. Even Craig looked disgusted.

'That's not a nice thing to say to Mum,' Craig said sadly with a shake of his head.

Jordan opened his mouth to apologise, but Claire silenced him with a look.

'If, *Jordan*, you think you'd be happier with your dad then feel free to track him down and see if he's willing to take you in. Go with my blessing. And while you're there,' she hissed, 'perhaps you could ask him where he's been the last ten fucking years of your life.'

With that, she left the room in a silence which lingered like a bad smell.

'You made Mum swear again, Jord. Mum never swears,' said Craig unhappily. 'I don't like you right now.'

The pain in his neck and lungs was nothing compared to the hurt he felt at that moment. His agony was exasperated when his phone burst into life and Wheeler's name flashed up on the caller ID. He ran up to his room quickly so he could take the call away from Craig, knowing that if he ignored it, it would only anger Wheeler more.

'Have you kissed and made up with shite-mouth yet? The one you stabbed?'

'Lewis. No. He still won't talk to me. Why?'

'The drugs supply I've got is bigger than I expected. We're going to need an extra pair of hands to shift it. Think he might fancy a bit of work?'

'I don't think it's the sort of thing he'd get involved with. After the stabbing, his mum–'

'Let me rephrase that, little-man. I need you to get him on board. We need an extra pair of hands. It's either that, or someone else you can trust. What about your kid?'

'Craig? No!' Jordan was up to his neck in it, there was no way he was getting Craig involved in Wheeler's world too. 'Leave it with me. I'll smooth things over with Lewis.'

'You're also going to be spending a bit more time with Taz. I don't trust him with the coke or ketamine, but he can shift some of the weed. Keep your phone on.'

With that, Wheeler hung up, leaving Jordan with a roiling stomach at the mention of Taz's name. The man was a baseball-bat-wielding lunatic. There's no way he was going back there to have his face licked again.

Jordan flopped onto his bed and howled into his pillow. He wanted to cry. Not only was he in physical pain after the beating from Wheeler, but he had run his mouth off and upset his mum and Craig. Now he had to try and recruit Lewis to help sell drugs, something which put the fear of God into him. Add Taz into the mix and the fact he could have killed an unborn baby and it was all too much. He had to find a way to make it stop.

He had to end it.

Claire lay under her bedcovers fully clothed, wishing more than anything she didn't have to go back on shift. A cup of tea was cooling on the bedside table. Craig had brought it up to her to cheer her up after Jordan's outburst, but it would take more than a mug of chamomile to take the sour taste from her mouth. The words had left her feeling raw. She didn't recognise her boy anymore. The deception and lying was one thing, but that? He had thrown the only thing in her face that he knew would really hurt her. And where the hell had he got those bruises because she didn't believe they were through playing.

She didn't even have the energy to cry. Nor did she even feel the justifiable anger she was due. She just felt raw and empty; thoroughly wrung-out. She had worked hard to provide a good home for her boys. A nice home, warm, clean, and full of food. A sanctuary that they would feel proud to bring friends back to. She had strived, alone – despite their dad not being around – to be a good person and bring her boys up to be the same, and this is how life repaid her.

'All will be well,' she said to herself as she sat up and tossed the covers away. She downed two paracetamols with a mouthful of the lukewarm tea and slipped her aching feet into her shoes. A quick spritz of perfume, a tidy of her chignon and she was ready to go again. Wallowing, like other things in her life, was a luxury she couldn't afford.

'I'm going,' she called down the landing. Craig responded but Jordan's room remained silent, the door firmly shut. Fine, if that's how he was going to be; he'd need her before she needed him. As she headed out the back door, she noticed his bike propped against the bins as always and a thought occurred to her. She placed her handbag on the floor and fished around in the small shed for the toolbox.

So, he was going to his dad's, was he? Fine, the useless waste of space could come and pick him up. He had always known where his boys lived but had chosen to ignore them; too busy chasing a lifestyle of his own that didn't have room for the inconvenience of family. She began to build up a sweat as she dismantled the bike's wheels. Stolen mobile phones, drugs, gangs, whatever Jordan was up to, good luck doing it with no bike to ride around on.

She smiled as she pocketed the bolts and, clutching her car keys, left for work.

37

———

Lewis was bored senseless. It was the weekend, and he was stuck at home with nothing to do, nowhere to go, and typically, no money to do anything with. His mum, as usual, was watching shit on TV whilst getting pissed on cheap cans of cider. His leg still hurt occasionally, but it was much better, and he would certainly have no problem having a kick about on it. The only problem was, Jordan had been his only real friend, so now he had no one to hang with.

Also, if he was honest, he was wary of knocking about with any of the other lads he knew because the stabbing had knocked his confidence. It had been a terrible experience, to be left in excruciating pain like that, consumed with shock and fear. At one point he honestly thought he was going to bleed to death there and then. And if he was *really* honest, he also knew that if he had been quick enough and managed to get the knife off Jordan, he would have had no hesitation about leaving his best friend lying bleeding on the ground. His dad had always told him it was a dog-eat-dog world.

Speak of the devil (another of his dad's sayings) Jordan's

number was flashing up on his caller ID. He had tried to ring him and speak to him several times at school, but Lewis had cut him dead. Today, however, a mixture of boredom and curiosity piqued his interest and caused him to answer.

'Ait?'

'Bro, can you speak?'

'Yeah, what d'ya want?'

'Look, I'm not gonna keep apologising because you know I'm sorry. I've got a proposition for you though. A chance to make some money. A way of making up.'

Lewis hesitated. Who didn't want to make money, but this was Jordan, and as his dad would say, he couldn't trust him as far as he could throw him. 'Make money how?'

'I'd rather not talk about it on the phone. Can you meet me?'

'Where?'

'The fields at Glendale?'

Lewis knew it like the back of his hand. It was a place they always played when they were younger. Close to home and just off the woodland trail, it could have been in the middle of nowhere because it was beautifully secluded, a solitary tree-lined sanctuary for playing hide-and-seek or football, away from nagging mothers and the threat of older kids.

'Yeah, okay. When?'

'Tomorrow morning. About ten?'

Lewis hesitated again as he rubbed his leg. He could hear Jordan breathing down the phone. What was the worst that could happen?

'Okay. In a bit,' he said as he disconnected the call.

Lewis dropped to the floor and peered under his bed, thick with dust and used cutlery. He reached under the bed where he had secreted a knife. He was curious to meet Jordan and hear about the money-making opportunity, but after last time, there was no way he was going unarmed.

If there was a risk of someone getting stabbed again, this time it certainly wasn't going to be him.

38

Jordan was feeling the pressure. He had already missed three of Wheeler's calls and been left a threatening voicemail. Wheeler had sounded completely unhinged screaming down the phone that Jordan needed to ring him back straight away or be at the flat by twelve or he would kill him. He was desperately hoping Lewis would agree to start working for Wheeler, so Craig wouldn't be dragged into the whole nightmarish business.

Jordan reached for his bag which had the drugs in and the cash that Ivo had given him. His hand hovered on the knife that Wheeler had given him. Should he keep it just in case he needed to protect himself? He thought back to how easily Lewis would have turned the knife on him if he had managed to get hold of it and he shuddered. He also thought of the talk in school assembly by the police who had warned them about how carrying a knife increased their chances of being stabbed.

He didn't even hear Craig open his bedroom door and jumped when he realised he was hovering behind him. He dropped the bag to the floor, hoping Craig hadn't seen the contents.

'What do you want?'

'Just to see if you want anything to eat?'

'No thanks, I'm going out.'

'Where?'

'Just out. I won't be long.'

'Mum's downstairs. You should say sorry after yesterday.'

Jordan nodded and his heart sank at the memory of Claire's face when he had carelessly mentioned their dad. 'I will do. I didn't mean it, you know. Things have been a bit hard lately, that's all, but I'm going to sort it. Promise.'

Craig mumbled something incoherent before heading back to his own room. Jordan guessed he'd not spotted what was in his bag or surely, he would have said something. He grabbed his bag and darted downstairs. Claire was sat in the lounge watching television and nursing a cup of her speciality coffee. She didn't even raise her head when he walked in.

'Mum?'

'What?' Her eyes remained fixed on the television.

'I'm sorry about what I said yesterday.'

'You must have meant it to have said it in the first place.' She still didn't look at him.

'I didn't. Honest. I was just in a foul mood. I shouldn't have taken it out on you.'

She turned to look at him. 'No, Jordan, you shouldn't have. I'm not the enemy.'

He opened his mouth to speak again, but the stony expression on her face suggested that whatever he said would be futile, so what was the point? He pulled his bag on his shoulders and glanced at his watch; he would be early to meet Lewis, but it was better than staying here. He opened the back door and stopped dead in his tracks when he saw his bike. The frame was propped against the bins, the wheels had been thrown against the shed.

'What the hell?'

He barged back into the house. Craig was hovering in the kitchen.

'What's up, Jord?'

'Someone's taken the wheels off my bike.'

'They could have fallen off.' Craig shrugged simply.

'Don't be so stupid, are you thick or what?'

Claire appeared stony-faced at the door. 'Don't you *dare* speak to your brother like that,' she said with a snarl. 'And for your information, I took your wheels off the bike.'

'Why?'

'Because nothing I say or do gets through to you, Jordan. If you're so keen to go and live with your dad, he can come and pick you up and perhaps he'd like to make a financial contribution towards his son's upkeep before he ships you off to the great blue yonder.'

Jordan wiped his hands across his face. 'God, there was no *need*,' he said as he slammed his way out of the house. He searched around frantically for signs of the bolts, even checking the bins, but there was no trace. This was the last thing he needed, how was he supposed to courier for Wheeler if he had no bike? How was he supposed to even *get* to the flat? If he was late, Wheeler would kill him. He glanced at his watch again and realised he'd have to be quick to meet Lewis on time.

'I *hate* you!' he screamed at the house as he barged his way out of the gate and set off for the fields.

He was too angry to realise he was being followed.

If the fields at Glendale could talk, they would boast of the halcyon days Jordan and Lewis had spent there over the years, bathed under the rays of a buttery sun. Had he been around, Lewis's dad would have described them as thick as thieves. The boys had whiled away the hours as cops and robbers, football stars, world-famous wrestlers and superheroes.

They would slope home coated in mud and grass stains, their faces tanned, sweat slicking the hair to their heads as the sun descended as softly as the duvets that settled on their sleeping forms. Most days, one of them, usually Lewis, would leave a coat or jumper behind. Half a makeshift goalpost left lying forlornly on the grass.

If the fields at Glendale could talk, they would say that they didn't recognise Jordan and Lewis as the same two boys. Yes, they were older, cracked voices had deepened and their gangly limbs were growing muscular, but it wasn't the physical difference that was alien, it was the distance between the two. The air had been charged with a frostiness that had nothing to do with the weather. Their body language spoke of aggression and mistrust. And they argued. The swear words they had coyly tested on each other aged ten, slipped from their lips with practised ease.

But it was what they weren't saying that bolstered their confidence as they stood toe-to-toe. One was unaware of the knife in the other's possession. The knife he had decided to carry 'just in case'. Just like thousands of other kids across the country and beyond.

If the fields at Glendale could talk, they would say that two boys arrived there that murky autumnal morning. They would say that there was nothing soft about the sun. She shivered and waned in the face of the mud-black clouds. The fields of Glendale would say that the sun scarpered the moment the knife was drawn. She reflected briefly against the flash of the blade. Then, the sun cloaked herself in the clouds, loath to be involved, leaving the fields of Glendale to witness the murder, powerless as they screamed in silent terror.

The fields of Glendale silently confirmed that two boys arrived that day. Only one of them would return home alive. The other was left on the grass like half a makeshift goalpost after sustaining a single, fatal stab wound.

39

Once the decision to house swap had been made, Maya, Spence and Chris decided there was no point in delaying. They all had a long weekend off work, so it was decided they would move there and then. Dominique was a willing volunteer and an extra pair of hands with a car, which was much more suitable than Maya's beloved, but for this purpose, unpractical Bonneville.

Spence's family also helped, and after a busy weekend of fetching and carrying they all concluded with a carvery and many drinks at Chris's local pub. That Sunday night, Maya slept better than she had in months. She was happy and contented, having enjoyed some much-needed family time and going to bed in a house that felt warm and welcoming and not tainted with fear.

The following morning however, the familiar feeling of trepidation enveloped her as she arrived for her counselling session with Jayne. Once ensconced in the lavender-scented room, Maya told her about the house move.

'That sounds like such a positive change for you,' Jayne said.

'And it's clearly helping already, you look so much lighter and less angst-ridden than you have previously.'

'That's because I've finally been able to sleep,' said Maya. 'Plus, I survived my first EMDR session, so I'm confident we're heading in the right direction.'

'So am I,' said Jayne. 'Shall we get to it?' She began the usual preparation work making Maya feel safe and grounded before recapping.

'Okay, so last session we left your younger self in the hallway, and you'd just pushed the living-room door open. When you think of that moment, can you rate your anxiety between one and ten please, remembering that ten is the most intense.'

Maya took a deep breath and closed her eyes as she visualised the scene. 'Eight. I saw the bloodstains, and someone was lying on the floor, but I could only see a hand. I think it's Mama.'

'Okay, let's go with that.' Jayne began to move her fingers and Maya allowed herself to be back in the hallway. She shivered involuntarily as she pictured it and allowed herself to move towards the lounge. She pictured opening the lounge door and seeing the bloodstains all over the carpet.

After a while, Jayne stopped. 'What are you feeling?'

'That I should go in the lounge. Mama's lying on the floor, which means she must be hurt. I want to go to her, but something's stopping me.'

'Stay with it.' Then hand movement continued.

Maya swallowed deeply as her eyes followed Jayne's fingers. There was so much blood on the carpet and a metal tang permeated the air. She couldn't bring herself to look at the hand properly, it was just a thing in the room that she was aware of being there. But there was also a threat in that room, something that terrified her.

'What are you getting?'

'There's someone in the room.'

'Okay, focus on your breathing for a moment and remember your safe space.'

Maya took a moment to take some calming breaths. 'I can do this. Let's carry on.'

The process continued as Jayne moved her fingers in the air more insistently. Maya imagined herself entering the room. A patch of blood on the floor was thick and gelatinous. Maya gasped.

'What are you feeling?'

'It's not Mama on the floor. I can see my grandad, and he's been badly beaten.'

The EMDR session had drained Maya more than the previous week. Picturing her late grandad lying injured on the floor had been a terrible shock. Jayne had stopped the session at that point and used the remaining time to help Maya work on her relaxation and manage her anxiety. Despite the stress of the session, Maya had managed another good night's sleep and she put it down to the sanctuary of being at Chris's.

'Honestly, if I carry on sleeping so well, you're never getting your house back,' she told him as they walked into Beech Field together for the start of their shift along with Elaine who had arrived at the same time.

'Hey, I'm in no rush. The takeaways near your place are amazing, I had *the* best kebab last night.'

Maya laughed. 'You do realise my kitchen is fully functioning, don't you? The cooker isn't just for show, it really works.'

'Yeah, but life's too short, I could be dead tomorrow. Plus, I like to think I'm doing my bit by supporting local businesses.'

'Not all heroes wear capes,' quipped Elaine.

'And it's not just the takeaways, I've never noticed how often the ice-cream van does the rounds near you, even at this time of year. It's bloody annoying though, every time I hear it chiming I react like Pavlov's dogs and suddenly crave a 99, but by the time I've got down in the lift it's gone. I'll catch it one of these days, you mark my words.'

They were laughing as they walked in the office and were met by a scowling Tara.

'Why do you look like you've been licking piss off a thistle?' Chris asked as he threw his coat over the back of the chair.

'Kym's in one of her moods and wanting everything done yesterday,' Tara said, sounding like a petulant child.

'In fairness,' Amanda offered diplomatically, 'she was only asking you to do your job.' Tara, who was notoriously workshy, didn't comment, choosing instead to bury her face in her computer and ignore everyone else.

'Much happening?' Maya asked.

Amanda shook her head. 'Surprisingly peaceful for now, but it's still early. Kym has asked if you can all get on top with van and equipment checks. Connor was called out to an assault last night and CID have got the victim's clothes from the hospital. They're soaked in blood so need to go in the drying cabinet.'

'Fair enough,' Maya said. 'Quick brew first while I check my emails and I'll get on with it.' She fired the computer up while the kettle was boiling and was pleased to see Sean had forwarded her an email from the forensic service provider who'd been asked to analyse the glove from the street robbery.

'Bugger,' she muttered as she reread the email a second time.

'What's up?' asked Chris.

'They've managed to get a full male DNA profile from the glove, but he's no match on the database.'

Chris shrugged. 'Shame, but not too surprising. Our witnesses said they thought he was a kid, so he's just not on there yet.'

'I'm just going to go and speak to Sean and see if they've had any success from their other enquiries.'

Maya managed to track Sean down, but was disappointed to hear there were no new leads on the case. She was heading back to her own office when she nearly collided with Jack.

'So sorry, all my fault. I was miles away.'

'No harm done. Did you hear that we've got a full male profile from the glove used in the baby Eden robbery, but no hit on the database.'

'Right, yeah, good,' said Jack, disinterested.

Maya frowned. 'Hey, are you okay?'

He shook his head. 'Have you read the night log?'

'Not yet, what's happened?'

'Lewis has been reported missing from home.'

'Lewis? Remind me...'

'Lewis Mellor, the kid who was stabbed.'

'Oh God, yes. How long has he been missing?'

'His mum rang us last night. He's not answering his phone and she reported him when he wasn't home by ten. Obviously not too late by most teenagers' standards, but on a Sunday night – a school night – and after the stabbing, she's understandably concerned.'

'And so are you.'

Jack shrugged. 'Do you think I'm being daft?'

'Not at all, I think you're being human. In this job we all come across cases, people, who get to us more than others. He's a teenager, he's probably just gone off with friends, lost track of time and fell asleep. He'll be home when he's hungry.'

'I hope so, I really do. I've asked Sean and Malone to go and speak to Lewis's mum and take it from there. Uniform took the initial missing-from-home report last night, but if he still doesn't turn up or arrive at school today, I want to leave no stone unturned.'

Maya squeezed his arm. 'He'll turn up. You know as well as I do that we get these cases all the time and they all come to nothing. Not every job becomes a murder enquiry. You know where I am if you need to chat.'

Jack nodded and she watched him go. Despite her well-meaning words of reassurance to Jack, she did not manage to convince herself. She was also genuinely worried and had a bad feeling that something serious had happened to the missing boy.

Sarah Mellor was already glued to the front window when Sean and Malone pulled up. Even though she had been expecting them, she was still dressed in her pyjamas with tea stains marring the top. Sean gave her a wave of acknowledgement as he parked the car.

'Jesus, this is going to be excruciating. She's going to start crying. I hate it when people cry. Jack should have paired you with Adila, not me. She's good with all that hand-patting bollocks,' said Malone.

'Trust me, mate, I'd rather be with Adila than you. And it's called empathy. As a parent yourself, you could try having some.'

Chastened, Malone followed Sean up the path where Sarah was now clinging to the front door as if it was the only thing from stopping her crumpling to the floor.

'He's still not back and he's not arrived at school,' she said with a sob. 'I've been ringing round everywhere I can fink of, but nobody has seen him.'

'Okay, Sarah, let's go inside. I want you to go through everything again from the last time you saw him. I know you've been through this with the officers who called last night, but it might help you remember a detail you could have overlooked. The more information we have, the better the chances of us tracking him down.'

Sarah nodded and led them through to the kitchen. An overflowing ashtray and stack of empty cider cans littered a grubby-looking draining board causing Malone and Sean to exchange a look.

'Take the weight off, love, and I'll make us all a brew if that's okay?' Malone said as he began to fill the kettle and move things around the dirty worktop.

Sarah reached for a cigarette before explaining how he'd gone out Sunday morning for the first time since the stabbing.

'Did he say where he was going?'

'Just said he was going out for a bit. I'd normally ask, but I was more surprised and relieved to be honest that he was going out at all. The stabbing has knocked his confidence and despite the bravado he likes to show, I know it's really scared him. I'm not working at the minute, what with me back and that, so I know he's been leaving first thing for school and coming straight back. Before the stabbing, I was having to ring him to get him back home as it was getting late.'

'Other than the stabbing, can you think of anything else that might have upset or worried him?'

'No.'

'Any reason you can think that he might want to avoid being at home? Have the two of you argued?'

'No, things been normal. I mean, he's a teenager so he has his moody moments, but we've not had a row or owt. I've always let him have his freedom and he knows he can tell me anyfink. It's the fact that he's not answering his phone. The bloody thing is never out of his hand.'

'Okay, tell me about Lewis's friends.'

'He has a few but Jordan Gaffney is his best friend and has

been since primary school. He's not seen him since the stabbing, but like I said he's been too scared to go out. I assume it was Jordan he was meeting, but I've rang Claire, she's Jordan's mum like, and she said he hasn't seen him.'

'Is Lewis's dad on the scene?'

'Nah, he left years ago and has been pretty shit about keeping in touch.'

'But does Lewis know where he lives, could he have gone there?'

'He has his number but not his address, he moved out of the area to Merseyside. My ex is a wrong'un, knocked me about a bit and that, so it was a relief when he left and wasn't too bothered about access. It made things easier for me. I know that sounds bad on Lewis, but I've always thought not having his dad in his life would be better for him long term. I'd be surprised if he has contacted him.'

'If you could provide his contact details and Jordan's too, it would be helpful.'

'Has Lewis got a girlfriend as far as you know?' Malone asked as he placed a pot of tea on the table.

'He's not mentioned anyone.'

'Would he?'

Sarah pursed her lips in concentration. 'Yeah, like I said, I've always let him have his freedom and that. I'd actually be chuffed if he brought a girl home.'

'Have you any reason to think he may be involved in drugs or anything like that?'

'He likes the odd cig and has a vape for school, which he's been caught with a couple of times, but show me a kid who hasn't. As for drugs, no. Definitely not, he's not the type. I don't mind him smoking but he knows not to do drugs, I'm a good mum.'

Malone nodded. 'Would it be okay if we looked in Lewis's room?'

'You're gonna search it?'

'No, just have a look around and get a feel for the lad and maybe see if anything stands out.'

'I've already been through his things to see if there's any sign of where he might be, but there's nowt. I don't fink any clothes have gone missing. His bag isn't there, but he takes that with him most places. You can have a look, but don't move anything. I want it kept as he left it, for when he comes home.' Sarah let out another sob as tears began to stream down her face.

'Top of the stairs, straight ahead,' she said in a strangled voice as the two detectives excused themselves from the kitchen table. Sean followed Malone up the uncarpeted stairs, with dust bunnies clinging to the skirting board. They located Lewis's room and the two of them took a moment to survey it from the doorway.

'Blimey, what a tip,' said Sean. 'And it stinks like a dog-shit bin.' The wardrobe doors and cupboard were jutting open with clothes spilling out of them. There were used cups, plates and takeaway containers still bearing food dotted on every surface as well as an overflowing wastepaper basket. The curtains were hanging from the rail, where at some point they had clearly been opened with too much force. The air was permeated with the stench of sweaty teenager, masturbation and unwashed feet.

Malone laughed as he clapped Sean on the back. 'Can tell you don't have kids, matey. This is all perfectly normal.'

'We can definitely rule out a girlfriend, no self-respecting female would ever come back to a room like this.'

'Your joking, aren't you,' said Malone as he began a cursory look in the bedside cabinet. 'Our Marcie's room used to be ten times worse than this. Bloody make-up and fake tan all over the place. She had twice as many clothes as this, plus jewellery and shoes. Not to mention all the perfume and hair products. Stood on her hair straighteners once and nearly burnt me foot off, she'd gone to school and left the sodding things turned on. Let me tell you, son, teenage girls might look well turned out but they're just as grotty and grubby as their male counterparts.'

'Think you've just talked me out of parenthood.'

'I wouldn't worry, you'd have to find a woman first, and there's slim chance of that.' Malone cackled as he straightened up. 'Look at this.'

He'd lifted a pillow off the bed to reveal a small metal pole lying on the mattress.

'S'pose it's a natural reaction after being stabbed,' said Sean. 'And at least if it's in here he's not carrying it. And it's not a knife.'

'Sure about that?' Malone shone the torch from his phone under the bed, which was thick with dust and more dirty crockery. There was a clean space on the dirty floor which matched the shape of a large kitchen knife.

'Looks like he's taken it with him which is unsurprising. Kids today, leave the house and pick them up as automatically as they reach for their phones. Silly little sod.'

'Shit.' Sean tutted. 'Right, let's go and have another chat with his mum and then I reckon we pay a visit to the best friend and try and get in touch with the dad.'

They paused at the top of the stairs as they heard crying coming from the kitchen. 'Good call,' said Malone. 'I made the tea; you can provide the sympathy.'

'Fuck's sake,' Wheeler mumbled as he opened his eyes. His head throbbed, his stomach swelled with nausea and his nose was raw and crusted. He heard Susie snoring softly at his side as he made his way to the bathroom.

He glanced at his watch and saw it was 2am. 'What the...?' He looked at his hands and shuddered at the sight of blood. It was streaked up to his wrists, embedded into the fingers and gnawed nails of his left hand. He balled his fists and punched his forehead several times.

He'd had the drugs in his possession for a few days and Wheeler had already succumbed to the trap most drug dealers fall into. He'd taken too much of his own gear. The coke mixed with the alcohol he loathed – but simultaneously sought comfort from, just like his mother – had not brought the relaxation and solace he had needed. If anything, it had made him even more aggressive and unpredictable.

He squeezed his eyes shut as he tried to remember the previous day. Little-man had eventually phoned him back and after that everything was hazy. He remembered leaving the flat to go and meet the kid and nearly getting jumped by a skank he knew worked for Ivo Zlatan.

After that, everything was hazy. He'd become heavy-limbed and sluggish through intoxication after exuding every bit of his energy on an act of bloodshed that left him spent. An act of violence he couldn't remember but that had clearly left him with plenty of blood on his hands, which he was now scrubbing at with Albert's worn old nailbrush. Then, careful not to wake Albert or Susie, he pulled on a pair of jeans, snuck into the kitchen to collect some things from the cleaning cupboard and left the flat.

Wheeler wasn't the only drug dealer feeling out of sorts. Ivo Zlatan also had a guilty conscience and blood on his hands. Things had got out of hand. It happened sometimes. It was par for the course in his line of work. But he still felt bad about it. The buck stopped with him. The stabbing should never have happened.

42

———

Bellies swilling with copious amounts of tea, Sean and Malone had eventually left Sarah Mellor, reassuring her that they would be in touch as soon as they had any news on Lewis's whereabouts. On the drive to Claire Gaffney's, both detectives remained quiet, lost in thought. Although a teenager missing from home was not uncommon, Lewis's recent stabbing was cause for concern and they both had an uneasy feeling.

'I'm guessing the lad is going to be in school, but his mum might be able to help,' Sean mused aloud as he stopped the car.

Claire had opened the door before they even had a chance to knock. She was wearing her carer's uniform but looked uncharacteristically dishevelled.

'Claire? Detectives Stevenson and Malone from Beech Field CID,' Sean announced as they both presented their ID badges.

'Thanks for coming so quickly, I only phoned in an hour ago.' Claire waved them in through the front door and led them to the lounge.

'Sorry, Claire, you've rang us?' Sean asked, confused. 'With news about Lewis?'

'Not Lewis, my son is Jordan. Jordan Gaffney.'

'I think we're speaking at cross purposes,' said Sean. 'We're here about Lewis Mellor. He's been reported missing by his mum. I believe she rang you last night to ask if Jordan had seen him and you said he hadn't. We've just got a few questions.'

'And I phoned you this morning to let you know Jordan is missing. I went to wake him for school before I left for work and he wasn't in his room. His mobile phone and bag are gone. He's never up before me, I usually have to shoe-horn him out of bed.'

'Okay,' Sean said as he opened his daybook. 'Let's take some details.'

'Have you checked with school and his friends?' said Malone.

'Obviously,' Claire said caustically. 'Sorry, I didn't mean to snap, I'm just worried sick.'

'Understandable.' Sean smiled sympathetically. 'As Jordan and Lewis are best friends, is it possible they could have gone missing together?'

Claire shrugged. 'I don't know, maybe.'

'Jordan and Lewis had fallen out,' said Craig. He had appeared silently in the doorway, his face as pale and drawn as his mother's.

'Craig, love, not now. Go on up to your room, please. I'll bring you a brew in a bit.'

'But the police might want to ask me something,' he said.

'They won't, love. Just leave it to me, okay?'

Craig hovered reluctantly at the door before eventually sloping off. Claire listened to his footsteps ascending the stairs and rose to shut the lounge door. 'He's very close to his brother and worried sick. I don't want him any more upset than he already is,' she explained.

'Had they fallen out?' Malone asked.

'Oh, don't pay any attention to Craig, he lives in his own

world a bit. The boys had a bit of a spat over something and nothing a few days ago, but it had all blown over.'

'Was it to do with Lewis being stabbed?'

Claire paled. 'Yes and no. Lewis has been dabbling in drugs, just weed I think and that's not Jordan's thing so they argued about it. I don't mean to be disrespectful towards Sarah or Lewis, we're both single mums and don't get me wrong, it can be bloody hard, but she's always given Lewis free rein. I've never been like that with my boys; they need boundaries and discipline.'

Sean and Malone exchanged a look. 'It was something we asked Sarah about, but she was quite adamant that Lewis wasn't into anything like that.'

Claire shrugged. 'She's his mum, we're always the last to know what our kids are into. Like I said, Sarah gives that boy too much freedom. She lets him do what he wants because it makes life easier for her.'

'And what's Jordan into?' Malone asked quickly.

'Sports, especially football. Ask his PE teacher. Ask any of his teachers. Jordan is a good kid,' she said adamantly, her eyes lit up with a flash of ire.

'Nobody is saying he's not,' Sean said diplomatically. 'We're here to help, Claire. We want the boys home safe and sound as much as anyone, but in order for that to happen, it would help us to know as much about them as possible. Warts and all. We're not judging you or your son.'

Claire's shoulders drooped as she sank despondently into the chair. 'Lewis was involved in something. I'm not sure what, but I caught Jordan with a load of mobile phones in his bag, there were eleven of them altogether. I asked him about it, tore a strip off him actually, but he told me he was minding them for Lewis. That he'd got involved with something or someone, and I shouldn't get involved as it could make things worse for

Lewis. I believed him. Lewis was that type of boy, but not my son.'

'When did you last see Jordan?'

'Yesterday morning before he went out. We've been short-staffed lately, so I didn't get home until one this morning. I always look in on the boys when I get home and he was in bed. They both were.'

'You're sure?' Malone asked.

'Yes.'

'You could see him in the dark?'

'The landing light was on and yes, I could see the shape of my boys asleep in bed. For God's sake, they're not toddlers, they both tower over me. Jordan is almost as tall as Craig.'

'Had you argued with Jordan? Has anything happened that might explain why he would want to leave home? Was he worried about anything? Like I said before, Claire, nobody is judging either of you, we just need to know,' Sean asked softly. Malone and Sean always worked well together in these circumstances. Malone's gruff cynicism was offset by Sean's gentler demeanour and surprisingly young looks.

Claire smiled at him, her eyes brimming with tears. 'I can't think of any reason. He was happy. He's a good boy.'

'I'm sure he is.'

A furrow plucked her brow. 'There is one thing. I noticed yesterday he had bruises on his neck. I asked him about it and he claimed he'd been playfighting, but I don't know, it looked really sore.'

'Playfighting with who, Lewis?'

'Possibly, he didn't say.'

'Would you mind if we just took a peep in his room? It's just procedure in cases like this.'

'Absolutely. Follow me and I'll take you up there.'

They followed her back down the tidy hallway and up the

pristine stairs and she hovered as they entered their second teenage boy's bedroom of the day. It was in complete contrast to Lewis's. It was tidy and surprisingly sweet smelling. They took a cursory look before heading back downstairs where they stayed for a further hour asking more questions and if they could take Jordan's phone with them so the digital investigators could examine it and see if it provided any clues to his whereabouts.

Claire looked thoroughly exhausted by the time she showed them out, clicking the front door shut by the time they had got to the gate.

'What are you thinking?' Malone asked once they were ensconced in the privacy of the car.

Sean sniffed as he nestled back in the seat and weighed up the exterior of the house. 'That bed hasn't been slept in. I suspect Jordan has been missing for longer than 1am, when she said she saw him in bed. Also, she said she'd rang his friend's, but knowing Lewis was missing, she hadn't rung Sarah, or surely she would have mentioned it to us earlier.'

'Agreed. Don't know where these kids are, but my money is on the fact that they're together and one of the mums is lying for whatever reason.'

'Which one?'

Malone snorted. 'Not judging but look at the difference between the two bedrooms and general state of the houses. One mum works, the other clearly doesn't. One mum "gives her kid freedom" the other has him on a short leash. You can quote all that cognitive bias bollocks at me if you want, but I know which one my money is on.'

Sean being Sean, diplomatically held his counsel.

43

Chris frowned at the computer. 'We might have a job.'

'I've got loads of statements to write,' Tara announced quickly, her usual excuse for shying away from anything that might take her longer than an hour. Maya and Elaine exchanged a smirk.

'What is it?'

'Male has been admitted to hospital with stab wounds. He's been dropped off by a mate at A&E and left. No ID on him, not currently conscious.'

'How old?'

'Teenager, dark hair, usual clothing. Nothing more than that.'

'I'll stick my head into CID and let them know.' Maya made a beeline for Jack, knowing they'd be on the same wavelength.

'You think it could be Lewis?' Jack said when she told him.

'Fifty-fifty chance.' Maya shrugged.

He grabbed his jacket off the back of his chair. 'Thanks for the heads-up. The others are all tied up on enquiries so I'll drive over there myself. It makes sense as I've met the lad and I'll know if it's him. If it is, we can get his mum there straight away.'

'We'll keep monitoring the log for updates on his condition and obviously if he comes round and can identify a scene, all the better.'

Jack nodded. 'I'll ring you as soon as I know.'

Maya returned to the office where Elaine and Chris were deep in conversation.

'Bloody stabbings every day,' grumbled Chris. 'Remember, Elaine, how Saturday or Sunday mornings used to be spent recovering ears?'

'Ears?' Tara poked her head above her computer monitor, her interest piqued. Maya had heard this before.

'Yeah, like I said, we rarely had stabbings back in the day, but people were obviously still getting tanked up and scrapping. We'd get reports of assaults where victims had their ears bitten off during a fight.'

'That's disgusting,' Tara said as she wrinkled her nose and returned to her keyboard.

'Noses too,' said Elaine. 'Bloody horrible thing to do; animal behaviour.'

'Aye,' agreed Chris, 'but nobody ever died by having the end of their ear or nose bitten off. Not like today with all these stabbings. All you need is to be in the wrong place at the wrong time and it's goodnight Vienna.

'And it's not just people involved in gang activity who are becoming victims. It could be me or you. We could be putting the bloody bins out and some idiot thinks you've looked at him the wrong way and you've had it. How is that right in a modern society? To me it's simple, don't carry one and you won't get hurt. All this bollocks about people carrying one for protection and they usually end up getting stabbed with their own blades. It's become a status symbol, kids posing with them on Snap-a-gram or whatever it's called.'

'Instagram and Snapchat,' Tara said with a roll of her eyes.

'That's the other thing with kids today, bloody social media. They spend all day obsessing about how they look and how they portray themselves; since when did it become cool to be a perpetually bored and superficial individual? No wonder none of them have any self-esteem or ambition. Who the bleeding hell thinks it's a great life choice to become an influence?'

'Influenc*er*,' said Tara.

'I tell you what, *I* should be an influencer. I'd tell them what they need to do to stay on the straight and narrow and teach them a few life skills for good measure. Get them off their phones and out into the world.'

'Yeah, you could start wearing your boxers outside your clothes and become known as Kebab Man. What teenager *wouldn't* want to listen to you,' Tara said nastily, and was promptly ignored.

'I tell you why I have an issue with all this Instagram crap. It typifies people these days and not just teenagers. We've become an insta-society, we want everything now; online shopping at our fingertips, fast food that isn't just fast, some other bugger will even deliver it for you. It's making us impatient and we have no time for what's real; art, books, nature, simply enjoying a moment with friends without having to capture it with a fake filter.'

Tara rolled her eyes and went to interject, but Chris cut her off. 'Even when it comes to falling in love and finding a partner, you're a prime example, Tara. The insta-shag generation. Dating apps at your fingers that will tell you who and how close your next conquest is. Whatever happened to wooing each other, the thrill of the chase, eh? Now it's all cock pics and fish pouts. Not for me.'

'Not for you? Maybe you shouldn't be too quick to dismiss it, late-forties and single, you're not doing so great without the apps,' sneered Tara.

'Well, even at my age, I haven't ruled out finding love. I really hope I do one day. I'd love to meet someone I want to settle with, to travel with, to share my life with. My point is, you're going to be my age, my waistline and single if the only thing you're relying on to meet Mr Right is those apps. They're just a quick fix, a quick bunk-up. Spend the time to find someone you truly connect with who excites you emotionally as well as physically. Learn to wait for something that's worth waiting for. Stop being so impulsive and narcissistic.'

Tara opened her mouth to retort but Maya silenced her with a raised hand. 'Please don't start ranting at each other.'

'What's up with you?' Tara asked haughtily.

'I'm just a bit concerned about this stabbing. I'm worried it might be Lewis.'

Tara shrugged. 'If it is, he's alive and in hospital. I'm sure he'll be fine.'

'Mmm,' Maya mumbled. 'But what if he isn't?'

While the team at Beech Field were putting the world to rights on the subject of knife crime, the fugitive was turning his attention to his own malevolent-looking blade. He took solace in regularly checking how razor sharp his knife was. Not only that, he liked to remove the knuckledusters he kept in his pocket and wear them whilst shadow boxing in the reflection of the window. The taser he pocketed was another piece of precautionary kit.

The day was growing closer. He was mere days away from exacting the revenge he was so desperate for. And then he could leave this place. He would go back to where they could never find him. If all went to plan, Maya would be the only person to see him. Then he could finally end things once and for all and slip back into the shadows.

189

44

———

Jack arrived at the hospital with a feeling of dread. He was worried sick that he'd get to the ward and be too late. That Lewis had passed away before his mum got to hold him one last time. He heard the familiar voice before he even saw him.

'Just patch me up so I can go home, innit.' The voice was loud, disregarding the fact he was surrounded by sick people and stressed, overworked doctors and nurses trying their best to help, despite being at their wits' end.

Without preamble, Jack ripped the cubicle curtain back and saw someone he had met many times over his police career.

'Nah, fucking dibble? I aint talking to you, man. Do one, bro.'

'Curtis Brady. What a surprise. Who's tried to turn you into a human colander this time then?'

The sallow nineteen-year-old turned away, pouting like a petulant child. Jack knew him as a burglar with a predilection for targeting pensioners, happy in the knowledge that if they ever disturbed him in action, he could knock them to the floor without a second thought. He was a common thief, thug and bully.

'What's his prognosis?' Jack asked the nurse, ignoring Curtis.

'He was unresponsive when initially brought in, but we believe that's because he was heavily intoxicated. It looks like he'd been self-administering pain relief with the assistance of street drugs and alcohol. Never a good idea,' she said pointedly to Curtis who ignored her. 'The stab wound is deep but relatively superficial.'

'Go on then, who did it?' Jack asked.

'No comment.'

Jack let out a sigh. 'For once, Curtis, you're not under arrest so you don't need to say that. Quite frankly, over the years, I'm sick of hearing it from you. You've been a victim of what sounds like a nasty stab wound. I'm here to help you, nothing more.'

'Fuck off.'

'I assume they were the clothes you were wearing at the time of the attack. I can arrange for them to be seized as forensic evidence.'

'Fuck off.'

'Also, once the bandages are removed, I can arrange for one of our SOCOs to take injury photographs which can be later used as evidence in court. Do you agree to that?'

'Fuck off.'

'You don't seem to realise the seriousness of this. You have received a deep stab wound. This isn't a black eye or broken nose, someone intended to hurt you, to cause you real harm. Either life-changing injuries or it could have proven fatal. Don't you want justice for your injuries?' Jack looked at the two nurses in the cubicle. 'Wouldn't you if you were in his position?'

They both nodded.

'Curtis?'

'Fuck off.'

Jack let out another sigh. 'In that case, can you just sign here in my notebook that you've been offered help and you're not interested in providing information that may help identify your aggressor or in pursuing any crime against them.'

Curtis took Jack's pen from him reluctantly and scrawled an illegible signature. Jack assumed he was going to pass him his pen back, but he volleyed it towards the bag of contaminated waste that contained blood-soaked material from where he'd had his wound treated. Knowing Curtis to be a drug user, there was no way Jack was chancing delving in there to get it back.

Jack turned to the nurse who was placing a bandage round his freshly-stitched arm.

'Is he in pain?'

'He's just had twelve stitches, so I assume so.'

'Good, the NHS is strapped for cash, so make a saving and hold back on his painkillers, eh?' said Jack. 'Oh, and Curtis, one last thing before I go.'

'What?'

'Fuck off.'

Dominique sat at her kitchen table clutching a lukewarm brew and gazing out at the grey day. Rain coursed down the window and it felt like the weather was mimicking her mood. She felt sick with worry. Every noise made her flinch, as she imagined Naylor stalking her and Maya, hiding in the shadows, waiting for the ideal opportunity to strike.

She knew part of the problem was because she had far too much time on her hands. She hadn't returned to her job as a community nurse since breaking her pelvis and didn't seem to be able to muster the energy or motivation to find something else to fill her days with. She felt uncomfortable at the thought of leaving the house and didn't even feel particularly safe in it despite all the security measures, lighting and CCTV she had in place.

And then there was Maya. She was relieved that she had moved into Chris's house for a while. She thought she would be safer there until Naylor was found and locked up. That's if he ever *was* found. It was the EMDR that worried her the most. She understood Maya's need to confront her past, but honestly believed that it would do her more harm than good.

Maya had eventually confided in her that she had remembered seeing her grandad lying, bleeding on the floor in the lounge and it had brought back the memory for Dominique too. She choked back a sob at the distant recall of seeing her dad lying injured and bleeding. The memory was overwhelming. He had been such a lovely, gentle man. He didn't deserve the violence inflicted on him or all the stress and worry he had endured.

Dominique glanced out of the window at the rain and shivered. Her past had caught up with her and was now very much in the present. It was only a matter of time before Naylor made his move. Part of her wished it would happen sooner rather than later, as waiting was agony. It was time.

She was ready for him.

45

———————

Maya's alarm sounded and rather than turning it off ready to start the day she made the fatal mistake of hitting the snooze button. As she dozed, her mind drifted toward the memory of her last EMDR session when she had realised it was Grandad lying on the lounge floor. Drifting in and out of sleep, she evaded the image and pictured herself stood in the sanctity of the hallway. Rather than facing the threat from the lounge she turned her attention to the cupboard under the stairs.

Partly asleep, partly awake, she allowed her subconscious to drift. The fresh memory grew and stretched out vividly, like a snake uncoiling. She didn't need Jayne or EMDR to recall what she knew, the memory returned intensely. If she opened the door to the cupboard under the stairs, there she would find a hidden panel. If she nudged it open, she would be able to see what was inside. She started as she woke, the memory sharp. In that cupboard was where Naylor kept a stash of drugs, a firearm and ammunition.

She was beginning to remember more.

~

'You've been very quiet this morning, everything okay?' Chris asked Maya as they carried out the van checks in the yard.

Maya had been reluctant to speak about her latest memory in case it sent it scurrying back to the recesses of her mind. She would wait until her next EMDR session to discuss it with Jayne and see if she could work on bringing it out more. She was aware that she was stalling exploring the threat of the lounge any further, but this new recall was too strong to ignore and as Jayne would say during the process, she would stick with that and go with it.

Maya smiled at Chris. 'Don't look so worried, I'm fine, honestly. I'm just starting to get really concerned about the missing boys. I'd hoped we'd hear from the morning briefing that both Jordan and Lewis were home by now. Surely someone must have seen them. And the weather last night was awful.'

'Which suggests they're staying somewhere safe and warm otherwise they'd be home,' said Chris.

'I suppose so. What did you get up to last night, anything nice?'

'I had a kebab for tea and ended up eating in and chatting to Emira,' Chris said coyly.

'Who?'

'You must know Emira. She owns the kebab shop. Lovely woman, really interesting and very funny. I'd gone downstairs to chase that sodding ice-cream van again, but missed it, so ended up calling in there instead. She sells pistachio ice cream and it's bloody gorgeous.'

Maya grinned as she nudged Chris. 'And so is she by the sound of it. Have you got a crush?'

'All the years you've lived at your place and you're seriously telling me you've never spoken to her?'

'Other than to give my order and thank her, no, but I'm not a takeaway addict like you. Some of us like to cook.'

Chris beamed. 'I was telling her about my famous shepherd's pie. I had to explain to her what it was, she'd never heard of it. I said I might make it for her one night.'

'You, cooking? For a woman? And since when did you ever make a "famous shepherd's pie"? I've seen you struggle to make a Cup-a-Soup, remember.'

Chris looked indignant. 'I do cook. Sometimes. Tell you what, I'll knock a batch up and you and Spence can try some. Let me know if you think it's okay.'

'Before you make it for the lovely Emira?' Maya teased.

'No harm in making an effort is there?'

'None at all, I'm pleased for you. Although I might need to pay her a visit and make sure she's worthy of you.'

The teasing continued as they returned back to the office, both laughing at the mutual banter, which stalled in their throats as they saw Kym emerging from her office and frowning as she squinted at the screen of Amanda's computer.

'Problem?' Maya asked.

Amanda looked up. 'We've just had a log-in, a distressed dog walker has reported finding a body covered in blood. He's described it as being a teenage boy.'

'Where?'

'The fields at Glendale. Patrols are on their way.'

'Do CID know?'

'Yes,' said Jack who had suddenly appeared behind her. 'I've got Turner and Adila on the way. We'd normally wait for confirmation, but as Adila has met both boys, both of whom are missing, it makes sense.' Jack looked uncharacteristically pale, no sign of his usual arrogant overconfidence.

'That's if there is a body,' Maya said in a desperate attempt to be reassuring. 'How many times do we get false calls?

Remember, Chris, that report of a human skeletal arm we had that turned out to be a dog chew?'

Chris nodded but looked as unconvinced as Maya felt. Jack gave her a wan smile and headed back to his office as the others continued about their business whilst waiting for an update.

'Eight-six-four-three foxtrot, show me state six with ambulance,' an officer shouted up. *State six* meant he had arrived at the scene.

The team were on tenterhooks as they waited with bated breath for an update, all willing it to be "false call with good intent'. An incautious dog walker mistaking fly-tipping for human remains. Time seemed to stand still, the air in the room hung heavily and oppressive.

After an age, the airwaves lit up again. 'Eight-six-four-three foxtrot, can you show CID at scene and for the log, ambulance have confirmed male deceased at this location. A scene log has been commenced.'

'Foxtrot to eight-six-four-three received the last,' replied the comms operator, 'are you able to provide an age or description please?'

'Appears to be white male, twelve to sixteen, dark clothing. CID have asked if you can arrange for the scene tent to be delivered.'

'Will do. I'll get more patrols to you to help with scene management,' comms replied as Maya turned the radio down. Everyone remained silent, the air began to crackle with the anxiety-fuelled energy that signalled a major incident was underway.

As the SOCOs waited for more information, they prepared their kit whilst Kym began to weigh up staffing. Brews were made, food quickly eaten, and any evening plans were quickly cancelled in anticipation of the fact that nobody would be leaving work anytime soon. All of it was playing for time as they waited for Jack to return with news, which he eventually did as he framed the doorway looking pale and shaken.

'I've just spoken to Adila.'

'Is it them?' Maya asked. 'One of the boys?'

Jack nodded.

Maya winced. 'Who is it? Lewis or Jordan?'

46

———————

'Now then, a nice cup of tea can make even the worse situations feel better,' Albert said as he placed a steaming mug on the coffee table in front of Susie. He cringed as he looked at the girl and the sight of the deep purple swelling which was blooming over her right eye.

'Thank you.' Susie smiled weakly. She winced as she leant forward to reach for the tea.

'Did he hit you anywhere else?' Albert asked, concerned.

'No, just my face. He didn't mean to do it, you know. He's just been so stressed lately. It was my fault for rubbing him up the wrong way. He does so much for us, all he asked me to do was to take his clothes and bedding to the launderette because they were bloodstained. I should have just said yes rather than arguing and demanding to know where the blood had come from.'

'He should never have hit you.'

'He won't do it again. He's apologised and said he's sorry and I believe him. I know he loves me and I love him.'

'Love should never hurt and certainly not like that,' growled Albert as he gestured towards her face. 'Now he's done it once,

199

he'll do it again. He's a violent man, why else is he covered in someone else's blood. And he would have strangled poor Jordan to death if I hadn't stopped him.'

'If he didn't love me so much, he wouldn't have reacted like that,' said Susie, numbly repeating the words Wheeler had said to her.

'You should go home. Pack your stuff now, while he's not here and go back to your mum and dad.'

'No.' Susie straightened up resolutely. 'No way. This is just a blip. The last thing I want is to go back there. That's what they're waiting for. Me to turn up with my tail between my legs proving them right that he's a wrong'un and I've made a massive mistake. They'd love nothing more than to rub my nose in it.'

'They wouldn't at all. You're their daughter, they love you and want the best for you. Now I've never been a parent as you know, but my mum and dad, oh I was so lucky, they were the best.'

'Tell me about them,' said Susie as she put her mug on the table.

'My mum was called Glenda. She was so pretty and feisty. You remind me of her actually,' Albert began. He settled back against the couch and lifted his arm so Susie could nestle into him. This had become their custom when Albert was telling her one of his stories and Wheeler wasn't around. Albert placed his arm protectively around the girl and continued to tell her about his parents.

The memories were bittersweet and brought tears to his eyes, yet he talked and talked until eventually he could tell by her breathing that Susie had fallen asleep. Even then he continued to murmur his stories into her hair, pausing only once to drop a gentle kiss on the top of her head.

~

Adila and Turner parked up outside the house. Turner killed the engine and let out a sigh.

'I'll do this one,' Adila said.

'You sure?'

'Yeah, it's my turn.'

'But it's a kid. This is the worst kind. I'm a sergeant, I get paid more than you, so I should be the one to live with the memory.'

Adila gave him a heavy stare. 'I think this is one we're both going to remember, don't you? "Oh hello, madam, sorry to bother you but we just wanted to let you know that we've found your missing son, but unfortunately he won't be coming home because he's dead".'

Turner let out a dry laugh. 'Christ, well if you're going to deliver it like that, I'm going to do the death message.'

'I'm joking,' said Adila. 'Honestly, I'm okay. I've got this one. I've met them before, remember – it feels more personal. She struck me as a good mum despite everything.'

For any police officer delivering the death message, the walk up to the front door was always the longest, weighed down by heavy shoulders and a heavy heart. Turner knocked on the door, but neither of them could look up. It was as if their load was so heavy, they couldn't physically raise their heads. Which is why as the door swung open, their eyes glanced down at a pair of shabby-looking slippers stood on the grubby hallway floor.

'Hello again,' said Adila. 'Would you mind if we come in?'

Sarah sat at the kitchen table, tears coursing down her face. She had never felt so much pain or desperation in her life. The need to hold Lewis in her arms was strong, a physical craving. She looked around the kitchen, but didn't see the dirty work surfaces, the overflowing bin, the empty cans that littered the draining board. Her mind was consumed with the things that she couldn't see that *should* be there. Lewis's coat on the back of the chair, his muddy football boots on the kitchen mat, a half-eaten Pot Noodle cast aside.

She couldn't countenance never seeing those things again. Couldn't imagine this house without the smell of his deodorant, his socks and shoes scattered everywhere. The relentless throb of his music vibrating from his room no matter how many times she told him to turn it down. All the dinners that were consumed seemingly within seconds despite the fact he'd eaten his body weight in snacks moments before. 'Hollow legs', as her ex would have said.

She couldn't stand the thought that he would never surprise her again by randomly turning to her for a kiss and a hug, just when she worried that he'd grown out of that stage for good.

She longed for one of those hugs now. One of those fleeting but tender moments that he would never in a million years display outside the confines of this house.

Sarah swiped away the tears and blew her nose noisily. The weight of her despair was all-consuming, so much so that she didn't hear it straight away, the click of the door, the steps on the hallway. And then by sheer miracle he was there. She was on her feet in an instant, arms wrapped round his neck. Waves of relief and anger simultaneously battered her as she slapped him, hugged him, slapped him again.

'Where the hell have you been, Lewis? I thought you were dead.'

Claire fussed around the detectives as she ushered them into the lounge, gathering up coffee cups and plucking a blanket off the sofa.

'Look at the state of this place, what must you think of me. I've not even mopped the hall. I normally keep a tidy house but the last day or so, well...' She tailed off as she stood despondently clutching the items. 'Tea,' she said eventually with a renewed vigour. 'Make yourselves at home and I'll put the kettle on.'

'Miss Gaffney,' said Adila as she took the cups off her. 'Claire, please, sit down.'

With unexpected strength, Claire snatched the cups back. 'I will in a moment. Tea first. And biscuits. I've a tin of nice ones that the boys bought me for Mother's Day and I never got round to opening them.'

'Claire...'

'Funny isn't it how we save things for the best. I hope they've not gone out of date, that would be a waste. I'll go and check.'

'We need to talk to you...'

'Sorry, I'm being rude. I assumed you'd want tea, but perhaps you'd prefer coffee.' Ignoring Adila she looked at Turner. 'You look like a coffee drinker.'

'It really doesn't matter. Like my colleague said, we really need to talk to you.'

Claire pushed past him and made her way into the kitchen, clicking the kettle on and fussing in the cupboards for the prized biscuits. The detectives exchanged a glance and followed her, watching for a while as she wrestled the plastic seal from around the edge of the tin.

'Please, can you just sit down,' asked Adila.

Claire rounded on her, her face puce with venom. 'No. I don't want to sit down, and I don't want to fucking talk. In fact, I'd like it if you could both just leave. Now. Just go.'

'Claire–'

'I said just fucking go!' she screamed as she hurled the tin at them. 'Because I know what this is about and I don't want to hear your platitudes as you tell me my son is dead. Because he is, isn't he? You've found him and he's fucking dead, isn't he?'

Adila couldn't bring herself to say the words, instead gave an imperceptible nod of her head. Claire let out a feral scream and fell to the floor as she began to rip at her hair. Adila was at her side in an instant, cushioning her in her arms as Turner looked on helplessly.

Maya and Chris worked tirelessly in the crime-scene tent as they examined Jordan's body. It quickly became apparent he had a large stab wound to the top of his back near his neck. He also had fresh facial injuries. Kym had attended the scene with them and they had identified a patch of grass where they believed

Jordan was stabbed before being dragged into the thicker shrubbery in a veiled attempt to hide his body.

Kym had been concerned with the lividity on Jordan's skin and pathologist Dr Granger had attended and confirmed that Jordan had initially been left lying face down after being stabbed and had been moved later where he had been left on his back.

Maya had commented that the attempt to conceal the body had been quite poor and the only conclusion they could come up with was that it had possibly been because it had been moved in the dark. Even with a torch the vast area of green belt would have been intimidating and difficult to manoeuvre, particularly if the murderer had worked alone. Bodies were referred to as a dead weight for a reason.

Kym had been on hand to write a strategy and arrange a time for the post-mortem, leaving Maya and Chris to work on the body. The pair continued prepping Jordan for the mortuary in silence, each knowing what the other needed as they worked in harmony exchanging swabs and exhibits.

Maya leaned forward with her camera to take a photograph of the seal that would secure the body bag. They had just finished placing Jordan in it and Chris let out a sigh as he stood up to stretch his back.

'You okay?' Maya asked.

'Yeah, just a bloody shame, isn't it? He's no age. Over the years I've been sad about the fact I've never been a dad. I think I would have liked to be, then you get a job like this and I'm grateful that I'll never know heartache like his mum will be feeling right now.'

'I never knew you wanted to be a dad; you've never told me that before.'

'It would have been nice but I've never met the right person. To be fair, nobody would put up with a cantankerous old sod like me. And our shifts aren't conducive to family life, are they?'

'You're hardly past it, there is still a chance for you. Maybe you and the lovely Emira will go the distance.'

'Steady on, we've not even been on a proper date yet.'

Maya nodded towards the body bag. 'What more prompting do you need that life is too short and you should go for it. That's what you'd tell me.'

Chris nodded. 'Maybe I'll text her after the PM.'

'No maybe about it. And for what it's worth, if you were my dad, I'd be the proudest daughter in the world.'

Maya could tell Chris was smiling under his face mask as he gave her a gentle nudge. 'Don't get me started, I'm already feeling choked up as it is.'

He bent down to zip up the body bag, pausing to place his hand tenderly on the boy's chest. 'Come on, son. We'll get you to the mortuary so we can find out who did this to you and then we can give you back to your mum.'

48

Wheeler was feeling the pressure of having so many drugs to sell. Despite his best efforts he couldn't seem to shift them fast enough and he hated the fact he had so many in the flat because, not only did he risk getting taxed by the likes of Ivo Zlatan, he also risked getting raided by the police. He was missing not having Jordan at his beck and call.

Then there was Susie. He would be the first to admit he had let things get out of hand when he hit her, but as he had told her, he was under enough stress without her not doing what he asked. They were supposed to be a team. He was working all hours to provide for her and the old man and where was the thanks and support?

Still, a bunch of chrysanthemums from the garage on the corner and a few crocodile tears had won her round. Women were so easy to manipulate. And here she was now, snaked round him as he lay in Albert's bed smoking the first joint of the day.

'Are we okay, babe?' he asked as he dropped a kiss on her head. He felt her nod into his chest.

'Good.' He closed his eyes for a moment and allowed himself

to relax, but then several seconds later, found himself bristling with irritation as he felt her shift. He opened his eyes and saw her propped on one arm, concern pinching her face. Her fake tan was too dark and patchy, it looked abrasive in the morning light and up close, he could see the grubbiness of her eyelash glue.

'Whose blood was that on your clothes and the bedding?'

'No one's.'

'Oh, so it was Mr Invisible's blood?' she snorted as she pulled away from him and began to pull on her clothes.

'Don't test me, woman.'

'Don't speak to me like I'm worthless. I asked you a question and I deserve a truthful answer. We're supposed to be a partnership.'

Wheeler let out a sigh as he watched her dress. He could tell she was riled with him as she purposefully kept her back to him as she pulled on her bra. Normally she would give him a flash, knowing it would keep him interested for the rest of the day.

'The thing is, sometimes the less you know, the better.'

'Really? We're living in a flat which looks like it belongs to Pablo Escobar. I think it's fair to say I'm already up to my neck, so I'll ask you again, whose blood was it?'

Wheeler stubbed out his joint and began to pull on his clothes. 'I don't know his name; it was a courier who works for Zlatan. He tried to tax me as I was leaving the flat, so I shanked him.'

'Is he okay?'

'How the fuck do I know? He walked away so I guess so and there's been nothing on the news.'

'Really? Are you sure about that?' Susie reached for her phone and held it aloft so Wheeler could read the breaking news bulletin that stated a teen had been found with fatal stab wounds on the Glendale fields.

'Shit,' breathed Wheeler. He scanned the report again, his eyes widening with shock and fear. 'Shit,' he said again as he pushed his way out of the bedroom and into the kitchen where he snorted a line of coke so he could think clearly.

Ivo Zlatan was also reading the news report and it fuelled his guilt about another stabbing that had left blood on his hands, albeit metaphorically. He had reluctantly recruited Curtis Brady as a favour to one of his boys who had been working for him for a while. Curtis was fresh out of prison having served a sentence for burglary offences. Personally, Ivo didn't like burglars, and really didn't like Curtis, but as he had always been known to keep his workforce happy, he had given him a job pedalling weed and vapes to the high-school crowd.

When he decided it was time to give Wheeler a warning, Curtis automatically came to mind. Subconsciously, he knew it was because there was a high chance Wheeler would be carrying and would act first and ask questions later. If that was the case, as his least favourite employee, it was preferable that Curtis got stabbed rather than one of his soldiers.

When the stabbing actually happened though, Ivo had felt a modicum of guilt. It had been fleeting, but guilt nevertheless. Still, his injuries weren't serious and could be considered payback for all the cowardly bullying acts Curtis had committed in the past. Ivo had done his bit giving him a job. Once he was out of hospital, he'd slip the lad a few quid as compensation and sign him off his payroll. Simple. Sorted. All was good, until he reached for his phone and read the breaking news story about a murder investigation at the Glendale fields. Then Ivo didn't feel so good.

~

'Well, this is concerning,' Dr Granger said. The pathologist frowned over his gold-rimmed glasses, his grey hair, as always sticking out haphazardly, reminiscent of Einstein. He stood back and peered at Jordan's eviscerated remains. Granger had conducted a subcutaneous dissection to display the underlying soft facial tissue and beyond, which in layman's terms meant he had peeled Jordan's face away to reveal his neck tissue.

'Lividity has masked it, but he has incredibly intensive bruising to his neck. It doesn't appear to have occurred too recently, certainly not as recent as the stab wound. If I were to hazard a guess, I'd say it definitely occurred in the last week.'

'Sorry, Doctor Granger, ignore my ignorance, but what have you deduced?' DI Redford asked through the intercom from the viewing room.

'This young man has recently been throttled. There is a lot of soft tissue damage and the bruising appears expansive and deep. He's certainly been in the wars.'

'And you think someone has tried to strangle him? It couldn't have been a suicide attempt?' Maya asked.

Granger shook his head. 'No, my dear. Suicide would involve a ligature and as you can see,' he said as he waved his scalpel over the general neck area, 'the bruising is substantial and not linear. I would suggest manual strangulation. In my opinion someone has tried to squeeze the life out of the poor boy.'

'And going back to the stab wound?'

'As I said before, a single fatal wound that has severed the top of the spinal cord. You're looking for a substantial-sized blade, I would suggest a large kitchen knife. Again, in my opinion, it could also be explained by the boy's sudden movement at the time of the attack, but the direction of the stab wound might suggest an offender with left-handedness, although that is my supposition and not something I would bet my mortgage on.'

'Right then,' said Chris. 'Then the poor kid has quite literally been stabbed in the back.'

'Yes. He might not even have seen his killer if he was being followed. There are certainly no defence wounds, which is surprising as it looks like he's been punched in the face which has caused the cut to his lip and nose.' Granger shook his head. 'What a waste. If it's any saving grace, I would say that death would have been relatively quick and as his spinal cord was severed, he may not have known what was going on or felt pain. It's not like fatal soft-tissue injuries that leave the patient bleeding out.'

'I appreciate it's early on in your investigation, but do you have any positive lines of enquiry when it comes to identifying our suspect? The advantages of such a cut means there is every chance of being able to match the murder weapon to the fatal blow, if you can recover it.'

'The scene is being held for another daylight search tomorrow, hopefully it will be there. Our victim is a teenage boy. They all seem too full of lies and deceit. The mother is understandably distraught and she can barely speak, so no, Doctor.' Redford sighed over the intercom. 'At this moment in time, we have no idea who the killer is, but trust me, I personally won't rest until we lock them up and throw away the key.'

49

———————

With Jordan being so young, the post-mortem had been arduous and draining to watch. Even Chris, who normally ate like a horse after attending one, wasn't in the mood to share a takeaway with Maya, choosing instead to head home with a ready meal. Maya herself was yearning company, and as Spence was working the late shift, she was grateful to have phoned Dominique and been invited round for dinner.

'I can pick something up or we can eat out,' Maya suggested.

'No, it's fine, love, I'll cook.'

'Are you sure, it's been ages since we ate out together.'

'Oh, it's too dark and wet to be venturing out. Besides, it makes a nice change cooking for someone.'

Although Maya appreciated the sentiment, she knew that Dominique was just making excuses not to leave the house. She had become even more isolated since the Naylor sighting and since the dark nights had drawn in. She had even resorted to online shopping and Maya had voiced her concerns to Spence that she could be becoming agoraphobic. Her thoughts were compounded as she arrived at Dominique's and saw how wan her mama looked.

'Are you okay, you don't look yourself.'

'I'm fine,' said Dominique as she enveloped Maya in a hug. 'You know the weather this time of year doesn't agree with me.'

'It's supposed to be dry and sunny at the weekend if you fancy driving out somewhere for a walk.'

'Maybe.'

'Pub lunch afterwards,' Maya wheedled.

'I said, I'll see,' Dominique snapped, then began to fuss over Maya to cover her brusqueness. 'Here now, here's some crisps to nibble on until dinner's ready. What do you want to drink?'

'Just water please.'

'How was your day?'

'Sad. A fourteen-year-old murdered.'

'Want to talk about it?'

'Not really, if that's okay.'

'Of course, I understand. So, are you still feeling settled at Chris's place?'

'I really am. We both love it there. Once Spence has finished his PT course and starts getting work, we're thinking of looking for a new place together.'

Dominique smiled. 'That's great news and a big step for you both.'

Maya shrugged. 'He's the one for me so I don't see the point in waiting.'

'Nor do I, he's a good man and it's obvious you make each other happy. Although, I never thought I'd see the day you'd sell your place.'

'Neither did I but I guess I've outgrown it. And it just doesn't feel safe or even like home anymore.'

'I can understand that. Oh, I miss our old house, I still wake up here and think I'm back there.'

'After everything that happened there though, did you not feel the same, unsafe and wanting to move?'

Dominique shrugged. 'No. Some bad things happened there of course, but a lot of good things too. I have happy memories of you growing up there.'

'*Some* bad things happened.' Maya laughed incredulously. 'What about Grandad lying bleeding on the floor and Naylor stashing drugs and a firearm there.'

Dominique looked up quickly, her face fraught with emotion.

'I remembered something else. I'm not imagining it, am I?'

'No, but I really don't want to have to talk about it. It's too painful.'

'That's what I'm saying, it's too painful, but you never thought of moving home and starting fresh somewhere else. I can't wait to sell my place and it pales into insignificance when I compare what happened.'

'It's not that simple, I didn't have the money to move. We always loved the garden and were lucky that we had nice neighbours.'

'But...'

'But nothing. He went to prison for a long time, so he was no threat to us. There was no need to move.'

Maya desperately wanted to ask more, to push more and see if it helped unlock any more memories, but she recognised the steely look on Dominique's face as she began to shut down. If she pushed her too far she risked alienating and upsetting her and she loved her too much to do either. Instead, she stood and hugged her mama, arms wrapped around her as she offered to make them both a cup of tea. She could feel Dominique trembling as she hugged her and felt guilty, knowing it was all her fault.

DI Redford was unable to switch off after the PM. He headed back to Beech Field, knowing that MIT would be taking over the investigation and wanting to prepare for the handover. He made a beeline for Jack's office and was relieved to see him still there.

'How was it?'

'Fucking awful,' said Redford as he relayed the findings.

'Strangulation,' mused Jack. 'Poor kid had really got on the wrong side of someone.'

'Yeah, I've asked the digital unit to prioritise his phone as a matter of urgency and we need to arrange another chat with the mum, see if she can shine any light on who Jordan was involved with. Have MIT been in touch?'

'Unfortunately, yes.'

Redford sighed, knowing by Jack's reaction the answer he would get. 'Which syndicate?'

'Three. DCI Chambers.'

'Course it is. God, that woman scares the shit out of me.'

'You and me both,' agreed Jack. 'There is some good news though. I didn't want to bother you while you were at the PM, but Lewis Mellor has returned home and he's reportedly safe and well.'

'Thank God for that. Have you arranged for him to be interviewed?'

'Yes, I sent Sean to collect him and bring him back here for a video interview so we can pinpoint when he last saw Jordan. It's going ahead downstairs as we speak.'

'That's good. Can you ask Sean to provide me with a full precis when he's done, I'll be around for a couple more hours yet. I need to try and form some semblance of a case before DCI Chambers and her team descend upon us. She likes nothing more than to accentuate how incompetent I am.' He sighed miserably. 'Being in the presence of that woman makes attending a post-mortem feel like afternoon tea at the Ritz.'

50

———

Sean was sat in the interview room on a sofa so low and spongy, that sitting up in it was like trying to get out of a bean bag. The interview room was purposely designed to make victims giving their evidence feel comfortable, with its pot plants, array of children's toys and abundance of tissue boxes. Unfortunately, as he had stood back to allow Lewis and Sarah into the room, they had automatically plumped for the detective's chairs, leaving him sinking into the sofa. He was very conscious of the fact that his pelvis had caused his knees to lift unnaturally high, leaving him peering over his policy book that he was struggling to balance as he wrote.

'Lewis, can you tell me where you've been the last few days?'

The boy muttered something incoherent into his chest, which Sean couldn't hear, so he had to ask him to repeat himself.

'I went to my dad's,' he said sulkily, and Sean noticed Sarah purse her lips with disapproval.

'From what I've read in the initial missing-from-home report that was taken when officers spoke to your mum, you don't, or certainly haven't had regular or even recent contact with your dad since he left home, is that right?'

Lewis nodded.

'So, what made you suddenly decide to get in touch and visit him after all this time?'

'Still me dad, isn't he?'

'Absolutely and no one is disputing that. We're just concerned as to why you wanted to get away and why you didn't let your mum know. A lot of people have been very worried about you.'

Lewis stared at the floor and Sean attempted to sit up straighter but ended up with his knees shifting even higher. 'Was it because of the stabbing? Is that why you wanted to get away? Your mum said she wasn't aware anything else was bothering you.'

'It just all got too much. The stabbing was awful, okay? I wouldn't let any of my mates know, but I can admit it in here, I was scared. Really scared.'

'Oh, Lewis,' Sarah said as she reached for his hand.

'I didn't want to tell you how I was feeling because it would only have made things worse for you. I know you've been worried; I can hear you crying at night 'n' that. I just thought if I could get away and clear my head, that things would feel better. But I couldn't tell you I was going to see him because I knew you wouldn't approve. I knew you'd be even more upset, and I couldn't face that. I was a coward and I'm sorry.'

'How did you even know where he lived?'

'I texted him and he picked me up from town.'

'How was it?' Sean asked.

'Okay at first. He told me on the drive there that I had a little brother–'

Sarah's head snapped up. 'What? And he's never thought to

let you know this nugget of information before? My God.' She shook her head and wrapped her arms around herself.

'I was curious at first and was looking forward to meeting him, he's only four and really cute, but he never stops. He's so energetic and so loud. Dad let me sleep on a blow-up mattress in his room which was okay but not very comfortable. Then, I kind of got jealous. It's like dad does everything for Kaiden and Melissa, that's his partner, but after the first night, didn't seem interested in me. I felt like I was in the way and that's why I came home.'

'Does he knock her about like he used to with me?' Sarah asked, venom in her tone.

'Dunno. They seem happy. Really lovey-dovey, but like I said, after that first night he seemed to have lost interest. I think he was disappointed or ashamed of me. I tried to talk to him about the stabbing, but he didn't seem to care, just said I should be careful who I hang about with in future. I asked him why he'd never kept in touch and he said it was your fault.'

'I never stopped him from seeing you. Don't get me wrong, I'm glad he didn't, but I would never have done that to you. If he would have proved himself to be a good dad, you could have seen him as much as you wanted.'

'I know, Mum. I knew he was lying. And that's when I decided I needed to come home, I didn't want to listen to him bad-mouthing you to Melissa and Kaiden when I knew what he'd been like when I was younger. It's like he's changed the way he is but doesn't want me in his life as a reminder of how things used to be.'

Sean nodded. 'I'm sorry things worked out with him the way they did; I appreciate how hard and upsetting that must be for you. I'm sure we can find you someone to talk to about all of this if it helps? But that aside, another of the reasons I've asked you here specifically, is to ask you some questions about Jordan Gaffney.'

'What about him?' Lewis asked.

'Jordan was reported missing around the same time as you. I wondered if you could tell me when you last saw him.'

'We weren't together. I went to Dad's on my own. I didn't know he was missing and I don't know where he is.'

Sean cleared his throat and with a Herculean effort managed to heave himself out of the sofa where he perched precariously, but in a more dignified manner, on the edge. 'I'm very sorry to have to tell you both that Jordan was found this morning–'

'Why are you sorry?' Sarah interrupted. 'That's good news, isn't it?' She glanced at Lewis and back to Sean. 'I mean, isn't it? What's wrong? Is Jordan okay, has something happened to him?'

'Preliminary investigations suggest that Jordan was murdered. His post-mortem is currently ongoing.'

Sean gave the pair a moment for the news to sink in. Sarah gasped with shock, her eyes brimming with tears whilst the colour drained from Lewis's face, as he sat wide-eyed and open-mouthed, reaching for his mum's hand.

'Where, when did it happen?' sobbed Sarah.

'His body was discovered at the fields near Glendale earlier this morning. I'm afraid that at this moment, I can't provide you with more information other than that. As you can appreciate, it's early on in what we're hoping will be a fast-moving investigation.'

Sean rose and poured them both a glass of water while they composed themselves. He had one eye on both of them at all times for any telltale signs that they knew something about Jordan's death. He knew there was a strong chance that Jordan had been murdered by someone he knew rather than a random attack by a stranger. He handed them a drink each and rather than allowing himself to be swallowed by the treacherous sofa, pulled out a spare chair in front of them.

'I just need to remind you both that this interview is being video-recorded. Are you happy to continue or would you like to seek legal representation?'

'Legal... no. God, no. We've nufink to hide at all have we? Obviously, we want to do whatever we can to help find whoever killed poor Jordan. The boys have been best friends since primary school, they've grown up together. I've *watched* them grow up together. Oh, poor Claire and Craig.' Sarah swiped tears from her cheeks with one hand whilst tightening her grip on Lewis with the other.

Lewis shook his head as he gulped down his water, he appeared speechless with shock, tears shining in his eyes. His face growing paper white.

'I appreciate this is upsetting for you both. When did you last see him?'

'He's not been round to ours for a while. Lewis hasn't been out since the stabbing for obvious reasons. He's been keeping himself to himself, haven't you, love?'

Lewis nodded as he took another gulp of water.

'That's perfectly understandable. So, when did you last see him?' Sean asked again.

'Can't remember.'

'Really? If you've not been out as much as normal, surely you can recall the last time you saw your best friend.'

Sarah tutted. 'Probably at school. You know what kids are like, they never remember what they've done from one hour to the next, let alone what day. And there's been all the upset with his dad.'

'If you could please give Lewis a moment to answer.'

Lewis shrugged. 'Yeah, like mum said, probably at school.'

'Can you remember when exactly? The time of day, was it end of school, during lunch or in a particular lesson, when?'

'I don't know.'

'Just take a moment to think.'

'I just... I don't know. You're asking me all these questions when I've just found out that my best mate is dead.'

'It's okay, love.' Sarah turned to Sean. 'Is this really necessary? You sound like you're hounding him.'

'Not at all. A boy has been murdered, it's important we establish the timeline of events leading up to that death as quickly as possible. It's certainly not my intention to hound your son and I'm sorry if that's how it seems. I appreciate the news of Jordan's death has been sudden and upsetting for you, so I apologise if my questions seem inappropriate but they are *necessary*.'

'And you must appreciate that my son – that *we* – are grieving. All this on top of the fact he has just been rejected by his estranged father and is still recovering from the trauma of being stabbed himself. In fact, perhaps I can ask *you* a question. It's been ages since Lewis was stabbed and you've not made one arrest despite him being brave enough to provide a perfectly good E-FIT of his attacker.'

'That is still very much a live investigation, sometimes these things don't progress as quickly as we would like.'

'I appreciate that, but I can't help thinking there's an anomaly here. Yes, you heard me right, an anomaly, I can speak in posh words just like you if I want to. I'm wondering why you're hounding my son over Jordan's murder when it could easily have been my boy that is having a post-mortem. My boy could have been murdered, yet you lot haven't arrested no one.'

'Mum...'

'No, Lewis, this needs saying. He's looking down his nose at us, at you because you've been in a bit of bother before and at me 'cause I don't talk so posh, I haven't got a job at the moment and me house doesn't look like somefink out of one of those fancy magazines. Whereas Claire has got her nice job with her uniform and her clean car. And yes, I know she cooks all her nice food and doesn't rely on ping meals like me. You're prejudiced, all you lot are, and we're not staying here any longer to listen to your shit. I'm taking my son home to grieve for his friend and if you want to ask anymore of yer fancy questions, you'll have to go through my solicitor.'

Sarah stood up and snatched her coat, ramming a cigarette in her mouth ready to be lit the moment she left the building as she physically dragged Lewis out of the room. The boy needed no persuading to leave.

51

———————

The following morning the conference room was a hive of activity. DCI Chambers and her team had set themselves up in it as a base for the investigation into Jordan's murder which was running under the title of Operation Scabbard. Redford and Jack had already had a gruelling meeting with the DCI and other members of the senior leadership team based at Beech Field. Redford had provided a list of actions that were already underway and had been left, not for the first time, with the feeling that although he'd tried his best, it just wasn't good enough.

Now the team were gathered waiting to receive further instructions. Chambers' sheer presence as always demanded attention. She was a tall lady with brunette hair tied efficiently in a French plait that hung down her back. Dressed in one of her many smart trouser suits, she had a reputation for not only being austere, but had a particularly grating habit of using business jargon.

'I've managed to touch base with those involved in the initial investigation and have been brought up to speed with where the investigation lies so far. You should all have had an update on the results of the post-mortem. Kym, where are we with regards to the crime scene?'

Kym, efficient as ever, didn't need to consult her notes. 'The priority yesterday was preservation and recovering Jordan's body for the PM. We also recovered his phone and this has been sent off for urgent analysis.'

Chambers made a note before raising her hand. 'Thank you, Kym, and was there anything else of interest in his school bag?'

'School books and a PE top, other than that, no.'

Chambers nodded for her to continue.

'We are confident that Jordan was stabbed on a patch of grass on the Glendale fields, but his body was moved later into a thicker area of shrubbery in an attempt to conceal it. We need to consider why that happened and try and ascertain if more than one person was involved.

'Jordan had bruising to his neck, which wasn't fresh, but the PM revealed it was incredibly deep and expansive as if someone had tried to strangle him. He also had fresh facial injuries suggesting he'd been hit, possibly punched. Dr Granger has suggested that the murderer could be left-handed, but this is only a suggestion, so he has advised caution and asked that we continue to keep an open mind. Thankfully, the weather is less inclement today, so Maya and Chris are going to return to the scene and take further photographs and we have POLSA on standby to conduct a search for the murder weapon.'

'Which I believe Dr Granger surmised is...' Chambers turned to Redford, but he was caught on the hop, swallowing a mouthful of coffee. The weight of her steely glare caused him to splutter, allowing coffee to dribble down his pristine shirt and Italian silk tie.

'Knife, ma'am,' Redford coughed as he tried to regain his composure.

'Yes, thank you, Phil, I think even those at the back of the class have been able to ascertain it's a knife, this isn't Cluedo. Can you provide any further information, are we looking for a fish, cheese or butter knife?' Her tone dripped with sarcasm as she watched him attempting to pathetically dab at his white shirt, which now bore a horrid brown stain.

He tugged at his jacket in an attempt to cover the spillage. 'Dr Granger surmised the murder weapon is a substantially large knife, which he has described as a kitchen knife with a blade sized approximately nineteen point five centimetres.'

'Something to bear in mind when we get boots on the ground and start doing house searches, although hopefully we'll find it at the crime scene. I also want digital chasing up today to see how they're getting on with Jordan's phone and see if they can bring anything to the table. Adila?'

'Yes, ma'am.'

'Are you still happy to act as family liaison officer? If not, I can allocate from my team?'

'I'm happy to stick with it, ma'am.'

'Good, thank you. Take DS Lund with you today to see if you can get any further insight into Jordan from the family and also consider having a more thorough search of the room. Consider seizing any laptops or iPads Jordan might also have had access to. Actions have been issued in relation to house-to-house enquiries and I want all bases covering.

'DS Adebayo,' she said, pointing to a tall black man who raised his hand, 'is going to the school to speak to teachers and get an insight into our victim. Remind me which of you is DC Stevenson?'

Sean raised his hand and Adebayo gave him a thumbs up as they had worked together on a previous case. 'You and me again, Weasley?' Adebayo called out, the nickname referring to the small red-headed boy from *Harry Potter* who Sean did bear an uncanny resemblance to.

'I want you both to get as much information from school then work on a strategy to interview Lewis and Sarah Mellor again. This time I'd prefer it if you didn't upset our witnesses,' she added, causing Sean's face to flush with shame.

'That's it for now, let's get moving and make sure we give it one hundred and ten per cent, people. I want quick results with this one, I'll be giving a press statement shortly in which I'll be offering my reassurances and that we are hoping an arrest will be imminent, so don't let me down.'

There was a flurry of movement as people began to head out of the conference room armed with their actions for the day. Kym turned to Maya and Chris and gave a perfunctory double clap. 'You heard the woman, let's get down to the Glendale fields and tear that place apart, see if we can find the murder weapon.'

Maya, Chris and Kym were grateful for the scant protection of the crime-scene suit. Although, they could be unbearable to wear in summer months, they offered some windproof protection in the winter. It was a crisp, sunny day with a layer of frost on the ground that glittered like diamonds and a wind that pinched through the double thermal layers they had on underneath.

'Jesus, me balls are trying to shrink back inside me it's that cold,' Chris grumbled as Maya took some additional scene photographs.

Maya smirked. 'It's definitely nipple weather, but don't let Kym hear, she'll tear a strip off us.' Kym was chatting to the POLSA sergeant at the end of the cordon as they discussed the search parameters.

'Thought she said they were bringing a search dog too,' Chris said.

Maya nodded. 'It's on its way but it's already been out this morning so it's having a snack and a rest before it's good to go again.'

'Bloody charming. The dog gets a snack and a rest and here's me literally working my bollocks off and I've only had one brew and no biscuits this morning thanks to Cruella dragging us out.'

Maya raised an eyebrow. 'Fourteen-year-old murder victim, remember?'

Chris looked suitably chastened. 'Yeah, course, I'm only joshing.'

'There's a pack of trail mix in my coat pocket.'

'Save that for the bloody dog. Hey up, Kym's waving us over.'

They joined her at the scene tape where she introduced the sergeant as PS Sadiq. 'Call me Mo,' he said as he shook their hands. 'I was just explaining to Kym, I'll get my lot to do a line search first, by the time we're done the dog should be here and we can run him through.' He produced a printout from Google Maps. 'Here's our location zoned off accordingly in three specific search areas: main scene, closest wooded perimeter and furthermost perimeter.'

He pointed a gloved finger at zone two. 'My guess is, if anything had been left in the main scene area you and your eagle eyes would have spotted it. If the weapon has been discarded, my money is on zone two, but I have been proven wrong before. Any findings, we'll let you know and then back off until you've done your recoveries.'

'I know it's a pain, Mo, but I do need your search team to fully suit up just to avoid potential contamination of any DNA evidence.'

Mo grinned. 'Already on it, that's why they're not over here yet, they're helping each other get suited and booted. It's like watching a classroom of playschool toddlers putting their own painting aprons on.'

As if on cue, the search team arrived all ensconced in white suits and looking like a budget version of the *Teletubbies* show, each clutching a search stick.

'Shaz,' Mo called to one of them, 'has COVID taught you nothing? Masks should cover your nose *and* mouth.'

He grinned at Kym. 'Don't judge them, they might look like they all share one brain cell each, but they're good at what they do.'

'I'll take your word for it,' Kym replied uncertainly and she then mumbled to Chris and Maya, 'Thank God we've got the dog.'

Mo assembled his group into three teams and sent them off to their respective zones from where it was a waiting game as Maya, Chris and Kym stood and watched as they moved in a methodical, thorough line, searching the grass and shrubbery with a fine-toothed comb.

While they were waiting, Chris fished his phone out of the scene suit and went onto the local news site.

'Chambers' press release has gone online and look, they've named and shared a picture of Jordan.' Maya and Kym leaned closer to look, both let out a sigh.

'He was a nice-looking kid,' Maya said.

'He certainly was, what a waste,' said Chris as he put his phone away again. 'Come on,' he willed the search team, 'bloody find it.'

They stood silently watching, shivering against the biting wind as they observed the slow but steady progress. After what felt like an age, a stick was held aloft and they could hear the cry, 'Sarge?'

'Hang fire, gang. What have you got, Shaz?'

They followed Mo to zone two where Shaz was holding back a thick piece of shrubbery. Protruding from it was the black handle of a seemingly large-looking kitchen knife. 'Good work, mate. Right guys, just hold back and let SOCO do their thing.'

Maya began to take more general shots to show the location of the finding whilst Chris and Kym headed to the van to bring supplies. They later returned with a yellow number marker, a scale, sterile brown paper, and a large weapons tube.

'I've got the Kastle-Meyer kit so you can screen it when you're ready,' Kym told Maya as they began to set up the work area using the sterile paper as a base to examine the knife on. Maya took care to clean her gloves before placing the marker next to the knife and photographing it.

'Certainly the right size,' mused Kym.

'Blood,' said Maya succinctly as she pointed at staining on the blade, which looked like there had been an attempt to wipe it.

'Let's not get our hopes up yet,' Kym said. 'Let's test it first.'

Maya cleaned her gloves again before reaching for the KM kit. She selected a piece of filter paper and folded it until she had a point and carefully rubbed it on a piece of staining along the blade, careful not to damage any latent ridge detail.

She squatted back on her heels and opened up the filter paper, placing it carefully on the edge of the work area. She carefully applied a drop of Kastle-Meyer reagent and waited several seconds before adding a drop of hydrogen peroxide. The filter paper turned a noticeable, startling pink colour, indicating it was positive for blood. The three of them grinned at each other under their masks.

'Good work,' said Kym. 'Get it packaged and I'll ask for the exhibits officer to get it fast-tracked while we carry on with the search.'

'Will do,' said Maya who had shone her torch on the knife. She turned to Chris. 'There's definitely some ridge detail on the blade. I've got a good feeling about this.'

He nodded. 'So have I, matey, so have I.'

52

———

Whilst the knife was fast-tracked for analysis, the search of the Glendale fields continued for a further two hours. In the meantime, Sean and Adebayo had arrived at St Mark's school and were being bustled into the head of year's office. She had poker-straight, brunette hair and sat stooped as if she carried the weight of the school on her shoulders.

'Shelly Clarke,' she greeted them, 'so sorry to have kept you waiting. A lot of the kids are naturally upset to hear about Jordan, so we've been trying to get as many as we can to engage with pastoral care.' Her office was warm and welcoming, in contrast to the bleak weather outside.

'It goes without saying,' she began, 'that we are all devastated to hear the news. To lose a pupil is terrible, but for a fourteen-year-old to be murdered,' she shook her head, 'it's unthinkable. Unbearable even. Anything we can do to help, either myself personally or as a school, please just ask. Mr Ramos will be joining us shortly; he's taught Jordan PE since he was in year seven and runs the school football team. Of all the staff here, he probably knew Jordan the best.'

'Thank you,' said Adebayo. 'We appreciate you taking the

time to see us as we know how busy you must be. As you can appreciate, it is early on in our investigation, so it would help us greatly if you could tell us everything you know about Jordan, his behaviour, friendship groups, if he'd been in any trouble or unusually absent lately. Anything you can think of at all that might help. However insignificant it might seem.'

'Of course. Well, prior to your arrival I had a look at the scores of recent assessments that Jordan had completed and academically, he was doing well, above average.'

'And behaviourally?'

'He was good.'

'Good?' said Adebayo. 'Forgive me, that sounds like quite a bland description. We really need to know as much about Jordan as you can tell us.'

Mrs Clarke fanned her hands across the desk. 'Let me clarify, there are over three hundred teenagers in my year. A small percentage of those kids are impeccably behaved and have grades that would happily secure them a place in Cambridge or Oxford. Equally, we have a small percentage of kids who are on the border of being expelled, who you and your colleagues probably know and see more of than we do.

'Then there are a larger percentage of kids who are just *okay*. Some may have had late marks, usually the teenage girls who arrive on time in the morning but are constantly late in between lessons because they can't drag themselves away from the toilet mirrors. Some may have detentions for missing homework or talking back to teachers, fighting with their peers, that sort of thing.

'Jordan was a good kid. He made the effort in lessons and engaged with teachers and peers. I've spoken to his friends and other teachers who agree he was a nice boy. Friendly, polite, well-mannered and trustworthy. More recently his attendance has been a concern. He's been late, which really isn't like him or he's had to leave early, claiming he had appointments. We do make a point of checking the validity of these claims, but kids can be conniving when it comes to doctoring the technology and with over three hundred kids, it's not always possible to keep track.'

'Had you raised concerns with the mum?'

'Yes, I had emailed her and she assured me she was looking into it and he would improve. It's hard for the parents sometimes, especially when they're on their own because if they're running round working shifts, it's not always easy to check where their kids are. What I can say is that Jordan was a good kid, which, as you said yourself does sound bland, but the truth of the matter is, that unless they stand out for being exceptionally gifted or are the type of kid we worry will burn the school down, they tend to stay under the radar if things carry on ticking along, which he was.'

There was a knock on the door and a tall, wiry-looking man in his late thirties with swarthy skin was invited in. 'Gentleman, this is Mr Ramos, Jordan's PE teacher. He can tell you much more about Jordan than I can.'

Mr Ramos shook the detectives' hands. 'It's such a sad state of affairs,' he said with genuine remorse on his face. 'Jordan was a genuinely nice and decent kid, I had a lot of time for him. He was one of my twenty-pound note kids.'

'Sorry?' said Sean. 'What does that mean?'

Ramos gave a sad smile. 'Myself and some of the other teachers have a saying about how decent a kid is. There are some you never feel safe turning your back on and then there are kids like Jordan. I'd happily leave twenty pounds of my own money lying around knowing the kid was trustworthy and wouldn't take it. Jordan was one of those kids. He was a good footballer too. He had talent and more than that, showed real sportsmanship, he was a team player.'

Sean smiled. 'You sound like you liked him a lot.'

Ramos nodded. 'I did. He was keen, chatty and funny. I enjoyed his company.'

'Mrs Clarke has said that his attendance hasn't been great lately. Would you say that was out of character?'

'Yes, he's always been a conscientious student. Also, I noticed he had bruising to his neck that looked quite nasty.'

Sean nodded. 'Yes, we're aware and were going to ask you about that.'

'When I asked him, he said it had happened playfighting, but he didn't elaborate who with. I assumed it was with his brother because a few weeks ago, the lads were showering after PE, I was passing through the changing rooms and noticed Jordan had a few bruises to his torso. It looked like he had been punched, I asked him about it and he said he'd been playfighting at home while his mum was out. I remember thinking it was out of character for the lad, because even though he was older and stronger than Jordan, Craig has always been a gentle giant.'

'Did you believe it was caused by playfighting?'

'He didn't lead me to believe it was anything else. I asked if everything was okay on both occasions and reminded him he could confide in me but he insisted it was nothing, just brushed it off.'

'Did you have the type of relationship that he *would* have confided in you if he needed too?'

Ramos didn't even need to think. 'Definitely,' he said in a split second. 'Like I said, I liked him and we genuinely got on. I knew his dad wasn't on the scene and Craig was never one for football, so he always made a beeline to talk to me about it because we supported the same team. He'd arrive early for lessons or practice and sometimes hang on afterwards for a chat, helping me clear stuff away whilst we had a natter.

'We'd always talk about what we were doing after school or the weekend, that kind of thing. He was always a chatty kid, couldn't shut him up some days, although when I look back now, he had been quieter the last week or so.' He wiped a hand across his eyes as he muttered, 'Why didn't I see it?'

'What about drugs, have you any reason to believe he was getting involved in anything like that?'

'No chance. That's certainly not his scene. I know his best friend Lewis Mellor was caught with a vape on the premises a few times and I once saw him smoking as I was driving home, but not Jordan. He was sporty and liked his football too much, he wouldn't do anything that affected his health so he couldn't play.

'He had his head screwed on. I can't imagine him even getting involved in anything like that. Plus, he adored his mum and Craig, he'd never risk doing anything stupid that would upset or worry them. He told me once that he wanted to do well at school so he could get a decent job and support them. He said he wanted to be a PE teacher like me. Like I said, a decent kid.' Ramos' voice was thick with emotion, and he had to look away for a moment while he composed himself.

'What about girlfriends, did he talk about anyone he was interested in?'

Ramos shook his head. 'No, it was all sport-related with us. Females never warranted a mention, and I never asked.'

'Jordan was reported missing from home before his body was found. Again, we believe this was out of character. Can you think of anywhere he may have gone or anyone he may have stayed with?'

'Other than one of his mates, no. Like I said, his dad wasn't on the scene and he never talked about any other family when we chatted about stuff we were doing at weekends, so I guess a friend's house is the only other place he would have to go. Jesus, if I thought the lad was in any kind of trouble, I'd have had him around mine in a heartbeat.'

'I see,' said Adebayo. 'What do you think of Lewis Mellor?'

'Bit of a shit if I'm honest.'

'Mr Ramos!' Mrs Clarke said, shocked.

'Oh, come on, Shelley. This is a private conversation amongst adults, you know better than I do that some of our kids are *challenging*,' he said, using his fingers as inverted commas. 'Lewis *is* a little shit. He gives backchat, he's always late and is forever pushing the boundaries. He's in detention most days. Him and Jordan were chalk and cheese. I know they were best mates but they couldn't be more different and I sometimes worried that Lewis would hold Jordan back.'

Mrs Clarke shrugged her shoulders as she thought about it, then nodded. 'I suppose you're right.'

'You've mentioned,' said Sean, 'that there was just Jordan, his mum and Craig at home. How did they seem as a family unit? Any problems there that we need to know about?'

'None at all,' said Ramos. 'Claire Gaffney is a committed mum, always engaged positively with school and encouraged both her sons. I don't know if you've met Craig.'

Ramos looked towards Mrs Clarke who offered, 'He is intellectually challenged.'

'Thank you.' Ramos nodded. 'I wasn't sure how to phrase it, as there are so many labels these days, but Claire never wanted Craig statemented. With support, he remained and did well in mainstream school which is what they both wanted. Like Jordan, he's a lovely kid. Nowhere near as chatty as his brother, but a dependable, honest lad.'

'A twenty-pound note kid?' asked Sean.

'Absolutely, one hundred per cent. Look, there are a lot of parents who don't support their kids through school. They believe behavioural issues are our problem and don't take their share of the responsibility. They're happy their kids come here so they can palm them off for the day but do nothing to support their education or aspirations. You must see as much as we do, that some families just don't give a shit about their kids. Claire Gaffney is certainly *not* one of those mothers.'

'What about Sarah Mellor?' Sean asked.

Ramos and Mrs Clarke exchanged a glance. 'I wouldn't like to be accused of casting aspersions, I'm sure you can come to your own conclusions quite quickly, detective,' he said as he splayed his fingers across the desk.

Neither Sean nor Adebayo had any further questions.

53

'What are you thinking, Weasley?' Adebayo asked as they started to drive away from St Mark's.

'Ramos was quite effusive about Jordan, that's for sure.'

'But certainly not about Lewis.'

'As kids we all had a favourite teacher, so I guess it works the other way and teachers have favourite kids.'

'There's favourite and then there's sainted,' snorted Adebayo.

'Be fair, he's just found out the kid has been murdered. Not everyone is as hardened and cynical as us.'

'I suppose so. Right, are you happy with the interview strategy for Lewis and Sarah? We'll tread carefully as I'm a firm believer that you catch more flies with honey than shit.'

'Agreed, you can take the reins with pleasure,' said Sean as they pulled up outside the house. They knocked on the door which Sarah eventually opened and she gestured with a grunt for them to follow her into the kitchen. The air was thick with cigarette smoke as she reached across the table for a fresh packet of fags.

Adebayo began to introduce himself and Sarah shrugged with indifference. 'Sit down then, you're making the place look untidy,' she said before shrieking, 'LEWISSSSS,' at the top of her voice. 'He'll be down in a bit,' she said with a sniff.

Sean coughed nervously and began to fuss with his tie. Overhead, they could hear noisy footsteps followed by the sound of Lewis urinating loudly before descending downstairs.

'FLUSH,' Sarah shrieked suddenly, causing Sean to jump out of his seat and Adebayo having to mask a grin. They listened to Lewis's heavy thuds as he returned upstairs, and the sound of the toilet being flushed. He emerged in the kitchen looking sleepy-eyed, his hair mussed, wearing stained joggers and a clearly lived-in T-shirt. He looked to Sean as if he'd aged ten years since having seen him the previous day.

'Ait,' he mumbled before reaching in the fridge for a carton of orange juice and joining them at the table. He noisily swallowed a mouthful before reaching across the table to Sarah who passed him the cigarette, allowing him a couple of drags before she snatched it back.

Adebayo smiled at them both warmly. 'Firstly, can I extend to you both my sincere sympathies. I can't begin to imagine how difficult it was to hear about Jordan's death and I apologise if you think Sean's questions were heavy-handed. For what it's worth, Sean is a very capable detective and we're currently doing everything we can to catch the person or persons involved in Jordan's murder.'

Sarah's head shot up. 'You fink he was killed by more than one person?'

'It's too early to say at this stage.'

'It's okay saying that, but I've no peace of mind. I'm worried that he, they, might come for my Lewis next. What are you lot gonna do to protect him? He's already been shanked once.'

'I can arrange for engineers to come and fit panic alarms to your house today. If you're at all concerned, all you need to do is press the button and it will signal straight through to the local police who will be with you in minutes. There are several target-hardening measures we can take to protect both you and your home.'

Sarah nodded. 'Yeah, that'd be good. Ta.'

Adebayo flashed her a smile. 'No problem. Now, Sean and I have been to the school today to chat to a couple of the teachers, and we just wanted to ask you both a few further questions as it's helpful to learn as much about Jordan as we can.'

'Which teachers did you speak to?' Lewis asked.

'Mrs Clarke and Mr Ramos.'

'Right cow she is and he's not right,' said Lewis as Sarah nodded in agreement.

'Finks she's something special she does.'

'What do you mean, "he's not right"?'

'Just the way he's always been with Jordan and that.'

'Which is how?'

'All over him all the time. Like, trying to be his mate. It's embarrassing. And he hated me.'

Adebayo frowned. 'Can you elaborate on what you mean when you say he was "all over him"?'

Lewis shifted awkwardly in his seat and glanced at Sarah who nodded for him to continue. 'Like, it was no secret that they got on and that Jordan was one of his favourites, but it was getting really embarrassing how he started singling him out even more lately. Not even being discreet about it. He called him one of his twenty-pound note boys for Christ's sake.' Lewis sucked his teeth in disgust.

'What do you think he meant by that?' Sean asked.

'Obvious, innit?'

Sean and Adebayo looked at him blankly, whilst Sarah reached for another cigarette.

'He treated the boys he liked with twenty-pound notes in exchange for, you know...' Lewis leaned back and made a rubbing motion near his crotch area before taking the cigarette off Sarah.

'Lewis, that is a very serious allegation. Just so we're perfectly clear and there is no misunderstanding whatsoever, are you claiming that Mr Ramos was requesting sexual favours off boys in exchange for money?'

Lewis nodded.

'Okay. We're going to have to look into this a little more and take a proper statement from you. Are you happy to do that?'

Lewis nodded.

'Everyone knows what a perv Ramos is. Even Clarke knows it, but they're like you lot, they don't grass on their own, do they? They all stick together and try and set people up too,' sneered Sarah.

'I know you won't believe me, but ask anyone in my class. There was this one time a few weeks ago, when we'd been in the shower after PE and Ramos couldn't take his eyes off Jordan. Next thing you know he finds an excuse to get Jordan in his office and kept him there for ages talking, so much so, Jordan missed lunch.'

'And how did you get on with Mr Ramos?' Sean asked. 'You said he hated you. Why?'

'Obvious, innit? Because I was Jordan's best mate and spent more time with him than he did. He was always hounding me at school, giving me detention for the slightest fing. He scared me sometimes, always shouting at me for no reason. There was one night me and Jord were leaving school together, the night I got stabbed. They stopped to chat and he could barely look at me. He said goodnight, like as an afterthought, but looked at me like he wanted to kill me. It was 'orrible, like, really sinister.'

Sarah reached her hand across the table and squeezed her son's. 'That's enough now. I don't want him upset again. Not after yesterday.'

'Absolutely,' Adebayo said. 'I agree. You've been really brave sharing all this, Lewis. I can see it hasn't been easy. We'll certainly be looking into it and we'll be in touch to pick things up from here. In the meantime, leave us to it.'

They showed themselves out and held their counsel until they were in the sanctuary of the car. 'What d'ya make of that then?' Adebayo said. 'Schoolboy gossip or potential hypothesis?'

Sean was eagerly scrawling through the emails on his phone. 'I'm always one to sit on the fence until we have concrete evidence, but this may well have legs. Look.' He handed his phone to Adebayo.

'What am I looking at?'

'An E-FIT provided by Lewis Mellor after he was stabbed in the leg by a male he claims was sexually predatory towards him. Someone who caused him serious damage and left him potentially bleeding to death. Someone he's clearly scared of and has given the clues hoping we can join the dots for him.'

Adebayo squinted as he studied the image again. The image was of someone older and scruffier-looking, but with a second glance, it was glaringly obvious that the E-FIT was the spit of Ramos.

54

Maya arrived at counselling, already exhausted even before the session had begun. She had slept badly, which was understandable after having attended Jordan's PM, but she was also going over the conversation with Dominique and felt guilty for upsetting her when she was obviously so fragile. She was becoming more and more concerned with how stressed she was becoming. She looked so brittle and jumpy all the time, barely recognisable as the strong powerhouse Maya had always known and loved.

And she couldn't remember the last time she'd seen her laugh. She wondered whether getting another pet would help. Their beloved cat, Jet, had been killed previously by someone acting on Naylor's instructions. Would a kitten act as a soothing distraction or a reminder of how vicious and hateful Naylor could be. Perhaps she'd ask Spence's opinion before broaching the subject with Dominique.

Her reverie was broken by Jayne calling her name. Once settled in the all too familiar room, she began to tell Jayne about the memory of the drugs and the firearm in the cupboard under the stairs.

'That's really good recall.' Jayne smiled. 'And it's common in talking therapies like this. Think of the memories like Jenga pieces, once you start to pull at one you can follow on with others until your whole subconscious comes falling down and reveals itself.'

'I wondered if we could concentrate on that memory today and see if we can further it.'

Jayne smiled again. 'We can, but the sceptical part of me suggests you're using avoidance.'

'Not really, I just thought it would be good to explore further.'

'It's a naturally occurring memory which may well continue to develop further on its own with time. If it remains fixed and causes you issues, we can certainly consider it, but it's not that particular memory that causes you anxiety and has been giving you flashbacks, is it?'

Maya grinned, contrite. 'Guess so. Back to the lounge?'

Jayne nodded. 'Back to the lounge. Okay, last time you were really brave and remembered going in there. It wasn't your mama lying on the floor covered in blood as you'd originally thought, it was actually your grandad.'

Maya felt the emotion welling in her and didn't trust herself to speak so merely nodded.

'Okay, just concentrate on your breathing and take a moment to picture your safe space. When you're ready, I want you to picture yourself back in the room. You can see Grandad, but it's okay, it's just a memory, remember. Stick with it.'

After a few moments, Jayne began the usual movement and Maya allowed her eyes to follow the swinging of her fingers until Jayne eventually stopped and asked her what she was feeling.

'Grandad looks unconscious, but he's breathing. I'm still too scared to go to him, to go further into the room because someone else is in there.'

'Stay with it.' The process continued. 'What now, Maya?'

'I feel so tense, I'm cowering, but I know I can't leave. I have to help him. I want to help him. That need feels stronger than wanting to run.'

'You're doing great. Carry on.'

Jayne let the process continue for longer before asking Maya again how she was feeling.

'I'm with Grandad. I'm at his side. I'm trying to cover him so no one can hurt him again. If I turn to the left I'll see him...'

'Stay with it.'

Jayne continued until Maya visibly winced. 'Remember your safe space. Can you tell me what you're feeling?'

'He's stood there. Naylor. He's in the room.' Maya shivered. 'He looks terrifying and he's furious. His eyes look weird, they're inhuman. God, I can smell him. The room stinks of him.'

'Go with it, Maya.'

Jayne continued as long as she could until Maya appeared too physically uncomfortable. 'What can you see?'

'He's coming towards me. He's screaming and coming towards me. I can't leave Grandad; I'm scared he'll hurt him even more if I do. But he's still coming towards me. And someone else is with him.' Maya squeezed her eyes shut. 'I run.'

Sean and Adebayo returned to Beech Field and made a beeline for Adila. 'Thank God you're still here. I was worried you may have left for the Gaffney's.'

Adila and DS Amy Lund were finishing a coffee. 'We thought we'd give Claire a bit of time, not that I imagine she's sleeping, but we didn't want to overwhelm her. We're setting off after this. What's so urgent?'

'The Lewis Mellor stabbing. We may have a suspect. Mr

Ramos, the boy's PE teacher. Lewis has made claims that he had sexual intentions towards Jordan and hated Lewis as he was jealous of their friendship. I'm curious about an interaction Lewis claimed they had as they were leaving school the night he was stabbed. You've got them leaving on CCTV, haven't you?'

'Yeah, sure. Give me a minute to access it.'

Sean and Adebayo hovered around the desk and read through the file whilst waiting.

'Here you go,' Adila said eventually as she turned her monitor in their direction. 'It's good footage, the camera was on the school fence, so it captures their interaction perfectly.'

The detectives watched the footage of Jordan and Lewis climbing on the bike. Jordan turns towards a black car, which leaves the staff car park and stops near the boys. Ramos is unmistakable as he puts the driver's window down and chats, clearly animated, with Jordan. Just as he leaves, he turns fleetingly towards Lewis and the look of vitriol on his face is unmistakable.

'Interesting,' said Adebayo. 'Fits in with what Lewis said, there really is no love lost between them two, whereas Jordan is clearly golden boy.'

'But that doesn't mean he's predatory. Lewis could be lying.'

'He could, but we can't ignore it any more than we can the fact that around the time Lewis is stabbed, the closest CCTV footage to the scene captures a car in the vicinity, which is also black,' Adebayo said as he tapped the image on the screen of Ramos in his black vehicle.

'We need to go and speak to the boss, but it's inevitable. Ramos is beginning to smell and we're gonna have to bring him in.'

55

'Is Jordan okay? He's not been round.'

Wheeler glared at Albert. 'What the fuck's that got to do with you?'

'Don't speak to him like that,' scolded Susie. She was sat at the kitchen table reluctantly weighing cocaine into snap bags, whilst Wheeler was preparing a fresh batch of deliveries.

'Well tell him not to poke his nose in my business. I don't like him in here while this is going on. Fuck off back in there and watch your TV or, nap or piss yerself or whatever the hell you old people do.'

Susie's disgusted pout angered him even more. 'You're a fucking walking corpse, old man,' he shouted as he kicked the door shut.

Albert lowered himself gingerly onto the sofa. His arthritis was playing up and his joints were agony. He'd become accustomed to Wheeler's hateful words and they bounced off him now; had long stopped to even resonate. Plus, he had bigger things to worry about. He reached again for the free local paper that had arrived that morning and devoured the article about the murdered teenager found stabbed on the Glendale fields. He had a bad feeling about it and was worried sick about Jordan.

He pursed his lips and recalled the night Wheeler had woken up about 2am. Albert had heard him go into the bathroom and heard the sounds of running water. He had pretended to be asleep on the couch when Wheeler had crept past him and collected something from out of the cleaning cupboard under the kitchen sink, before leaving the flat.

Albert had been dozing on and off when he heard him return ninety minutes later. He waited until he could hear snoring coming from his bedroom before he got off the couch and stepped into the hallway. Wheeler's sodden trainers had been kicked into the corner, his coat hung on the peg, dripping rainwater all over the floor.

Albert wondered where he had been at that time of the morning. He didn't need to wonder what Wheeler had been cleaning up, as the following day the argument had ensued when he had asked Susie to take some bloodied clothing to the launderette for him. Albert wasn't a betting man, but would put his pension on the fact that Wheeler was involved in the murder. He only hoped and prayed that wherever Jordan was, he was alive and safe.

In the harsh light of the interview room, Guy Ramos looked the epitome of a startled rabbit. Sean and Adebayo had rudely awoken him at 5am with a warrant to search his address as they'd advised him he would be interviewed under caution. Adebayo had accompanied Ramos up to his bedroom and supervised him whilst the PE teacher had dressed.

He had then been brought to Beech Field custody where he

had been photographed by Elaine. He had then had his clothing seized and replaced with a humiliatingly tight grey tracksuit and the type of black plimsolls that, ironically, primary school children wore during PE. He was now sat looking pale, unshaven and dishevelled, practically cowering under the weight of Adebayo's stare.

Ramos' duty solicitor was a plump-looking woman with raven-black hair tied back into such a tight ponytail her eyes looked pinched at the corners. During their initial consultation prior to interview, she had looked at Ramos with disdain as he had professed his innocence as she had assured him, without much conviction, that it would all be ironed out in no time.

Ramos had listened avidly as Adebayo had reiterated his rights and formally introduced himself and Sean for the benefit of the recording. He noticed his solicitor had already begun to take notes and he found this spurt of professionalism reassuring, until he glanced down at her pad and discovered she had done nothing more than begun to doodle a circular pattern.

'Mr Ramos, you last met my colleague and I at St Mark's school where we also met with Mrs Clarke. Can you recall that occasion?' asked Adebayo.

'Of course. I'm hardly likely to forget it. You came to talk to us about Jordan Gaffney after he'd been found murdered. It was an awful, truly sad day.'

'On that day you spoke very highly of Jordan. Can you sum up for me what you thought of him?'

'With pleasure, he was an amazing kid, probably one of my favourites, which might not be a professional thing to say, but I genuinely cared for the kid. We spent a lot of time together and I enjoyed his company.'

Adebayo nodded and made a note of what Ramos had just said, before carefully rereading what he'd written and tapping the book with his pen. '"We spent a lot of time together". Can you describe further what you mean by that?'

Ramos' face flushed as he straightened in his seat and slapped his palm on the desk. 'Oh no, I know where you're going to go with this and you're bang out of order. No!' He turned to the solicitor who eyed him blankly. 'They're going to suggest that my relationship with Jordan was inappropriate. No, that's not fair. You're barking up the wrong tree completely. Jordan's killer is out there right now and you're wasting your time with this shit?'

Ramos let out an incredulous laugh before sinking back into the chair and looking utterly defeated mere moments after the start of the interview.

'When did you last see Jordan?' Sean asked as he smiled pleasantly at the teacher.

'Last Thursday I think, but that would have been during our PE lesson as he told me he couldn't make football training that evening because of a dental appointment. I'm trying to recall if I saw him at school on the Friday but I'm a bit too flustered now to remember clearly. I'd hazard a guess and say I didn't as I would have asked him how the dentist went and would have remembered.'

'You must care a lot about your pupils if you ask how they went on after a dentist appointment.'

'I do care.' He saw the solicitor make a note and glanced at the pad, devastated to see the circular spiral developing leaves and limbs.

'About all your pupils or just certain ones?'

'Well, all of them obviously, it goes with the job, as a teacher you're *in loco parentis*.'

'What do you think about Lewis Mellor?'

Ramos sighed and shook his head. 'He's one of our more challenging pupils.'

Adebayo made a show of flicking back through his book and thumbing down a page. 'When we met you and Mrs Clarke, you actually described him as "a little shit". Do you recall making that comment?'

'Yes, but you're taking it out of context. I explained that compared to Jordan, Lewis was a shit. He gave backchat all the time, he was continuously late and disruptive in class.'

'And Jordan?'

'Keen, conscientious, well-mannered and a generally nice kid.'

'You enjoyed spending time with him?'

'Yes, I've said so. There was nothing sinister about it, not like you're suggesting. We got on, we had football in common and he was such a chatty kid we'd talk about things we got up to outside of school. He knew I liked swimming and playing squash. I'd also taught his older brother Craig and knew his mum too, so used to ask how they were getting on. There's no law against it, is there?' He turned to the solicitor who looked at him blankly as if they'd not met before and Ramos began to wonder if he was in some twisted parallel universe.

'Are you in a relationship at the moment?' Adebayo asked.

'What? No. I mean that's nothing to do with you. It's not relevant.'

'Would you mind telling me what your sexual preferences are?'

'Absolutely not. For Christ's sake!' Incredulous, he looked at the solicitor again and was relieved to see that she looked like she'd finally woken up.

'I don't see how my client's sexual preferences have any relevance. Perhaps if you'd like to get to the point, detective.'

'When we spoke last, you described Jordan as one of your twenty-pound note kids. What did you mean by that?'

Ramos swiped a hand through his hair. 'I told you. It meant

that I would trust a kid like him around twenty pounds of my own money. Confident he wouldn't take it. He was trustworthy.'

'And Lewis Mellor? Is he a twenty-pound note kid?'

Ramos snorted. 'Wouldn't trust him with twenty pence.'

'I'm going to get straight to the point. Have you ever offered a child twenty pounds in exchange for sexual favours?'

Ramos leapt from his chair and slammed the desk. 'Fuck's sake, no. Never!'

Adebayo's hand was wrapped around his forearm in an instant. 'Sit back down please, Mr Ramos.'

The teacher did as he was told, swiping away tears of frustration that suddenly stung his eyes. There was a lull in the interview while he calmed himself down.

'Going back to Jordan, you mentioned last time we spoke that you observed bruising to his torso whilst he was getting changed after showering?'

'Yes.'

'You claim you asked him about it and he said he received the bruises when playfighting with his brother Craig.'

'Yes.'

'Where did you have this conversation?'

'I called him into my office as he was leaving the changing rooms because I was concerned about the lad.'

'And how long did the conversation last?'

'Ten minutes.'

'Is that all?'

'Yes.'

'Are you sure, Mr Ramos, because we have witnesses that say they didn't see Jordan until the next lesson. It was lunchtime after PE, yet he never met up with his friends in the dining hall.'

'No. I asked him about the bruises and made sure he was okay. That conversation only lasted about ten minutes. Then I noticed the time and was worried he'd be at the back of the lunch queue. I could hear his tummy rumbling and he had just done PE. The kids don't get long for lunch and I didn't want him going hungry, so split my lunch with him, I always make too much.'

'Very generous of you.'

'*In loco parentis*. If you saw a kid you knew was hungry and you had food to share wouldn't you do the same?'

'Where did Jordan eat his lunch?'

'He stayed in my office. We were chatting about football and then I got the latest fixtures up on my laptop so we could discuss which teams were playing next.'

'Has Jordan ever been to your house?'

'No.'

'Did he know where you lived?'

'No,' Ramos paused. 'Yes.'

'Sorry, sir, which is it – yes or no.'

'He knew I lived near the leisure centre because I mentioned that I went swimming and played squash there. He asked me in passing one day which street, as he had a friend that lived there, and I told him it was Jasper Avenue.'

'Did you tell him the number?'

'No, it wasn't relevant. He has never been to my house.'

Adebayo studied his notes again. 'Only when we met last, you commented, "If I thought the lad was in any kind of trouble, I'd have had him around mine in a heartbeat". I'm wondering how that would have happened if he didn't know where you lived? Did he have your phone number?'

'No, that's not allowed, it's a school rule obviously. And he knew which street I lived on; I've told you that. I guess he could have figured out which number if he saw my car on the drive.'

'Oh, so he's been in your car?'

'No, I didn't say that. He's seen me driving in and out of the staff car park, so he knows what I drive.'

'Where were you on 2nd November?' asked Sean. The sudden change of subject startled Ramos. 'I, erm, I honestly don't know. I'd have to think.'

'If it helps you recall, it was a Thursday.'

'Oh, I imagine I would have been playing squash then.'

'Who do you play with?'

'My friend, Tom Barrow.'

'So, if we ask Mr Barrow he would be able to confirm where you were.'

'Yes. Oh no, hang on. The 2nd? I remember now, I was supposed to play but cancelled last minute.'

'Why?'

'I had an upset stomach.'

'So what did you do?'

'I stayed home obviously.'

'Did anyone see you? A neighbour, delivery person, did a friend or family member call round?'

'No.'

'So you don't have an alibi?'

'An alibi for what? I cancelled my squash game and stayed at home because I had the shits. I didn't realise I'd need witnesses, or I'd have recorded every bowel movement, and trust me, there would have been a lot of footage.'

'It was also the date that Lewis Mellor was stabbed.'

'Oh. Well, I can assure you that had nothing to do with me.'

'Can I show you some footage of that evening from St Mark's as you were leaving school?'

'Certainly.'

They all watched the footage of Ramos pulling over in his car and chatting animatedly to Jordan. The footage was paused as he turned to reluctantly acknowledge Lewis. The look of contempt on his face spoke volumes.

Ramos glanced helplessly at the solicitor. He glanced down at her pad again. The spiral shape had been elegantly transformed into a flowering blossom tree. He sighed heavily.

He was fucked.

56

Adila and DS Amy Lund arrived at the Gaffney's house with a carrier bag full of tea bags, biscuits, milk, cheese, bacon and bread that Adila had bought on her way to work.

'That was kind of you,' Lund said as she nodded towards the shopping bag.

'Least I could do. There are no family on the scene and Claire hasn't left the house since she heard about Jordan, so someone has to look after them,' Adila said as she knocked on the door.

Claire eventually answered. She was ensconced in a dressing gown and looked stooped and broken.

'Hi, Claire, we've picked you up a few bits to keep you going. Have you managed to eat today?'

'Not yet, I just can't face it. Thanks for the shopping though, I appreciate it.'

'How about a bit of cheese on toast, or bacon? I'll make it for you if you like while we have a chat? Perhaps Craig would like some?'

'Maybe later. Come through to the kitchen and I'll put the

kettle on. Please don't bother Craig, I've just looked in on him and he's finally asleep.'

They followed Claire into the kitchen where she carefully shut the door so their voices wouldn't travel upstairs and disturb Craig. Claire began to fill the kettle despite Adila offering to take over. 'I'll do it, it helps to keep busy,' said Claire. 'Amy. Tea, coffee, hot chocolate or I can even offer you a hot Bovril.'

'Bovril would be lovely, I've not had that in years. It's just the thing on a cold day like today.'

'It's Jordan's favourite, personally I can't stand the smell.' Claire winced. 'It *was* Jordan's favourite. I can't ever imagine getting used to saying that. There are so many reminders, it's like he's still here. Like I'm dreaming my worst nightmare and any minute it's just going to stop. Except it isn't, is it?' Grief physically weighed her down. She was a husk of a woman, so drained she didn't even have any tears left.

'I promise you, we're doing everything we can. The laptop you gave us last time has gone to digital forensics and we're expecting a result back from Jordan's phone later today. We're currently looking into a number of lines of enquiry, we're going to find out who did this and get you closure. It's the very least you deserve.'

Claire began to prepare the drinks and Lund frowned at Adila when her back was turned. It was wrong for her to promise something like that as there were never any guarantees in any investigations. Adila shrugged back at Lund helplessly. She knew as she'd said the words it was wrong, but the poor woman looked so broken, she wanted to offer some reassurances.

'When we talked last time,' said Lund, 'you told us about Jordan's friends. Is there anyone else you can think of who Jordan might have confided in?'

'He's close to Mr Ramos at school. He teaches PE and runs the school football team. Neither Craig or I are into sports, so he's always chewing Ramos's ear off about football.'

'Have you met him?'

'Yeah, loads of times. At football matches and cross-country training mainly. Jordan never stops talking about him.'

'What's he like?'

'He's a lovely man, clearly got a soft spot for Jordan. He used to teach Craig too and he's always struck me as a decent and dedicated teacher.'

'Okay, this is a little delicate, but an accusation has been made that Guy Ramos might have been, erm – inappropriate – towards some of the boys. Had Jordan ever indicated that that was the case?'

'God no. Absolutely not. Whoever has suggested that is lying. I honestly believe Guy Ramos is a good man, a genuinely caring teacher and someone who has always been a fantastically supportive role model to Jordan. I don't believe that for one second, whoever has suggested that is twisted.'

'And as far as you're concerned, Jordan's relationship with Mr Ramos was confined to school. He would never have visited his house or met up with him after school, other than at a school sporting event.'

'No. That's a horrible suggestion. I have absolutely no concerns about Mr Ramos's integrity.'

'What about Lewis? Did you ever hear him speak about Ramos?'

Claire snorted. 'Lewis Mellor never had a decent thing to say about anyone in that school and I assume the feeling was mutual towards him. Don't get me wrong, Lewis has always been polite towards me, but he's a cheeky kid and I know he's always in trouble at school. I overheard him moaning that Mr Ramos had given him a detention on a few occasions and made claims that he was always picking on him, but he said similar about other teachers too.'

'Has he ever made any claims suggesting that he thought Mr Ramos was being inappropriate?'

'Never.'

'If, and from what you've told me, it's a big if, Ramos had overstepped the mark with Jordan, would he have told you?'

'Definitely, but I am adamant that nothing like that ever happened. Jordan certainly showed no signs of anything like that and I *know* Mr Ramos, trust me he certainly isn't the type. I can't imagine him ever being inappropriate towards a student.'

Adila and Lund returned to Beech Field in time for the daily MIT briefing.

'For what it's worth,' said Adila, 'Claire has convinced me that the accusations about Ramos are bullshit. I'm curious to know how Sean and Adebayo got on in the interview.' They settled themselves in the conference room and waited for DCI Chambers to gather updates from the day's various enquiries.

Adila and Lund listened avidly to Adebayo's account of Ramos's interview, and exchanged a look, both agreeing that there was no concrete evidence that showed anything untoward had happened. As it stood, the accusations were nothing more than pure speculation.

'And what was the result of the house search?' Chambers asked.

'We found nothing of note but have seized his phone and iPad for submission to digital,' said Sean.

'Speaking of which, ma'am,' came a voice from the back of

the room, and everyone turned to look at Jack. 'I've just received an update from Jordan's phone. Apparently, it looks like his phone ran out of charge and the battery died Sunday afternoon, but before that happened, earlier that morning he made and received phone calls to two people who they have identified as being Lewis Mellor and Guy Ramos. They've also had a preliminary look on Ramos's phone and one of the latest images he has, is the photo of one of his pupils.'

Chambers' eyes lit up. 'Give Adebayo and Sean details including times and length of calls, then get back down to custody and let him have it.'

Ramos was marched back into the interview room and Adebayo reconvened without preamble.

'Earlier we asked you if Jordan Gaffney had your mobile number. You claimed he didn't, that it would be a breach of school rules.'

'That's right.'

'I'd like to ask you again. Did you and Jordan exchange phone numbers?'

'No.'

'I'm going to show Mr Ramos a printout of data and ask him if he can identify either of the phone numbers listed.'

Ramos visibly paled as he looked at the sheet in front of him.

'Do you recognise the number listed here?'

'No comment.'

Adebayo raised an eyebrow at Ramos as he continued. 'How about the second number?'

'No comment.'

'The first mobile number is yours and the second is Jordan Gaffney's, isn't it?'

'No comment.'

'On Sunday morning, Jordan rang you, didn't he? The call lasted approximately five minutes. What were you talking about?'

'No comment.'

'Did he ring you to say he was available to meet you?'

'No comment.'

'Was it a secret assignation that you had instigated earlier in the week? At school? Jordan had been missing a lot of school lately, was that because he was avoiding you? Were you pressurising him, coming on too strong?'

'No comment.'

'And then, an hour later you called Jordan back and spoke for a further two minutes. Why did you ring him back? Had you arranged to meet and he hadn't turned up? Were you ringing him to let him know you'd arrived? Because we know from *your* phone data that the second call, when you rang Jordan, you were in the area of the Glendale fields.'

'No comment.'

'It's a big place, did you phone him because you were struggling to find him?'

'No comment.'

'Did you arrange to meet him at the Glendale fields because you knew it was an isolated area where not many people go? Is that why you suggested meeting there, so you wouldn't be disturbed?'

'No comment.'

'We have seen the photo of the lad on your phone. Have you anything to tell us about that?'

'No comment.'

'The photo was taken near the Glendale fields, wasn't it?'

'No comment.'

'Were you having an inappropriate relationship with one of your pupils?'

'No comment.'

'Mr Ramos, did you murder Jordan Gaffney?'

Ramos began to cry.

57

The fugitive believed in the adage, 'patience is a virtue'. It had taken him a long time to track down the address. It's not as if he could follow Maya there, that would be far too risky. He would stand out far too much and risk being seen. Some things took a little more work and investigation than others. Fortunately, a lifetime of being surrounded by criminals had taught him the skills to do what he needed to do.

Now his patience really was being tested as he took one of his biggest risks yet. He couldn't chance hanging around the house waiting to see if he had her new address. It was one of those places where the neighbours were prone to curtain twitching, and in their absence, the fish-eyed CCTV lens would blinkingly observe and record his every movement.

After doing a reconnaissance of the area with the help of Google Maps street view, he had known what to do. He knew how he could get eyes on without anyone paying him a blind bit of notice. Hiding in plain sight was his preferred choice and the darkness and gloomy weather would help mask his presence. The inclement weather was his friend; no nosy dog walker having been battered by the wind and rain would stop to talk to him when a warm house and hot drink were beckoning.

He had procured a nondescript work van and telecommunications tent which he positioned outside the convenient green fibre box. It was an innocuous piece of street furniture that few people gave a second glance, and he was confident that likewise, he would go unnoticed and unobserved.

To match his façade, he had a makeshift toolbox in which he had also secured a small pair of binoculars, the knuckleduster, taser and knife. He was leaving nothing to chance. If anyone decided to get involved they would just have to become collateral damage. Once he was finished here, the tent and the van would be discarded in such a way that not one single piece of forensic evidence would remain.

The rain battered the tent, the wind plucking at its hem as he remained squatted on the foldable plastic stool. He didn't flinch, shiver or shift with discomfort, he remained motionless – other than his eyes which scanned the house for signs of movement. He knew she was in there, in order to confirm he did have the right address, he just needed to see her leave.

As he sat and waited, surveying the property, he wondered what had prompted her to move here. Oh, he had so many questions, but there was no guarantee he would have time to ask them let alone her answer them. When the time came for them to be together it would be short but oh-so sweet. He grinned to himself as he instinctively slipped a gloved hand into the toolbox and felt for the blade.

And then at last, his patience was rewarded. From his vantage point he heard the clicking of locks resound across the street, the sound carried to him by the wind. He watched her glance nervously up and down the street and smiled to himself, she was right to be cautious. She darted out of the front door like a mouse from its hole, snatched up the bottle of milk and disappeared back inside, where he could hear the locks turning again. At last, he had his confirmation.

This was Dominique's new address.

58

———————

Lewis and Sarah were brought back to the interview room to be questioned by Malone and Turner. Both the Mellors radiated their usual hostility, but with an edge of nervousness.

'Lewis, last time my colleagues spoke to you in here, you were asked when you had last seen Jordan. Have you remembered yet?'

'No.'

'Despite having time to think about it since you were asked. Despite finding out that your best friend has been murdered. Think again please, Lewis, when did you last see him?'

'I've told you, I dunno.'

'Remember,' Sarah interjected, 'he's been under a lot of pressure, what with the stabbing, the fing with his dad and like you said, finding out his best friend has been murdered. His head is all over the place.'

'I appreciate that,' said Malone, 'but it's not a difficult question.'

There was a stony silence.

'Perhaps,' said Turner, 'it's easier for you to remember when you last spoke to Jordan, or even texted him.'

'I dunno.'

'You've got your phone with you, perhaps you'd like to check?'

Lewis shrugged.

'In fact, what we *can* do is ask our experts to look at the phone for us and they'll let us know.'

'You're not having me phone.' Lewis glanced at Sarah and she squeezed his arm reassuringly.

'Okay, in that case I'll tell you when you last spoke to Jordan. He rang you and you both had a three-minute conversation on Saturday afternoon. You then texted him on Sunday morning at 10.15am asking where he was. He replied he was ten minutes away and you sent another text telling him to hurry up because it was freezing at Glendale and you were fed up of waiting.'

A hushed silence descended as Lewis and Sarah exchanged a glance.

'In short, Lewis, the information from Jordan's phone puts you in the location he was murdered and with the time and date of these messages, suggests you were one of, if not the last person, to see Jordan alive.'

'Fuck this!' screamed Sarah as she lurched towards Turner, waving a finger in his face. 'Fuck you. You're try'n'a set him up.'

Turner gave her a level stare which made her sit back down. 'I'm doing nothing of the kind. I'm presenting him with the facts. If you carry on like that, I'll have you removed and ask for another appropriate adult to sit in on the interview.'

'All right yeah, you're right, he did ring me and we did meet. I didn't tell you before 'cause I knew you were gonna be like this, and like me mum said, gonna set me up.'

'That's not what we're doing, Lewis. We're only interested in the facts and lying to us is going to stop us finding Jordan's killer. You don't you want that, do you? He was your best friend.'

Lewis looked red-eyed as he folded his arms and stared at

the floor. 'He rang me on the Saturday and asked me to meet him at Glendale. We'd not been getting on and he said he wanted to talk to me. I got there at ten and there was no sign of him so after a bit I texted him and he replied that he was on his way. I was fuming when he eventually turned up, 'cause it was freezing and he'd left me waiting after asking *me* to meet him.'

'Did he say why he was late?'

'Somat about his bike being damaged so he'd had to walk.'

'Then what?'

'We talked.'

'About what?'

'Why we'd not been getting on. Jordan could be a bit stuck-up sometimes, like a proper brown-nose and I thought he was starting to look down on me. I wanted to do stuff he wasn't interested in.'

'Like what?'

'I dunno, just hanging about the precinct and that. Having a laugh. Jordan just wanted to play football and be with Ramos.'

'Can you explain what you mean by "be with Ramos"?'

'Yeah, like, I told you Ramos was all over him, that's why he hated me. Me and Jordan argued 'cause I said I knew there was somefink going on between them both and it was wrong. He started getting all defensive about it, and being really nasty. And he looked like he'd been proper leathered, like he had all these bruises around his neck and they looked really sore.'

'Did he say how he'd got them?'

'No, I asked if Ramos had done it and he just went nuts. Proper kicking off with me, so I left. I didn't know I wouldn't see him again, did I?'

'Did you fight?'

'No.'

'Are you sure? It's important because we also know that in

addition to the stab wound, Jordan also appeared to have been hit in the face as he had a cut lip and bloody nose.'

'I didn't hit him, we just argued. I really wish we hadn't, or he might still be here.' He looked down at the table as tears brimmed in his eyes. He sniffed noisily and wiped his nose with his sleeve. 'I was gutted that we'd fallen out. I missed him and was hoping we could make up. Everything felt, I dunno, hopeless, so that's when I rang me dad and went to his. I just wanted to get away, I hate it round here.'

'And you left Jordan there?'

'Yeah, I fink he started walking back too, but I dunno, I didn't look back.'

'Did you see anyone else as you were leaving?'

'No.'

'Anybody at all, any dog walkers, other kids?'

'No, we hardly ever do, that's why we've always gone there 'cause it's always dead quiet.'

'Just to be really clear here, and think very carefully before you answer, are you absolutely sure that you did not see or speak to anybody else at Glendale when you met Jordan?'

Lewis exchanged a fleeting look with Sarah and rubbed a hand over his mouth. 'No.'

'Okay, let's take a break for now. We'll go and get you some more drinks.'

Malone and Turner left the room and huddled conspiratorially in the corner. 'What do you think?' Malone asked.

'That we need to search Lewis's *and* his dad's. We only have his word that he didn't hurt Jordan. They'd been arguing so he had motive. And it would make sense why he suddenly decided to disappear to his estranged dad's after all this time. Personally, I don't believe him. I think he's lying, his body language is giving him away, did you see him cover his mouth when he said no?'

'Yeah.' Malone nodded. 'He's definitely hiding something.'

Turner glanced down at his phone. 'The boss has just texted, she's called a briefing, apparently something has come back on forensics. Let's go.'

Those free to attend the briefing, who weren't involved in interviews or other enquiries, filed into the conference room with eager anticipation. Maya and Chris flanked Kym as they joined her at the front next to Chambers.

'People, thanks for taking time out to listen to the update. Before we go ahead, has anyone had anything pertinent so far?'

Turner raised his hand and gave the headlines from Lewis's interview so far. 'In brief, ma'am, I think we need to go through the Mellors' address and Lewis's dad's.'

'Agreed,' said Chambers. 'We'll get the wheels in motion and I'll notify Merseyside Police too for his dad's address. Kym, can you provide SOCOs for the Mellors?'

Kym nodded. 'I have Connor currently available as Tara is busy examining Ramos's vehicle. We can sit down after this and discuss the strategy if you like.'

'Thank you, and the forensic results so far, what have we got?'

'First of all, I have spoken to Dr Granger in light of the suggestion that Ramos had sexual intentions towards Jordan. He has confirmed that the PM did not find anything that confirmed these claims. That's not to say that nothing untoward has ever happened between them, but shall we say, there were no signs of recent sexual activity.

'As for the forensic results, there is good news and bad news as is often the case, I'm afraid. The blood on the knife has been confirmed to be Jordan's so both Dr Granger and I am happy we have our murder weapon. There is a mixed DNA profile from the handle which is indistinguishable. There is also some ridge detail, but unfortunately it is only a partial amount and not enough for searching on the fingerprint database. There is possibly enough for a direct one-to-one comparison.'

'That's better than nothing. I'd like both Lewis Mellor and Guy Ramos's prints comparing, please.'

Kym nodded and turned to Maya and gave her a gesture to continue.

'Ma'am,' said Maya as she produced a copy of her crime-scene notes, 'the other week, Chris and I attended the scene of a street robbery where a heavily pregnant woman was brought to the ground during an attempt to steal her phone.'

'Yes, baby Eden's mum. I'm sure we all saw the news footage of that incident at the time. How is it relevant?'

'A glove was seized from the crime scene and submitted for DNA. A full male profile was extracted, but no match on the database. A hit has just come back that confirmed Jordan Gaffney's DNA on the glove.'

A hush descended on the interview room as they all took a moment to process the information.

'Well, well, well,' said Chambers. 'I didn't see that coming. So, it transpires that Jordan wasn't the perfect teen everyone has professed him to be. The plot thickens.'

59

The cocaine was making Wheeler paranoid and tense. Plus, even he had started to notice he was putting a dent into the supply, more so than he was selling. He knew he should start laying off, but he needed the clarity and the energy rush it gave him. Reilly was on his back constantly and was threatening to send Sully for a visit, just to pile on even more pressure. Wheeler had managed to persuade him it wasn't necessary, but as he uttered the words, he was well aware of the fact he was only buying time.

He still had a shitload of gear to sell, Susie and Albert were like an albatross around his neck and then there was Jordan. He thought back to the last time he had seen him when he had gone to meet shite-mouth Lewis. The kid had looked terrified, pleading with him to take Lewis on as a courier instead of Craig. Wheeler had set them a challenge and given them both five bags of coke and said the first to sell all five and produce the most cash would win.

If Jordan won, Wheeler promised to leave Craig alone and would delete the video of him stabbing Lewis as well as giving him the knife back. He would keep Jordan on as a courier but would pay him in future. If Lewis won, he'd be taken on as a courier and would be paid well for the privilege. Both had motivation to do well. How was he to know things would turn out the way they did? He wasn't to blame for everything, it wasn't his fault. Was it?

Ramos was reminded of his rights under caution before the interview recommenced.

'Are you feeling calmer?' Sean asked.

Ramos took a sip of hot chocolate. 'Yes, thank you.'

Ramos's solicitor cleared her throat. 'My client and I have had another consultation and it is his wish that he is open and transparent about why he and Jordan Mellor exchanged mobile numbers.'

'Can't wait to hear it,' said Adebayo. 'Before you do, I'd like to remind you that we *know* Jordan rang you from near home on the Saturday and you later rang him back from the location of the fields at Glendale.'

Ramos nodded. 'It happened like you said. And I know I was fundamentally wrong to exchange my personal number with Jordan, but I promise you there was nothing sinister or predatory about my intentions. I trusted the boy implicitly which is why I broke the rules. We had a match with The Lowry a few weekends ago. The day before, the Friday, Jordan told me he wasn't feeling well so I gave him my number and told him to text me if he was no better by Saturday morning and if he wasn't going to make the game.'

'Don't you have a school mobile for things like that?'

'Yes, but I wanted to know sooner rather than later. He's my star player so if he wasn't going to show I needed time to rethink match tactics. Plus, I knew his mum tended to work weekends, so I genuinely wanted to know if he was okay in case he was on his own. I know I was crossing a line, but like I've said I knew I could trust Jordan to be discreet. You've got my phone; you can see that there are no other messages or calls between the two of us.'

'Have you ever used alternative phones, ones just for you and Jordan?'

'Christ, no. You're making this sound so much worse than it is.'

'We currently have a SOCO searching your car and we will also be searching your classroom, so we just need you to be sure in case we find anything.'

'I'm sure. Search whatever you like, I've got absolutely nothing to hide.'

'What can you tell me about the photograph on your phone?'

Ramos groaned and ran a hand through his hair. 'It's a photo I took of Lewis Mellor at Glendale. The day Jordan rang me, obviously.'

'What happened?'

'Jordan rang me at home in the morning in quite a state. He wouldn't go into detail, but he said that he had got himself into some trouble and his mum had taken the wheels off his bike as a punishment. He was very apologetic about phoning me but asked if he could borrow mine. He knew I had one gathering dust as it was a standing joke that I'd tell him I might go out on it at the weekend and come the following Monday morning, of course I never did.'

'And you agreed?'

'Yes, I asked him where he was and he said he was meeting someone near the fields at Glendale. That's quite far from my house, so I offered to take the bike to him. Again, I know it was wrong, but I wanted to help him. I'd told him often enough he could rely on me, so I felt obliged.'

'The photo?' Adebayo prompted.

'Ah, yes. I arrived and was about to get out of the car when I saw Lewis Mellor heading away from the fields. Thankfully he didn't see me. He looked... I don't know, flustered and angry. He was clearly in a rush the speed he was walking.' Ramos tutted. 'He's never been a good runner, and he's even worse at football.

'Anyway, I took a photo of him. I honestly don't know why really, I guess it was because I was concerned for Jordan and seeing Lewis like that, I assumed they might have had a fight. I knew they hadn't been on good terms since Lewis was stabbed. If they had fought, I wanted proof that Lewis had been there. I didn't really think it through, it was instinctive.'

'Because you always think the worst of Lewis?'

Ramos nodded. 'Probably, yes. That's a fair comment.'

'Then what?'

'After Lewis had gone, I phoned Jordan to let him know I was there. He apologised for messing me about and said he didn't need the bike anymore. He sounded genuinely sorry. I asked him if he was okay, and he assured me he was. He said sorry again and then told me he would see me on Monday. Obviously, he didn't because something else happened after that and he was killed.' Ramos began to tear up.

'When you spoke to him the second time, did he sound like he was on his own or was someone else with him?'

'I assumed he was on his own. I couldn't hear anyone in the background.'

'This is the murder investigation of a boy you openly admit you genuinely cared for and you haven't thought to tell us any of this earlier?'

'No, because you started straight away suggesting I was some kind of sexual predator. I'd broken the rules exchanging numbers with Jordan and I knew you'd jump on it and twist it into something it wasn't as well as making me look like the number one suspect when you should be out there looking for him, not wasting time on me.'

'Him?'

Ramos looked exasperated. 'Jordan's killer.'

'What makes you say "him"?'

'Oh God, I don't know. See, this is exactly what I mean, you read too much into everything. I just *assume* it was a male. Statistically it's inevitable if nothing else.'

'You saw Lewis leaving the scene and didn't mention this earlier. That could have been relevant, he could be a potential suspect.'

'How? I spoke to Jordan after Lewis left and he sounded fine. Plus, the fact that as I was driving home I saw Lewis again at a bus stop near Bridgewater Road and he was getting on a bus going towards town. I've made it perfectly clear I think Lewis is a lot of things, but I don't believe he was involved in Jordan's murder.'

60

'**G**ood morning, everyone, thank you for your attention,' said Chambers. Despite working around the clock like everyone else involved in the investigation, she looked as polished as ever without a hint of fatigue shadowing her face.

'We managed to cover a lot yesterday. In brief, Guy Ramos has been released on bail and he has also made a convincing plea that he believes Lewis Mellor isn't culpable. Which brings me to your team, Kym, how did they get on at the Mellors' house?'

'Well, I wouldn't be too quick to cast Lewis off as a suspect. Connor recovered a burner phone in his bedroom which he had taken great pains to secrete at the back of his radiator.'

'Suspicious,' said Chambers.

'Exactly. He also discovered a hooded top at the back of the wardrobe with blood on the sleeves and down the front. When I say the back of the wardrobe, I mean the wardrobe had been pulled away from the wall and it had been tucked down there.'

'Well, well, well.'

'Both have gone for analysis so watch this space.'

'Good work, thank you. I spoke to Merseyside this morning

and they have drawn a blank at the dad's house. The dad was quick to say that when Lewis left he made sure he took all his stuff with him and he's not welcome back. The other thing that doesn't add up is the time he rolled up at his dad's. It was nearly midnight before Lewis got there apparently, so he has some explaining to do as to where he was since leaving the fields and going into town. I don't think we'll get more from the dad; he's made it abundantly clear that Lewis means nothing to him.'

'Nice guy,' muttered Adebayo.

Chambers turned on him. 'Are you offering an update?'

'Yes, ma'am, as you said Ramos is out on bail and just when we think we may be a suspect down, we have someone else in the frame.'

'Don't beat about the bush.'

'Digital confirmed there has been no other communication between Ramos and Jordan, but another number has come to light. Jordan rang someone else on Saturday afternoon from Glendale. Intelligence suggests that the number he rang belonged to a renowned drug dealer named Ivo Zlatan.'

There was a stunned silence in the room. 'So, our squeaky-clean murder victim has been stealing phones off pregnant ladies *and* was in cahoots with drug dealers. This is the case that just keeps giving.'

'We're trying to track Zlatan down,' said Jack, 'but our experience of past dealings with him have shown that he can be a very slippery fish.'

'Understood but let's make him a priority, please.' She looked at Adila and Lund. 'Can I have a word with you both after the briefing. We're going to have to go and talk to Claire again at some point. I appreciate how hard things are for her, but we need to start digging deeper so we can get to know the truth behind Jordan. Let's go back and speak to friends and neighbours again first. Something is not sitting right and the only way we're going to get to the bottom of this is to find out exactly what Jordan has been hiding and why.'

Maya had missed the morning meeting as she was due at her next EMDR session. Thoughts of the case consumed her and were a much-needed distraction. With each session, she felt like she was getting closer to remembering the past, and although her anxiety levels were dropping every time, she still felt the usual trepidation. Anticipation, when it wasn't connected to something nice, was a stressful feeling.

The session picked up where it had left off last time, with Maya's realisation that it wasn't just Grandad covered in blood on the floor and the terrifying image of Naylor stood in the lounge. To visualise him so clearly in such a familiar room after all these years would normally be terrifying, but the EMDR process had masked her anxiety, so much so that she felt ready to continue.

'Last time you said you were going to run, stay with that.'

Maya concentrated on the movement of Jayne's fingers. 'What are you feeling now?'

'I run. Or at least I try too. My legs won't work. It's the sensation of dreaming when you know you need to get away, but you can't move your legs. I'm rooted to the spot with fear. Naylor is still screaming and coming towards me and I know there's someone else in the room with him.'

'Keep going.' Carefully monitoring that Maya wasn't in too much distress, Jayne continued the movement for longer this time, really allowing Maya to recall the memory. She eventually stopped.

'Okay, what have you got?'

'I've moved away from him. To the other person in the room. I can barely recognise her. She kept her hair long in those days.'

'Who did, Maya, who's in the room with you?'

'Mama.'

'She's screaming at him. And she's covered in blood too.'

'Steady your breathing, everything is okay. Do you need a minute?'

'No. It's okay. I go to her because I know she's going to stop him. I've never seen her like this. She looks feral, she's screaming at him and swearing. Awful words. But I know she's going to keep us safe. I know she's not scared of him now and she's going to stop him.'

'Why is that, Maya?'

Maya shrugged simply. 'Because she's holding a baseball bat and she's screaming that she's going to kill him.'

61

____

Operation Scabbard seemed to hit a wall. It truly was a case of one step forward, two back. Chambers was itching to have Lewis interviewed again but was reluctantly holding off until she had results back from the burner phone and the blood on the clothing. Detectives were also turning over every stone to flush out Ivo Zlatan who was at the top of the suspects list on a par with Lewis.

Unfortunately, despite their best endeavours, Zlatan was currently nowhere to be seen, or he was too well protected in the underworld that he had built around himself. Guy Ramos had been pretty much exonerated, although suspended from school and with strict instructions to report daily to Beech Field police station.

Lund and Adila arrived at the Gaffneys' house ready to talk to Claire and update her on what they had discovered about Jordan. This was not going to be an easy conversation and they were both dreading it.

'I'll take the lead with this,' Lund said as they waited at the front door. 'She may well get agitated when we present her with the new information. I'd rather get the flack for it and you can remain impartial so it doesn't impact on your relationship as FLO.'

Adila nodded and broke into a smile as Claire opened the door. 'Morning, did you manage to sleep?' she asked as they followed Claire into the lounge.

'A little, thanks. The tablets from the doctor helped, but I'm wary of taking them, I don't want to get too dependent.'

'Can I make us all tea?'

'If you don't mind. I'd do it, but it just seems too much effort today. My limbs feel like lead; I feel like I'm drowning.'

'It's not a problem. You just let me know if I can do anything else while I'm here. I'll put a wash on before I go, eh? Maybe some fresh clothes will help? Is Craig up yet?'

'Yes, he's gone out for a walk to the fields. I was worried at first it was too macabre, but it seems to settle him. People have left flowers and balloons at the entrance for Jordan and he likes to look at them. Anyway, it's a bright day, the fresh air will do him good,' Claire said robotically, slipping into parent dialogue.

She looked terrible, every movement seemed to cause her physical pain and her stature had withered. She was clearly ensconced in the chemical fug of the sleeping tablets. As Lund watched Adila head to the kitchen she knew she would have to tread very carefully with the information she had to share.

'Claire, I appreciate how much you're suffering at the moment and believe me when I say that the last thing I want to do is add to that, but there are a few developments that have come to light which have made us question the type of things Jordan was involved in. Before I tell you though, I want you to know that everything we have heard about Jordan, everything you, his teachers, friends and neighbours have told us paint a picture of what a wonderful, caring, decent boy he was and nothing can ever taint his memory.'

What little colour Claire did have in her face drained away. She opened her mouth to speak but didn't have the words. She merely gestured with her hand for Lund to continue.

'Also, bear in mind that there may be perfectly reasonable explanations for the information we have received. My job is to present you with the facts we have so far, I'm not casting aspersions and I'm certainly not accusing Jordan of anything untoward. I'm on your side and want more than anyone to find out who killed Jordan. Do you understand?'

'Just tell me.'

'A few weeks ago, there was an attempted street robbery where someone tried to snatch a phone out of a lady's hand. She was heavily pregnant and fell during the struggle.'

'Baby Eden? I read about that; it was shocking,' Claire said, wide-eyed. She covered her ears. 'Oh, no. No, don't say he–'

'A glove seized from the offender was sent for DNA analysis and a full DNA profile has come back matching Jordan.'

'No, no, no.'

Adila appeared at Claire's side and placed an arm around her trembling shoulders. 'Like Amy said, we're just presenting you with the facts. There could be a number of innocent explanations.'

'What if someone else – the mugger – had taken Jordan's gloves?'

'Well, yes. That's one line of enquiry that would explain it.'

'Lewis,' said Claire adamantly as she slapped the top of her legs. 'My Jordan wouldn't hurt a fly let alone a pregnant lady. He was the type of lad who would have offered to carry her shopping bags, he'd never hurt her in a million years. He'd never harm a baby; he was great with little ones.'

'But Lewis?'

'Lewis could easily have taken Jordan's gloves and used them for the mugging.' She looked up suddenly, eyes shining. 'It makes perfect sense now. I told the two detectives, one was called Sean, can't remember the name of the older one. They came to see me after Lewis had been reported missing and I assumed they were here because I'd just reported Jordan.

'I told them I had found a load of mobile phones in his schoolbag. I went mad when I saw them because I knew it wasn't right. He said he was minding them for Lewis and not to make a big deal of it. He said he needed to give the phones back to Lewis so he wouldn't get hurt.

'Naturally that scared me because, as you know, Lewis had already been stabbed in the leg. I have no doubt that was because of whatever it was he'd become involved in. I've known Lewis since he was in reception class, and I care about the lad, so I didn't want to make things worse for him. Plus, I thought if I stopped Jordan returning the phones then he'd get dragged into Lewis's mess too.

'Now you've told me about the mugging, it makes sense that Lewis must have been wearing Jordan's gloves when he mugged that poor woman. It's the sort of thing Jordan would never do, but Lewis certainly would.'

Lund referred to her notes. 'We do know a string of similar offences were reported in the area leading up to the baby Eden job. Witnesses have described a teenage boy wearing all dark clothing, face covered with a hood and mask and riding a bike.'

'There you go then. With such a generic description, it could be any teenage boy in the UK. I have no doubt it was Lewis, wearing Jordan's gloves.'

'Does Lewis have a bike do you know?'

'I think his last one got stolen outside their house back in summer. He either gets the bus or Jordan gives him a backie. He may well have borrowed Jordan's bike while he was at football practice. Jordan is the sort of boy– sorry...' She closed her eyes as she winced in pain.

'Jordan *was* the sort of boy who would give you his last penny. Lewis clearly took advantage. It wouldn't be the first time. When I think of the number of Jordan's things he's borrowed over the years...' She shook her head. 'And those things that *have* come back have never been in one piece. He never looked after things like Jordan did.'

Adila went to the kitchen to fetch the drinks whilst Lund finished making some notes.

'That's really useful information, thank you. The other thing that has come to light is a phone call Jordan made on the day he was killed. We know that, according to his phone he would still have been at the fields when he made it and the call lasted about fifteen minutes.'

'Who was it to?'

'A man named Ivo Zlatan.'

Claire shook her head as she took a cup of tea from Adila. 'Never heard of him. It's an unusual-sounding name to me, I'd certainly have remembered if Jordan had mentioned it in the past. Maybe he's got something to do with the football team? Mr Ramos will know.'

Adila and Lund exchanged a look. 'No, Claire,' Lund said. 'Our records show that Ivo Zlatan is a prolific local drug dealer.'

Claire's hand shook as she placed her cup on the table and they waited for her to speak.

'There you go then,' she said eventually. 'It all makes sense. This is Lewis again. He must have called him from Jordan's phone. It was Lewis that Jordan met and the night before he disappeared, we argued.'

'About?'

'I could smell cigarette smoke on his coat. No, not just cigarettes, I could smell weed, you know, cannabis. I asked him about it and he said he wasn't smoking it but a few of the kids he was hanging around with were. I've mentioned before how

Jordan and Lewis had fallen out because Lewis had started to dabble in drugs and Jordan wasn't interested. He was always too absorbed in football and other sports to mess with that stuff. This is the kid who used to insist I cut the fat off his bacon for goodness' sake because he didn't want his arteries clogging.'

She gave a dry laugh which died in her throat as she stared despondently at the carpet.

'We know what time the call was made from Jordan's phone. We also know what time Lewis left the fields. Jordan made the call after Lewis left.'

'How do you know what time Lewis left?'

'We have a witness. We can't disclose details at this stage, but we trust the veracity of that person's claims.'

'Okay.'

'This witness evidence suggests that when Lewis left the scene, Jordan was still alive. We believe Jordan made the phone call to Zlatan.'

'Or somebody using Jordan's phone?' she said sharply.

Lund faltered. 'Well, yes that's another consideration. I just wanted to present you with the facts so far so we can get an insight into Jordan's movements. Like I said before, I'm on your side.'

'I know,' said Claire wearily. 'I'm sorry.'

'There is something else we needed to ask. We know from the eyewitness that Lewis left on foot. I assume Jordan walked to Glendale too. Is that his bike in the yard, the one that's broken or did he have another? If so, we're conscious of the fact it may have been stolen from the scene and it will be useful to do a press release with a description of the bike, preferably with a photograph if you have one.'

Claire gasped suddenly and looked like she'd been winded. She struggled to catch her breath. In an instant Adila had knelt in front of her and taken hold of her hands. 'It's okay, slow, steady breaths. Take your time, I've got you. Copy me and take nice easy breaths, in through your nose and out through your mouth.'

'Is she okay?' Lund asked.

'Panic attack,' said Adila succinctly as she exaggerated her own breathing for Claire to copy.

Feeling helpless, Lund went to the kitchen to fetch a glass of water and for some kitchen roll to stem the tears that were streaming down Claire's face. She left them on the table and sat and watched as Adila managed to calm Claire down. She sat shaking, looking worse than ever, as Adila placed a blanket around her shoulders and held the glass for her as she took small sips.

Eventually the sobs subsided and Claire sniffed. 'Mum used to say that grief makes invalids of us all. She was right, look at the state of me.'

'What's upset you?' Adila asked softly.

'The bike. It's all my fault. I told you how we'd argued the previous day and I took the wheels off his bike to teach him a lesson.'

'That doesn't make you a bad mum,' cooed Adila.

'It fucking does,' spat Claire. 'If he'd not been on foot he would have cycled to the fields and away from whoever killed him. If it wasn't for me Jordan would still be alive.'

It was 2am and Zlatan was armed and ready to strike. He had his three best soldiers in the car with him and they were just waiting for the perfect moment. They had been parked outside the flats for an hour. Before that one of Zlatan's men had eyes on and had reported the comings and goings. The last sighting of Wheeler had been ninety minutes ago when he had arrived back and walked unsteadily to the building. He had been seen to take a line of coke before he exited his car and headed into the block.

Zlatan knew drugs and he knew there was nothing more foolish than a dealer that took his own stock. By now, rather than making him sharper, the excess of coke and weed he had ingested during the day would have numbed Wheeler's brain. Not that he had much to numb. The man had aways been and would always be nothing more than a walking cum stain.

He had been pleasantly surprised to hear from Jordan on that Sunday morning. The lad had phoned him, pleading and desperate. He had told him that he was up to his neck in it with Wheeler and he wanted out. He said Wheeler had promised he would let him go if he could sell five bags of cocaine for the maximum value. He had begged and pleaded for Zlatan to take the drugs and give him the cash. Zlatan had assured him that such a transaction could occur quickly and easily, and he would even deliver the boy to Wheeler's door so he could collect his prize.

At a price.

First, Zlatan demanded to know the set-up in the flat, if Wheeler had any weapons concealed in there and any idea of what time he would typically come and go. The boy had sung like a canary, which was why Zlatan and his boys were now sat outside the flat knowing anytime now was the perfect time to tax it.

The second condition was that Jordan would come and courier for him. Jordan had agreed.

Zlatan watched a rat scurry across the road and began to gorge itself on the remains of a dead pigeon. Vermin. Zlatan hated vermin. They relied on predating on the weakest to survive. They preyed on the dead and dying. They were scum.

'Balaclavas on, lads. We'll give it five more minutes and we're away.'

He reached into his jacket and felt the reassuring weight of the machete tucked in there. He felt the swell of adrenaline and allowed himself to ride its wave. The only drugs he needed were adrenaline, power and money.

Once they were out of the car that was it, no going back. They were committed. He knew the old man and the girl were in there, but that wasn't his concern. If they had any sense they'd stay out of the way. If they didn't, then, well, collateral damage was inevitable in his line of work.

He was about to give the nod when his mobile rang. He cursed as he lifted it out of his pocket. He clocked the number and swore again, considering whether to hang up. Instinct kicked in and he answered, knowing that this particular soldier would never bother him with anything that wasn't life or death.

'Hey.'

'Have you gone in yet?'

'No, just about to, 'sup?'

'I've just had a call. Filth are looking for you all over, man.'

Zlatan's eyes widened. 'What for?'

'There was a kid murdered on the fields near Glendale.'

'So?'

'Kid called Jordan Gaffney. Filth are saying you were one of the last people he called.'

'Fuck.'

'It's a reliable source, man. You know I wouldn't bother you with shit.'

'No, man. I know, bro. Thanks for the heads-up, speak later, yeah?'

Zlatan hung up and started the engine.

'What's up, boss, we not going in?'

'Nah, man. We're getting the fuck away from here. From this flat and this town.'

'How long for?'

'Fuck knows.'

62

There was an electric buzz coursing through Beech Field. The team were exhausted but new leads brought them renewed vigour and fresh sense of purpose as Lewis Mellor was brought in under caution. Turner began the interview without preamble.

'Did you murder Jordan Gaffney?'

'What the fu– no! Of course not, he was my best mate, why would I do that?'

'Jealousy?'

'Me, jealous of Jordan? No chance. Why would I be?'

'He was successful at school, academically above average, popular, and a renowned sportsman. No offence, Lewis, but from what we have heard, you spend more time in detention than you do in class. And then there's his home life. What do you think of Claire?'

'She's all right. Nice if not a bit stuck-up. She's always been good to me.'

'She seems a good mum. The house is spotless and even though she works all hours, there's always a home-cooked meal to come home to. Not something you've ever had, is it? When was the last time your mum cooked for you?'

'Don't start on my mum,' he said, a flash of anger rising to the surface.

'I do feel like you're bating my client. Need I remind you he's only fourteen,' said the solicitor, whilst the appropriate adult, Audrey, who was glued to his side, nodded agreement.

Malone smiled placatingly. 'Lewis, could you talk us through again what happened when you met Jordan that Sunday.'

Lewis tutted and sighed heavily. 'We arranged to meet the previous day. I texted him to see where he was 'cause he was late and it was freezing. He replied saying he was nearly there and he arrived on foot, which was odd because he's always on his bike. He said something about it being broken, I dunno. We started chatting and I was hoping we were gonna make up, but he was acting weird. He had these bruises around his neck and I asked if Ramos had done it and he went mad. Proper kicking off at me, so I left.'

'Did you hit him?'

'No.'

'Are you sure?'

'Well yeah, we just argued. I didn't do nuffink to him.'

'Okay,' said Turner, 'when we searched your house, our SOCO found a hooded top shoved between the back of your wardrobe and the wall. For the benefit of the tape, I'm showing a photograph of exhibit number CD3 which is a black hooded top. Is that yours, Lewis?'

'Dunno. Maybe. I'm not sure. I borrow my mates' clothes sometimes.'

'Our SOCO noticed some blood on the sleeves and front of the top. It's not immediately obvious with it being such a dark top, but under a strong light source you can make it out. Here's another picture taken with a torch concentrated on the area to show you what I mean. There's quite a lot isn't there? That blood has been analysed and is confirmed to be Jordan's blood.'

Lewis looked at Audrey and then his solicitor before shrugging. 'Me and Jordan was always playfighting. If it is my top, it could have happened any time.'

'We know that Jordan sustained a facial injury before he died, did you hit him?'

'I've told you, no.'

'He was bigger and stronger than you. It would make sense if you were arguing. You might have felt like getting the first punch in to defend yourself.'

'Didn't happen.'

'You were together nearly thirty minutes. It's a long time to argue.'

Silence.

'What did you do after you left Jordan?'

'Got the bus into town then decided to go and see me dad.'

'You see, this is what gets me. You've been estranged from him for years and all of a sudden you choose that weekend, that *day* to go and see him. What were you running away from?'

'Nuffink,' he sniffed, 'I just wanted to see him. I missed him.'

Audrey passed him a tissue and asked if he was okay, throwing Turner a venomous look. 'He's a fourteen-year-old boy who missed his dad, it's not too difficult to understand.'

'Did you go back to Glendale later to meet Jordan again?'

'No.'

'We know what time you left, we have a witness who saw you, but this was your stomping ground wasn't it, a place you were comfortable. You see, we'll be checking if you were in town and how long you stayed there because we know you didn't get to your dads until midnight. I think you planned town as a cover for yourself and knew you were going back to meet Jordan again.

I think your phone records will show you went back to the field twice that day.'

'I didn't. You can check what you want, I went into town and on to me dads.'

'You're a compulsive liar, aren't you?'

'Steady on,' said Audrey.

Turner ignored her and continued. 'I'm now going to show you a picture of exhibit CD4, which is an Alcatel mobile phone we discovered at the back of the radiator in your room.'

Lewis didn't flinch.

'It's what we call a burner phone,' Malone added as he tapped the image with his pen. 'It's just a cheap phone with prepaid minutes and no contract so it can't be traced. It gives the user anonymity. Typically, they're used by drug dealers.'

Lewis remained impassive.

'We've analysed the phone and it certainly appears from the nature of the text messages on there that it has been used for dealing. Is this your phone, Lewis?'

'No.'

'Have you been involved in drug dealing?'

'Did you find any in my room?'

'No, but that doesn't mean you're not dealing. If you're working for someone, we know that you'll collect the drugs from them and sell them on.'

'I'm not dealing.'

'Why do you keep a metal bar under your pillow?'

'Because it's just me and me mum, innit? In case someone breaks in and that and I need to protect her.'

'Could you do that? Use force against someone?'

'Yeah.'

'Do you always carry weapons with you?'

'No.'

'Did you threaten Jordan with a weapon?'

'No.'

'Did you hit him?'

'No.'

'You see, I think your lying, I think you did and that's how you ended up with blood on a top of yours that you then went to great pains to hide. In fact, I think you did more than just hit him. You were jealous of Jordan, which is why you fell out.

'You did meet up with him again later that day, didn't you? You planned it when you first met in the morning. It was the second time that you argued. Because you were recently stabbed, I think you were carrying a knife with you for protection, just like you have that metal bar under your pillow.

'I don't think you intended to use it, but when Jordan in your own words "just went nuts... proper kicking off", you were scared because he was bigger and stronger than you. You punched him in the face but it didn't stop him. It probably made him angrier. Did he go for you then, is that when you remembered the knife? Did you threaten him with it? Did he back off, start to run away? Did you follow him and stab him in the back? Is that what happened, Lewis?'

'No.'

'Are you left- or right-handed, Lewis?'

They were met with a wall of silence.

'Was it a shock when you realised he was dead, or did you just stab him and run off? Did you go and lay low somewhere while you tried to decide what to do?'

Lewis stared at the table.

'Did you go back to see if he was still there and then moved his body when you realised he was dead? Before you went to your dad's?'

Lewis didn't reply.

'Did you murder Jordan Gaffney?'

'No comment.'

63

———

Wheeler had no idea how close he had come to being taxed by Ivo. If Ivo had his way, Wheeler would have the imprint of a machete blade in the back of his head and a flat without so much as a gram of powder in it. Rather than waking and embracing the joy of the day however, Wheeler was in a foul mood and was already being riled by Susie.

'There's nothing to eat. Like literally nothing.' She pouted as she leant into the fridge, removing a bit of cheese and tomato that had grown fur.

'I'll get some stuff later.'

'But we're hungry now. Albert hasn't had anything since last night.'

'Make him a brew then.'

'There's not even any milk.'

'Fuck's sake, tell him to drink it black.'

'I'm not even asking you to go. Just give me some cash and I'll go.'

He turned on her. 'I've told you, you ain't leaving this flat until the gear is gone. It's asking for trouble. Just two or three more days.'

'It's okay for you, you can live on gear and booze, but honestly, I'm so hungry and Albert is too. It's not good for him having to miss meals at his age.'

'I said I'll go in a bit, now give it a rest.'

He went to walk out of the kitchen, but she grabbed his arm. The rage came out of nowhere as her voice turned into screeching white noise. He backhanded her across her face, sending her reeling. She clutched her cheek, her mouth a perfect O of shock.

'I told you to give it a rest.'

He went to walk away again, but she persisted. He decided later, when he looked back on it, that it was all her own fault; he had warned her not to push him and she had gone too far as usual.

'No, you don't get to do that again, you said it was a one-off.' She grabbed at his arm again to stop him from walking away and the next thing he knew she was pinned to the wall by her throat. She was scrabbling frantically, trying to pull his hands away. He had lifted her off her feet and her toes were trying to reach for the floor.

Her long, acrylic nails tore into the back of his hand causing stinging welts to rise. It angered him further, so he head-butted her to make her stop. His hands wrapped around her throat even more, but suddenly it wasn't her face he could see, it was Jordan's and his fingers dug into her neck, gripping and squeezing her tighter and tighter.

A sudden blow to his side was not enough to hurt him, but enough to cause him to lose his balance and it gave Susie the leverage she needed to dive away from him.

'You leave her alone, you.' Albert was posturing like a prize fighter who had forgotten he was an octogenarian. His fists raised, he shuffled on his slipper-clad feet. 'I mean it. You touch her again and your ears will be ringing.'

Wheeler let out an incredulous laugh. 'Fuck off, old man.' Wheeler mimicked the posturing as he bounced on his feet, making playful jabbing motions at Albert, who tried to block them but missed. The inevitable punch when it came ricocheted around the room as Wheeler's fist connected to Albert's cheekbone causing his head to snap back. With a moan, Albert landed in a heap on the floor and Wheeler was on him instantly, raining kicks at the old man's head and torso.

'Stop it!' Susie let out what would have been a scream, but it came out as more of a guttural croak after being strangled. She threw herself on top of her friend to protect him from the kicks. The sight of her draped over Albert, blood streaming from her face where he had head-butted her, brought Wheeler to his senses, just in time.

'Shut it, okay, just shush.' The mist had lifted as quick as it arrived and he was mortified as he looked at her. 'I told you to give it a rest. Neither of you listen.'

Albert winced as Wheeler reached for him and a pit of shame fluttered in his stomach. 'Come on, get on the couch.' He hauled the old man to his feet and Susie reached for him as she settled him, tears streaming down her face as she cooed to him that he was okay.

'Clean yourself up and make him a brew, yeah? I've got a few drops to do then I'll get some shopping in. I'll get you both a takeaway and some beers, yeah? Make up for it, like.'

He grabbed the gear, his phone, keys, knife and coat and left the flat without a backward glance.

'Are you okay?' Susie asked as she swiped the blood away from her face with her sleeve.

Albert's skin was the colour of wallpaper paste, his voice weak and scared. 'It's my hip, I think I've done something to it.'

Her heart broke as she looked at him. This innocent, gentle old man had shown her nothing but love, kindness and friendship and Wheeler had broken him. It was one thing for him to hurt her – truth be known, if this hadn't happened, she would have forgiven him again and settled into a routine of a lifetime of violence from him – but to hurt Albert was going too far. The cuckooing, drugs and violence was one thing, but she had learnt to love this old man and would protect him with her life.

'Try and stay still, everything's going to be okay, I promise.' She reached for her phone. 'I'm going to call for an ambulance and then do something else I should have done a long time ago.'

'What?'

'Report that animal to the police.'

64

Maya and Chris arrived for the late shift and were being brought up to speed with Operation Scabbard by Kym.

'MIT still have a lot of work ahead of them, but they're concentrating on obtaining CCTV footage that shows Lewis travelling towards town and then later heading back to the fields for another prearranged meet with Jordan. It's the only hypothesis we have at the moment unless something else comes to light. Something between that first and second meeting made the boys snap.'

'If there *was* a second meeting. How can we be sure?' Maya asked.

'We can't yet. What we do know though, is Lewis's top is covered in blood. We checked with Ramos and he said he didn't notice any on him when he took the photo. We've looked too and there's nothing obvious but it isn't the best quality, and he also had his hands tucked in his pockets.'

'It's a black top though, *would* it have been obvious?'

'We just don't know. But it makes sense to me that if he had no blood on him then, he got it later when he went back to meet the second time and *that's* when he attacked Jordan after they'd argued like he said they had initially.'

'Lewis goading Jordan about Ramos?' asked Maya.

Kym nodded. 'That's one possibility. At the moment it's not definite, just guesswork, we'll have to wait and see what we can get from Lewis's phone. The truth of the matter is, we might never know what went on between the two boys. When Lewis realises the odds are stacked against him, he may continue to give *no comment* interviews and it's for the court to decide.

'It'll come down to CCTV and his phone to prove his movements, and if it's his ridge detail on the knife, even better. Jordan must have been killed by someone he knew and Lewis was there, he had motive and he's clearly lying to us.'

'What's his mother had to say?'

'She's still maintaining his innocence, but I guess she would, wouldn't she? You're always going to protect your own. One thing that has come to light is that she's confessed to not really knowing much about Lewis's movements that Sunday as she'd had a skinful. She let that slip in the interview when she was kicking off.'

'Which backs up the theory that Lewis could have returned home, swapped his clothes and then scarpered to his dad's. He could have marched a herd of elephants down the hall and she wouldn't have known,' Chris said.

'Exactly.' Kym nodded. 'We're not there yet, but my money is on Lewis. It'll be interesting to see if the mum continues to protect him when the evidence is eventually presented. I suppose she'll continue to stand by him.'

'Would you though, if you knew your kid had killed someone? I mean, this isn't like shoplifting or burglary, this is as bad as it gets. I know what you're saying, she wants to protect him because she's his mum. I'd want to protect someone I loved unconditionally, but I don't know if that includes protecting a murderer,' Maya said.

'I'm with you,' said Chris. 'I'd forgive someone I loved with time, no matter how bad it was, but murder is pretty unforgivable. Let's hope we're never in that situation, eh?'

Redford appeared at the door and stopped the conversation.

'Hello, Phil, what can we do for you?' Kym asked.

'Log 1447 if you will. It's going to be keeping us busy for this evening.'

Maya turned to the computer and read out loud for Chris and Kym's benefit. 'Call to ambulance and police stating that this is the flat of an elderly man, Albert Bennett, who is the victim of cuckooing by a local dealer. The offender is a man named Owen Walsh aka Wheeler, he has left the scene having assaulted his girlfriend and the elderly occupant. Police and ambo are on scene and have confirmed the male is seriously injured and there is a large quantity of class A drugs in the kitchen.'

'Where's Wheeler now, do we know?'

'No, he's gone out to sell. A description has been circulated of him and his vehicle. Obviously when you guys go, I'll ensure officers remain at the scene so we can lock him up the minute he returns.

'I'll do some background checks on him and the other occupants and pop back in for a chat so we can agree on how to approach it. We've got the cuckooing aspect, drugs and assault, so we need to decide on the best strategy. The female is being seen to by paramedics then being brought in for interview and the old man is on his way to hospital and a patrol is following.'

Redford left and Chris slipped his coat on and began to follow him out of the office.

'Oi, where are you going?' Maya called.

'You heard the man, it'll keep us busy all night that,' he grinned, 'I'm going for food while I can.'

65

While Maya and Chris were waiting to receive more information before going to examine Albert's flat, Wheeler had returned home. He drove his car towards the car park, saw the heavy police presence and promptly did a U-turn.

'Fuck,' he muttered as he drove away and reached for his phone to call Susie. It went straight to voicemail and he knew there and then that she had turned him in. He had gone too far with the old man, and she had double-crossed him as a result. 'Bitch.'

He drove away as quickly as he could without drawing too much attention to the vehicle. No doubt she had provided his registration number. They were probably hunting for him right now. He headed to an area he knew well. It was slightly off the beaten track, with no prying eyes or CCTV cameras.

It was where he usually brought any cars he stole. He kept a stash of registration plates he had stolen previously, and he would swap these with the original plates of the stolen car. Then he would leave the vehicle parked up for twenty-four to forty-eight hours and if it hadn't moved in that time, he would sell it on, confident it had no tracker on it.

He pulled over and lit up a joint to help him concentrate. The thought of Susie double-crossing him made his blood boil and his hands shake with rage. He took another pull on the joint and willed himself to stay calm. He couldn't afford to lose his head now, he needed to think clearly. So far, he had two problems: to avoid the police and to think about what he was going to say to Reilly. He certainly knew who he was more scared of, but for now, the police were his biggest threat. He had to stay under the radar until he decided what he was going to do.

The thought of facing Reilly and Sully and telling them the drugs had been seized by the police was a no-no. It was time to cut his losses there. He'd grown weary of the intimidations and the beatings anyway. It was time to move away and start again fresh. Maybe down south, as far as London initially, then on to Brighton, that was a good scene to be able to deal. Then perhaps he could think about moving abroad, he could get his hands on a false passport quite easily.

But all that would cost money and he didn't have enough on him to be able to move straight away. He did, however, have plenty of favours he could call in. He was confident he could get a fair amount of cash and some legitimate wheels within twenty-four hours. Then tomorrow, just as it was getting dark, he would slip away. He fired off a quick text to Reilly to let him know that sales were booming, and he'd be in touch tomorrow. That would get him off his back and buy him some time. Then he finished his smoke and went to the boot of the car.

He had a bag packed with spare clothes and other essentials, just for occasions like this. He fished out a stash of unperishable food from the shopping he had bought for Susie and Albert and stuffed that into the bag. He slipped on his thicker winter jacket and pulled the hood tightly around his face and slipped on a face mask for good measure.

He felt for the handle of the knife tucked down his waistband and felt reassured by its presence. He was ready to go. He needed somewhere close he could hide out for twenty-four hours. Somewhere secluded, where nobody could find him.

He set off on the walk to the Glendale fields.

Albert had been made comfortable at The General. He'd been given pain medication and was waiting to go for X-rays. A young police officer was sat with him and he was grateful for her cheery company. She reminded him of Susie who he was longing to see. He was also grateful because he was terrified Wheeler would come bursting into the ward any moment.

He removed the oxygen mask he'd been given. 'Where's Susie? Is she okay? She's not gone back to the flat, has she?'

'No, Albert. Remember I told you she's been checked out by paramedics and she's fine. She's gone to Beech Field police station to give a statement and to help us find Wheeler. Forensics are at your flat at the moment. Once they're done the council will get it cleaned up for when you're ready to go home.'

'I'm not going home,' he said sadly, and she didn't know whether he meant because of his injuries or because he was too scared to. She decided not to ask. She didn't want the poor old boy to get himself into a state.

'Pop that mask back on, Albert, and just stay calm and comfortable, okay?' she said as she stroked his hand. His black veins stood proud against liver-spotted skin, the frailty of him saddened her.

'That thing,' he said, pointing to her body cam. 'Can it record me?'

'Yes, why?'

'I've got something I need to tell you. It's important. It's about Wheeler.'

'We'll take a proper statement off you when you're better.'

'No, now. These painkillers are already making me forgetful and if I need an operation or something, God knows how I'll be. I could be totally doolally by then.'

She laughed. 'Honestly, it can wait. Nothing is more important than getting you sorted.'

'It's about the murdered boy, Jordan Gaffney.'

The smile fell from her face and she started recording. The red light turned to green on her body cam. 'Okay, Albert. What do you want to tell me about Jordan Gaffney?' she said.

'Not long after Wheeler codded his way into my flat, a young lad rolled up looking for him. It was Jordan. When he first knocked on the door I tried to shoo the lad away but Wheeler wasn't happy with that. Poor Jordan was terrified of Wheeler and was selling drugs for him. I don't know why, because it was obvious he didn't want to. I think Wheeler was blackmailing him or something. Whatever Jordan's dealings with Wheeler, he was doing it under duress.'

Albert placed the oxygen mask over his nose and closed his eyes in pain as he took a few breaths. 'He was a nice lad, Jordan. Polite and kind. He should never have been anywhere near the likes of Wheeler. I was devastated when I read in the paper that he'd been murdered. But I think Wheeler had something to do with it.

'The night before, he came home covered in blood. Ask Susie. The first time he hit her was because he wanted her to take his clothes and bedding to the launderette. Anyway, later that night, I heard him creep out in the early hours. I was sleeping on the couch and heard him go into the cleaning cupboard. He was gone for a while and when he came back his clothes were wet through. It had been raining you see.'

He took another gulp of oxygen. 'I think he killed Jordan and went back later to hide his body. Please look into it. It's important Jordan's mum knows the truth. He was a nice boy.'

The police officer had a list of questions she wanted to ask him, but he'd grown ashen, so she settled him back and placed the oxygen mask over his face. Just then, the nurse arrived to take him to X-ray. She waved him down the corridor and radioed up, asking to speak to CID as a matter of urgency.

66

—————

The creeping sunlight woke Wheeler from his stupor. He couldn't call it a sleep really, despite the amount of weed he'd smoked, he'd just dozed intermittently. The outdoors gave him the creeps, all the unfamiliar noises and the damp that rose from the ground, chilling him to the bone regardless of all the layers he'd pulled on.

He'd slept rough many times before, but in the city where he felt safe. The countryside was no place for him. He'd called in his debts, which he would collect in a few short hours and then he would go to London where hopefully he wouldn't see a single blade of grass. The idea of Brighton after that was growing on him. He could easily sell enough gear there to be able to set himself up abroad and out of Reilly and Sully's way for good.

He sat up, groaning as his joints resisted against the cold and damp. He stretched, farted and took himself for a piss. Then he lit up another joint which he smoked quickly. He rooted in the bag for some food and ate a chocolate bar and packet of crisps, washed down with an energy drink. Sated, with the sun now risen and casting a weak lemon pall across the fields, he began to take in his surroundings. It had been too dark when he arrived last night to be able to get his bearings.

In the distance, not too far, he could see helium balloons bobbing weakly in the damp air. Their gases had been exhausted and they were drifting more towards the ground than the sky. Dipping like deflated lungs on shiny red ribbon away from heaven and towards hell. He realised this was part of the memorial shrine left for Jordan and felt a fleeting murmur of guilt, which he shrugged off as if he was batting a bluebottle away.

He realised now how close he was to where he had last met Jordan. Instinctively his eyes scanned the ground for traces of blood. He knew there was none, that it would all have been washed away when the crime-scene tape was removed, so why was it he could imagine spots of it glistening back at him from the wet grass? Like drops of Pinot Noir splashed on the ground.

Jesus, the coke was making him paranoid. He vowed, when he got settled down south, he would never touch it again. Ever. He would start to lay off the weed too. He smoothed his clothes down and adjusted the knife in his waistband. He might as well pay a quick visit to Jordan's makeshift memorial whilst he was here. He would pay his respects, clear his conscience before he moved on to pastures new.

Because of the cordon protecting the crime scene at the Glendale fields, Jordan's memorial had started at the entrance. Craig liked to walk to it and read the messages people had left for Jordan. It helped to know how much his brother had been liked; to see how popular he was. Since the crime-scene tape had been removed, he also liked to walk the fields and see if he could sense Jordan's soul being carried on the breeze.

As he neared the memorial, he saw a familiar face also approaching, from across the fields. Someone who he'd not seen for a while, but he'd recognise anywhere. Wheeler had seen him too and hesitated briefly, as if he was going to run back to the direction he came from. Then he regained his usual swaggering posture and ambled towards Craig.

'Ait,' he said, extending a hand. 'Good to see you, bro. Look, I'm really sorry to hear about what happened to little-man.'

Craig looked down at Wheeler's hands with utter disdain, his hands remained in his jeans pocket. 'You're not my bro. Jordan was. You can't even say his name. You're not worthy of saying it.'

'Woah, where's this coming from? I get you're upset, man, but don't go giving me beef.'

'I know it's all your fault. Jordan was fine until the day you texted him. Then he changed, he was different. I know it's all on you. You killed him.'

'No way, man. No way. Yes, I knew Jordan and he did the odd favour for me, but I didn't kill him. Watch your mouth.'

Paranoid as ever, Wheeler looked around to see if anyone was about who might have overheard the exchange. The second his face was turned away, Craig raised his fist and swung a punch at Wheeler. Within moments, they were rolling around in the wet grass, exchanging kicks and punches. Craig was bigger and stronger and quickly had the advantage as he pinned Wheeler to the ground and began to punch him, ceaselessly.

All Wheeler could do was protect himself against Craig, using his right forearm to deflect the blows as his left hand reached into his waistband and closed around the handle of the knife.

~

'Craig?' Claire called as she climbed down the stairs. 'Do you want a brew?'

Her head was thick with sleep and felt muggy, her tongue furred. Although the medication helped her sleep so she could temporarily numb the pain, she didn't like how she felt on waking. She felt sluggish, the pain of grief enveloped her the moment she woke, forcing her out of an otherwise comfy bed. The yearning for Jordan was so visceral it was a physical ache.

'Craig?' she called again as she peered into the empty lounge. He wasn't in the kitchen either. She looked at her watch and realised he must have gone for his morning walk to the fields. She could check on her phone tracker. That's when she noticed he had left his mobile on the kitchen table and panic gripped her. The fear of not being able to see where he was and get hold of him...

Mother's instinct saw her reaching for her car keys and, still clad in her nightwear, haring towards the fields. She knew something was wrong. The sense of threat was real; like a white noise whose source she couldn't place. She pulled up at the entrance and ran towards the fields, car door still hanging open. She could hear the shouts before she saw them and was already ringing 999. As she rounded the corner, she could see Craig pinning Wheeler to the ground, but Wheeler made a practised movement which flipped Craig off him, and the tables were turned.

She let out a feral scream as the scene played before her eyes in seeming slow motion. Wheeler pulled the knife from his waistband and was jabbing it towards Craig. Her screams stilled them both as she hurtled towards them. But there was something about Wheeler, his face didn't look human, his eyes were animalistic as if he was lost in a red mist. She had to stop him, but she was too many paces away.

Out of nowhere, a figure raced past her and leapt at

Wheeler, knocking him away from Craig and pinning him to the grass. Guy Ramos wrestled Wheeler to the ground as Claire arrived in time to pick up the knife and move it out of harm's way.

'Are you okay?' she asked Craig, who nodded as he helped Ramos keep Wheeler pressed to the ground, while they waited for the sirens that would result in Wheeler being caged, finally where he belonged.

67

Wheeler was subdued during his interview, clearly aware that his actions had finally caught up with him. It's not as if, now he was arrested, he was free of any threat from Reilly and Sully, they could easily get to him inside. He had to come to terms with the fact he was going to have a rough ride in prison, which is why he decided he was going to confess to everything; the drugs, cuckooing, and assaults. With a good sob story prepared by his solicitor, his guilty pleas would surely diminish his sentence.

Adebayo had partnered up with Malone for the interview. Malone would clear up the drugs and cuckooing, and Adebayo would address Albert's claims that he believed Wheeler had murdered Jordan. So far Wheeler had already confessed to the cuckooing and assaulting Susie and Albert.

He also confessed to selling drugs but was adamant that the gear in the flat was all the supply he had, that there had been little more than that. He didn't name anyone else in the chain, he wasn't that stupid, throwing Reilly and Sully under the bus would be like signing his own death sentence.

'Tell me about Jordan Gaffney,' Adebayo said.

'Not much to tell. He did a bit of work for me, sold a few bags.'

'From what we know about Jordan, that doesn't sound like his scene at all. He was a good kid apparently, so how did he get involved in working for you?'

Wheeler shrugged. 'I can be persuasive.'

'You're looking at a long stretch already,' Adebayo tapped his paperwork, 'this is bigger than just drugs and cuckooing. This is a murder investigation and right now you're looking like you had motive *and* opportunity.'

'No! No way, man. Okay, truth. I met him and Lewis on the night they had a falling out. Lewis bad-mouthed Jordan and I said he had to defend himself. Told him to shank Lewis, which he did. I recorded it and kept the knife which was persuasion enough for Jordan to run some errands and keep me sweet.'

'Blackmail?'

'If you want to call it that.'

'It's what it is,' spat Malone. 'You preyed on a fourteen-year-old kid. A good kid.'

'Were you ever violent towards Jordan?' asked Adebayo.

'He wound me up a couple of times.'

'When?'

'First time I asked him to steal phones, he wouldn't do it, so he took a bit of persuading. The only other time was when I heard about the baby-momma that got hurt when he mugged her. I lost my shit, I admit it, I might have knocked him about a bit.'

'A bit?' said Malone. 'The post-mortem revealed he had extensive bruises to his neck. You strangled him.'

'I know, right. I feel bad, yeah. I just snapped, I kicked myself for it after, 'cause like you said, little-man was a good kid and I went too far. I'm sorry about it now. God's honest truth.'

'When did you last see Jordan?' Adebayo asked.

'Last Sunday afternoon. I met him at the Glendale fields with his mate Lewis. I needed an extra pair of hands and Jordan said Lewis might do it. I gave them both some drugs and said whoever sold the quickest for the most amount of money would be courier. I told little-man if he won I'd delete the video of him shanking his mate and give him the knife back. I left them to it, I was busy.'

'Who won?'

'Dunno, I didn't hear from Jordan again. Obviously now I know why, because he'd been killed. Lewis rang me though, using a burner phone I'd given Jordan. Said he'd given Jordan a smack and took the phone off him because he thought I'd be impressed. I told him he was a snide for snaking on his mate and I wasn't working with someone like that.'

'And that's the last time you saw Jordan.'

'Yeah, last time I saw either of them.'

'Did you see anyone else as you were leaving the fields?'

'No, I was in a rush. If there had been anyone else, I probably wouldn't have noticed.'

'What did you do the rest of the day?'

'Had some errands to run so I was in and out of the flat.'

'By errands, you mean dealing.'

'Well, yeah, you know that.'

There was a knock on the door and Adebayo paused the interview and excused himself as he stepped outside. An awkward silence followed where Wheeler, his solicitor and Malone avoided eye contact with each other. After a while, Adebayo returned and exchanged a look with Malone that Wheeler couldn't read.

'Sorry about that. On the Sunday that you say you saw Jordan, did you assault him?'

'No. I've told you what went on.'

'So nothing happened on that day for Jordan to have sustained bleeding injuries whilst you were in the vicinity?'

Wheeler sighed. 'You're asking about the blood on my clothes, Susie and Albert have told you. Test it, that's not Jordan's blood. Someone tried to tax me as I was leaving the flat, so I shanked him as a warning. Nothing too serious. To be honest, I was out of it that night, I'd been on the gear myself, I carried on with my deliveries, got back and went to bed.'

'Did you go anywhere else after that?'

'Yeah, I woke up at some point, must have been the middle of the night, later even. I realised I still had blood on my hands and clothes and went to wash it off. I'd sobered up a bit by then. I got some cleaning stuff and went to the car park at the back of the flat where I'd stabbed the geezer. There was blood everywhere so I did what I could to clean it up, then just as I'd finished, it pissed down anyway, really heavy, I was soaking by the time I got to the flat.'

'Okay, thanks for your transparency so far. Is there anything else you can think to tell us that might help with finding Jordan's killer?'

'No, absolutely nothing. What I can say is it had nothing to do with me. I swear down. I admit I knocked him about. I hold my hands up to the drugs and knocking Susie and Albert about too, I'll do my time for all that. But, Jordan, no way did I kill him. If you ask me, it was that Lewis. The kid's snide, the way he took Jordan's burner phone and he had motive because he wanted revenge for being stabbed in the leg.'

'Okay, that concludes the interview for now, but I do need to tell you something else and I need you to listen carefully. I'm going to take you back to the custody desk and you're going to be rearrested under suspicion of murder.'

'What? What the fuck, man. No way. I just told you; I didn't kill Jordan.'

'This has nothing to do with him. I've just taken a call from the hospital and been advised that Albert Bennett died forty minutes ago.'

68

———————

Adila and Lund had arrived at the Gaffneys' as soon as they heard about the altercation between Craig and Wheeler. Ramos was also there, his arm supportively around Claire as she gave her version of events.

'And why were you there, Mr Ramos?' asked Lund.

'I'd gone to take some flowers to the memorial for Jordan and to pay my respects before I went to sign on at Beech Field. I saw the way Claire's car was parked and knew something wasn't right, with the door being open. Then I heard the commotion. I didn't know who it was, but I just ran anyway and then I recognised Claire and of course Craig and Wheeler. Wheeler was going to stab Craig. It was terrifying. This family has been through enough.'

'Guy has told me that you've interviewed him and I can assure you there's no way he would ever have hurt Jordan or done anything untoward,' said Claire. 'I've told you before and I stand by it, he's a good man and a good teacher and has been nothing but kind to me and my boys.'

There was a knock on the door. 'That will be my colleagues, Maya and Chris who I told you about. She's come to take some initial photos of Craig's injuries, but we might need more if the bruising develops further,' Adila said.

Claire answered the door and Maya and Chris introduced themselves. Claire gestured to the stairs. 'He's in his room, he's expecting you.'

Craig appeared on the landing and Maya and Chris headed up, nodding to Adila and Lund as they passed the lounge.

'Hi, Craig,' said Maya. 'We've come to take some photographs of your injuries; I believe you've got some cuts and bruises.'

Craig nodded. 'My hand too,' he said as he showed her his bruised and severely swollen knuckles as Chris primed the camera.

'Blimey, that looks sore, I bet it hurts.'

'I didn't really notice at the time. I was too angry at first then scared when I saw the knife. It's easier to stab someone than punch them, you know.'

'Is it?' said Maya rhetorically as she examined his hands.

'Yeah, it takes effort and it really hurts when you punch someone, but knives go in people quite easily.'

Maya and Chris exchanged a look whilst Maya studied his hands again. 'Are you left-handed, Craig?'

He nodded.

'I punched him a few times. I was so mad because it's his fault Jordan was involved with drugs. And it's like mum said, if she suspected that he was involved in drugs, stealing or gangs. As much as it killed me, I would rather take a knife to Jordan myself than sit and wait for some bloody stranger to do it.'

Tears began to fill his eyes. 'Because that's how it always ends.'

69

———

If Adila and Lund thought Claire had looked broken before, it was nothing compared to what was left of the husk of the woman they were interviewing now.

'What's going to happen to my Craig?' Her voice was barely a whisper.

'He's okay, Claire, I promise. He's being spoken to now and assessed to establish whether he has capacity. It's in his best interest and yours if you tell us what happened.'

Claire let out a heavy sigh. 'On the Sunday morning when Jordan was going out, he realised I'd taken the wheels off his bike. I heard him scream "I hate you" and he left. I heard Craig follow and just thought he was going to give him a piece of his mind for the way he'd been speaking to me lately.

'Craig had been gone a while, about an hour. I was in the kitchen making lunch when he came in and he dodged past me. Tried to go upstairs without me seeing. It was awful, he was covered in blood. I asked what he'd done, but he was almost comatose with shock. He said he'd done what I said would happen if Jordan was involved in drugs and he'd killed him. I knew they'd gone to the fields, so I locked Craig in and drove there.'

She began keening as she wrapped her arms around her stomach and began to rock back and forth.

'I knew before I even got to him that he was dead. I've found enough of my old people like that to know it was too late. He was gone, there was nothing I could do for him. I threw the knife in the bushes and looked in the bag and saw a load of drugs and cash. I pocketed it and went back to the house. I know that sounds bad, but like I said, he was *gone*, I had to protect Craig. I can't lose both my boys.

'When I got home, I asked Craig what had happened. He had seen Jordan in his room earlier and saw drugs, money and a knife in his bag. When Jordan came downstairs, Craig looked in his room, and saw the handle of the knife sticking out under the bed, so he took it and followed Jordan.

'He saw him meet Lewis and later Wheeler arrived too. Craig said he saw Wheeler slip them both some drugs. Wheeler left and he saw Lewis and Jordan argue. Lewis punched Jordan and stole a phone off him that Craig hadn't seen before. Craig said he nearly went over at that point, but Lewis left, and Jordan looked okay. Well, he was panicking, but not too injured.

'When Jordan was left alone, he made a phone call. Craig managed to get closer without being seen and heard him begging someone to buy the drugs. He said Jordan looked really scared and as he was leaving the fields, he stabbed him because of a comment I'd made previously. He takes things literally, you see. In his own way, he was doing a good thing trying to stop Jordan. He wouldn't have realised he was actually going to kill him. He loved his brother.

'I made Craig shower and bagged his clothes up with the drugs and money and took him to work with me so I could keep an eye on him. One of my old ladies is incontinent, so when I put her bedding in the washing machine, I put Craig's clothes in too and hid the drugs and cash at the bottom of her bin below all the adult nappies.'

She began to cry again and Adila stepped outside to fetch her a fresh tea and they waited until she was composed, knowing there was no point pressing her. She would tell the truth in her own time.

'I finished my rounds as quick as I could. It's all a blur, I just went through the motions. I blocked everything out and concentrated on being normal so I wouldn't give us away. Craig was exhausted when we got home. He went to bed and I waited until he was asleep and went back to the fields. I know it sounds stupid, but I wanted to say goodnight to Jordan. It was pitch black and raining. I couldn't stand the thought of him lying there exposed to the night, so I moved him. I tucked him away in the shrubbery, covered him over a bit.' She started to cry again.

'I tucked him in for the last time and went home to check on Craig. In the morning, I reported him missing and the rest you know. I told Craig we couldn't tell the truth or you would take us away from each other. Then I tried to make sure he was out of the way when I knew you were coming.'

'Okay, Claire, let's take a break for now.'

'You've both been kind to me. I'm sorry I lied but don't you see, I had to protect Craig. Like I said, I knew Jordan had gone. Craig is all I have left. Memories of Jordan are in Craig too, all the more reason I couldn't let him go. I honestly don't know what hurts the most, being the mum of a murdered kid or the mum of a murderer. Either way, my life, that stupidly I once thought was hard, is over now. I'll never hold both my boys together again.'

70

Sarah and Lewis stood hand in hand at Jordan's memorial. He remembered the last time he and Jordan had met at the fields. They'd argued about the drugs and getting involved with Wheeler. Lewis had wanted to earn easy money and decided that Wheeler was the key to that. So, he'd punched Jordan as he wrestled for the burner phone. Blood had poured from Jordan's nose and mouth and covered Lewis's top.

He'd left him then, later feeling shame for treating his best friend so badly. The self-disgust had been so strong, especially after he had phoned Wheeler who had said he didn't want to work with someone as two-faced as him. He realised then that he had sunk to an all-time low if someone like Wheeler didn't want to know him.

He had headed home, hoping to speak to his mum, but she had been comatose on the couch after another bout of binge drinking. It was then he decided to grab some stuff and go to his dad's. Even that hadn't worked out as his dad had made it perfectly clear that there was no place for Lewis in his new family nest.

Sighing, Lewis gently placed the football top of Jordan's

favourite team in amongst the flowers, teddies and balloons. He took a moment to stare at the photo of Jordan, broken by the sight of such a familiar face. One he would never see again. The boy he grew up with would remain fourteen forever while Lewis would one day become an old man. Even then, he swore he would still remember Jordan.

Wiping the tears from his face, he stood up and Sarah gathered him into a hug.

'You okay, son?'

'That could have been me.' He nodded to the shrine.

'I know. For a moment I thought it was. I dunno what I'd do if I lost you.'

'It's not going to happen. Jordan died because I messed up. I caused him to get dragged into things he didn't want to do. I'm gonna turn it around and be better, be more like Jordan. I'm gonna make him proud and be the man he would have been. I don't want his death to be for nothin'. I've got a lot of making up to do. When we get home, I'm going to start by writing a letter of apology to Mr Ramos.'

Sarah smiled at him. 'I'm proud of you for saying that. I'll help you be the best you can be. Fresh start for both of us. It's never too late to change. I'm gonna lead by example and start being a better mum. I think this has been a wake-up call for both of us. Whatever happens to Claire and Craig, we'll be there for them too. Do whatever we can to help and support them. For Jordan's sake.'

Lewis nodded at the photo. 'Be back to see you soon, mate. Sleep well.'

Then he linked his mum's arm and they both walked home together.

~

'Prick,' said Sully as he passed Reilly his phone and showed him the news report that detailed Wheeler's guilty plea in court earlier that day.

'Don't worry, he's not heard the last from us,' Reilly said. 'He'll keep. It's not as if he's going anywhere. Look at you, all tense,' he said, his soft Gaelic tone surprisingly carefree despite knowing he'd lost the biggest link in his supply chain. 'Let's take a drive and go and pick up a McDonald's.'

'I'm not hungry.'

'You can always manage some fries,' said Reilly. 'Plus, the last few times I've been there I've noticed this kid hanging around hoping for scraps. He only looks to be about thirteen and clearly has no one waiting at home for him.'

'He sounds perfect,' said Sully with a Machiavellian grin as he reached for his jacket. 'Let's go.'

'Dave the Bastard' was also reading the news and was unimpressed with how the report was written. He would have done it ten times better and there was so much more to this story to pursue. He'd have hunted Wheeler's girlfriend down by now and talked her into giving him an exclusive.

This story had legs and Dave's journalist instincts were itching to be all over it. He hadn't yet accepted that his dismissal whilst being investigated for harassing Maya was permanent. It was just a blip. A lead like this would be just what he needed to get back into Peter's good books.

He reached for his mobile and attempted to call his boss, but it wouldn't connect. Strange. He rang the newsroom and asked to be put through to Peter but was intercepted by his secretary who told him that any communication with the newspaper in future would be via HR and his solicitor. His items had been boxed up and would be couriered to him imminently and he was to hand over his press pass and work ID so it could be returned the same day.

To say Wainwright was outraged was an understatement. He hung up and tried Peter's number again. This couldn't be happening. What an overreaction. When the call wouldn't connect a second or third time, reality hit Wainwright. Peter had blocked his number. Bastard!

If Wainwright had contacted Susie for an exclusive, she would have provided one quite happily. He would, in fact, not have been able to shut her up. She would have taken the opportunity to warn naïve girls like herself to stay away from 'bad boys', to say that, as tempting as they might seem, people like Wheeler were nothing but scum. They were users and manipulators, and by being with them, you were supporting and enabling their actions.

You'd start off turning a blind eye to the fact the flashy car you were driving in was stolen, or that the nice perfume or new necklace you were wearing was bought with the proceeds of selling drugs to kids and addicts. Next thing you know you'd be bagging up drugs and watching someone you loved being beaten in their own home.

Susie would have told how she wished she had listened to her parents. How she wished she'd realised they weren't nagging but were doing the right thing warning her to stay away. Susie would have told how Wheeler slowly but gradually coerced her into losing contact with her family and friends until she was isolated from the people who loved her and was solely dedicated to him. A man who brought other knife-carrying dealers to the door. A man who embroiled her in a world she never wanted to be part of.

Susie would say that despite regretting ever getting involved with Wheeler, the one thing she was grateful for was her friendship with Albert. And then she would talk even more as she sang the praises of what a wonderful man he had been. She would share all the stories he'd told her about his life, his family, his adventures. She would keep his memory alive by sharing his stories and telling everyone about him, and despite not having any family of his own, he would live on in Susie's.

As Albert used to say to her when he talked about people he had loved and lost, as long as they are remembered they're never truly gone. Albert and Jordan would never be forgotten.

71

———————

For the SOCO team, the conclusion of the case came with a sense of closure. All they had to do now was write their witness statements and provide copies of their scene notes to MIT, then wait for the next inevitable job.

In the meantime, Maya entered Jayne's office for her weekly EMDR session. After a quick catch-up of how each other's week had been, Jayne began.

'We went really deep into your recollection last time. You remembered being in the lounge with Grandad unconscious and covered in blood lying on the floor. Marcus is in the room too and you were about to run out until you realised your mama was also there. She's screaming at him. And you said she was covered in blood too.' Jayne looked up from her notes.

'That's right. I recall running to her because I know she was going to stop Marcus. I've never seen her so angry. She looked feral, screaming and swearing. She was saying that she was going to kill him and she had the baseball bat in her hand.'

'All of this would have been terrifying for a twelve-year-old, it's no wonder your mind has blocked such trauma out. Okay,

Maya, take a few deep breaths. Take a moment to remember your safe space.' Jayne hesitated for a few moments before holding her fingers aloft and swinging them from side to side whilst Maya's eyes followed. 'Fall back into that moment and stay with it.'

November 2005

'Mama?'

She doesn't even see me at first. Her eyes are glazed with anger and something else that I've not seen before, a kind of chemical rage. Spittle flies from her mouth as she screams vitriolic words. Threats of violence and pure hatred spew from her lips. With every syllable she swings the baseball bat in the air, emphasising each sound and sending droplets of blood cascading across the room. Marcus dodges away from her and screams at her to put the bat down. That's when she realises I'm in the room.

She reaches for me, pulling me into her side, burying my head against her chest as I sob wildly. She flings the bat towards the door where I had been stood so she can wrap both arms around me. I've had a growth spurt so have to crouch as she comforts me like I was a much younger child. I certainly feel like a terrified six-year-old, not a pre-teen, as I dig my nails into my mouth and tear my cuticles with my teeth.

'Is Grandad okay?' I'm so scared I can barely get the words out.

'Yes, he's fine, baby. He's fine. Go back to bed now and let Mama make everything okay again.'

Terrified, I peer out from under her arm, anxious to know if Marcus is still in the room. He is, and more horrifying than that, he is standing over Grandad. I'm frozen with terror as he leans forward and lifts his head up whilst feeling frantically around his face and neck, before dropping him back to the floor. There's a muffled thump as Grandad's head hits the carpet.

Marcus straightens up and nudges his torso with his foot.

'Christ, Dominique, you hit him too hard. I told you to stop. I think he's dead. You've fuckin' killed him.'

'No!' I scream as I tear myself away from Mama and run towards Grandad. I drop to the floor and bury my head in his chest, shouting his name again and again. A sudden wave of liquid covers us both. Ice-cold cider splashed from a glass across Grandad's face, covering the back of my head and shoulders. The sudden chill and the sound of my voice causes Grandad to stir, and I gasp with relief as his eyes flicker, and I catch the murmur of my name on his lips.

I turn to Mama and see her stood frozen with fear. Marcus is looming over us with the empty cider glass in his hand. He's so close I can smell him. Alcohol, cigarettes, garlic and sweat.

'See, he's okay,' he says as he reaches out a hand to place on my shoulder and pull me away. I jump from him so he can't touch me. He's so close, I feel physically sick, and it's not just because he smells of alcohol and sweat.

It's the sheer presence of him. Everything about this man exudes hatred, intimidation, and violence. His every breath extenuates the fact I do not – and never will – mean anything to him. In this moment he catches my eye as I flinch from him. I see the pure hatred he has for me.

I had been so much younger when I first realised he didn't like me. That had been hurtful enough, but when you're young, with time, everything becomes normal. Whilst other dads swung their children in the air, hugged them after school, cuddled and kissed them, mine was just there. A reluctant, resentful presence. A shadow in the house who went missing for weeks, sometimes months at a time. Those absences were a breath of fresh air; his absence was probably the only kindness he ever showed me.'

As each period without him grew longer, the hope that he would never return would bloom like a spring bud. But inevitably came the day when a sickening sensation would settle in my stomach as I padded down to breakfast. The house was contaminated by his presence, his noise, his smell. Mama would change, becoming glassy-eyed and stupid – malleable in his presence.

There were times I knew he hurt her though, physically and emotionally. He loved nothing more than to taunt her with mind games. He abused her love and trust, her adoration for him turned her into a puppet whose strings he could pull at will. There were times she would stand up to him and then the fighting would start. The screaming caused me to cower as I braced myself for the sound of slaps, the rumble of furniture being displaced.

Each would give as good as they got. But even this, the violence, the manipulation, things that would break a relationship only seemed to fuel her love for him as he would eventually storm out, vowing never to return, leaving her keening like a broken animal.

Now as he glared at me with unadulterated hatred, it is a light-bulb moment. If you think about the force of pure love shared between parents and their newborn child. That love is physical, visceral, overwhelming, everlasting. The birth is bloodied and brutal. Now reverse that. Think how it feels as a child to suddenly realise that a parent hates you, or to experience parental estrangement for whatever reason. It is physical, visceral, overwhelming, everlasting. The hatred is bloodied and brutal.

The split second I flinch from him, and we make eye contact, it's a moment of rebirth for me.

'I fucking hate you,' I say, the swear word alien on my tongue. 'Stay away from my grandad.'

He stills momentarily, shocked by my swearing. Then throws his head back and begins to laugh. Instinctively, my hand drops to the floor and wraps around the baseball bat. In an instant I have it gripped in my hand as I swing it towards his head. It makes an ineffectual glance across his jawbone.

The laughter freezes in his throat as he reaches for the end of the bat and snatches it from my hand.

'Well, look at that!' he screams as he turns towards Mama, gesturing at me with the bat. 'Isn't this little bitch truly her mama's daughter?'

He swings the bat towards us and we both scream. Miraculously, Grandad manages to stir again and sit up.

'Marcus, no.' His voice is weak, but the deep timbre carries across the room and causes Dad to freeze.

'You go now and I'll say nothing more about it,' he says as he struggles to sit up.

'You should learn to mind your own business, old man, then you wouldn't get hurt,' Marcus says as he reaches in his jeans pocket for a pack of cigarettes.

'You have made it my business by dragging my daughter into your dirty world. She was a good girl until she met you and now you've dragged her into this,' Grandad says as he leans against the wall and begins to pull himself to his feet.

His hand waves towards the large bay window ledge. The curtains are drawn and as I glance over, I can see white powder, weighing scales and bags. I've seen the powder before.

There are lots of brick-shaped, cellophane-wrapped parcels in the cupboard under the stairs — some brown , some white. I remember seeing them weeks ago behind a false panel that had loosened at one side. I had been in there looking for my old roller skates that I'd promised to give to my friend's little sister.

I suddenly remember there was something else in there too. Something that made me back away and push the panel back. Pretend I'd never seen it. Something that made me too scared to carry on looking for the skates. Something that looked too surreal to be in our house. Something that I'd only seen in television and films. But not like one I'd seen in toy shops, this gun was real.

Suddenly, Grandad is lurching towards the window ledge. His hand outstretched as he reaches towards the powder that covers the surface and sweeps it to the floor.

Mama screams and dives forwards.

Marcus reaches for Grandad and pulls him away, throwing him back to the floor.

Mama dives towards the carpet, frantic as she blocks one nostril and tries to hoover as much of the spilt powder as she can with the other. Marcus kicks her away as he reaches for the bags and tries to refill them. I freeze, horrified; confused and disgusted by what I see.

Panicked, I look to Grandad, waiting for some sense or an explanation. He looks back at me, equally frantic as he makes a telephone gesture with his hand and mouths the word 'Police.'

I flee into the hall, my feet cold against the floor as I snatch up the landline telephone and dial 999. I shout garbled words down the phone. I assume later that it's the screaming and shouting from the lounge that the call-taker can hear in the background that causes her to send as many units as quickly as she can.

It feels like hours but can only be minutes. There's a pounding on the door and I run to open it – through the glass I can see the fluorescent jackets of my saviours. Then a flurry of activity as uniformed figures storm the house. Shouting, screaming, swearing, banging follows.

I cower in the cupboard under the stairs, shaking. I cover my ears but it's futile as I can still hear the mayhem. I remove the panel to reveal the hidden stash of drugs and the gun. I sit guarding it until a police officer sticks her head into the cupboard when she realises I'm there and I point mutely to the contraband.

She places an arm around me and gently pulls me into the hallway. She shields me as Marcus is dragged kicking and screaming from the lounge. He's handcuffed but still resisting. He sees me cowering behind the police officer and clocks the open door to the cupboard under the stairs. He knows then that I've revealed his secret and his expletives are then fired at me as he screams that he is going to kill me.

Mama is guided from the lounge with care as she is accompanied into the kitchen. She passes me and stops to hug me briefly, before she breaks into noisy sobbing and she's settled at the kitchen table. An ambulance, its siren screaming, arrives outside and paramedics dash down the hall carrying a defibrillator.

I break away from the police officer and run to the lounge and watch, horror-struck, as they begin to work on Grandad, connecting pads to his exposed chest and passing instructions to each other. I'm screaming now and shaking with shock, hitting out at the police officer who tries to pull me away as she pulls the lounge door shut so I can't see.

I can't stop the screaming. It's like it has taken on its own entity and I am just the vessel that allows its sound to exude through the house. Another paramedic arrives in the hallway. He's thickly built, salt-and-pepper eyebrows frame his face. He tries to calm me; he seems immune to the screaming which I can't seem to stop. It's like the fear inside of me is trying to climb out.

His reassuring words bounce off me like hailstone. The trauma is too much. A stream of urine pours down my leg just as my brain responds to the shock and my consciousness is swallowed into a merciful void.

The paramedic catches me as I collapse.

~

'What are you feeling?' Jayne asks as she stills her hand movement. 'What can you see?'

Maya blinked back tears. 'Everything. It all makes sense

now.' She reached for her glass of water and gulped it down as a laugh of hysteria rose in her throat and bubbled over. Her laughter filled the room until eventually she calmed herself and eyed Jayne levelly.

'I've seen it all and I remember *everything*.'

72

———

Maya arrived at Dominique's in such a rage, that by the time she was pounding on the front door, she couldn't recall a single thing about the journey there.

'What's wrong? You nearly put the door through. I thought someone was trying to break in the way you were banging.' Dominique clung to the door, looking jumpy. She took one look at Maya's face and reached for her. 'Darling, what's happened? Is it Spence?'

Maya batted her hand away as she pushed into the house. 'It was you. It was you all along who hurt Grandad. You hit him with a baseball bat for Christ's sake, your own father.'

Dominique's eyes widened and her mouth hung open. 'Maya... it's not what you think. I can explain.'

'You've been so jumpy since that sighting of Naylor, but now I know why. First of all, the thought of him coming back means he risks exposing your dirty secret, how you were helping him sell drugs and taking them yourself. And it's also why you were so opposed to me having EMDR, isn't it? It had nothing to do with wanting to protect me from the past, it's all about not wanting me to remember the truth.'

Dominique began to cry silent tears as she shook her head slowly.

'Well, I remember it all now. I know the truth. I *see* you.' Dominique was cowering in the hallway, Maya towering over her as her rage built.

'Please just let me explain. That night, it was a catalyst for me. It was a wake-up call for how involved I'd become. The thing is, back then I loved Marcus. He was like an obsession to me, *he* was the drug. He was everything I wasn't, a risk-taker, chancer, free-spirited. He was exciting and he made me feel alive for the first time in my life.'

'Listen to yourself, you were a grown woman, not some lovesick teenager. You're pathetic.'

'But that's how he made me feel. It was intoxicating. I knew he had a bit of a reputation for being a bad boy, but I didn't care. It made me want him even more. And he wasn't into anything too bad at first. Things just grew over time. By the time I found out how deeply involved he was, how much he had crossed the line into a world of criminality, we already had you and I was in too deep.'

'I'm so sorry I got in the way,' Maya spat venomously.

'No, darling, please. You were always wanted, I loved you the minute I found out I was pregnant.'

'He never did.'

Dominique sighed and raked her hand across her head. 'He was jealous of you. I know it sounds pathetic, but he resented the time I spent with you.'

'Pathetic? It's fucking embarrassing. *You're* an embarrassment. I've always thought you were one of the strongest people I know, but as I said I see you now and you're weak as well as a liar. How did Grandad ever let this happen?'

'Grandad never liked him or trusted him from the start, but I was young and foolish and didn't listen. I swear to you though, I never dealt drugs for him. Yes, I turned a blind eye to what he was doing–'

'That's even worse,' shouted Maya. 'You were still culpable. Do you know how many lives that shit ruins?'

Dominique wiped her face with her hands. 'Yes of course. And it was never my thing. Not really. He slowly introduced it to me. Made it seem daring and fun. It was just a bit at first but then it became a habit. Looking back now, I realise he had coerced me into taking it so he could control me.

'Grandad had noticed a change in my behaviour. He said I seemed more erratic than usual. I was training to be a community nurse at the time and he put it down to the stress of the job. That night he called round unexpectedly. The timing couldn't be worse. Marcus was preparing a delivery for a dealer he knew. He was bagging it up. That's why the baseball bat was in the room with us, in case any rival dealers broke in while the stuff was there.'

Maya snorted incredulously and shook her head.

'He saw the drugs and understandably went ballistic. Then he started threatening to call the police if Marcus didn't leave. I know I acted badly, but you've got to understand, Maya, in that moment I thought he was going to take everything away from me. If he rang the police I would lose Marcus and you would probably have been taken away from me too. We'd been drinking and taken some stuff. I know it's no excuse, I'm just explaining why I did what I did. I wasn't thinking rationally, I just reacted.

'He started to leave the room; I begged him not to phone the police. Asked him to stop and just talk to me, but he wouldn't. I had to stop him. He was risking everything I loved.'

'Including the drugs?' Maya was astounded by what she was hearing.

'I know you don't want to hear it, but yes, back then, even the drugs. He turned his back on me and I just snapped. Next thing I knew, I had the baseball bat in my hand and I was hitting him, screaming that I hated him and was going to kill him. I honestly didn't want to hurt him, I just had to stop him from ruining my life.'

'And the drugs and gun in the cupboard under the stairs?'

'Honestly? I swear to God I didn't know anything about that. I didn't know they were there. I only found out when the police officer told me you'd showed them. By then I didn't care, I just wanted to get to hospital to make sure you and Grandad were okay.'

'Really? You cared after you'd taken a baseball bat to him?'

'Yes of course. I loved him. I love you. Like I said, that night was a wake-up call. It was like I'd been under Marcus's spell all those years and the shock of it all brought me out of it. Marcus refused to comment in interview or in court and I realised he wasn't going to say anything about me. Whether that was out of loyalty to me, I don't know. I doubt it, he just wanted to protect his own skin, didn't want to go to prison being known as a grass.

'Grandad and I talked and we agreed to keep things between us. I didn't want to risk having you taken from me or my career being ruined. Grandad promised to help and support me as long as I got clean, which I did. It was obvious that the trauma of that night meant you didn't remember what had happened, and with time, we moved on and things became normal. We were happy.'

Maya shook her head, disgusted. 'Who even are you? Have you heard yourself? You were actually glad I experienced a trauma so frightening that I couldn't remember anything. You're sick. Call yourself a mother – you're as bad as him – I don't even know who you are anymore, and more to the point, I don't want to know.'

Dominique reached for her, but Maya slapped her hand away and walked to the door.

'Maya, please don't go. We need to talk. Please, let me just explain. I want to make things better.'

Maya turned on her, their faces so close they were nearly touching. 'Don't,' she hissed. 'I don't want to hear another word. I have *begged* you to tell me the truth again and again. You know how ill not knowing has made me and all you have done is been hellbent on keeping your sordid secrets. My entire life has been based on your lies. From now on, you're dead to me.'

She wrenched open the front door and stalked towards her bike. She could hear Dominique begging and crying, screaming for her to stop and come back. She could hear the desperation and pain in her voice.

For once, she was completely impervious to it.

73

———————

The next few days passed in a blur. Maya took leave as for once, she couldn't bear the thought of going to work. She just wanted to cocoon herself in the house and lick her wounds. Jayne had been able to offer her a couple of emergency sessions to help her come to terms with what she had remembered, and although it helped in part, she was left feeling more drained and exhausted as she pieced the horrendous pieces of her childhood back together.

Spence had phoned Dominique and asked her not to try and contact Maya. He explained that she needed some time to come to terms with things and that she would probably speak to her once she had calmed down. As he had said the words, Spence wasn't convinced himself. He had never seen Maya so angry and so adamant that she didn't want to see her mother again. All he could do was be there for Maya, to be a sounding board for her. He wasn't going to risk alienating her by making her talk to Dominique before she was ready.

Even Chris, for once, didn't have any words of wisdom, other than to tentatively remind her that her faith meant she should show forgiveness. He also assured her that she needed time to process things first and that she would know when the time was right. He went to see her after every shift and kept her company on the evenings Spence was at work, allowing her to just talk about how she felt.

'I don't know how you can stand to come around here all the time listening to me moaning on,' she said one evening.

'You'd do the same for me – and you're not moaning. For Christ's sake, Maya, you're coming to terms with a lot. It's been a huge shock and there's a lot you need to get your head around. It won't always feel like this though, just keep talking to me, Spence and Jayne, and I promise you, what you're feeling now, the intensity of it, will start to fade.'

'I just feel like I'm in such a dark place right now and the fact it's winter is compounding my mood.'

'Well, I tell you what might lighten it for you quite literally,' said Chris, 'how about putting the Christmas decorations up?'

'It's still November,' Maya replied incredulously.

'It's the twenty-fifth today which means it'll be December a week today. All the lights have been up on the high street for days and there's been decorations in the supermarket since September. C'mon, you love Christmas. I've loads of stuff in the loft. Have a mooch through and see what you can find. Put whatever you want up.'

A smile appeared on Maya's face. 'It would be lovely to have some lights up. I've got a beautiful plug-in star which would look great above your fireplace.'

'There you go then. Call round tomorrow and collect it. I'll be out in the afternoon.'

'Where are you off to?'

Chris grinned; a flush of colour pinched his cheeks. 'Lunch with Emira.'

Maya clapped her hands. 'At last, a date. And I'm glad you're taking her out rather than risk cooking for her.'

'So, it's agreed then? This time tomorrow the place will look like Santa's grotto.'

'Agreed,' said Maya as they clinked glasses. She could feel a frisson of excitement. Chris had made a fantastic suggestion. She did like Christmas, and it would be fun to decorate his place. 'I'll call at the apartment tomorrow afternoon and raid my Christmas supply too.'

~

Maya slipped her key into the lock and stepped into the hallway of her apartment.

'It's only me,' she called in case Chris hadn't yet left for his lunch date with Emira. There was no answer, so she headed for the kitchen and left two bottles of mulled wine and a box of mince pies on the counter for him. It had been his idea to get her into the Christmas spirit, the least she could do was return the favour.

Habitually, she started to unload the dishwasher, humming to herself to fill the silence. Being back here made her realise it was no longer home. It didn't feel like home. And it wasn't just because it was now full of Chris's things that made it alien, it had too many bad memories. She had felt scared and unsafe here and knew, no matter what happened in the future, it would never be home again. She was ready to think about selling.

She stood on the balcony and looked down on the city stretched below her. She had always loved this view, but even that now felt tainted. She shivered and stepped back inside, locking the balcony door. She headed into the spare room and began to root through the boxes of Christmas decorations, looking for the star and any other bits she thought might look nice at Chris's house. She filled carrier bags with various items and got ready to leave the flat. Her phone rang as she was getting ready and she struggled to answer it. Weighed down by bags, she hooked her foot round the edge of the door to pull it shut behind her.

'Hi,' Spence said. 'Just ringing to let you know Mum is cooking a roast today and has offered to plate some up for us if you'd like?'

'That would be great. I love your mum's cooking.'

'I know you do. She knows you wanted to do the decorations today, so said it would save us having to cook later.'

'She's the best. Tell her I'll cook next time and she can come to us.'

Maya continued the conversation as she waited for the lift. She was too absorbed in the call to realise that the apartment door hadn't closed properly.

Chris arrived back from his date with Emira on a high. It had gone better than expected and he couldn't wait to see her again. They'd eaten at a tapas restaurant in town, then called at various pubs for a few drinks. Quite a few drinks if he was honest. He was the first to admit he was feeling a little worse for wear. He blamed the tapas, those little dishes weren't enough to fill anyone, which is why he'd picked up some chips on the way home.

He staggered up the hall, placing the chips on the kitchen table, He grinned at the sight of the mulled wine and mince pies on the counter. He reached for his phone and called Maya so he could thank her.

'Thanks for my present. This afternoon has been amazing.' He could hear himself slurring as he spoke but didn't care. He was happy. 'Honestly, Maya, *she's* amazing.' He headed for the lounge so he could turn the lamps on but froze as he stepped back out in the hallway. He sobered instantly and screamed in terror. 'Maya, he's here! Maya–'

It had taken several hours but finally the house was decorated. Maya and Spence stood together looking at the lounge. It looked perfect.

'There is one thing we've forgotten,' said Spence as he pulled her towards him.

'What?'

'This!' He reached into his back pocket and pulled out a sorry-looking piece of plastic mistletoe. They grinned at each other and began to kiss, eventually falling towards the floor, wrapped in each other. Maya's mobile rang and Spence groaned as she reached for it.

'It's Chris,' she said as Spence littered kisses along her neck. 'He'll be ringing to say thanks for the wine. I'll call him back.' She turned her attention back to him, Chris temporarily forgotten.

Later they lay wrapped in each other's arms, covered in the throw from the sofa and dozing in front of the television. Spence yawned as he looked at his watch. 'Right then, I'll go to Mum's and collect our roast dinner.'

They reluctantly peeled themselves away from each other. Maya began to set the table as Spence left the house. She returned to the lounge and began to neaten the throw, when she saw her phone and remembered to call Chris back. He'd left a voicemail message. She began to smile as she listened to it, then her face froze as she heard the sudden panic in his voice. She pressed the phone to her ear and listened. 'Maya, he's here! Maya–'

Chris's screams continued as he pleaded for mercy. Her

blood turned to ice as she listened to her best friend's cries and the grunting of Naylor's exertion as he attacked Chris. After what felt like an age, everything grew eerily quiet. Tears streamed silently down her face as she strained to listen. A crackling sound as the phone was picked up from the floor.

'Daddy's home, Maya!' Naylor panted down the phone before hanging up.

Panicked, she tried to ring Chris back. She listened to his phone ringing out. She hung up and rang nine-nine-nine as she grabbed her helmet and reached for her keys when there was a sudden pounding at the front door which froze her to the spot. It was loud and insistent. Whoever was outside, was intent on getting in.

74

Maya was numb with shock. She couldn't comprehend what she was hearing. The Christmas lights that had looked so pretty a couple of hours ago, seemed to be mocking her as they flashed and flitted through the wave cycle. Jack had been on duty when he heard the news. His immediate concern had been for Maya's safety, and he had arranged for uniformed patrols to make their way to Chris's address and ensure she was safe.

Maya had been convinced it was Marcus at the door trying to force his way in. It was only when she noticed the blue lights and fluorescent jackets, visible through the front door, a repeat image of all those years ago back at Dominique's. She had flung the door open shouting anxiously about Chris. It had been Jack, who had arrived next in a plain car who had sat her down to tell her the news. Spence had arrived back at the same time, food abandoned in the passenger footwell as he had run into the house, the sight of police cars had terrified him as he thought something had happened to Maya.

Spence had held Maya while Jack had explained how Chris had been found by Maya's neighbour Keith. He had arrived home and been concerned to see the door slightly ajar. He had called out, and after getting no reply, had popped his head into the hallway to see if everything was okay. He saw Chris lying in a pool of blood in the hall.

Keith had rung for an ambulance and tried to give Chris CPR, but it was obvious he was already dead. It looked like he had been stabbed several times in the chest and stomach with what they believed, due to the nature of his injuries, was a zombie knife. It would have had an ornamental handle and the blade would be serrated, making it even more lethal than a normal knife.

Maya had played the voicemail message Chris had left her and they had all listened with horror.

'It should have been me,' Maya said eventually. Up until then, grief and shock had left her mute as she sat trembling, tears coursing down her cheeks as she had listened to the nightmare unfold.

Jack couldn't make eye contact with her, because he knew what she was saying was the truth. Marcus Naylor had arrived at her flat today with the intention of hurting her. Chris had been cannon fodder.

Maya looked at Spence. 'I was so distracted on the phone to you, consumed with the thought of doing the decorations. I don't think I shut the apartment door properly.'

'You can't blame yourself, love,' said Spence as he squeezed her hand.

'Oh, I know exactly who's to blame. We know who's done this.' She glanced at Jack who nodded. 'I should have realised it would be today. The 26th November is the date he was released from prison last year.'

'We're doing everything we can to find him,' Jack said.

Maya let out a brittle laugh. 'He's been on the run for nearly a year. Nobody found him in that time, so why would it be any different now? He knows how to hide. He's going to go to ground now more than ever. He's taken a chance to come and kill me, he won't risk it again. My bet is that he'll be out of the country by the end of the day.'

Her legs shook as she stood up and wrapped her arms around herself. 'I don't even want to *think* about him. I don't care where he is. He's won. He's caused me the most pain possible. He's murdered – mutilated – my best friend.'

Spence went to hold her, but she moved away. 'You don't understand. It hurts too much. I can't believe he's gone. I'm never going to see him ever again. Never going to talk to him, laugh with him, confide in him. Hug him.'

Tears streamed down her face; her body was wracked with sobs. 'I can't cope with the fact I won't see him next week, let alone for ever.'

75

It had been a week since the murder and Maya, who hadn't left the house since then, finally felt up to seeing her team. She needed to be with other people who had loved Chris. Maya arrived in the office and hugged her colleagues. Kym shut the office door so they wouldn't be disturbed.

'Under the circumstances, top office have given us time to be non-operational. We're monitoring jobs and passing them on to staff at Cedar Lane,' Kym told Maya.

'Who dealt with my apartment... I mean, who dealt... who recovered Chris?' Maya asked as tears filled her eyes. She couldn't bear the thought of him being bundled into a body bag and taken to the mortuary.

'Willow Grove dealt with everything,' said Amanda. 'The staff from there hadn't had many dealings with Chris over the years so it made sense. It wouldn't have been right for someone who knew him to go.'

'And a Home Office pathologist came up from Birmingham, so Dr Granger didn't have to do the PM,' said Elaine.

'It's just so quiet without him,' said Kim.

'And there's still a full packet of biscuits on the side that haven't been touched yet,' said Connor, which despite everything made them smile.

'He'd say he might as well eat them as he could be dead tomorrow,' said Tara. 'He was always making comments like that. It was as if he knew.'

Kym threw her a caustic look and was about to say something until Amanda diplomatically interjected.

'Here,' she said to Maya as she opened her desk drawer and fished out the keys to her apartment. 'Cleaners have been in and there's no sign that... Well, if you do feel like you can cope with going back there, everything is in order.' Amanda said as she handed them over.

Maya touched her hand as she reached for the keys and suddenly, she was holding Amanda as the two of them began to cry. Elaine embraced them both and was joined by Kym. Tara and Connor exchanged a look and in seconds had their arms around each other as they joined the others. Sobs wracked the office as the team stood in a huddle, united in grief and their love for Chris.

Maya arrived back at Chris's where Spence was anxiously awaiting her safe return. She began to pace the kitchen, unsure of what to do with herself. She was feeling antsy and suffocated.

'Can I get you anything, love? How about a brew, or I could run you a bath?' Spence asked as he pulled her into a hug.

Angrily she pulled herself from his grip. 'No, I don't want a brew or a bloody bath. I just want all this... this *shit* to stop. And don't keep grabbing at me all the time. I can't bloody breathe,' she snapped.

'Whoa, okay.' Spence took a step back and held his hands up. 'I know how much you're hurting right now, I really do, but don't shut me out, Maya, please.'

She sighed and shook her head. 'I'm sorry, I didn't mean to. It's not you. I just feel like I'm drowning right now.'

She reached for her helmet and keys and he raised an eyebrow, concerned. 'Where are you going now?'

'Just for a ride to clear my head. Don't look so worried, I'll be careful. It'll do me good.'

Spence hesitated, instinctively he wanted to stop her,

worried she'd be too distracted to concentrate while on the bike. Plus, he couldn't stand the thought of her out there on her own with Naylor still on the loose. But he also knew Maya. She knew her own mind and right now she was going through hell. He needed to let her have her own space or he risked alienating her.

'Just be careful, okay?'

Maya wrapped an arm around his neck and breathed in the familiar scent of him. She was about to pull away when she added as an afterthought, 'I love you.' She didn't know why, but she had a fleeting sense that she was saying goodbye to him for good.

She roared away on the Bonneville, in a futile attempt to outrun the pain she was feeling.

Maya didn't plan it, but after riding around familiar streets, past her old school, friends' houses, places she had worked, church and her and Dominique's old house, she found herself parking up at Miller Court. Her last stop. She felt numb as she rode the lift to the eleventh floor. She hesitated outside her apartment as she closed her eyes and rested her head against the door. With trembling hands, she reached for the keys and unlocked the door like she had countless times before.

She hesitated in the hallway, her eyes scouring the floor and walls. The cleaning crew had done a thorough job, there were no telltale arrows marking blood spatter on the walls and the floor was clean. No fingerprint powder remained on any of the surfaces. Other than an unfamiliar chemical smell, the place looked the same as it had on the day she'd called to collect the Christmas decorations.

She wandered into the kitchen where one of Chris's jackets was slung over the back of a chair. She reached for it, burying her nose into the fabric hoping to find his scent. A hint of aftershave lingered but it was faint. Before long, she realised, it would fade altogether. Another trace of him gone. The pain was somatic as it suddenly gripped her, sending her bent double on the floor as her body became wracked with sobs.

The sense of loss was unbearable. To have lost someone she loved in normal circumstances was bad enough, but to have him taken so violently by an animal like Naylor was horrendous. He had been such a loving, caring man who did so much for others, he didn't deserve to end his life like that, bleeding out terrified and alone. No one did.

She thought of Jordan lying on the Glendale fields and imagined how Claire must have felt when she discovered that one son had murdered another. Maya properly imagined it, in a way that, as a SOCO she could never allow herself to feel, as she needed to remain desensitised to cope with the job. She allowed the shock and pain to compound her own grief. She couldn't desensitise her feelings for Chris's death, and the feeling was alien to her. She had become so used to being able to switch her emotions off, but this was so personal.

Now she was faced with the most distressing time of her life, and she was terrified to realise she couldn't cope. Yes, she had been devastated when Grandad died, utterly inconsolable in fact, but he had lived a good, long life, which was the correct order of things. He hadn't been brutally murdered in his prime. Maya shuddered as bile flooded her mouth.

Pulling herself up, she headed to the sink and took gulps of water straight from the tap. She was shaking with fear and grief, overwhelmed with Chris's death as well as remembering her past. It was all too much. Sobbing, she reached for the balcony keys and stepped out into the biting air, gulping in lungfuls like a drowning woman, which was how she felt.

The emotion was like a white noise in her head, hammer-jacking into her skull. She looked down at the familiar sight below her, the city at dusk. Her city. Her home. Soon, night would cloak the city, allowing the lights below to twinkle like stars in their own right. How things could change so quickly. There was a time she would love to sit out here, sipping wine on the balcony in summer while reading a book. Wrapped up on Bonfire Night or New Year's Eve watching the fireworks punctuate the sky with a chorus of multicolour.

Now, she knew she could never feel content again, let alone happy. Her best friend was dead and she could never imagine living without him and the agonising pain that accompanied his loss. Her family was in tatters, her mother now as estranged to her as Naylor had always been. What was to stop her turning into them and what family did she even have left? Nobody. The knowledge that she shared DNA with a monster like Naylor made her want to claw at her own skin.

Then there was Spence. Already she could feel herself pulling away from him. Flinching from his touch; irritated by his platitudes. She loved him beyond measure but how long before she would deliberately sour their relationship and push him away to avoid any more heartbreak? How long before the scales would fall from his eyes and he would see her for what she was? Marcus Naylor's daughter, a scourge, a plague, something toxic to be avoided as misery followed her everywhere. And soon her friends and colleagues would see the same. She had to make it all stop. She had to end it.

She was oblivious to the tears streaming down her face as she placed her hands on the balcony. The lights below were starting to twinkle and from up here, they looked so peaceful. Almost inviting. As if they were beckoning to her. With a grunt she heaved her leg over the edge of the balcony, her eyes fixated on the lights...

77

S pence had called to see Dominique the day after Chris's murder, to let her know what had happened. She had been devastated and shed tears for the grief she knew Maya would be feeling as well as for the loss of Chris. She had asked Spence if she should go and see Maya, but he had cautioned her that it might still be too soon and that Maya would be in touch when she was ready.

'Perhaps losing Chris will give her fresh perspective and persuade her to come and talk to you,' Spence had suggested and Dominique desperately hoped he was right.

An urgent manhunt was underway for Naylor, and fresh appeals had been circulated requesting the public's help in tracking him down. Dominique thought like Maya. He had evaded capture so far for nearly twelve months. He would have gone into hiding again now he had killed Chris, so he had even more reason not to be caught. As far as Dominique was concerned, the only good thing to come out of Chris's tragic murder was that it meant Naylor would go back in hiding for good.

She just longed to be able to speak to Maya. She wanted to

hold her, comfort her and help ease the pain she knew she would be feeling. Chris had been such a special, important part of her life and she didn't know how Maya would cope without him. She didn't know how she could cope with not being there for her daughter when she needed her the most.

Sighing, Dominique began to tidy the kitchen. Cleaning always soothed her mind. She realised the kitchen bin was full and removed the liner. She unlocked the kitchen door and began to slip her feet into the garden shoes so she could run to the wheelie bin. Then the doorbell rang. Tutting, she checked the CCTV and saw the postman, huddled against the battering wind and rain in his red jacket. She left the bin bag on the floor, propping the kitchen door open as she hurried to the front so she wouldn't keep him waiting in the driving rain.

78

—————

The wind whipped at Maya's curls as she braced herself to swing her other leg over the balcony. Then all she had to do was tilt her body weight forward, keep her eyes fixed on the twinkling lights, open her arms and allow herself to fall towards the ground and sweet oblivion. She was about to raise her leg when a noise below was carried to her on the wind.

It was only faint, but she paused, straining to hear against the gusts of wind that whipped around her. There it was again. Quiet but unremarkable. She dropped her leg, feet planted firmly on the floor. Suddenly the wind stilled and she could hear properly now. The unmistakable chime being played from an ice-cream van. She backed away from the rail, her back crashing into the door behind her. She leapt back into the apartment, locking the door behind her and hurling the key from her as if it was on fire.

She clutched her chest as she gasped with shock at the realisation of what she had been about to do. She was hyperventilating and called on one of the techniques Jayne had taught her until it subsided. Her strangled breaths eventually turned into a harrowing laugh. She'd heard about people all the time sending messages from the other side in the guise of robins or white feathers. Only Chris could thwart her suicide attempt using an ice-cream van.

She laughed raucously, tears mingling with snot which she swiped away with her sleeve. The realisation of what she had nearly done hit her and she was so grateful that whether it was Chris or just good timing, she had come to her senses when she had. However bad she was feeling, suicide was never the answer – she had attended enough of them to know that.

She thought about the pain she would cause for those left behind if she had gone through with it. She thought about how precious life was and how much Chris wanted to live – what right did she have to even contemplate taking her own? It was too precious. She thought about Dominique. Then she recalled the conversation they had had in the office with Kym when they were discussing whether you could forgive someone for murder. She remembered Chris's words clearly: 'I'd forgive someone I loved with time, no matter how bad it was.'

Dominique had done wrong in the past, but hadn't she turned things around since? She had clearly made amends for all her mistakes because she had been a good mother. She had always worked above and beyond in her job as a community nurse and had given back to the community tirelessly. She had cared for Grandad towards the end too, when he had grown sick, weak and needy like a lost child. Losing Chris was too much, could she afford to lose someone else she loved, just by being stubborn.

Now, having just faced the lowest point of her life, she knew where she needed to be.

79

The wind and rain battered Maya as she rode to Dominique's. She parked the bike and Maya ran up the path and rang the bell, shivering as she waited on the step. Dominique opened the door slightly and peered through the crack. She looked wide-eyed and frantic.

Maya raised the visor of her helmet. 'Let me in, Mama, it's freezing out here.'

Dominique shook her head and moved to shut the door, but Maya blocked it with her hand. 'What's wrong with you? We need to talk. Now.' Maya pushed against the door as Dominique lurched backwards. Tutting, Maya turned to shut the door as she pulled her helmet off.

She looked up and froze in horror at the sight of Marcus with his arm around Dominique's neck and a zombie knife pressed to her throat. He was wearing a red postal worker's jacket, which looked ludicrous given the severity of the situation.

'Living room, now.' He indicated with his head.

'Why did you come, you should have stayed away,' Dominique sobbed.

'Shut up. I said living room, NOW!'

Maya did as he asked and they followed behind her. The room was dim, the thick curtains had been pulled shut and there were no lamps on. Marcus pushed Dominique away from him towards the sofa where Maya joined her. They both clutched hands as they stared at him.

Other than the photograph, it was the first time Maya had seen him since she was twelve years old. She would have recognised him anywhere. He had grown his hair and beard, now streaked with silver, so looked nothing like the photograph the police had released. He had the same evil-looking eyes although now they were deeply lined with crow's feet.

'Well, isn't this nice,' he said. 'The three of us together again after all this time. A lovely family reunion.'

'You're not family, you're scum,' spat Maya. Dominique squeezed her hand to signal to her not to rile him, but here was the man who had murdered Chris and it was all she could do not to leap up, grab the knife off him and plunge it in the place where his heart should be.

'Still feisty like your mama, eh? I always said the apple didn't fall far when it came to you two.'

He gestured towards them with the knife as he spoke and Maya was devastated to notice that even in the dullness of the room, there were traces of blood still visible on the blade. The sight of it caused her to gasp.

'What's up with you? Oh, I see.' He looked at the knife and laughed. 'It's still got your fat little mate's blood on it.'

Maya and Dominique stiffened with shock and disgust as they watched him run his tongue along the flat side of the blade, before flashing them both a manic grin.

'Why?' said Maya.

'Why what?'

'Why did you kill Chris? He was a good man. He didn't deserve to die.'

Marcus shrugged nonchalantly. 'Wrong place, wrong time. I went there so I could wait for you. The plan was to carve you up and I was going to record it to make her watch later,' he said as he nodded towards Dominique.

'You're a sick fuck. Chris was more of a man than you could ever be.'

'Oh, I'm so sorry to disappoint you, Princess Maya, but I'm here now. Daddy is back and where is he? Lying in a giant fridge starting to rot away. You know about death, Maya, you know what will happen to your precious Chris as he starts to decompose, putrefy, bloat and decay. You won't be wanting daddy cuddles off him then, will you?'

Maya screamed and leapt from the couch, but Dominique pulled her back with an unsurprising strength and hissed for her to sit down.

Marcus laughed again. 'Listen to your mother. Try that again and I'll cut her up in front of you if you so much as move a muscle.'

'You're going to do that anyway,' said Maya. 'To both of us.'

Marcus nodded reasonably. 'I am, but you're going first.'

'No,' shouted Dominique as she gripped Maya's arm. 'There's money upstairs. Just take it. I'll come with you. Do whatever you want to me, but please, don't hurt Maya. Just let her go, she hasn't done anything wrong.'

'Oh, I know she hasn't. All of this,' he gesticulated around the room, 'is on you, Dom. I went away for years because of you. My mum died before I got the chance to say goodbye, because of you. My *brother* died because of you. All *because* you put her first. You were supposed to love me, but the minute the police showed up, you sold me down the river and left me to rot. You chose her when it should have been *us*.

'Things were perfect before she came along. We were a team but that wasn't enough for you, was it? You chose her. As payback, precious Maya is going to die and you're going to watch. I always knew the only way to get to you was through her. To take away the only thing you ever genuinely loved. Because it was never me, despite what you said.'

'You used and manipulated me all those years,' said Dominique. 'I didn't realise how badly until you were no longer here and I got clean. I thought I had a life when I was with you. It was only later I realised it had all been a lie.'

'That's not true, we were good, we had it all. We were perfect together – she changed things; you changed after you had her. She came between us.'

'She's our daughter,' Dominique cried incredulously.

'She's *your* daughter.'

There was an impasse as Marcus and Dominique stared at each other, and Maya for the first time ever, experienced a glimpse of what had once been between them. A raw, furious, passionate lust between two people who mistook the feeling for love. Two people who would always be hellbent on destroying each other with the toxicity of their relationship.

Marcus broke the silence. 'I'll do you one last favour, my darling Dom, just because it's you. For old times' sake. I'll make it quick. I won't gut her like a fish and leave her to bleed out like I did with her good friend Chris. If she comes to me now, like a good girl,' he made a slashing motion across his throat with the knife, 'I'll make it quick. And Maya, if you do behave, after Mama has watched you die, I'll make it quick for her too. I'm a man of my word, I promise you both.'

'Okay,' said Maya as she stood up, wiping her palms down the front of her trousers. 'I agree.' She smiled sadly at Dominique. 'I love you, Mama.'

She held her hand up as she walked slowly towards Marcus. 'Let's end this.'

80

——————

Each step felt like a mile as Maya walked towards Marcus. She felt empty and broken as she walked towards him. She had nothing more to give. She just wanted it all to stop.

'Maya, no!' shrieked Dominique. 'Baby, don't. Please come back.' She began to sob with terror as Marcus reached out with one hand towards Maya, the zombie knife primed and ready in the other.

A scream filled the air as Marcus suddenly fell to the floor, gripping his neck while his body thrashed and spasmed. The fugitive stood over him, with a smile on his face and a taser in his hand.

'Lurch,' panted Maya, 'thank God you're here, but how?'

From their vantage point on the couch, they had seen the man-mountain appear, unseen by Marcus, in the hallway. He had pressed his finger to his lips to indicate silence, and Marcus had been too distracted by his ramblings to notice that both pairs of eyes had flickered over his shoulder.

Now Lurch, or Sydney as he had also been known, reached for Naylor by the scruff of his coat and hauled him to his feet, slamming him into the doorframe.

'Later. First, what do you want me to do with this?'

Marcus began to thrash against his assailant until Lurch pressed the taser against his neck a second time and sent him crumpling back to the floor. 'I'll keep doing that until you learn,' said Lurch as Maya approached and moved the zombie knife out of harm's way.

'I've always kept a lookout for you.' He smiled. 'I heard that this scum had been released and then about the fire.' He nodded towards Dominique. 'I heard a rumour from a friend of a friend who'd been hiding him that he was planning on coming back to finish you both. I owe you for giving me my life and my freedom back so I knew I had to come back and stop him. I've been following you as best as I can. The kitchen door was left unlocked, so I crept in. It's the least I could do,' he said with a shy smile. 'I loved you once, Maya.'

'But you're taking a big risk being back here. If the police catch you–'

'They won't.' Without flinching or breaking eye contact with Maya, he raised his leg and booted Marcus in the stomach, causing him to groan in agony. 'I'm too careful. I've learnt a lot since I've been away, and look,' he said as he removed his hood, 'don't I look different?'

The hair transplant had transformed him and that's when Maya also noticed something else about him that was new. 'You've got teeth!' she said with a laugh. 'Sorry, I didn't mean to be rude.'

'You're not,' said Lurch as he proudly tapped his veneers, before giving Marcus another kick. 'It's amazing what money can buy.' His cheery façade left his face and was replaced with thunder. 'I'm so sorry about Chris. I've been watching your apartment so I could be there if you needed me. I realised too late that you'd swapped houses otherwise I would still have been at Miller Court. I should have been there to stop him.'

'I know you would have. Thank you for doing this, risking everything for me.'

'I owed you. What do you want me to do with him? I already have a place I can take his body that no one will ever find.'

'Yes,' said Dominique. 'God help me for saying it but yes. Dispose of him like the trash he is.'

Lurch nodded and turned to Maya. 'Is that okay with you?'

Maya hesitated. She thought of how easily he would have slit her throat given half a chance. Then he would have done the same to Dominique. Then she thought of Chris and how Marcus had left him to bleed out alone and terrified.

'No,' she said eventually. 'He lives. If you kill him that makes us all as bad as him and I couldn't live with that thought as well as having his death on our conscience. My faith alone wouldn't allow it. We'd be haunted by it forever. He has to pay for what he's done to Chris. He should be caged, back where he belongs.'

'But, Maya. He's been imprisoned before and still got to us,' said Dominique. 'While he's alive, he will always be a risk to us.'

'Not if he's broken,' said Lurch with a shrug. 'Take away his power and he's got nothing.'

Before Maya could speak, Lurch had dragged Marcus to his feet again and with a few sudden movements and a loud crack from his neck and back, Marcus dropped to the floor like a stone.

'That should have paralysed him,' said Lurch.

The three of them stood back and looked at Marcus who had grown eerily silent, his face deathly pale, nothing moving from the neck down.

Dominique gasped and Maya glanced at her, unsure what to do. She had been adamant that she didn't want Lurch to murder Naylor, but this was just as bad. How could Lurch do something so horrific without so much as flinching. Surely Naylor would be better off dead than this.

She looked down at him and caught his eye. It was still there – that look of sheer hatred. Despite being left paralysed on the floor, that superseded everything. He would never change. Lurch was right, the only way to stop him other than kill him was to take his power away. He couldn't hurt them now. He wasn't physically capable. He would be stuck motionless in his own twisted world until the day he did die.

Lurch had done what he had to protect her and Dominique. He had shown mercy, something that Naylor hadn't shown Chris and wouldn't have shown her and Dominique had Lurch not arrived when he had.

'I have to go, for good this time,' said Lurch as he smiled at Maya.

'Where to?'

'Back to the sunset. That's all you need to know. I won't be back. I've done what I wanted, righted a wrong and got revenge for you. Be happy, Maya, live a good life.'

He nodded at Dominique and just like that he was gone. He flitted away as quickly as he'd arrived. He left barely a scent in the air.

Locard be damned.

81

———————

On the day of Chris's funeral, St Mary's church was bursting at the seams with mourners wanting to pay their respects. It truly was testament to what a popular man Chris had been; someone who had left them far too soon. Maya had clung to Spence throughout the service, unable to comprehend that her friend, someone she loved so deeply, who was larger than life and such a huge presence, was now nothing more than a body in a coffin.

Maya had shed fresh tears every time she raised her head and saw the photograph of Chris that sat on the casket. She didn't think she would ever come to terms with him being dead, and she had felt truly broken when it was time to walk away from the crematorium knowing even his body would soon be gone for good. She wanted him back so desperately; it was a physical pain in her gut.

Being at Chris's funeral reminded Maya how close she had come to taking her own life, and how desperately glad she was that she hadn't gone through with it. Life was such a precious gift. Her job as a SOCO reminded her on a daily basis how easily it could be snatched away. Chris's murder was testament to that fact. She would never take it for granted again.

She thought fleetingly of Naylor and whether he wished *he* was dead rather than paralysed. He was currently in hospital but it was only a matter of time before he was returned to prison. Once there his existence would be miserable as the staff wouldn't have the resources to provide the care he needed, despite the prison governor claiming they *could* provide round the clock care. And whilst inevitably the disability liaison officer would try to protest to improve his quality of life inside, bureaucracy was so slow that Naylor would be left to rot. No more than what he deserved.

Maya had heard a sob to her right and looked at Dominique, who sat on the other side of Spence. Things were far from perfect between mother and daughter and Maya wondered if they would ever be able to fully rebuild their relationship back the way it had been. Jayne had agreed to spend time working with both of them and at least they were able to talk openly and honestly. In the meantime, Maya was glad Dominique was here to offer support on one of the hardest days of her life.

Later they had gathered at The Eagle for Chris's wake. Agency staff had been brought in to work the bar and the pub was opened exclusively for the funeral party. Spence had gone behind the bar to fetch some bottles of wine and Dominique offered to check that everything was okay with the buffet and brought out the first platters of food as Maya ushered everyone in.

As Kym walked past her, Maya grabbed her arm and nodded towards Tara and Sean who were approaching the pub hand in hand. 'I didn't see that coming.'

Tara, knowing she was being talked about, hovered near them as she walked by with Sean. 'What was it Chris said? "Spend the time with someone you truly connect with who excites you emotionally as well physically".' She winked at them both. 'It's surprising how sometimes you can't appreciate what's right under your nose.'

Coats were removed and chairs shuffled around tables which became quickly laden with food and drink. Maya headed to the jukebox and selected several of Chris's favourite songs. She knew he would have loved nothing more than to replace the sombre atmosphere of the funeral with a party ambience so people could celebrate his life. 'Mr Brightside' began to play and instantly the mood lifted.

Spence appeared at her side with two pints of lager. 'Here, I thought we could toast him with his favourite drink.'

Maya smiled and they clinked glasses. 'To Chris,' she said. 'Rest in heavenly peace, my friend.'

Spence slipped an arm around her shoulders as they sipped their drinks and looked around the busy pub. Everyone from the office was crowded around one large table, either chatting noisily and animatedly, or singing and bouncing to the lyrics. Dominique was deep in conversation with Kym, telling her something that was clearly amusing her boss. Chris would have loved it.

'Hey,' said Spence as he brushed a curl from her cheek. 'Are you okay?'

Maya swallowed a mouthful of lager before she answered. 'Honestly? No. I miss him so much. I've never known pain like it and life right now feels so empty without him. But, for the first time ever, I'm not scared of Naylor anymore. He's no longer a threat and never will be. I don't need to think about him ever again.

'What I want to concentrate on is remembering Chris and fixing things between me and Mama, not just for our sake, but because it's what he would have wanted.' She nodded towards the table where Dominique was sat with all her friends and colleagues.

'To answer your question, I'm not okay but I will be, because I've got that lot, a job I love and more importantly,' she leant forward and kissed him gently on the lips, 'I've got you. And as long as we're together all the rest will fall in place.'

'That's a lovely sentiment,' he said as he leant to kiss her gently on the mouth. Suddenly, from outside, a burst of sirens could be heard as police cars drove by, screaming to the latest emergency. Instinctively, Maya's interest as a SOCO was piqued as she wondered what was happening now. Because one thing was inevitable, crime stopped for no one and it would be only a matter of time before police tape was being strung to preserve the latest crime scene.

THE END

AUTHOR'S NOTE ON EMDR

In 2017 I was diagnosed with PTSD. Although I have suffered with anxiety and depression in the past, this was by far the worst experience of my life. I was having vivid, terrifying nightmares that felt so real they stayed with me hours after waking, making me a nervous wreck. I couldn't work and was struggling to function daily, merely going through the motions.

I couldn't understand what the root cause was. By then I'd worked fifteen years as a crime-scene investigator, so it was easy to assume my trauma was job-related, particularly because of the nature of my nightmares, but I couldn't associate it to anything I had dealt with. I was anxious, depressed and quite frankly, terrified.

Fortunately, I met my very own 'Jayne' through force welfare. With her help and support and after a successful period of EMDR, my trauma was unlocked and dealt with. It is no exaggeration to say that the treatment and 'Jayne' literally saved my life and I'll be forever indebted to her and grateful for the therapy. Without EMDR, I would never have got to the root source and unlocked something, that in comparison to the nightmares, was relatively tame. It is common for a patient to laugh after EMDR, once the trauma is identified and unlocked, as it's such a visceral relief, which is why Maya does when her own trauma is unlocked.

When I first started to plan this trilogy, the one thing that I knew for certain plot-wise, was that Maya would suffer with PTSD. I wanted to share this experience through my protagonist in the hope that if it helps only one person who reads this, then it has been worth digging deep and revisiting a very distressful time. It hasn't been easy, but I hope it's been worth it.

Although I have taken some poetic licence in Maya's case, I have written as closely to the memory of my own treatment as best as I can recall. I wanted to be candid about this and share 'our' experience in the hope that, if you, or someone you know is suffering with something similar, please speak out and get help. PTSD doesn't have to be a death sentence and I promise you that things can and *will* get better.

ACKNOWLEDGEMENTS

Firstly, thanks to Betsy and all the team at Bloodhound Books for having faith in me and bringing the Maya Barton trilogy to fruition.

Special thanks to editor extraordinaire, Ian Skewis for having what can only be referred to as 'eyes like a shit-house rat'. There's a huge compliment in there somewhere, I promise you. Thank you for all the work you've done on the trilogy.

Thanks to Jennifer Susan Smith for bidding in the Bloodhound Books charity auction to raise money to help the people of Ukraine. Jennifer is also known as Susie and won the chance for her name to be used in this book.

Huge thanks to Lindsy Slamon for her unwavering support and for giving the time to read, comment and crime-scene manage all the Maya books. You're an absolute star – love you, Crazy Legs!

Also, thanks for the continued support, advice and friendship from my partner in crime, Graham Bartlett and my friends in the reading / writing community including Christie Newport, Brian Price, Samantha Brownley, Swanwick Writers and the UKCBC community.

Huge thanks to my readers, especially those who have already taken the time to comment so kindly on the previous books. Your support is greatly appreciated and believe me, it makes my day whenever I hear a kind word or positive review.

To my daughters Sophie and Elissa, thank you for putting up with the craziness of having a Mama who writes! Thanks for the cuddles and encouragement as well as the constant interruptions when I'm trying to concentrate 😊. I love you both.

Finally, to the love of my life, Gary. Thank you for the relentless encouragement and for believing in me when I don't believe in myself. Thank you for all your support and for being the best husband ever – and that's not just cupboard love! I appreciate you so much and am forever thankful and grateful that you're mine. I love you.

ALSO BY KATE BENDELOW

Definitely Dead (Maya Barton #Book 1)

~

Shattered Bones (Maya Barton #Book 2)

~

<u>Non-fiction</u>

The Real CSI: A Forensic Handbook for Crime Writers

A NOTE FROM THE PUBLISHER

Thank you for reading this book. If you enjoyed it please do consider leaving a review on Amazon to help others find it too.

We hate typos. All of our books have been rigorously edited and proofread, but sometimes mistakes do slip through. If you have spotted a typo, please do let us know and we can get it amended within hours.

info@bloodhoundbooks.com

9 781504 086677